a TARTAN *love*

the EARLS *of* CAIRNFELL
book one

NICHOLE VAN

Fiorenza Publishing

A Tartan Love © 2025 by Nichole Van Valkenburgh
Cover design © Nichole Van Valkenburgh
Interior design © Nichole Van Valkenburgh

Published by Fiorenza Publishing
Print Edition v1.0

ISBN: 978-1-949863-25-3

To Megan,
a shooting-star of a woman.
Thank you for making the world sparkle
with the light of your brilliance.
Welcome to the family.

And to Dave,
because after twenty-six years of marriage,
you're still my favorite person.
I love you.

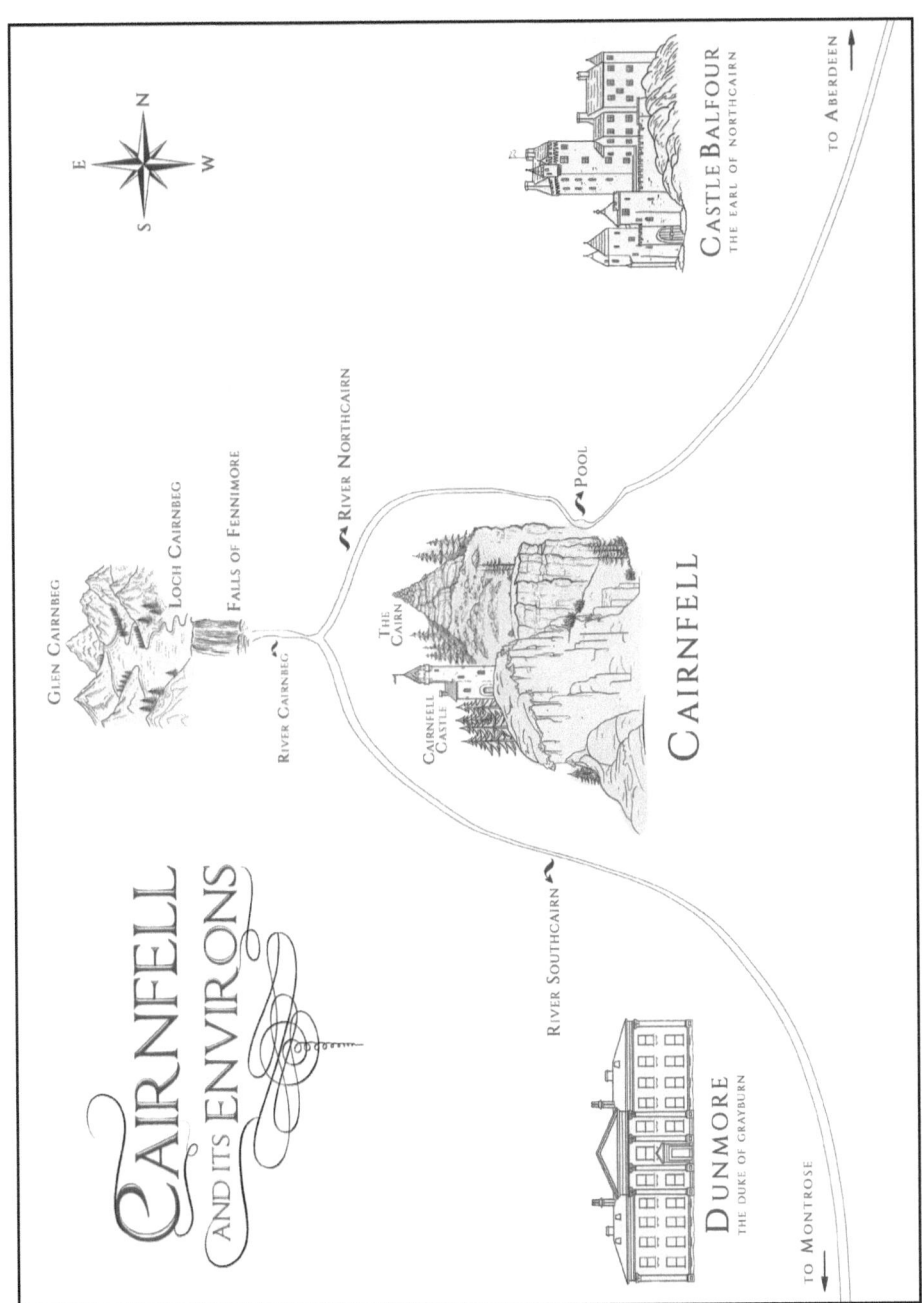

CAIRNFELL AND ITS ENVIRONS

N
E · W
S

GLEN CAIRNBEG

LOCH CAIRNBEG

FALLS OF FENNIMORE

RIVER NORTHCAIRN

RIVER CAIRNBEG

POOL

THE CAIRN

CAIRNFELL CASTLE

CAIRNFELL

RIVER SOUTHCAIRN

CASTLE BALFOUR
THE EARL OF NORTHCAIRN

TO ABERDEEN

DUNMORE
THE DUKE OF GRAYBURN

TO MONTROSE

PROLOGUE

August 12, 1808
The parish kirkyard
Pettercairn, Scotland

The boy was weeping.

Lady Isla Kinsey might be only fifteen years of age, but she recognized the signs of a good *greit*.

He knelt before a grave—palms braced on the ground, spine hunched—the earth beneath his knees still black and fresh. Even thirty feet back and peering between tombstones, Isla could see gusting sobs wrack his shoulders. They were quiet things, those sobs. Dramatic visually but soundless. As if the young man were accustomed to grieving in silence.

The thought ached and sighed through her bones.

She recognized him, of course. Even if the grave marker had not proclaimed his identity, his reddish hair, the expensive superfine of his coat, and the black mourning band tied around his right arm all but shouted his name—

Mr. Tavish Balfour.

Isla placed a gloved hand on the wall of the parish church beside her.

She should leave.

No good would come of him seeing her here.

And yet . . .

She had wandered the churchyard often enough to know the words etched into the grave marker before him:

Mary Balfour, Lady Northcairn
Beloved wife of Douglas Balfour,
8th Earl of Northcairn
Born May 22, 1768
Died February 10, 1808

Tavish Balfour wept for his mother, gone these six months.

Something raw and scalding lodged in Isla's throat. Her eyes darted left, seeking out her own mother's grave in the opposite corner of the kirkyard. Unlike Lady Northcairn, Mamma's grave loomed over the other tombstones—a rectangular, granite box raised four feet off the ground and covered in carvings of vines and angels.

Isla had cast off her mourning blacks over two years ago, but the passage of time hadn't lessened the sting of her mother's death. It was why she was here today, was it not? Why she had cut a large slice of Cook's brandy-soaked pound cake and wrapped it in a handkerchief before slipping out the door, unnoticed.

Today was Isla's fifteenth birthday—the third birthday without Mamma's cheery laughter and rose-scented gifts. A third birthday spent in the echoing silence of her loss.

But Isla still wished to pass a part of today with her mother, leaning against the cool stone of her tomb, eating cake and listening to the starlings quarrel overhead—

She glanced down at the piece of cake in her hands. It truly was monstrous. Decidedly enough to share.

Mr. Balfour was sitting back on his heels now, scrubbing at his eyes with both fists.

Isla's father, the haughty Duke of Grayburn, would be furious were he to learn she had spoken with a Balfour under any circumstance, not to mention alone and unchaperoned.

Normally, Isla would never disobey her father.

But the words *compliant* and *timid* circled like vultures above her head.

Several years ago, Isla had overheard her governess, Miss Farnsworth, use those adjectives to describe her to the housekeeper—*"Lady Isla? Ah, she is a timid, compliant girl. She never gives me a whisper of trouble."*

Isla had beamed at the compliment. At the pride in Miss Farnsworth's voice. She had immediately looked up both words in Dr. Johnson's *Dictionary of the English Language*, wanting to understand these praiseworthy attributes of her person.

> *COMPLIANT: Yielding; bending.*
> *TIMID: Fearful; wanting courage.*

Isla had glared at the definitions.
Yielding.
Bending.
Fearful.
Wanting courage.
This was what Miss Farnsworth found noble in Isla? That she allowed her personality to be molded like clay? That she lived her life in cowardice and fear?

The portrayal of her person was anything but flattering.

Peeking between the gravestones, Isla knew ignoring Mr. Balfour would be the *timid, compliant* thing to do.

But today, as she faced down all fifteen of her years, Isla found she no longer wished to be *passive*—a kissing-cousin to *timid* and *compliant*.

And so, she pushed off the church wall and crossed the graveyard.

Mr. Balfour whirled at the sound of her pelisse brushing the low-cut lawn.

Their eyes caught and held as Isla continued to approach.

Blushing, he scrambled to his feet. He scrubbed his cheeks with his coat sleeve, but the tear streaks remained, smudging the skin beneath his red-rimmed gray eyes.

He was . . .

Oh, dear.

He was handsome.

Tall and lanky, he topped her by several inches, but the soft down on his cheeks proclaimed him to be a boy still. And though his hair was decidedly ginger, his skin lacked the ruddy tones and freckles of a typical redhead. His features looked to be chiseled in marble—sharp jawline, long nose, wide cheekbones, square chin bisected by a deep cleft.

Only his lips, she noted, appeared soft and full. The sort that made one wonder how they would feel to kiss.

She blushed at the indecent thought.

Isla had no memory of studying Tavish Balfour before now. She knew only that he was a Balfour and therefore to be avoided.

The animosity between their families was the stuff of legends. The Kinseys and the Balfours had once been family in truth—both lines descended from twin brothers born to Robert Balfour, Lord Cairnfell, over two hundred years past. Back then, Lord Cairnfell had ruled his lands from atop Cairnfell itself, a rocky crag jutting upward from the gentle fields of Angus.

The twin brothers, Daniel and David, fought side-by-side with King Charles II during the Great Civil War, and His Majesty rewarded them handsomely. Daniel, the elder brother, was given the title of Earl of Northcairn, after the river that ran through the traditional family lands north of Cairnfell. David, younger by only nine minutes, was granted the title Earl of Southcairn, in honor of the river that ran south of Cairnfell. Southcairn was also granted a large swath of land around his namesake river.

It should have been harmonious—brothers thriving on adjacent properties, the height of Cairnfell rising between them. However, each brother felt slighted by oversights in the king's generosity and blamed the opposite party. Though Northcairn had been elevated to an earldom and granted money to build a new castle, he had been given no additional territory. Southcairn, however, had received new lands and property, all of it more arable and productive than his brother's.

And so, twin brothers who had played together—fought together, defended king and country together—became bitter rivals. Two centuries of backstabbing, betrayal, and contention followed. The sort of vitriol only a family could sustain.

Southcairn had used his wealth to marry into the English aristocracy, change his surname, and climb to the title of Duke of Grayburn.

Northcairn had built Castle Balfour north of Cairnfell and upheld the family's tradition of laird and clan, shepherding their people.

Each side detested the other.

Isla knew this history, yet . . .

As Tavish Balfour straightened beside his mother's grave, she was hard pressed to see him as an enemy.

No.

He looked like a person just as lost and solitary as herself.

"Hallo," she said, Scotland making an unwelcome appearance in her vowels. As a rule, the Kinseys did not tolerate even a whiff of a brogue. Miss Farnsworth, with her dulcet English tones, would have a fit of the vapors if she heard Isla at the moment.

Mr. Balfour said nothing. Merely stared.

Swallowing, Isla soldiered on, wincing as that trace of Scotland remained. "I couldn't help but notice ye here, uhm . . ." She drifted off, glancing at the grave beyond his shoulder. Heat climbed her cheeks at an alarming pace. "Anyhow, today is my birthday, and I've come to visit my own mamma, over there." She pointed in the direction of her mother's tomb. "And I brought a wee bit of cake. Enough to share, if ye'd like."

She held out the cake in its bit of muslin, hating the tremble in her fingers.

His gaze left her face, dropped to the cake, and then lifted back to her eyes.

"'Tis your birthday?" he asked.

He did not ask her identity. Like herself, he surely knew she was a Kinsey, even if they had never spoken a word to one another. Unlike herself, Scotland sang unapologetically through every syllable of his words.

"Yes."

"Today?"

"Yes."

This gave him pause. He blinked.

"The twelfth of August?"

"Yes. That is the date today." She smiled brightly. Was he a bit addled in the head?

He blinked again. "Today is my birthday, too."

A laugh startled out of her. "Truly?"

"Aye."

"We are birthday twins!" She grinned. "How old are ye today?"

"Sixteen."

"Hah! I turned fifteen. Well then, we shall definitely be sharing this cake." She lifted the bundle in her hand. "Birthdays should not go uncelebrated, I say, regardless of circumstance."

Without waiting for an invite, Isla sank into the grass beside his mother's grave and patted the ground.

He glanced around the kirkyard, as if nervous their clandestine meeting might be observed, before folding his long legs and sitting beside her.

He looked at the cake in eager invitation.

Isla opened the handkerchief and broke the slice of cake in two, handing him the larger half.

"Thank ye." He smiled—a tentative, quiet thing.

And then, he promptly unhinged his jaw and took an enormous bite of the cake. It was a bit like watching a grass snake devour a mouse.

Isla's eyes went wide as saucers.

It was . . .

Words escaped her. She would have to consult Dr. Johnson for more.

Her own brothers were a bit older than herself, so she had no true recollection of them as younger men. Certainly not as rag-mannered lads.

But watching Mr. Balfour eat . . . the long slide of his Adam's apple as he chewed, the muscles bunching in his jaw . . .

Well.

It was rather educational.

Mr. Balfour did not miss her stunned expression.

"It's goo' cake," he said with his mouth full.

It was such . . . *boy* behavior.

Isla giggled, the sound dropping out of her like water flowing over the Falls of Fennimore.

He continued to chew—unrepentant, those plush lips of his curling at the corners.

His nonchalance only made Isla laugh harder. She pressed a palm to her mouth to staunch the sound, but the pressure made her snort. Loudly. Like a sow with its piglets.

With anyone else, the noise would have been mortifying, but his presence was a light thing, welcome and accepting.

Isla collapsed into giggles. Hilarity shook her shoulders and filled her blood with bubbles so light she could imagine her heart soaring away on a merry wind.

He swallowed and then joined her in laughing, his baritone voice rumbling.

"Ye be Lady Isla, am I right?" He popped a smaller piece of cake into his mouth.

She liked how he said her name—AYE-la—dragging out the initial *A* sound. Why there was a silent S in *Isla*, no one had ever adequately explained to her.

She nodded. "And you're Mr. Tavish Balfour?"

"There's an honorable before that, I'll have you know—The *Honorable* Mr. Tavish Balfour." He winked.

Isla laughed again.

Oh! This simply would not do. She had never considered herself to be the sort to giggle and blush over a handsome boy.

And yet . . . here she was.

She was learning all sorts of illuminating things about herself today.

"Ye be alright for a Kinsey," Mr. Balfour said.

"Pardon?" Isla nibbled at her own slice. *Dainty bites*, as Miss Farnsworth would admonish.

"We all think ye be a bit too proper, you Kinseys. Ye keep to yourselves there at Dunmore. Avoid mixing with us clan folk and the townspeople."

Isla had never thought of her family quite like that. She just assumed that . . .

Well, what had she assumed?

It was true that her brothers never attended the local *ceilidhs* or assembly balls that the maids whispered about. Surely, her family was invited.

They simply . . . didn't mix with the local clan folk, as he said.

"Life is rather boring at Dunmore," Isla confessed.

"Aye?"

"Ayyyye," she drawled just to see him smile again. He did not disappoint, his lips stretching wide.

There was something arresting about this boy. The way that he looked at her, the angle of his head as he spoke, the quiet earnestness of his gaze combined with the rough masculinity of his frame.

Never before had she been so aware of her own body as female and another's as male. It shook something awake within her belly. Like standing in the midst of an electrical storm, the current buzzing along her skin.

"We shouldn't be speaking," she said.

"Nae, we shouldn't."

"Why do our families hate each other? I don't understand."

"Me, either. All I know is my da' would whip me if he caught me here."

"Mine would lock me in my room for a week."

"Would he now?"

Isla shrugged. "Perhaps. I actually don't know what he would do as I've never . . ."

She left the rest dangling, but she was fairly certain she heard the words *timid* and *compliant* whisper on the wind.

Lifting an eyebrow at her, he deliberately took another obscene bite of cake, holding her gaze the entire time.

A challenge, she realized.

Isla stared, unable to look away.

Still chewing, he waggled his eyebrows and then glanced meaningfully at the slice in her hand.

I dare ye, his eyes said.

Isla pursed her lips, a grin tugging at the corners of her mouth. She had only been in this boy's company for ten minutes, and she already knew he was incorrigible.

He swallowed and licked his lips.

"Go on, then." He nudged his chin toward her slice. "The biggest bite ye can manage."

"Why?"

"Why not?"

"That is decidedly poor logic."

His eyebrows lifted. "Because life is meant to be lived. Not constantly harrowed up by our fathers' *shoulds* or *shouldn'ts*."

"Mmm. A bit better."

She glanced down at the cake.

Oh, heavens.

She was going to do this. She was going to take an enormous bite and swallow *timid* and *compliant* right down.

On a breath, Isla opened her mouth as wide as she could and sank her teeth into the cake.

It was . . .

Gracious!

The taste of brandy, vanilla, and sugar exploded on her tongue.

How did he chew and breathe at the same time?

It scarcely mattered. The whole experience was divine. Like dunking her head in the frigid waters of the River Southcairn on a hot summer's day.

"There ye go, lass." He took another bite. "We'll unearth your Balfour roots yet."

Isla managed to swallow.

"Ye have a wee bit of cake . . ." He pointed to the edge of his mouth.

"Where?" Isla brushed her fingers across her face. "Here?"

He stared at her lips for a moment. "Allow me."

Reaching out, he pressed his thumb to the edge of her mouth. It was the briefest of touches, scarcely more than a whisper, but Isla felt it everywhere—in the gooseflesh that flared down her spine, in the burning heat where his thumb had been, in the rabbit-thump of her heart.

Hand dropping, he popped the remaining bit of cake into his mouth and flashed a smile before gazing out over the cemetery.

As if that brief touch had affected him not at all.

Isla's lungs reminded her to breathe.

"Thank ye." He glanced at his mother's grave behind them. "Thank ye for making today a wee bit more bearable."

"The first birthday without them is the most difficult. It gets easier after that."

He nodded.

Voices drifted in . . . people walking up the street.

They both turned toward the sound. His body tensed.

Mr. Balfour clearly had the same thought as Isla—no one could see them here together.

Pivoting back, he leaned toward her. "If I never speak with ye again, know that I consider ye a right bonnie lass."

Her cheeks burned even as she smiled too wide.

"And—" He leaned even closer. Close enough that she could see the flecks of silver in his gray eyes and feel the warmth of his breath. "Happy birthday, Lady Isla."

"Happy birthday to ye, as well."

With another wink, he sprang to his feet and vaulted over the stone fence that encircled the kirkyard, disappearing into the trees beyond.

Isla watched him go.

She likely *would* never speak with him again. Their families wouldn't permit it, not even an innocent friendship.

But neither her ducal father nor Miss Farnsworth could control Isla's daydreams. In her own fantasies, she could be as *un-timid* and *non-compliant* as she would like.

And abruptly, Isla knew she would see Tavish Balfour's face in each one. Every day, she could remember his joyful bite into her cake, envision his laughing eyes, the way his thumb brushed away the crumb on her lip, his voice as his head dipped toward hers with a low, *Happy birthday*.

Daydreaming about him would be simply that—a dream.

After all, it wasn't as if she would marry him.

1

NINE YEARS LATER

JULY 15, 1817
CAIRNFELL
PETTERCAIRN, SCOTLAND

He had arrived back at the beginning.

It seemed fitting, Captain Tavish Balfour supposed, that his path should take him here—across the River Southcairn at the shallow west ford and into the shade of the ancient Caledonian forest before sending him up the slopes of Cairnfell.

Yes. Returning to this place was good. To remember before confronting . . .

Well . . . everything.

The towering Scots pine dripped with moss as he urged his horse,

Goliath, up the narrow path. Clouds raced overhead, blocking the sun and promising rain later. Wind tugged at his hat and snapped his greatcoat, bringing with it the scent of damp earth and whispered memories.

The trail crested the hill, the trees receding.

In the middle of a clearing, the ruins of Cairnfell Castle loomed—the abandoned ancient seat of his family, the Earls of Northcairn. Four stories of stones so old that ferns and lemon-colored marsh marigolds clung to them. Only the impressive oak front door guarded by an iron yett and the first two floors with their panes of glass showed any signs of habitation in the past century. Generations ago, Tavish's family had built the roomier Castle Balfour to the north, leaving Cairnfell Castle to be slowly reclaimed by the elements.

Beyond the tower house, the hill rose a final time to an area of bare ground. There an ancient cairn stood—the cairn atop the fell—an enormous pile of stones over thirty feet high.

In short, climbing the path to his ancestral lands felt like traversing through History itself.

Or perhaps it was merely Tavish's own history, specifically. The ghosts he had returned home to banish.

This reckoning had been long in coming.

He swore he heard laughter on the wind. *Her* laughter. A giggling sound that had always clung to his senses like the sweetest honey.

Swinging out of the saddle, Tavish looped the reins around an obliging post beside the castle. He and his older brother, Callum, had driven the post into place when Tavish had been fourteen.

"Can't leave our horses untethered while we . . ." Callum had drifted off with a suggestive lift of his eyebrows and a sideways glance at the castle, slamming the post into the loamy earth.

"While we what?" Tavish had asked, holding the oak pole steady.

His brother had rolled his eyes. Callum was nearly seventeen, and Tavish knew he had been spending far too much time with Farmer McKay's bonnie widow.

"Ye'll figure it out soon enough," Callum had replied.

Tavish *had* figured it out—both Callum's meaning, as well as what his brother had been up to with Widow McKay and other lasses at Cairnfell.

More history. More pain to be confronted.

At least Tavish had gotten Goliath out of Callum's penance. He patted the horse's neck before checking his Baker rifle and saddle bags—the muscle memory of a soldier too long at war.

All secured, Tavish turned for the tower house. He pulled on the yett—the metal gate protecting the oak front door—only to find it locked fast.

Huh. Here was something new.

The yett had never been locked, but now its iron bars appeared recently cleaned and oiled. At least someone was tending to the place. Mariah, most likely. His eldest sister had always been the first to address a need.

The laughter came again, tinkling and happy.

He frowned. Truly, this place could play fae tricks.

Walking around the corner of the castle, he looked to the cairn beyond. The views were always the best from its summit. Perhaps the higher elevation would give him some metaphorical perspective—

A shushing sound had him looking left.

Later, Tavish would wonder how that particular faint rustle had garnered his attention. But as a former officer of the 95th Rifles, a regiment of snipe shooters, he had spent years honing his instincts—slipping through forests like a phantom, attentive to the slightest noise.

Regardless, that soft swish stood out as significant.

He froze.

As if summoned, she emerged from the surrounding trees.

Tavish's . . . she.

Lady Isla Kinsey.

A jolt pinned him into place. Like lightning shocking his muscles and stealing his breath.

She looked ahead, eyes on the cairn. She certainly didn't see him, pressed into the shadow of the tower.

Why was she here, a Kinsey on Balfour lands?

His pulse pounded against his eardrums.

Tavish cataloged her differences. The passage of years had changed everything . . . yet nothing.

She was older, obviously—her expression more firm, her face settled into the defined lines of womanhood, the curves of her body more pronounced and, well, curved.

Unlike the girl she had been, Lady Isla now wore the height of current fashion—a blue satin spencer over a white gown of flowing muslin with a matching blue satin bonnet on her head. An ensemble that only the most expensive of modistes could create.

Lady Isla had spent considerable time in London, he realized.

Eejit. Of course, she had. What did he think she had been doing all these years? Sitting in the vast drawing room of Dunmore, embroidering bed curtains and swapping bonnet trimmings?

Lady Isla was the previous Duke of Grayburn's only daughter and sister of the current duke. No doubt, she was the most sought-after heiress in Polite Society. While Tavish had been urging his men through the muddy slop of the Peninsula—fighting hunger, low morale, and French rebels in equal measure—she had attended dinners and routs and balls. Watched the fireworks at Vauxhall and danced the night away in silk slippers. Surely some half-drunk swain had stolen a kiss or two.

The thought curdled his stomach.

Naturally, the clouds decided in that moment to part. The sun blazed through . . . illuminating Lady Isla in a beam of light.

Tavish nearly rolled his eyes. *Truly?* he longed to ask the Universe. *Isn't this laying it on a wee bit thick?*

Enough.

She was the reason he had returned here. They had unfinished business, the two of them. Why put off until tomorrow what he could accomplish the now? Tomorrow was hardly a guarantee. *Carpe diem* thoughts—those of a rifleman too accustomed to living in the shadow of Death.

Pushing off the stone, he walked toward her.

She startled—her gaze whipping to him, a hand pressing to her stomach in surprise.

Drawing near, he noticed her eyes were, as ever, the pale blue of Loch Cairnbeg in winter. And the framing bits of blonde hair on either side of her face still militantly refused to hold their curl, hanging defiantly straight.

Even seven years on, Lady Isla remained the bonniest lass he had ever seen—pointed chin, button nose, a smattering of freckles atop her cheekbones.

Tavish stopped a respectable four feet in front of her, his heart thumping against his ribs.

Lady Isla blinked, a slow up and down of her long eyelashes, as if she believed him a ghost and needed to verify his tangible being.

How odd. Not even a word said, and he could read her thoughts.

"Lady Isla." He lifted his hat in greeting.

"Mr. B-Balfour," she stammered. She did not, he noticed, dip her head or bob a shallow curtsy in greeting. Nor did she call him *Tavish*, as had once been her wont.

Either he had spooked the manners right out of her, or she rightly viewed him as beneath her notice. He felt every inch of his shabby greatcoat and scuffed boots.

"*Captain* Balfour," he couldn't help but correct. "I may have traded in my uniform, but the military remains."

"Captain," she whispered. "With the Gordon Highlanders?"

"The 92nd Regiment?" Tavish frowned. "Nae, I only enlisted with them initially. I was transferred to the Rifle Corps, the 95th, shortly thereafter."

"You are . . . *were* . . . a rifleman?"

"Aye."

A damn fine shot, too.

He didn't add that bit.

Her eyes darted to the faint scar across his upper right cheekbone. If the saber tip of Napoleon's *chasseur* had slashed even an inch higher, Tavish would have lost his eye.

"H-how . . . or r-rather *why* are you here?" she stammered.

Her accent was melodic and achingly English, courtesy of years of governesses and elocution lessons. Once, there had been faint traces of Scotland. Now, their homeland had been scrubbed out of her. Just as memories of him had surely been scrubbed clean.

He managed a weak smile. "There are . . . *matters* here to be settled, as well ye know."

Her chin lifted two inches, acknowledging the hit.

"I see."

"Never fear, I shan't be home long. Just . . . long enough."

"Oh."

That's all she said. *Oh.* Lips pursing into a perfect circle. As if they were discussing the weather and not the enormity of everything that lay between them.

"Isla—" Tavish stopped himself and cleared his throat. "That is, *Lady* Isla, if ye could spare a minute, perhaps we might discuss—"

A shadow flickered in the trees behind her.

Her elder brother, the Duke of Grayburn, strode from the tree line— walking stick swinging, clothing immaculately pressed and styled.

Time had changed the man not at all.

Grayburn still had the mien of an insufferable arse.

Why were two Kinseys on Balfour land?

Head down, the duke watched the ground, placing his feet with care. Tavish noted the deep sole of the man's right boot—nearly two inches thicker than the neighboring left one. Grayburn might be a duke, but he had to pay Hoby, his boot maker in London, a wee fortune to balance out the length discrepancy between his two legs—a defect that had plagued His Grace since birth.

Sometimes, Tavish was petty enough to take comfort in the man's deformity.

Today was one of those days.

"Look who has come home, Gray," Lady Isla said.

Her brother's head snapped upright.

Tavish nearly chuckled as he watched a series of emotions flicker across the duke's face—curiosity, shock, horror, before finally settling on fury.

Given that Grayburn was usually the picture of sangfroid made the entire display even more delightful. As ever, the duke's temper flared when he had to interact with a Balfour.

Some things remained as predictable as the tides.

Grayburn stopped at his sister's side. Unlike Lady Isla, his features were sharp. As if God took a chisel and hammer to a block of granite to form him—knocking off great slabs to create large eyes under a stern brow ridge, the thick slash of wide cheekbones, and a patrician nose.

That His Grace's nose sported a permanent bump courtesy of Callum's fist only added to the charm in Tavish's view.

The duke gave him a slow up and down—a sort of contemptuous, pitying appraisal. Surely Grayburn noted the three subtle repairs in Tavish's greatcoat—neat stitches done by his own hand during the days and weeks of mindless nothing between battles. Tavish might be an earl's son, but there had been little money for over a decade now.

"Balfour." Like his sister, Grayburn did not dip his head in greeting. "Same as ever, I see."

His words dripped with decades of derision. Generations, really, of spite and animosity.

Once, Tavish might have reacted to the slight.

But seven years of war—of watching friends blown apart in cannon fire, of hearing the shrieks and cries of the dying in his dreams at night—had tempered him.

Unlike the boy he had been, he now knew when to draw a sword, literal or proverbial. He would not spend energy fighting unless it became necessary.

"Grayburn," Tavish returned. "Out surveying enemy territory? Plotting your attack, perhaps?" He might not draw a weapon, but needling an enemy was a well-proved battle tactic.

Predictably, Grayburn stiffened, his eyes drawing down in a murderous manner.

Ah.

Cairnfell still struck a nerve, it seemed.

It was common knowledge that Grayburn wanted Cairnfell for his own, which likely explained His Grace's presence today. The large hill—the common origin of their two families—rested between their estates.

The fell had passed between their families several times over the years. The most recent exchange had occurred just over fifty years ago, when Tavish's grandfather had won Cairnfell from Grayburn's grandfather in a game of faro. Locals referred to the incident as the "Infamous Jack of Hearts" after the winning card. Northcairn had declared it a divine message from God, blessing his ownership of Cairnfell. Grayburn stormed out, shouting allegations of cheating.

The current Grayburn wanted revenge for this past slight and aimed to reacquire Cairnfell for his half of the family.

His Grace drew in a slow breath and darted a sideways glance at his sister. Tavish could practically see a vitriolic response clinging to the duke's tongue, but ever the gentleman, he refused to release it in a lady's presence.

"I was unaware you had cashed out of your regiment, Balfour," Grayburn parried instead. "Or, at least, I suppose you cashed out."

The implication being that Tavish was somehow stripped of his captaincy and tossed out on his ear.

"Aye, well, with the French Menace having been resolved at Waterloo, the army has been aggressively reducing the number of troops. I had a chance to sell on my commission, and I took it."

"He is a captain now, Gray . . . Captain Balfour." Isla gave her brother a tight smile.

Grayburn's eyes never left Tavish's face. He had the impression that the duke would bite off his own tongue before calling Tavish anything other than an *unmitigated bastard.*

"Sister, please return down the trail to the carriage. I shall join you in a moment. But first, I would like a private word with *Mr.* Balfour."

Even Isla raised an eyebrow at Grayburn's deliberate slight.

"As you wish. Though do not be long." She gave Tavish a pensive look before turning away.

Grayburn watched until she disappeared into the trees before whirling back to Tavish. "I thought my instructions were exquisitely clear the last time I conversed with you."

"Och, aye, they were. *If I ever see ye again, I'll put a bullet through your heart.* It was perfectly articulated and impressively melodramatic." Tavish rocked back on his heels.

Color climbed Grayburn's throat. "Then why . . . the *hell* . . . are you here?!"

"I'm on my family's land, Grayburn. How was I to know ye would be trespassing upon it today?" Tavish spread his arms wide. "I'm permitted to visit my family, particularly after an absence of seven years."

"You promised to stay away from my sister."

"And I have kept to that promise up to now. Ye lot be the ones to find me here today, not the other way around."

The duke's nostrils flared, red spreading from his neck to his cheeks. Soon the tips of his ears would be glowing like a blacksmith's forge.

"Lady Isla has never been for the likes of you. Maintain your distance, or I will hold to my part of the bargain."

"And put a bullet through my heart?"

"Precisely. I beg for you to give me an excuse."

Grayburn pivoted and followed his sister down the path, anger evident in how his gait slipped from a smooth glide into a subtle limp.

Tavish took petty comfort in it.

Sighing, he turned for Goliath.

Swinging into the saddle, he caught a glimpse of Lady Isla through the trees, looping her hand through Grayburn's elbow as they continued down the trail. The duke shot a murderous glance over his shoulder.

Tavish tipped his hat in farewell, knowing Grayburn would find it irritating.

The duke's returning glare did not disappoint.

Chuckling, Tavish nudged his own horse for the trail that led north toward Castle Balfour and home.

Thankfully, he hadn't actually agreed to steer clear of Lady Isla.

That would prove impossible.

Because one secret truth remained—

Lady Isla Kinsey was already Tavish's wife.

Isla could scarcely think, much less string sentences together, as she followed Gray down Cairnfell. Her thoughts had taken on the shape and density of wool batting.

Tavish has returned.

Returned, returned, returned . . .

The word looped through her mind, tangling her powers of speech.

Fortunately, Gray was speaking enough for them both.

"A captain! Hah! The nerve of that—" Her brother broke off, censoring his tongue.

He needn't have bothered.

Isla had no difficulty filling in the rest—*arse, bastard, blackguard.* And that was just the beginning of the alphabet. She supposed Gray would happily work his way through to *wastrel* before he finished.

He was limping. Badly. As ever an excellent barometer of his foul mood.

Only three things needled her normally level-headed brother to the point of rage:

Mention of their deceased mother,

Any interaction with the Balfour family,

And even a whiff of scandal touching the Kinsey family name.

Unfortunately, encountering Tavish Balfour encompassed the last two and had faint echoes of the first.

In short, Gray was furious.

"How dare that . . . that *man* approach and speak with you!" He swung his walking stick in an arc, slashing through a patch of nettle. "The brazen nerve of those Balfours never ceases."

Isla declined to point out the obvious: She and Gray *had* been trespassing on Balfour land. Propriety demanded that Tavish acknowledge and greet her.

Seeing her husband after an absence of seven years had been . . .

Isla hardly knew where to start. The Tavish of her memories was barely eighteen years old, untried and untested. A youth on the final cusp before manhood.

But the man she had encountered atop Cairnfell just now . . .

He is huge.

That had been her first thought. Had he always been so tall, so broad of shoulder?

Her Tavish had worn his heart on his sleeve, his gaze open and warm. It was one of the things she had loved best—the easy way he loved others.

But Captain Balfour had been armor-wrapped steel for all the emotion he showed.

No.

The body of Tavish Balfour had come home, but Isla was rather certain that *her* Tavish had died right along with their love.

"Balfour's return will bring difficulties, of course," Gray was saying, cane still slashing about.

Difficulties? Hah!

Her brother, in his ignorance of her marriage, didn't quite grasp the understatement of that.

"I had almost convinced Northcairn to sell Cairnfell to me, but who knows now?" Gray continued. "One word from the conquering hero, and I'm sure the old Scot will choose to hold to his pride and his poverty."

To hear Gray talk, only Northcairn's status as a Peer of the Realm kept him from debtor's prison. The earldom was on the verge of bankruptcy. And as the Northcairn estate was currently unentailed, the present earl—Tavish's father—could sell off chunks to pay his debts.

It was no secret Gray wished to buy Cairnfell. To avenge the "Infamous Jack of Hearts" card game and bring their ancestral lands back under his own control.

And he didn't care who he trampled in the process.

Isla had learned that bitter truth more than once over the years.

It was the primary reason she hadn't told Gray about her marriage. The knowledge that, when the topic of the Balfours reared up, her ducal brother could be cruel.

Isla and Gray reached the carriage, a coachman and two footmen standing at attention. Gray handed her inside before stepping in himself. They hadn't intended to stop here today, but a visit with local acquaintances had been cut short, and Gray wanted to have a "tramp" around Cairnfell before returning to Dunmore.

Return.

That word again.

Synonyms chased it—*reemerged, come back, resurfaced.*

Isla bit her lower lip, anything to tame the jittery energy banding her chest.

Why, after all this time, had Tavish chosen now to return home? And her most pressing question—did he intend to publicly claim her as his wife?

Her pulse thumped, anxiety acrid on her tongue.

"Do I need to order you to steer clear of Balfour?" Gray asked as the carriage lurched into motion.

"Of course not." Isla stared out at the green hills and the purple heather just beginning to flower . . . anything to prevent Gray from seeing her rising panic. "I have no intention of repeating the indiscretions of my youth."

That was only a partial truth.

Isla would never rekindle the wild, frenzied affection she had once felt for Tavish Balfour. It had scarcely been love at all. More like a fevered madness. A reckless slide into starry-eyed infatuation that, in her youth and inexperience, she had labeled *love*.

Could any girl know her heart at barely seventeen years of age?

Now facing her twenty-fourth birthday, she rather thought not.

In hindsight, Isla considered it a mercy that she and Tavish had shattered apart as spectacularly and quickly as they had fallen in love. Or, at least, that was how she envisioned it—a torch to a powder keg, obliterating the whole in one violent billow of flame and ash.

However, staying away from Tavish would be impossible given the pesky matter of their marriage—a fact known only to herself, Tavish, and the doctor and his wife who witnessed and signed the lines of their handfasting. A marriage that Isla had long regretted.

She now had a clear understanding of her own desires for the future.

One that would not involve a Balfour.

She could only pray Tavish felt the same.

Please feel the same!

Gray stared out his own window, a muscle twitching in his jaw. He tugged irritably at his constricting neckcloth. Despite his finery, her brother loathed the feeling of clothing tight against his skin. On an irritated huff, he ran a hand through his hair, turning it from respectable to a lion's mane, tawny-colored and shaggy around his face. His inner anger was fast unraveling his exterior.

It was astonishing, really, how quickly a Balfour could get under his skin.

In London, Gray relaxed into an urbane gentleman. He smiled with ease and always said the proper thing at the proper moment. He laughed over dinner and bestowed ladies with the exact right amount of charm. He tended to his responsibilities in the House of Lords just as meticulously as he managed his lands and tenants.

But when at Dunmore, that gentleman became harder for Gray to capture. The constant presence of one Balfour or another in the village of Pettercairn, combined with the lingering memories of their mother at Dunmore, had him frequently on edge.

"Are you still considering Colonel Archer and his suit? He would make you an excellent husband," Gray finally said, voice level.

Ah. Changing the subject, I see.

"I agree." Provided Isla could convince her current husband to divorce her and somehow keep the fact of their divorce quiet. "I am eager to deepen my acquaintance with him."

"Excellent. As I mentioned earlier, we have been invited to a house party with Colonel Archer and his parents at their hunting lodge in Aberdeenshire in about two weeks' time. I shall send them our acceptance."

"Please do."

Isla clasped her hands together, anything to mask the fine tremor that had started there.

Colonel Edward Archer was the second son of the Earl of Milmouth. Despite the similarity of title to Tavish—both men being the second sons of an earl—the Archers were everything the Balfours were not, namely English, wealthy, and highly respected.

Isla had met Colonel Archer last autumn in London. He was all a lady could wish in a suitor—kind, handsome, genuine. The consummate gentleman. Theirs had been a slow courtship, moving from acquaintances to friends at a snail's pace—Isla terrified to encourage him too much as she knew her former marriage to be a barrier. She refused to add "bigamy" to her list of sins.

Gray approved of the match as he was eager to form an alliance with Lord Milmouth and gain a powerful ally in the House of Lords.

Gray's support meant Isla would retain her dowry.

Which meant Malton Hill would be forever hers.

Malton Hill guided most of Isla's decisions at present.

In the wake of Gray discovering her attachment to Tavish—and in turn, Tavish permitting Gray to irrevocably separate them—Isla had fled south to England and Malton Hill, the small estate tied to her dowry.

She had arrived bereft, her heart an open wound. There, she discovered an estate as devastated as she felt. A place that needed her attention and love.

Over the following months and years, Isla had become a tigress, dragging Malton Hill back from the edge of ruin, defending her lands and people. And in the process, she reassembled the shattered pieces of herself into a new form. Into a woman who finally left behind the words *compliant* and *timid*. A woman who stood tall in adversity and no longer mourned the loss of a boy.

She loved the woman she had become.

If Isla remained married to Tavish Balfour, she would not see Malton Hill again, much less retain ownership of it. She would lose that vital piece of her sense of self. Her brother would never cede a farthing of her dowry to a Balfour. She only kept Malton Hill if she married with Gray's approval.

But with her erstwhile husband returned home, she could finally take measures to dissolve her marriage. She could attend the house party, smile and flirt with Colonel Archer, and accept his courtship with a clear conscience.

Despite her feelings as a young girl, sometimes *complying*—always a variant of that word—to the role laid out for her by family and tradition was not ill-advised, particularly when her dowry and the ownership of Malton Hill hung in the balance.

First, she simply needed to convince Tavish Balfour to grant her a divorce.

"I am pleased with this house party," Gray said. "It will allow me to formalize my alliance with Milmouth, and give you a chance to see Archer in his native environment and decide if you will suit."

"Native environment? At their hunting lodge in the Highlands?" Isla couldn't help the touch of asperity in her voice. She could scarcely imagine Colonel Archer in any sort of rough or tumbledown setting. An ancient drafty lodge in the foothills of the Cairngorms did not strike her as his "native" environs.

"Kingswell House is hardly a hunting lodge." A faint smile touched Gray's lips. "Lord Milmouth's mother was the only daughter of a wealthy Scottish lord. The estate came into the family as part of her dowry. It is anything but a hunting lodge."

Ah. A Palladian palace, then, something akin to the Earl of Dalhousie's stately home outside Brechin.

"You will find the place charming and restful," Gray continued.

"I look forward to it." Isla prayed Gray couldn't hear the quiver in her voice.

She breathed in a slow breath. Anything, really, to mask the agitated pounding of her heart.

One week.

She had just one week to run Tavish to ground and somehow convince him to set her free.

Isla stared out the window at the slashes of purple-shadowed earth rolling past—a field left fallow, exposing the red-brown soil of this corner of Scotland, as if the very dirt itself were rusting away. So unlike the rich loam of Malton Hill, eager to sprout roses and feed spring lambs.

She called up the house, nestled into the Gloucestershire hills. The gleam of sunlight in her study as she pored over the estate books with her steward. The sparkle of crystal and china as she laughed over dinner with friends in the dining room. The fiery light of the woman she was within those walls.

A life that was a vast cry from the uncertainty and mayhem Tavish had proposed seven years ago.

"We'll run away, you and I. Make our own fortunes in the world. I have a bit of money set by. We can use it to start our life together. Do you fancy New York City?"

In her youthful folly, Isla had thought the idea a grand adventure. Tavish had nearly shone with love for her, and her for him . . . until Gray, until those shredding words, until—

There was no point in reliving their ending.

She had been thirty ways a fool.

A flaw she had no intention of revisiting.

ARRIVING HOME, GRAY collected his afternoon post off a silver platter in the entry hall and disappeared into his study—limping, wrenching off his neckcloth and unbuttoning his collar. No doubt he was already penning a letter to his solicitor, venting his frustration over Captain Balfour's return and its implications for the purchase of Cairnfell.

Walking into the drawing room, Isla flipped through the letters that had arrived for herself—missives from friends and an update from Mr. Cranston, her steward at Malton Hill. Apparently, the west fields had flooded, and he had questions about measures to improve the drainage there.

Like Gray, she should retire to her writing desk and pen a reply.

If only her hands would stop shaking.

Tavish had returned.

Returned. Returned.

Isla helplessly replayed the events of the afternoon.

I shan't be home long, he had said. *Just . . . long enough.*

What did that mean? Long enough for *what* precisely?

Panic raced in her veins as she contemplated the options. Tavish could claim Isla as his wife—assert all legal power over her life—and drag her away with him unwillingly. Or, worse, denounce her as his wife and then abandon her to Gray's fury. Or, perhaps worst of all, simply do nothing and leave Isla in this in-between place for another seven years.

Unable to contain the nervous energy, her feet wandered the quiet rooms of Dunmore, the tap of her boots and the tick of cabinet clocks trailing her steps.

Built around eighty years ago when the family had grown tired of their ancient, drafty castle, Dunmore was a grand palace—the sort of estate more at home in the Wiltshire downs than their corner of northeast Scotland. The famed architect, William Adam, had designed it to impress—a central pedimented block with two wings connected by curving galleries. Enormous symmetrical windows punctuated the gray granite exterior, rendering the interior rooms light and airy on even the most dreary of days.

Seeing Tavish earlier had shaken Isla's moorings, and now memories echoed off the walls with each footstep.

There was the sofa where Mamma had loved to sit with a needle and thread when she was home. Given that the former duchess was rarely at home, the moment had always been a holy one. Isla would gather her small embroidery basket and curl up beside her mother, content to work in companionable silence and the soothing scent of Mamma's French perfume.

Ah, and here was the table where Gray had once discovered her hiding. Piers—she had called him by his first name then—had been around fourteen; Isla, eight.

She had found a kitten in the stables and claimed it as her own—much as she had claimed Tavish that fateful first meeting in the cemetery, come to think of it now. She found something to love, and so she loved it.

At the time, it hadn't even occurred to her to ask for permission to keep the kitten, any more than she had asked for permission to keep Tavish. Her parents were usually gone, and her brothers scarcely paid attention to her.

But the kitten had jumped out at the duke's feet as he tread the stairs, startling him. Her father's rage had burned hot. The kitten had been cast back to the stables, and Isla berated—everything from her slovenly manner to the hint of Scotland in her vowels—until she crumbled to sobbing tears.

Piers had found her huddled under a console table in the music room, face splotchy from crying. He crouched on the ground before her—neckcloth missing and shirt unbuttoned, as was his wont.

"Ah, poppet, you look a proper fright," he had said. "I'm sorry about your kitten. You should have been allowed to keep it."

He sat on the floor and opened his arms.

Isla crawled from underneath the table, instantly collapsing onto his chest.

She could easily recall it now. The steady thump of his heart. The soothing *shush-shush* as he quieted her tears. The upswelling of love in her heart for her older brother. Here was a person who cared about her. Who would defend her.

And he was. And he did.

Until Tavish or some other Balfour entered the picture. Then, all semblance of a loving brother disappeared.

That lesson had been bitterly learned.

Now, just as Cairnfell held the memory of Tavish, Dunmore reminded Isla of all the people who had abandoned her in one way or another. Her mother through death. Her father through his coldness. Gray through his deliberate actions and harsh threats.

Only Matthias, her other brother, remained at her side. Matt might never be her advocate, but he at least did no harm. And when she had needed a supporting arm, Matt had lent her his.

Eventually, her pounding heart and anxious feet led her to the library. It was a properly grand room, occupying the entirety of the central floor of the west wing of the house. Three walls boasted bookshelves between large windows. A sitting area, a map table, and a desk dotted the floor. Dust motes hung in the air, breathless in the golden sunlight.

Perhaps Isla should have written Tavish at some point. During their final argument, she had made him swear not to write her, and he had been true in that. Pity, he hadn't been true in his belief in her and their supposed "love" before that point.

Regardless, writing him had always felt too risky, too fraught. Besides, by the time she had recovered from the pain of their breaking, she was immersed in her work at Malton Hill. She hadn't wished to encourage his affections when hers had changed so utterly. Her impulsive marriage had been a fatal mistake—the reckless offering of an adolescent's heart. And therefore, she had buried the weight of it deep inside until it became a small thing—a smooth, light stone easily avoided.

But if she had written him, she might now understand his reasons for returning.

As it was, her heartbeat refused to settle in her chest, preferring instead to mimic the *ratatat* of a military tattoo.

Crossing the soft Axminster carpet, Isla opened a long drawer and stared at its contents—past issues of the *London Gazette*. Seven years' worth, to be precise.

Gathering them, she spread the papers atop the map table. The *Gazette* helpfully supplied the general movement of regiments, rank advancements, as well as lists of the officers who were wounded, captured, or killed in each battle.

All this time, Isla had thought Tavish to be in the 92nd—a regiment she had followed with an almost unholy attention. After all, a lady needed to know if she had become a widow.

With every new special issue, she had searched for Tavish's name—heart a pulse on her tongue.

But she had never once found him. Certainly not among the wounded or dead. No rank advancements, but also no mention of him in battle, either. Based on this, she had assumed that he had simply done his duty and nothing more. That he had never seen any true action and, instead, spent his time rusticating in a barrack well away from the fighting.

On occasion, though, she would wonder if he had ever journeyed to the front line. And if he had—if he spent long nights under a quiet sky of stars, fellow soldiers sleeping around him—did he ever look upward and think of her sleeping under the same heaven?

But, as it turned out, she had been looking in the wrong place.

Flipping through the pages of the *Gazette*, she charted the fortunes of the 95th regiment. The Rifle Brigade.

Even Isla had heard of the Rifles. Their bravery and brilliance in battle were a common topic. No soldier could enlist directly into the Rifles. A man had to prove his mettle and marksmanship and only then would he be asked to join their distinguished ranks.

And Tavish had become one of them. Had he even known how to shoot a rifle when they married?

It was only a matter of minutes before she discovered his name in the *Gazette*.

Lieutenant Tavish Balfour had fought in the Peninsular War and had been lightly wounded in the Battle of Badajoz. In 1813, he had advanced from Lieutenant to Captain. There was no mention of him at the Battle of Waterloo.

Sparse facts.

But more than she had known before this moment.

His face from earlier today rose before her, the white scar stretching beneath his right eye. Was that the "light" wound he had received in Badajoz? She could scarcely stop herself from imagining it. Tavish in a military uniform, covered in blood and gore, jaw set, rifle lifted to fire and defend himself. Or, perhaps, to be used as a club to bludgeon an enemy assailant.

She had seen such a thing once. Not a true battle, of course. But a pair of farm hands at Malton Hill, bared to the waist and attempting to bloody each other with their fists. It had been brutal and violent, and then to imagine Tavish in a similar situation, face twisted in rage, bayonet raised to—

Snick.

The library door opened.

"There you are." Matt nodded in greeting.

Unlike Gray, who saturated a room with the importance of his august person, Matt had a gentler energy.

Though nearly of a height with Gray, her brothers were only vaguely similar in looks. Where Gray was sandy-haired and hazel-eyed, Matt's hair was darker with matching soft brown eyes. Where Gray held his head like a general about to bark orders at troops, Matt had the mien of a monk—quiet and contemplative and set on retiring from the world. He rarely left the grounds of Dunmore, no matter Isla or Gray's pleading. Only once, when Isla had needed rescuing after Tavish's abandonment, had Matt asserted his will, bundled her into a carriage, and set forth.

It had taken Isla a long while to understand that Matt *needed* to control how he interacted with the world. Or, rather, how the world saw him.

The source of his discomfort was obvious—the bottom half of his right arm was missing from the elbow down. The same birth deformity that had resulted in Gray being born with his right leg slightly shorter than his left had denied Matt a right forearm and hand entirely.

Today, like every day, saw him with his right coat sleeve pinned up. Both Isla and Gray had pestered Matt to simply have his tailor cuff his right sleeve at the elbow, but their brother wouldn't hear of it.

"My appearance is already odd enough. Allow me the normality of seeing what my arm could have been," Matt had said on more than one occasion.

Unfortunately, Isla rather thought that summed up how Matt saw his life in general—*what could have been.*

"Matt," she nodded.

"Taking in some light reading, I see." He glanced meaningfully at the *Gazette.* His sharp gaze missed nothing. "Gray told me about Captain Balfour. Ranted, rather. I assume you are merely verifying the evidence."

"Yes. Rather."

They never spoke of this, she and her brothers. Matt and Gray had never asked for specific details about her tempestuous relationship with Tavish Balfour, and she had certainly never volunteered anything. The whole was all very English and stuffy, but Isla was glad of their silence. Her brothers only knew that there had been some brief attachment between herself and Tavish—an attachment that Gray had successfully disrupted. Matt likely understood the depth of that attachment, but she doubted his mind had ever leapt to matrimony.

"What have you discovered?"

"Captain Balfour was in the Rifles, it turns out. Not with the Gordon Highlanders, as I had supposed."

"Ah." Matt peered over her shoulder, reading the text. "Balfour made captain in 1813 after the Battle of Vitoria. A dreadful number of men died at that time."

Though her brother said nothing more, she could feel the weight of his questions: *Are you still entangled with Balfour? Will you kindle Gray's wrath once more?*

Isla swallowed as her answers to his hypothetical questions would be *Yes* and *Most likely*.

She needed to speak with Tavish first and understand why he had returned. *Matters to be settled*, he had said. God-willing, that referred to her and the knot of their handfasting. She prayed he intended to pick apart the tartan ribbon that had once bound their hands together. Isla knew little of what was involved—only that divorce was possible, as Scottish marriage law was decidedly more forgiving than English—but she assumed it would require the help of a man to sort. *Matters* always did.

If Tavish agreed to dissolve their marriage, they would eventually need to involve Gray to help keep their divorce as secret as their marriage had been. Only the might of a duke could ensure the divorce happened behind closed doors and hidden from scandal-hungry journalists.

More to the point, Gray was one of the most powerful men in Britain. *Ergo* . . . no Scottish judge would rule on her marriage without consulting her brother first. The second her name crossed a magistrate's desk, Gray would be informed of the truth: His sister had married a Balfour. And if her brother hadn't been told before that point . . .

Isla shuddered.

The only thing more terrifying than an angry Gray was a *humiliated* and angry Gray.

He must be told. It was simply a question of when.

But Matt . . .

At the moment, her confession hung on the tip of her tongue . . . to tell Matt of her handfasting and beg for his help in untangling it. No matter how inconsequential she considered the weight of her marriage, even the tiniest stone, when caught in a slipper, could leave the flesh abraded and raw.

And right now, her psyche stung. Anxiety stuffed her lungs and rendered her breathing tight.

Matt had always been the peacemaker. If she asked him, Isla knew he would keep her confidences as much as he deemed possible.

That was, until her confidences required him to set foot off Grayburn lands and possibly interact with a solicitor or some official in person. Yes, Matt had rescued her once, but over the years since, her brother had become even more set in his ways, more of a recluse. If she told him, he would likely wince and then urge her to confess all to Gray.

Thinking of which—

"McPherson?" Gray's voice echoed in the entryway, calling for the butler.

"I recommend hiding the evidence of your curiosity, Sister." Matthias glanced toward the open door. "You know how he gets over these matters."

Swallowing, Isla gathered the papers together and dropped them back in the obliging drawer, shutting it with a soft clack.

Would that disposing of her past indiscretions were so simple.

F or Tavish, traversing the road between Cairnfell and Castle Balfour felt like a journey back through time—each rock and tree ringing with the memory of Isla Kinsey and everything he had tried so very hard to forget.

There was the sheltered copse where he had been wont to steal a kiss.

The deep pool where the River Northcairn curled into itself, and Tavish had taught Isla to swim.

The rutted road—scarcely more than a track—that he would dash along in his haste to reach her. The same road Isla had raced down to throw herself into his arms.

Her past jubilation was the precise opposite of the poised, withdrawn lady he had just encountered atop Cairnfell.

Where had she gone, that vibrant lass?

It hardly mattered now, he supposed.

Lady Isla hadn't been happy to see him. No smile of surprise, no spark of delight. If anything, her expression had been one of dread and worry. Clearly, the passage of time had not softened her heart toward him. Battle-weary soldier that he was, Tavish understood when to raise the white flag of surrender.

Unfortunately, Lady Isla wasn't the only difficulty to be confronted today. There was still the matter of his family and their role in all this.

Tavish turned the last bend in the road and stopped. Castle Balfour gleamed in the sinking sunlight, a tattered banner flying from the west tower.

After seven years away, the view turned his throat tight.

He had hoped to feel nothing more than nostalgia upon arriving home. Instead, an upwelling of resentment, anger, and grief greeted him—emotions he had assumed long dead and buried. However, the feelings were precisely where he had left them—here, in this castle, echoing off the granite walls and crumbling battlements.

Returning had, perhaps, been a miscalculation on his part. Or, if he had visited with more regularity, maybe the surge of emotion wouldn't sting like a sharp slap.

Like himself, Castle Balfour was a bit worse for wear.

Ducking under the arched gateway and cantering into the courtyard, Tavish noted the masonry missing here and there atop the crenelated walls. Ivy appeared to be taking over the south wing entirely. Straw, mud, and animal refuse coated the flagstones.

Swinging off Goliath, Tavish handed the reins to a groom.

"See that my saddle bags are brought up to my room," he said.

The boy blinked, obviously having no idea who Tavish was or why he might be staying at Castle Balfour.

Aye, he had perhaps been away too long.

Tavish didn't wait for a reply.

Instead of pounding on the front door for entry—and letting one and all know he had returned—Tavish slipped through a smaller side door and up a staircase to the back of the entrance hall. From there, it was a simple matter to creep up the wide spiral staircase and across the great hall.

His entire family was seated at dinner, talking loudly over one another along the large table, pets scattered around the room. Meals had always been informal affairs at Castle Balfour. Children were not relegated to the nursery. So it was no surprise to see his two youngest siblings sitting with their elders.

Tavish stood in the doorway, waiting for someone to notice him in the chaos.

Naturally, his father sat at the head of the table, hair grayer and face more lined. Lord Northcairn's ruddy complexion showed signs of dissipation, and his waistcoat buttons strained to contain hi s girth.

Callum, Lord Cairnfell, Tavish's older brother, sat to their father's right as befitted his position as heir. Like Tavish, Callum had red hair and a deep-chested, muscular build. Unlike Tavish, Callum was quick with a laugh and compulsively flirted with any woman foolish enough to come within earshot.

Opposite Callum sat Mariah, their eldest sister. Unlike her brothers, she had dark hair that curled and bounced as if it would spring from her head at the slightest jolt. Efficient and organized, she still had the mien of a general, marshaling troops. Mariah gave orders, and they all listed to obey.

Case in point, at just that moment, Mariah bent to say something to the two children beside her, their youngest siblings—the twins, Edmond and Elsie. Edmond scowled but straightened in his seat. Elsie primly lifted her fork.

Heavens, how the twins had grown. They had been only three years old when Tavish left, barely out of leading strings. And now here they were—ten years of age and poised to sprout upward like a pair of silver birches reaching for sunlight.

Only Alice and Kenneth were missing. Alice had married nearly four years ago and lived in Aberdeen with her solicitor husband and two children. Or so Mariah had written. Tavish hadn't met her husband or his new nephews.

Kenneth was currently reading law at St Andrews University in Fife.

There had been other siblings. In particular, a pair of sisters between Kenneth and the twins who had died of a lung ailment over a decade past.

And, of course, their mother. A lady as dark-haired and fierce as Mariah and similarly quick with a hug or a firm scold. Bloody hell, but he missed her.

Tonight, dinner was their typical merry mayhem. That, at least, had not changed.

Edmond poked Elsie, who predictably complained to Callum. Mariah said something to their father, who nodded and poured more wine. Three dogs snuffled around the table, whining for scraps. They were hardly the most observant of fellows, as not one of them had yet noticed Tavish. A black and white cat stretched on one of the vacant chairs, claws pricking into the embroidered cushion. And was that a rabbit twitching its nose in the corner? Why the sudden onslaught of animals?

Finally, one of the dogs, a gray Scottish deerhound named Wallace after Scotland's famous hero, realized that another family member had joined them. With a woofing whine, he raced to greet Tavish, tail wagging furiously, his entire body nearly twisting in half with joy. The dog raised onto his hind legs and attempted to lick Tavish's face as the rest of the family jumped to their feet.

"Tavish!" Mariah cried.

"Son!" their father smiled.

"At last," called Callum.

"That's Tavish?" Edmund asked Elsie.

Tavish caught Elsie's soft words. "I suppose so."

And then Edmund's reply. "I thought he would be taller, the way Mariah talks."

Mariah rounded the table and, pushing Wallace aside, wrapped Tavish in a tight hug.

"Ye wretched man!" she said in his ear, shaking him slightly. "Ye didn't say even one word in your last letter about this. I would have been waiting at the window in anticipation!"

"Hallo, Mariah." Tavish returned her hug, lifting her off the ground. Her small frame always surprised him. Mariah was such a force of nature, he thought of her as a giant when, in fact, she was a mere wisp of a woman.

Pressing a kiss to his cheek, she pulled back, tears pooling. "Regardless, I'm glad ye be here."

The emotion lingering in Tavish's chest constricted.

"Enough. Ye will both be *greiting* like a pair of mawkish débutantes next." Callum pushed Mariah aside.

For all his brusque words, Callum grasped Tavish in a tight embrace.

Huh. They were the same height now. Before, his brother had always been a wee bit taller.

"Figures ye would grow another two inches, ye *bawbag*," Callum said good-naturedly. "Welcome home, brother."

And then the twins were upon Tavish, demanding his attention though they surely had no true memory of him.

Edmund climbed his legs as though they were tree trunks, while Elsie tugged on his coat. Both battered him with questions.

"Will you be here for long, Tavish?" That was Elsie.

"Did you kill a hundred Frenchies in the army?" That was Edmund.

"Edmund!" Mariah swatted the back of his head.

"What?! He was a soldier, Mariah."

"Would you like to meet my pet rabbit? Her name is Josie—"

"Josie is silly! Ye should see my frogs, Tavish!"

"Children! Enough!" Their father clapped his hands.

Lord Northcairn used a cane now to walk, Tavish noted. But the man's gaze danced as lively and heedless as ever.

Reaching up, he pulled Tavish's head down, pressing a gentle kiss to his cheek. "I praise God ye have arrived home safely to us, Son."

"It's good to be home, Da'."

"Jameson!" Lord Northcairn called for their butler. "Let us have a bottle of Madeira to celebrate."

The twins whooped and raced around the room, setting the dogs to yipping. The cat leapt onto the sideboard, upsetting the gravy boat and tracking brown paw prints across the tablecloth. Mariah rapped the table, calling for order, which the twins—no doubt to their peril later—blithely ignored. Callum rolled his eyes. Their father laughed and went back to his food, tossing the cat to the floor. The beleaguered Jameson arrived and summoned a footman to help clean the mess.

Home was precisely as Tavish remembered—mayhem, laughter, and affection flowing atop undercurrents of resentment and pain.

As ever, he drifted along in its wake.

THE FOLLOWING HOURS passed in a rush.

The twins were beside themselves to finally meet their long-absent older brother. This meant they had to show him everything in their world. Tavish admired the frogs—one was likely a natterjack toad, not a frog, which the twins debated at length—as well as a smooth snake, a rabbit, and a litter of kittens. Apparently, the snake had a habit of eating the frogs. No surprise there.

Once the twins had been banished to the nursery—complaining mightily that they were not tired and Tavish still hadn't seen the spider nest in the back garden and would he spend the day with them tomorrow?—Tavish joined his father and Callum in the library for a dram of whisky.

The fire burned low in the hearth, casting eerie shadows up the bookcases. Originally the dining hall of the medieval tower house, the library featured a high-barrel vaulted ceiling and the family coat of arms carved into stone above the mantelpiece—three holly leaves flanked by two knights under the family motto, *sub sole sub umbra virens,* which translated as "flourishing both in sunshine and shade."

"So what brings ye home now of all times?" Callum asked once they were each holding a glass of the fine Bracklamore whisky Tavish had brought with him. "This whisky is excellent, by the way."

Tavish saluted him with his own glass.

As usual, Callum vibrated with energy—one knee bouncing, body shifting in his chair—some part of him always in motion. To be truthful, it surprised Tavish that Callum was here at all. His brother always appeared more at ease outside of family obligations, chasing some dangerous pursuit or another. Daring curricle races in London. Sailing a boat across Montrose Basin in a tempest. Climbing the sheer face of Cairnfell without a rope.

The more perilous an activity, the more certain it was that Callum would seek it out. Boredom was the true enemy of his existence.

"I'm right glad ye like the whisky." Tavish stretched his feet toward the fire before returning to his brother's question with, "I have a spot of business in Aberdeen." A secret marriage to address, rather, but his family knew nothing of his history with Lady Isla. "And I am planning on meeting up with a pair of army friends for a week of hunting near Corgarff and finalizing plans for America."

"Ye still set on heading to Pennsylvania then?" his father asked.

"Aye. I enjoyed my time in the States. And there is significantly more opportunity there."

After banishing Bonaparte to Elba in 1814, a portion of the 95th rifles had been sent to assist efforts in defending British interests in Florida and Louisiana. Though the British had eventually admitted defeat and returned home, Tavish had found the States themselves to be an alluring mix of economic possibility and lofty idealism.

"What is your plan then in Pennsylvania? Live on the frontier in a log cabin and farm the land?" Callum pushed to his feet and began pacing. "That sounds like a rather dreary life for an earl's son."

Of course Callum would think so.

Anger, well-worn and familiar, spiked Tavish's pulse. Bitter words stacked on his tongue:

Aye, opera dancers and gaming hells are rather thin on the ground in rural Pennsylvania, so of course ye would think the place a dead bore.

From long habit, Tavish breathed through the sudden rush of fury and bitterness.

Callum's compulsion to seek thrilling pastimes didn't harm only himself. The rest of the family had suffered because of it over the years, Tavish in particular.

He had forgiven Callum—he *had*—but as Tavish still dealt with the consequences of his brother's folly, resentment festered.

One of a myriad of reasons why Tavish had delayed returning home.

"I assure ye, Pennsylvania is a mite more sophisticated than that. Have ye not heard of Pittsburgh?" Tavish pasted on a stiff smile. "My friend, Captain George Ross, is the son of a prominent whisky distiller. Bracklamore whisky in Moray, to be precise." Tavish raised his glass. "He knows everything there is to know about growing rye and turning it into the best whisky inside or outside of Scotland."

Callum fixed him with a pained look. "Ye intend to become a whisky distiller? Is that what we Balfours have been reduced to?"

Tavish merely lifted an eyebrow at Callum's tone. *No thanks to yourself,* that eyebrow said.

Callum at least had the decency to look away.

"Aye. I have some capital from the sale of my commission and an understanding of the lay of the land in the States. Ross has the knowledge to create the whisky. And we have another friend, Fletch, who has promised to invest the rest of the monies needed. We'll hammer out all the finer details when we meet at the end of next week. Our thoughts are to give the whisky producers in Kentucky a run for their money. True Scottish whisky made like it is in the old country. None of this apocryphal Irish nonsense they get up to in Kentucky."

Lord Northcairn sipped his glass appreciatively. "It's excellent whisky, Son. Ye shall have to send me a case of your first bottles."

Their conversation drifted off after that, wandering first to corn futures and wool prices before becoming lost entirely in Lord Northcairn's musings on a horse he had an eye to purchase.

With what money? Tavish longed to ask.

Neither Callum nor their father asked Tavish any further questions.

But then, that had always been the way of things with them. Northcairn had his heir in Callum, and Tavish was merely an afterthought. If he told them he had spoken with his secret wife at Cairnfell this afternoon, they would likely respond with polite noises. Maybe ask Tavish how he was going to support her. Nothing more.

Well, until Tavish informed them that his wife was Lady Isla Kinsey. Then, the vitriol and recriminations would fly. The talk of Kinseys enraged Balfours, just as much as Balfours infuriated Kinseys.

What a bollocking mess this had all become.

In the end, it was Mariah who knocked on his bedchamber door just after he retired for the night. She came bearing a tray of hot chocolate and shortbread.

"I thought ye might like a wee go at supper before bed," she said with a wan smile.

"Ye know me too well." Tavish motioned her into his room.

Sitting before the fire, Mariah poured them each a cup of chocolate, sipping with a quiet groan of appreciation.

Initially, they spoke of inanities.

Yes, the twins were a handful.

Yes, Kenneth was enjoying his studies.

No, they had no plans to visit London or even Edinburgh. Though Alice might come for a visit from Aberdeen over Michaelmas.

Tavish had never told Mariah about his marriage. Not because he worried about her reaction—she would love and accept any lady he married, Mariah's heart was so huge.

No, he simply refused to add one more burden to the already heavy load of worry his sister carried.

"How bad is it?" Tavish finally asked.

Mariah didn't pretend not to understand. She set her cup down with a sigh and tried to give him a bright smile, but it emerged as a pained grimace. It was an expression he remembered their mother wearing, as well. An attempt to put a brave face on difficult circumstances.

"That bad?" Tavish continued.

Tilting her head back, his sister studied the ceiling, as if willing her tears to drain back into her eyes.

"I never cry over it," she whispered. "It's merely been so long since . . . since . . ." She trailed off.

Since I had help or a sympathetic ear, Tavish easily supplied.

Guilt nipped at his heels.

"Ye needn't feel guilty, Tavish," Mariah continued, accurately reading him. "There is nothing ye could have done here except be a drain on our limited financial reserves, and that is the truth of it. In some ways, it was fortunate that your regiment never returned to Britain during the War. No one could have reined in Callum's excesses or changed the events that happened before your departure or since."

Tavish snorted. "I could have put a bullet through Grayburn's black heart."

"And swung from a hangman's noose for it? I think not. At least Callum is home now, attempting to make amends."

"Are you positive there is nothing I can do to assist ye?"

"Quite."

They sat in silence for a long moment, coals settling on the fire.

"And yourself?" Tavish asked. "What of your prospects?"

Mariah gave a bitter laugh. "Nothing has changed there. I am as ruined as ever. I am so beyond the pale that even eligible gentlemen farmers cross the street when they see me coming . . . fearful that the taint of my reputation might touch them from twenty paces off."

Tavish ground his teeth. Of all the unfair things he had experienced over the years—and heaven knew he had seen aplenty—the fact of his older sister's ruination stung the worst. Though Grayburn hadn't actually done the ruining himself, the duke had been the puppet master pulling strings to ensure it happened.

"And Da'?" Tavish had to ask.

Mariah shrugged. "The same. His health declines year over year because he does nothing to curb the worst of his drink and appetite. Moreover, there is a widow he visits with some regularity outside Stonehaven. Everyone speaks of it, as our father is incapable of discretion. Alice, thank goodness, is married. Ken will do well as a solicitor, perhaps venturing into politics eventually. Edmund is resourceful and will make his way in the world. But my heart breaks for Elsie. I cannot imagine there will be much of a future for her. She is barely ten years old and already saddled with a lack of a dowry, looming poverty, and a scandal of an older sister. Who will marry her?"

"Callum will ensure she is taken care of."

"Will he, though?" She sipped her hot chocolate.

"I'll thrash him if he doesn't."

"So confident of your abilities? Ye rarely bested him in the past."

Tavish stared into the fire. "Seven years of war change a man. I assure you, Callum wouldn't stand a chance."

He said the words quietly, but given how Mariah flinched, she caught the steel behind them.

"But ye dodged my question," Tavish continued. "What of your own future?"

"Mine? Hah!" Mariah set down her cup and stared into the low flames, expression bleak. "I merely hope that Callum has a nursery full of children who need a loving aunt to tend to them. That is the best my life can bring."

"Perhaps my new adventure will be fairy-kissed, and I will earn enough selling whisky that I can provide ye with a future of comfort."

His sister shot him a side-eye, rife with her own disbelief.

"The same good fortune that, seven years ago, saw a distant 'uncle' purchase you a regimental commission at no small cost? An uncle with whom we have never spoken, before or since?"

Tavish acknowledged the hit with a lift of his chin. Yet one more secret he kept from his family.

"'There are more things in heaven and earth, Horatio, than are dreamt of in your philosophy,'" he quoted, setting down his teacup with a faint clink. "Sometimes miracles happen when they are most needed."

"I stopped believing in miracles years ago," Mariah snorted. "Someday ye will tell me the truth of how your regimental commission came to be."

"Someday," he agreed. He owed his sister as much. "But not tonight."

4

EIGHT YEARS EARLIER

AUGUST 12, 1809
PETTERCAIRN, SCOTLAND

Today was his seventeenth birthday.

Tavish kicked at the stones lining the base of Cairnfell Castle.

Another year without his mother.

And this year, his father, sister, and older brother were absent as well. Lord Northcairn had taken Callum and Mariah to London to launch Mariah into society with the help of their aunt.

In short, no adults were present to celebrate his birthday.

Had his mother still been alive, she would have planned something for him. Even if she had needed to be in London, she would have anticipated his birthday.

Instead today, like most other days, saw Tavish forgotten.

Cook had taken pity on him and baked his favorite dessert—a large clootie dumpling that she had first formed into a ball and boiled in a cheesecloth sack before leaving it to dry by the fire.

Tavish had eaten his fill and then stolen another large wedge and wrapped it in a bit of muslin. Slipping out the back gate of Castle Balfour, he had stopped by the kirkyard to blow a kiss to his mamma and leave a discreet note partially tucked into a crevice of the opulent monument of the former Duke and Duchess of Grayburn.

Then, he made his way up Cairnfell to wait.

Tavish often came here, resting in the quiet of the ruins. The place where, centuries past, the Balfours and the Kinseys had been a single, united family.

He hadn't spoken a word to Lady Isla Kinsey since their birthdays last August. Granted, he had been at school for most of the year. But he had finished his studies in June, and he didn't intend to continue on to university. He hadn't the temperament for law or the church.

What he wanted, at the moment, was to see Lady Isla.

Over the past year, she had gone from a person he scarcely noticed to the lass he saw everywhere. He watched her stroll down High Street in Pettercairn with her governess, the bespectacled Miss Farnsworth, stopping at the haberdashers and the milliners. Her bonneted head was directly in his line of view during church services on a Sunday. He had caught snatches of her in Grayburn's carriage, swathed in black, mourning the death of her father just four months past.

This would be her first birthday without her father.

And, like his family, her older brother was in London for the Season.

If all their kin were currently in residence, Tavish wouldn't have dared to arrange a meeting with her. Callum smacked the back of his head if he caught Tavish so much as looking in Lady Isla's direction.

But Tavish had to try. His sense of fairness forced him to return the compassion she had shown him last year. To bring some happiness to what was surely a difficult birthday for her.

Knowing she would likely visit her parents' grave today, he had left a straightforward note there:

A wise person once told me that the first birthday is the hardest. If you wish a compassionate ear, meet at the base of Cairnfell Castle this afternoon.

He had not signed it.

If she didn't realize the note was from him, then the connection he had sensed last year clearly had been one-sided.

Better to know now. As it was, she already occupied too many of his thoughts.

Was she as vibrant as he recollected? The girl last year had nearly sparkled with an untamed energy. Her bubbling laughter haunted his dreams.

Tavish waited for an hour.

Then two.

Just when he thought she might not show, a dark figure emerged from the surrounding forest, walking toward him, a determined lift to her chin.

The mourning black of her gown did dreadful things to her complexion, dimming the roses in her cheeks and lending her skin a sallow color.

Their eyes met, and his heart thumped . . . perhaps its first true beat in a year.

With a start, he realized that Isla was taller than he had supposed. Not looming for a female, but taller than average. Enough that he wouldn't have to bend too far for a kiss.

Not that he was going to kiss her.

He shouldn't. He wouldn't.

But he was a seventeen-year-old male, so kissing and all its attendant activities were rarely far from his thoughts.

She stopped six feet before him.

He doffed his hat and gave a lavish bow—the one his mother had drilled into his manners.

"Lady Isla," he intoned.

"Mr. Balfour." She curtsied, elegant and smooth.

"Thank ye for coming." He grinned, his most winsome expression. Or so Mariah told him.

Lady Isla had been crying, he noted. Her red-rimmed eyes could mean nothing else.

His smile faltered.

"Have you come to cheer up my day?" she asked. He detested the wee warble at the end of her sentence.

There was less of Scotland in her vowels this year. That English governess of hers was erasing all traces of their country.

"Aye, lass. I consider it my sacred responsibility. The proper duty of a birthday twin, as it were. I shan't consider your birthday properly celebrated until I hear ye laugh."

She smiled, but not a true one. More of an impoverished cousin to a smile.

Hands clenching into fists, she gave him a bold look, far more direct than he thought her capable. More bold than any other lass of his acquaintance.

"Do you think to use me for revenge?" she asked.

Her question punched the air from Tavish's lungs.

"Revenge?"

"Yes. Against my family . . . Do you attempt to befriend me in order to wound them? We are enemies, after all."

Tavish's jaw worked for a few seconds, unable to form words. The thought hadn't once crossed his mind, but he could see how his actions might appear to her.

He simply considered her a bonnie, interesting lass whom he would like to know better. And . . . maybe laugh with on occasion.

"Never," the word coming out more forceful than he intended. He shook his head. "I would never use any woman, much less yourself, so abominably."

Still, she hesitated, suspicion in her gaze.

He liked her all the more for her careful consideration. It showed spirit and backbone and a strong sense of self. Attributes he applauded.

"I swear it, lass. Upon my mother's grave." He crossed his heart. "Are ye using myself?"

"And if I were?" she asked, voice cool.

He mimed a dagger to the chest. "Best to get it over with quickly, then."

She shook her head, but a genuine grin picked up one corner of her mouth.

"Come. Let us set aside our familial enmity today of all days." He beckoned. "I have set a humble birthday party of sorts."

He led Lady Isla around the base of the castle to a clearing between the towerhouse and the cairn. Here, he had placed a small table and two chairs, all taken from the lower room of the castle. Atop the table, he had arranged his large slice of clootie dumpling in the muslin and a jug of small beer he had pilfered from the cold larder.

He held out a chair for her, helping her to sit, before taking his own seat.

"My lady, may I offer ye a wee slice of the best clootie dumpling in this corner of Scotland?"

She smiled again, slightly broader this time. "I should like that."

"Unfortunately, my hostess skills have not extended to china or cutlery, so we shall have to make do with our hands."

He broke off a piece of the pudding, several currants and a lone sultana tumbling to the muslin. Peeling off her gloves and retrieving a handkerchief from her sleeve, she set her slice atop it, nibbling at a bite, head bowed.

Tavish detested the wee quiver he noted in her bottom lip. This lass was made for laughter and sunshine. How the stern Kinsey family had birthed a daughter who shone like fairy light, Tavish hadn't the faintest idea.

"Happy birthday, lass."

She sniffed. "Thank you."

Breaking off another piece, she lifted it to her lips before wiping a tear from her cheek with a knuckle.

He wanted to thumb the teardrop from her face himself, to pull her to his chest and let her weep her grief.

"I am sorry about your father," he said.

She nodded, taking another nibble of cake and wiping yet another tear.

"I would have thought my tears would send a gentleman scrambling for the hills," she sniffled. "I know my brothers cannot leave the room quickly enough when they find me crying."

"I ken a wee bit of emotion to be a good thing. My own mamma said a soul suffers when feelings stay locked tight inside. Feelings are something ye *feel*. If ye refuse them, they can fester and poison ye from within."

His words sent more tears tumbling down her cheeks. She wrestled with them, breaking off pieces of the dumpling.

"Can I tell you a . . . feeling?" She raised her head. "I cannot speak of this to anyone else and, yes, it festers within."

"Of course."

"You will think me a terrible person."

"Impossible."

The opposite, he didn't add. *I think you the loveliest thing.*

She sat back. "I'm not sure my father liked me much."

This surprised him. "How so?"

"My mother was a social creature. She craved the company of others and was always off visiting this place and that. But when she chose to appear in the nursery, she was a warm presence. However, my father . . . my father was a stern, distant figure. He only spoke to me when he found something to criticize." She poked at her bit of dumpling. "He definitely showed more interest in my brothers, but I supposed that was to be expected. They're male—the heir and the spare. I was female and therefore lesser."

"Regardless of the reason, that's a right terrible thing to bear."

"Perhaps, but the day after our father died, Piers . . . or rather Grayburn, as I suppose I must call him now, became just as distant as our father. It was as if a fae spirit had stolen in overnight and replaced kind Piers with dreadful Grayburn."

"Truly?"

She nodded. "He hasn't said a kind word to me since. For example, I asked him if I looked ghastly in my mourning blacks. Gray looked me up and down before shrugging and walking away without a word. As if I were of no more note than a buzzing gnat."

Tavish wanted to whisper that the mourning black itself was, indeed, dreadful, but only because she belonged in colors like those of meadow flowers.

"Piers would never have behaved so abominably," she continued. "He would have put an arm around me and told me I looked lovely. But now that he is Grayburn, his former kindnesses have simply . . . vanished. Like a candle being blown out. Is it a requirement when becoming a duke? To put a barrier between yourself and your female relations?"

"I cannot say."

"Is your father distant and cool toward your sisters?"

Tavish envisioned his father—his larger-than-life Da' with a boom for a laugh and arms open to sweep anyone and everyone into a hug. That was part of the problem, Tavish reckoned. His father was rather indiscriminate with his affections, as barmaids, lonely widows, and the occasional London actress could attest. The man had been anything but discreet since the death of Tavish's mother.

"Nae. My da' is open and loving to a fault."

Lady Isla swallowed, nodding her head again.

Neither of them said anything for a long moment.

"I greatly dislike that our families are enemies," she said at last.

"Me, too."

"We should be friends, you and I." She pinned him with her blue eyes. "Set a good example for our families. Show them kindness is better than hatred."

Again, so bold.

"I should like that." He wiped his hands on his breeches and then extended his right hand across the table. "Friends."

She slipped her slim hand into his.

The warmth of her bare skin against his sent fire licking up his arm.

And yet, her bones were so fragile in his grasp.

A tremendous rush of protectiveness surged through him. If her brothers were not going to look after her properly, Tavish was more than willing to do the job.

"If we are to be friends," she said, "then we must have a better way of communicating. If someone else had found your note to me . . ."

"Aye. What do ye propose?" Because even if he didn't know this lass that well, he guessed she might have a knack for planning.

"My governess spoke of ciphers last week as we were discussing Caesar's campaign against the Gauls. Perhaps we could devise one of our own."

"A Caesar cipher—the sort where you merely shift the letters of the alphabet by three letters or so, like A becomes D and so on?"

"Or perhaps we create one that is more random. Any learned person would see the scrambled text and assume it to be a Caesar cipher. We can be more intelligent than that."

"Agreed." Tavish grinned. Bloody hell, but he adored the quick turn of her mind.

They spent the next hour deciding what their cipher would be. Something simple, but complex—each letter of the alphabet substituted with another letter, seemingly at random. They wrote it out with a bit of charcoal on the muslin cloth of the clootie dumpling.

And Tavish did make her laugh in the end—a rollicking story about Callum getting drunk off sour whisky and tumbling into Farmer McLeod's pig sty.

The sound of Lady Isla's giggles twined through the trees of Cairnfell and filled Tavish's heart with such happiness, he feared the organ would burst.

Isla sat immaculately still as Reverend Stronach preached on the certain damnation of liars and deceivers—every word flying like a barbed arrow straight to her heart.

She bore it all without a hint of a blush or a telltale clutch of her reticule. Given the weight of her guilty conscience, it was an acting performance worthy of Drury Lane.

Isla felt inordinately proud of herself.

Another sin to repent of, no doubt. The good reverend would assuredly have strong opinions on the evil of feeling pride over one's ability to hide iniquity.

Voices whispered behind her, followed by a giggle. Gray scowled and shifted in his seat at her side, gaze remaining militantly forward.

The Balfours were seated one pew behind them to the left. If Isla canted her head the tiniest bit, she could see the graying head of Lord Northcairn seated beside Lord Cairnfell and Lady Mariah. Captain Balfour sat closer to the aisle between the twins, Master Edmund and Lady Elsie.

The twins giggled again. A muscle in Gray's jaw twitched.

Isla resisted the urge to fidget.

She *needed* to tell Gray about her illicit marriage. Every day she delayed was one more nail in her coffin.

And yet . . .

Fear was a powerful motivator, she pondered for not the first time. Gray burned hot when it came to the Balfours.

Another giggle sounded, chased by a loud shush.

Gray took in a slow breath at her side, his hands flexing where they held the brim of his hat.

Isla could feel the leashed energy in him. Just sitting in the same room as Tavish had Gray itching to toss the entire Balfour clan out of the kirk. And that was without knowing Isla had married the man. How incandescent would her brother be once he learned the truth?

She could imagine Gray rising to his feet and shouting her perfidy from the rafters, denouncing her before pointing a finger at the Balfours and demanding justice. Tossing her to the wolves without so much as a scathing look in her direction.

Unbidden, a memory rose. The three of them—herself, Matt, and Piers—lounging in the drawing room together on a lazy July afternoon.

Piers was maybe sixteen and down from school. As ever when with family, he wore only loose breeches and shirtsleeves. Even then, he had seized any opportunity to discard as many layers as possible.

Matthias, at fifteen, was the opposite. He was always immaculately attired, his right sleeve neatly folded and pinned. With every passing year, he had become quieter and, more often than not, refused to leave the house. *Everyone stares*, he had whispered to Isla.

Isla, at age ten, had sensed change on the wind. Both their parents had been more and more absent, but never at the same time together. The duke was currently in London doing whatever dukes do in London. Their mother was in Shropshire, visiting friends.

"I think our parents have abandoned us," Matt said. "It's easy to see why." He lifted his right arm with its pinned sleeve at the elbow.

Piers had snorted. "Our parents aren't here because they are a sorry lot and prefer to escape their duties rather than face them. It has little to do with us."

"Do you truly think that, Piers?" Matt asked.

"Of course. Mother refuses to tolerate Father's presence. Father pines for her instead of seeing to his lands and bemoans his fate to all who will listen. Both of them heap scandal and ridicule on our family name. Gossip that the Balfours are far too eager to discuss with our neighbors. All the things I will not tolerate once I'm duke."

Piers sat up, bracing his elbows on his knees and causing his shirt to gap open at the collar. His keen hazel eyes met first Matt's and then Isla's.

"I won't be able to correct the wrongs thrust upon our family by myself," Piers said. "I will require your support. We need to band together, us three. To be as unbreakable as we can. What say you?"

"You will always have my support," Matt said on a rush. "Why would you think otherwise?"

"I don't. I guess I . . ." Piers let out a slow breath, dragging a hand through his tawny hair. "I guess I simply wanted to hear that nothing would ever change between us."

How like Piers, Isla had thought at the time. *Thinking of others.*

"I will always love you, Piers." Isla had rushed to hug him. "You and Matt will always be the bestest brothers."

He had laughed and hugged her back.

Of course, once Piers became Grayburn, his promise of support had really only strung in one direction—from Isla and Matt to Gray. Her ducal brother's approval came with rigid stipulations and expectations. As long as Isla didn't deviate from those, Gray would back her.

But the moment a Balfour came into the picture . . .

Gray held no room in his heart for calamitous errors in judgment, such as Isla's marriage.

No. He would never forgive her for it.

Only Matt, with his own demons and struggles, had remained true to her. The only person to witness her fracturing after Tavish enlisted and left. The only person to stretch a hand into the darkness and plead with her to grab hold.

After all, Matt had been the one to take her to Malton Hill.

ISLA HAD ARRIVED at Malton Hill a mere shell of a person, prone to staring into space for hours on end. Even eating had become an unwelcome chore.

Her love affair with Tavish had disintegrated mere weeks beforehand. Melancholy clung to her back, a gremlin she hadn't the energy to cast off.

Matt knew something had occurred with Tavish Balfour to kindle Gray's wrath. But Matt had never asked her about it. Perhaps Gray had told him. Or perhaps, in his quiet way, Matt knew that the minutiae of her relationship with Tavish were rather moot now he had accepted an officer's commission and exited her life.

Regardless, Matt had accompanied her south to Gloucester.

"A change of scenery," he had insisted. "A new place with new memories hovering in the wings."

Though Malton Hill was promised to her in her dowry, Isla had never visited the place. She needed a male guardian to accompany her and, as the estate was far from both Scotland and London, none of her male relations had been interested in escorting her there. Until Matt, that was. She knew leaving the sanctuary of Dunmore had cost him dearly, but for her, he had done it. She would love him forever for the sacrifice.

Isla could easily recall that first glimpse of Malton Hill—its honey-colored limestone aglow in the warmth of an English sunset, gables contouring the light and painting windows in streaks of gold and rose. The house had hummed with an ancient promise, as if anticipating her arrival.

It had been, Isla realized years later, a moment of genuine rebirth. A crack in her chrysalis, one just big enough for her to glimpse a new world.

No one at Malton Hill knew of Tavish Balfour. They didn't know she had once loved a gray-eyed boy with a laugh like summer sunshine. They didn't know her heart was an open wound, throbbing in her chest, or that she lay in her bed at night, staring at the canopy overhead, desperate to think of anything but him.

No one at Malton Hill had any preconceived notion of her at all. She wasn't the sum of the mistakes Gray laid at her feet, or a host of charms to watch grow into womanhood.

To most, she was Lady Isla, the elegant mistress of an elegant estate. The aristocratic owner who had finally arrived to address problems that had been ignored for too long.

Though the estate was to be Isla's, her father had badly neglected it. The old steward was indolent in his duties, cruel in his collection of rents and slow to authorize repairs. The land languished, and tenants suffered.

For herself, Isla had never been taught how to run an estate as a whole. A household? Yes. An entire estate? No.

When faced with the enormity of it all, she discovered something about herself:

She wasn't timid or compliant.

She might be unsure and untrained in this particular task, but determination roiled in her breast.

So, despite feeling desperately young and out of her depth, Isla had rolled up her sleeves and set to work. She was intelligent and capable. She merely needed to learn estate management. Matt, as ever, refused to deal with people or leave the house, but he had an excellent listening ear and provided advice. He propped her up as she learned to spread her untried wings.

The old steward was let go and a new one hired—a younger man, Mr. John Cranston, who brimmed with energy and clever ideas for modernization that assisted tenants instead of penalizing them. With Matt and Mr. Cranston guiding her actions, Isla authorized repairs and mediated disputes. She discussed planting schedules and tallied account sums until her eyes ached. Some days, it felt as if all she did was breathe through one catastrophe after another.

But slowly, through trial and error and an astonishing amount of work, she brought the estate back to life. Leaking roofs were rethatched, and crumbling harling refreshed. Crop yields dramatically increased, and her tenants smiled more readily.

Most importantly, witnessing the changes filled Isla with an almost holy sense of purpose and protectiveness. She had begun the task as a way to channel her grief over Tavish Balfour. But it had ended with Isla discovering entirely new horizons within her heart, as well as carving out a place for herself in a new community.

She became a favorite with Dr. and Mrs. Sumsion and always praised his Sunday sermons. She took Mrs. White's advice on how to improve the health of the damask roses in the back garden and Sir Arthur's recommendations on excellent sheep breeds for the home farm. She hosted an annual fete each October and awarded prize ribbons for foot races and laughed when Mr. Johnshaven told her the same tired joke for the twelfth time. She wept with Lady Wintrose when word came that her son had been killed at the Battle of Vauchamps. She held Mrs. Peterson's hand as she drew her last breath after a catastrophic apoplexy.

In short, Isla became one of them, a trusted pillar of the community. She shed her old life—Tavish Balfour and their crazed "love"—and grew vibrant wings, launching into the sunshine of her future. *Timid* and *compliant* stopped nipping at her heels. She embodied stronger words— *brave, intrepid, resolute.*

Malton Hill became the bedrock of her existence.

Isla would do whatever it took to retain ownership of the estate, and by extension, the new person she had become there. Anything to ensure she didn't lose her community or the woman she was at Malton Hill. She would beg Tavish for a divorce. She would dance to Gray's tune and marry where he dictated. Anything, really, to secure her dowry in full.

Because giving up Malton Hill was the one thing Isla refused to contemplate.

REVEREND STRONACH ENDED his sermon with a loud *Amen*.

Gray shifted beside Isla as they sang a hymn in closing, his bass voice steady.

Services finished, Isla stood. Gray murmured something about needing a word with a local squire before adding, "I will meet you in the carriage momentarily. I shan't keep you waiting long." He walked off, his gait smooth. At least seeing the Balfours in church hadn't overset him.

Matt, of course, had not come to church. Years ago, he had refused to attend, claiming that someone had to keep their Grandmama company while Gray and Isla were away. Their English grandmother had held rather inflexible opinions about the Church of Scotland and preferred to attend "regular" church (as she called the Church of England) when they were in London. But after Grandmama had passed on, Matt hadn't resumed his attendance.

Gray no longer at her side, Isla pivoted and scanned the gathered villagers and parishioners.

The Balfours easily stood out. Not only were Lord Cairnfell and Tavish some of the tallest men in the congregation, but their good looks and charming manners always elicited smiles and shy blushes.

Certain facts would never change.

Some might consider it surprising that two families, sworn to bitter enmity, would attend the same parish church. However, the joint attendance was rather by design. When King Charles II elevated the Balfour brothers to the titles of Northcairn and Southcairn, he ordered them to worship in the same space, thereby forcing the families to maintain a veil of civility. Upping the ante, the King's charter also decreed that they each contribute to the cost of the church, as well as the minister's salary.

From Gray's lengthy diatribes on the subject, Isla gathered that Northcairn hadn't paid his portion in more than a decade.

Just one more black mark in the never-ending quarrel between their families.

The knowledge didn't quell Isla's urge to stare and stare at Captain Balfour across the church nave, to catalog every minute change that had taken him from her Tavish to this towering man. But to do so would generate curiosity from their neighbors and censure if Gray learned of it.

So instead, as Isla made her way toward the door, she flitted a brief gaze over the assembled Balfours.

Captain Balfour boldly met her eyes. As if he, too, were unable to ignore her presence.

He slid his eyes subtly to the right.

Oh, gracious.

She had nearly forgotten about that. Their signal. The way that they communicated with each other when around others.

I left you a note, his look said.

She blinked once, slowly, and then glanced away. *I will collect it.*

Exiting the church, Isla greeted a few acquaintances and then casually made her way around the building to her parents' impressive grave monument—two carved granite tomb boxes arranged side-by-side. Gray had added a marble canopy over the whole, complete with gothic arches and finials. It was all rather fussy and ostentatious.

Isla placed a hand on the granite, as if communing with the dead. Leaning forward, she braced a gloved hand against the stone and pressed a kiss to her mother's name engraved on the side of her tomb. The motion allowed Isla to palm the scrap of foolscap slid into a small gap between sculpted decorations.

She waited until she reached the safety of her bedchamber before unfolding the paper with trembling fingers.

EQQV EQ YV VPQ OCOYW . . .

It was written in the cipher she and Tavish had memorized years before. How appalling that after seven years, she easily substituted the letters, words jumping out at her.

> *Meet me at the usual place and time, if you can. There is much to discuss.*

Nothing more.

Isla swallowed. Why were her hands shaking and her heart thumping? Why, after everything, did Tavish Balfour have any sway on her emotions?

Also . . . how arrogant of him to simply *assume* that she would remember their "usual place and time." She did, of course, but still—

This had to cease.

Much to discuss, he said.

Yes, there was. Namely, how quickly she could rid herself of him as husband.

She would meet him, insist on a divorce, and finally—*finally!*—put the follies of her youth behind her.

Malton Hill awaited.

Often, Isla wondered if her love for the estate rivaled that of a mother for her children—the willingness to fight tooth and nail to nurture and protect.

In this, Isla perhaps found an unexpected kinship with the returned Captain Balfour. They were both soldiers, battle-hardened and prepared to defend their people.

EIGHT YEARS EARLIER

November 3, 1809
Pettercairn, Scotland

Isla raced up the steep path leading to the top of Cairnfell.

Please, be there!

She was late to meet Tavish, but Gray had been in such a temper today—it had been impossible to slip away unnoticed before now.

Rain drizzled from the sky, making the path slippery under Isla's boots. She staggered sideways before righting her footing.

Almost there.

She and Tavish had been trading notes via her parents' tomb for months now. Clandestine meetings on Cairnfell, usually discussing nothing of import and, yet, everything of importance to them both—her opinion of current skirt lengths, his views on Napoleon and the war on the Continent, the likelihood of Widow James marrying for a seventh time. It felt like no topic was too small, esoteric, or scandalous to discuss. Unlike her brothers, Tavish treated her as an equal, not a child to be coddled.

But today, Isla needed answers.

Did Tavish know what had happened? Could he fill in the silences that punctuated Gray and Matt's conversations whenever Isla wandered into the room?

Something had occurred in London. Something dreadful. Something that involved Tavish's family—his older sister, Lady Mariah, in particular. Gray had brawled with Lord Cairnfell over it, and Tavish's older brother had badly broken Gray's nose. The physician had set it, but they all knew that Gray would now have a bump in his previously patrician feature.

Finally, Isla crested the hill and strode into the clearing of Cairnfell Castle, lungs heaving with her exertion.

And there he was. Tavish. Her friend.

Her *best* friend, if she were honest with herself.

His clothing appeared dashed together—a loose coat and wrinkled waistcoat over a pleated kilt, neckcloth carelessly tied. As if Tavish had been in a rush to reach her and hadn't cared to fuss about with his attire.

Though Gray always tossed off his coat and neckcloth as soon as he returned home, her ducal brother wouldn't dream of appearing in public without being properly starched and pressed within an inch of his valet's life. Matt . . . well, he never left Dunmore, and he *still* dressed immaculately every day.

Tavish, however, seemed more . . . oh, how could Isla explain it? More comfortable in his skin, perhaps? A man would have to be to wear a kilt with such insouciance.

For Gray, close-cut superfine coats and embroidered waistcoats were akin to armor—a layer of protection between himself and the world. He might despise the feel of them on his body—too tight and uncomfortable, he had once told her—but he would never forsake them in public. In a certain sense, the clothing wore him, not the other way around. Or, maybe, better expressed—without his expensive tailoring, who would the Duke of Grayburn be? It was as much a part of his ducal persona as impeccable manners and stern orders.

But Tavish . . . his clothing seemed almost an afterthought. Not that he wasn't well-dressed as befitted an earl's son. No, it was more that you would notice a hundred things about him before caring what he was wearing. The wide brilliance of his smile and the warm openness of his gaze. The soft timbre of his voice and rolling hum of his Scottish brogue. The quick leap of his thoughts and kindness in his manner. If anything, his coat served the purpose of highlighting the breadth of his shoulders while the blue of his waistcoat brought out the silver flecks in his eyes.

At sixteen, Isla was rapidly realizing that members of the opposite sex found her attractive. She had initially attributed that attraction to her status as Lady Isla Kinsey, sister to the wealthy and powerful Duke of Grayburn. But she was observant enough to recognize that such attention might have another source. Boys, and even some men, stammered when introduced, blushing and staring before bowing over her hand with reverence. They handled her with hushed tones and deferential care as if she were made of Venetian glass.

But never Tavish. He never saw her as anything other than Isla.

Waving, he jogged across the clearing to her, kilt snapping behind him.

"There ye be, lass." He took her hands in his. "I was beginning to be right *worrit*."

"I am . . . well . . ." she gasped, trying to catch her breath.

"I've lit us a wee fire. As large as I dare without anyone seeing the smoke. Come."

Glancing around to ensure no one was about, he tugged her through the large door of the tower house and up a short spiral staircase to the ancient great hall. She had only been inside a handful of times, finding the place dark and unwelcoming. But today, a fire popped in the hearth. The hall was rudimentary at best—stone damp with small panes of glass in the three windows, one for each wall but the fireplace. The furnishings weren't much better—an aging table in one corner and a pair of wooden chairs set before the fire. There was a second room through a door to the left of the fireplace that appeared to house a bed with a moldering straw mattress.

Isla sat in one of the chairs, pulling off her gloves and stretching her chilled fingers toward the flames.

"You must tell me the news," she said without preamble. "Something dreadful has happened, has it not?"

"How do ye know?"

"Please! I can practically feel the tension radiating from your shoulders."

It was the truth. He sat stiffly in his chair, spine straight. But even without seeing him, she would have heard the bleakness in his voice.

"Am I that easily understood?"

"By me, you are."

He narrowed his eyes at her.

"Also, my brother sports a broken nose that I overheard a footman blame on your brother." Isla rolled a hand. "Please, talk to me."

Tavish's expression turned desolate, like a chill wind stealing one's breath. He pressed his palms into his eyes, rubbing. "I can scarcely countenance what has happened."

"Then tell me!"

He stared into the fire for a moment. Trying to decide how much to tell her, Isla was sure. Sometimes, reading his thoughts was as easy as understanding her own.

"Tell me all," she urged.

"I'm sure ye recall that Mariah became betrothed to Lord Stafford in August."

"Of course. You are all eager for the match. Lord Stafford is a decent-enough fellow. He is one of Gray's old school friends and has visited Dunmore once or twice."

"Aye. He met Mariah during his last visit to Grayburn at Dunmore and was quite taken with her. Stafford was eager to court Mariah once she arrived in London."

"I can imagine. Your sister is lovely."

A gentleman would have to be blind to miss Lady Mariah's striking beauty—dark hair and eyes the color of summer sky. Isla had always envied the glittering joy that Tavish's sister trailed wherever she went. Heaven knew, Isla had caught even Gray looking Lady Mariah's way more than once. Every gentleman swiveled to stare when she passed, such was the power of her loveliness.

"Has there been a hiccup in the wedding plans?" Isla asked. "The marriage contracts are already set, correct?"

"Aye. Set in stone."

"Then what has occurred?" As far as Isla understood things, once the marriage contracts were signed and in place, the marriage was as good as done. To break a marriage contract at this stage would result in a heavy lawsuit.

Tavish took in a stuttering breath, as if the weight of what had occurred was nearly drowning him.

"Apparently, your brother . . ." He drifted off.

"Gray?"

"Aye. When Grayburn learned of Stafford's impending nuptials to my sister, His Grace was displeased, to put it mildly. He didn't approve of his friend's decision to marry into the Balfour family. So much so that Callum claims your brother began a systematic campaign to convince Stafford to break off the betrothal."

Isla gasped. "Gray? Truly? What did he say?"

"Callum didn't elaborate. However, I can guess Grayburn gave a blistering litany of all the defects of my family and Mariah, in particular."

"Truly? But . . . Gray would never . . ." Isla drifted off, words of denial freezing on her tongue.

Given how Gray's behavior toward herself had cooled over the past year, she could hardly protest that her brother would never do such a dastardly thing. The Piers she had known would never willfully destroy a lady's reputation, even a Balfour. But Gray as he was now? So hateful toward Northcairn and his family? Isla wasn't sure what Gray would do if he deemed it necessary.

"Please tell me Gray was unsuccessful," she whispered instead.

But she already knew the answer. Tavish's stricken expression said it all.

"Stafford reneged and has refused to marry Mariah."

"Oh, Tavish!" Nausea churned in Isla's stomach. "Poor Lady Mariah!"

No wonder Cairnfell had broken Gray's nose.

"Callum challenged Stafford to a duel over the whole affair, but Stafford refused, saying Callum wasn't enough of a gentleman to tempt him to duel."

Isla gasped. Such a slight was nearly beyond the pale.

"Your brother is determined to ensure that no one in my family is ever received again. And as he is a duke, he will succeed." Tavish sat back, arms folded, a muscle ticking in his jaw.

"But what of Lady Mariah?"

Here, Tavish pinched the bridge of his nose. "She . . ." He swallowed. "She allowed Stafford to convince her to anticipate their marriage vows."

Isla pressed a hand to her mouth. She knew such things happened, but for Lord Stafford to lay with Lady Mariah and then refuse to marry her . . .

"What is to be done? Lord Stafford must marry her before news of her disgrace is broadcast."

"That horse has already bolted from the barn, so to speak," Tavish laughed, harsh and bitter. "No one can be forced to the altar, unfortunately. Stafford has refused, publicly claiming that he didn't know she was a lady of poor reputation before proposing to her."

"Balderdash!"

"Aye, but as Stafford has Grayburn's support, he is unlikely to suffer a loss of his own reputation over this, the bastard. Regardless, Mariah has filed a lawsuit of five thousand pounds against Stafford for breach of promise."

"Good! That miscreant should pay for his actions and cowardly betrayal! Such a sum would go far to helping Mariah establish herself."

"Aye, it would. But the trial won't begin for months yet, and because the sordid details were published in the lawsuit filing, all of London now knows that Mariah is a fallen woman."

An icy chill chased Isla's spine. She knew the outcome before Tavish said it.

"My poor sister is utterly ruined. Not a rumored or hearsay sort of ruination. But thoroughly destroyed. Mariah has no reputation to speak of. She will no longer be received nor ever marry."

Isla pressed a hand to her stomach. The shock of it. The horror.

And Gray had played a central role.

No gentleman would do such a thing to a lady, no matter how provoked. It was the rankest behavior on Lord Stafford's part . . . and Gray's, too. Without her brother spewing vicious lies, Isla doubted Lord Stafford would have reneged.

Emotions bucked and roiled in her chest—betrayal, disappointment, helplessness. How could Gray have done this?

She closed her eyes, trying to keep herself from screaming.

"Ye should let it out."

Isla snapped her gaze to Tavish's.

"All that ye be feeling." His gaze burned into hers. "As I've said before, ye should let it out."

She gave a harsh laugh. "How? Slash Gray with a dagger while he sleeps?"

He cocked his head, as if examining the thought before casting it aside with a quick shake. "Nae. Something less bloody that won't see ye hanged."

He stood and offered her his hand.

Isla took it without hesitation.

Tavish led her out the door and into the forest beyond. Within minutes, they reached the cairn itself. It towered overhead, slate stones darkened with rain. The downpour had tempered to a light sprinkle, but the wind lashed the ends of Isla's pelisse and snapped Tavish's kilt and bent the Scots pine.

"Come on. We have to go to the top."

Their hands clasped for balance, they scrambled up the slippery stones—feet sliding with every other step, wind chafing Isla's cheeks. It took several minutes before they reached the summit.

"Now." Tavish dropped her hand. "We bellow our rage."

Bending at the waist, he drew in a long breath and then roared into the wind. The sound whipped around Isla, racing down the hill and blending with the clamor of the tree branches. The sound was primal and angry and felt so very vital.

Mouth opening wide, Tavish bellowed one more time, a guttural shout of fury. The wind clapped back with blasts of arctic air.

He turned to her, gray eyes wide, red hair plastered to his head and dripping water into his eyes. He appeared elemental. A handsome *kelpie* determined to lure her to her doom.

"Your turn," he said, a wild grin on his lips.

Isla surveyed the landscape, the tops of the pines disappearing into the rising mist and cutting off any further views of Dunmore to the south or Castle Balfour to the north.

"Scream, lass! Pull the air deep into your gut and then let it fly . . . all your rage and frustration at the damnable injustices of life."

As ever, Isla thrilled at his swearing. Tavish never saw her as something to be coddled. In his eyes, she was a fledgling eagle, ready to take flight.

And so she bent forward, sucked in all the air her body could hold, and roared into the wind. The sound scoured her lungs and scraped her throat and sent sharp prickles of energy along her skin.

"Brilliant!" Tavish shouted. "Again!"

Isla screamed, dragging the fury and helplessness and heartache from her lungs and flinging it into the tempest—all the emotions that wanted to flatten her, to snuff out her will to resist.

Yet as the rain beat down and the sky flashed silver and the very elements raged, *You are nothing!* . . .

Never had Isla felt so alive.

July 23, 1817
Cairnfell
Pettercairn, Scotland

Given the momentous occasion of the morning—after all, it wasn't every day that one spoke with one's husband after an absence of seven years—Isla felt it rather unfair of the weather to be so amiable. Puffy clouds floated across a blue summer sky, carried on a breeze just strong enough to ensure the heat was delightfully pleasant and not a whit stifling.

It was all decidedly intolerable.

A billowing tempest would be more appropriate to her mood—towering thunderheads and torrential rain. A bit of lightning would not go amiss. The present cheerful sunshine felt like an assault on the crown of her head.

Lifting her skirts, Isla continued to trudge up Cairnfell. How many times over the years had she made this journey? Crossing the fields from Dunmore and traversing the old stone bridge before summiting the fell itself?

Like then, her heart pounded a steady drumbeat in the back of her throat. Once, she would have labeled this emotion as excitement or anticipation. Now, she knew it to be dread.

Unlike then, she no longer had a governess to thwart, and Gray felt Isla's wandering to be safe, as long as she stayed close to Dunmore. Little did His Grace know.

Isla had slept poorly last night, her nerves refusing to settle in anticipation of meeting Captain Balfour. She *had* to convince him to grant her a divorce, and she wasn't above employing hysterical tears, if necessary.

It had taken her three years after Tavish's departure to summon the courage to brave the memories of Cairnfell. Even now, she longed to summit the cairn and scream her frustration and worry to the wind. But like everything else, she refused to permit him to dominate her memories of this place. Even if she did see him peeking out from every hollow and tree as she crested the hill.

Captain Balfour was precisely where she expected him to be, leaning against the side of Cairnfell Castle, arms crossed over his absurdly broad chest, one foot bent at the knee and resting on the stone behind him. His kilt—the blue and yellow of the Balfour tartan—fluttered in the slight breeze.

His head lifted as she stepped into the clearing.

Their first meeting here with Gray, Isla had been too stunned to study him.

During church services, she hadn't dared.

But now . . . she looked her fill.

Of course, the passage of seven years had only rendered him more handsome, the wretch. His hair had settled into a polite auburn, while his skin still avoided the ruddiness of most redheads. As ever, his chin held that alluring deep vertical dent, and his lips—lips she could still easily recall touching her own—were absurdly full . . . a pair of pillows framing his mouth. Pillow lips, those.

Worse, the scar on his upper right cheek did nothing to detract from his good looks and, instead, made him appear distinguished with a hint of danger. Though he certainly had shaved this morning, his skin already sported night whiskers.

The most striking change, however, was in his height and weight. His chest and shoulders were broader and heavy with muscle. She refused to even contemplate how they would feel wrapped around her. His calves bulged against the garters fastening his woolen stockings just below his knees.

He had to have grown at least an inch or two. Before, Isla hadn't strained to kiss him. A mere press to her toes would see the job done. But now, she figured she would need to drag his head down to meet hers, even on tiptoe.

He had left a boy.

But this . . . this was a man.

And *whywhywhy* was she even *thinking* about kissing and Tavish Balfour in the same breath?

He watched her approach, eyes surely cataloging her differences. The cool poise of her head. The militant erectness of her spine. The prim clasp of her hands, reticule dangling from her wrist.

She stopped well in front of him.

"Captain Balfour." She curtsied.

"Lady Isla." He bowed.

A repeat of their meeting just a few days ago.

This time, however, she squarely met his gaze.

Tavish had been a friendly, tender-hearted boy. The sort to wear his proverbial heart on his sleeve. An idealist and a romantic. Attributes she had loved with a mad passion.

But the man before her . . . gaze cold and expression withdrawn. He appeared as hard and unyielding as the granite of the Cairngorms themselves.

It felt as if Tavish—her Tavish—had died long ago. And now this strange man had appeared, wearing Tavish's face and speaking with his voice, but displaying not an ounce of the open warmth of the boy she had loved. Gone were his easy smiles and clear-eyed happiness.

This man had seen horrors. Likely even committed them.

Had *her* Tavish reappeared, Isla might have worried that her heart would again succumb to his allure. That she would once more tumble into reckless love with him and, in the process, lose Malton Hill and the woman she was there, abandoning her people to an uncertain fate.

But, no. She had no fear that any ounce of her would pine for this stony-faced soldier.

Captain Balfour . . . not Tavish.

Isla's only desire was to sever every tie that bound them.

"You wished to speak with me?" she said, forcing herself to work through niceties before demanding answers to her questions.

"Aye." He motioned for them to walk toward the cairn. "There is much to discuss, I ken."

Isla nodded. Nothing in his demeanor tipped his hand as to his thoughts.

He proffered her his arm. No matter what had befallen him, his manners did not falter.

She shook her head.

Touching Captain Balfour in any capacity would be ill-advised. And given the faint flicker of relief in his eyes, he felt the same.

Yet, as they walked the uneven ground, the heat of his large body pulled at her senses. As if just his simple presence agitated something deep within. A tug. A whisper of the girl she had been, throwing herself over and over into his arms.

Her body still remembered the animal attraction of him. She grimaced at the thought.

Instead of climbing the cairn itself, he led her around the base to the back side. Unlike the eastern face of Cairnfell with its gradual rise, the western edge plunged down great black-slabbed cliffs to the plain below. A small bench fashioned out of logs rested at the base of the cairn. A place to sit and admire the expansive view.

Isla sat, and Captain Balfour took a seat beside her, leaving a decided two feet of space between their bodies.

She felt the thrum of him anyway. He had never worn fragrance before, but now he smelled of sandalwood and other exotic spices. Scents to lure women who were not her.

How many had there been? It was a terrible thought, but one that had occupied more than one sleepless night over the years. Surely, he had kissed and wooed and perhaps even bedded other women. His loyalty to her had undoubtedly been short-lived. The thought turned acidic in her throat if she pondered it overlong.

It wasn't as if she had completely honored their marital vows herself. She had permitted the occasional London swain to claim a kiss during her Seasons in Town. Colonel Archer had been the most recent at just two months past—a very pleasant kiss stolen under a bower in the back garden of his parents' townhouse.

The tense silence between her and Captain Balfour stretched and pulled, a thread of black treacle dangling from a spoon and waiting for the slightest wobble to snap.

What are your intentions? she longed to shout. Anything to release the nervous pressure in her chest.

He spoke first.

"I have always appreciated the view from here," he said, voice calm as if this were a social call. "On a clear day like today, ye can even make out the rise of Ben Tirran." He pointed in the direction of the peak.

"Yes. It is lovely," she managed to choke.

And it was. The wild landscape of the Angus glens extended before them, lush forest and shrubs, the Falls of Fennimore glittering in the distance.

For Isla, the view had always been a summary of their families. Beyond the waterfall, the shores of Loch Cairnbeg shimmered. The River Cairnbeg rushed out from it, tumbling down the Falls of Fennimore. From there, the river rambled along Glen Cairnbeg until it crashed into the rising might of Cairnfell. There below, the river dashed itself against the fell's granite base, splitting in two: Northcairn and Southcairn. Running wild around the mass of Cairnfell, the rivers took very different paths to the ocean—the River Northcairn meandered toward Aberdeenshire in the north, while the River Southcairn angled toward Angus and found its way to the ocean near St. Cyrus Beach.

Two rivers, once one, but now divided and forging separate paths. Just as their families had done. Just as she and Tavish—hopefully, prayerfully—would soon, too.

Isla rallied her nerves, swallowing down her agitation. Enough vac-illation. Malton Hill hung in the balance, and she would fight for her future.

"Come, Captain." She lifted her chin. "Let us discuss that which must be discussed."

She dared a glance at him.

A pained smile tugged at his mouth.

"Still direct, I see."

"Pardon?"

"Your manner. Ye were never one to ease gently into a difficult con-versation. Ye jump in with both feet."

Isla stared. Was that true? She considered her younger self the sort to avoid confrontation and discord. But, perhaps, he was correct. With him, she *had* been more forthright.

"I choose to take that as a compliment," she said.

"Good. It was meant as one."

They looked at each other for a moment. Isla hated it . . . the lack of her Tavish in his eyes. They were blank and polite and utterly unreadable.

Where did you go? she wondered. *Or were you never truly real?*

It scarcely mattered now, she supposed.

"Ye be referring to our marriage?" he asked.

"Yes." Isla's heart pounded. She resisted the urge to lick her lips. "I wish for the knot of our handfasting to be untied."

"Do ye?"

She nodded just once, a crisp up-down motion. It was all she could manage through the anxiety pulsing at her fingertips.

"Well." A long pause. "I suppose that would be for the best."

Isla's shoulders nearly collapsed, relief flooding her veins.

God be thanked!

"Ye needn't appear so liberated." His eyebrows flew to his hairline. "A gentleman does have his pride."

She froze. "You cannot believe we would continue in this farce of matrimony? We are all but strangers to one another."

Not a single muscle in his face twitched at her harsh words.

Yes. Granite, this man.

"Nae, I assumed we would pursue a divorce. I just wished to ensure that ye felt the same." His voice radiated calm. As if this conversation were of no particular note.

"And if I had said I wish to continue in our marriage?"

He shrugged. "Then I would honor my vows to yourself."

Unbelievable.

As if staying married or divorcing were one and the same to him.

Isla shook her head. "I shan't require you to fall upon your sword for my sake."

He lifted an eyebrow and gave her a slow perusal, eyes skimming her person from the brim of her straw bonnet to the toes of her boots. The heat of his gaze ignited tiny sparks across her skin.

He cleared his throat and looked away. "'Twould be no hardship, I assure ye."

Isla willed a blush at bay. Her Tavish had never been so bold. Or had he? She supposed he had never been shy about his attraction to her. But it had never taken on this edge of . . . of what? Sensuality?

Or perhaps it had always been thus with him, but she had been too young to understand the undercurrent of his meaning.

"I am more than the sum of my appearance, Captain," she replied with a snap. She had more than enough experience in repressing the unwanted advances of forward gentlemen.

If she thought to offend him, she was disappointed. A smile tugged at his lips, and some emotion finally glinted in his eye.

There's my lass, his expression seemed to say.

Isla didn't know what disturbed her more. That he would see her contrariness as proof that she hadn't changed beyond recognition. Or that she understood his emotions so easily.

She wanted none of this.

"Ye have always been more than the sum of your appearance or your familial connections, Lady Isla," he rumbled in his deep brogue.

His words didn't conjure her Tavish per se, but it was a reminder of why, once upon a time, she had fallen in love with him.

Because . . . in this, he was correct.

He had never seen her as the daughter of the Duke of Grayburn with a pretty face and dowry to acquire. A possession to be passed from one man to another.

No, to Tavish, she had always been Isla—a woman who was defined by her own unique dreams and ideas.

She didn't know how to reply to the compliment. How many gentlemen had flattered her over the years with fawning comments about her beautiful eyes or genteel manner?

None had ever seen beyond the surface of her.

Only Tavish.

Being near him was more painful than she had supposed it would be. She had thought to feel nothing.

Instead, a terrible sort of grief welled up. For the devastated girl she had been. For everything that had been splintered in the wake of his betrayal and abandonment.

He had broken them. Broken her.

And then he had left, galloping off into the world, forcing her to pick up the pieces.

TAVISH HATED THAT he still found Lady Isla so captivating.

I am more than the sum of my appearance, Captain.

The words evoked the girl he had known—fierce and determined. A shooting star of a lass, blazing through his life as rare and brilliant as a comet.

Surely that girl was still inside, clamoring to be freed from her cage of ice. And once free, how would that girl merge with the woman she was now?

As in years past, his emotions pulled at the tight reins of his control—*curiosity, lust, fascination.*

That hadn't changed.

She is not for yourself. Ye have no means to support a wife, much less the daughter of a duke.

More to the point, Lady Isla no longer harbored any feelings of tenderness for him. Her relief at the prospect of their divorce more than confirmed this.

"What is your plan then?" She sat so primly, so still, back ramrod-straight, eyes fixed ahead.

The picture of a tightly-contained English lady.

Grayburn must be so proud, Tavish thought bitterly. He would regret to his dying day that he hadn't bludgeoned the duke when he'd had the chance.

Aye, Lady Isla wasn't the lass he had left, but then, Tavish was hardly the lad he had been. It scarcely mattered now. Soon, they would be free of one another, and he would be an ocean away.

"I take it Grayburn remains unaware of our marriage?"

Lady Isla flinched. "Of course. As you well know, my brother's wrath burns white-hot over any matter involving a Balfour."

"Aye, but we both know his help will be required, if nothing else to prevent the news of our divorce from reaching an ambitious newspaper editor. Grayburn might rage a wee bit, but he will be motivated to see our union disbanded."

"Agreed."

"Then . . . may I ask why ye haven't told him as of yet?"

"Given that you were half a continent away and fighting for your life on a daily basis, I did not see the point in raising the matter until it became absolutely necessary."

In summary: *You were far away, and I kept hoping you would die and render the entire situation moot.*

Tavish pushed away the sting of her words.

"I would argue that *now* is a fairly necessary point."

"Yes." She raised her chin. "Hence my presence here."

Something in her manner gave him pause. The way her tongue rushed through words and her fingers strangled her reticule, knuckles white with tension.

There was more to this with Grayburn. Tavish knew it as surely as raising a rifle to his shoulder and sighting down the barrel, intuitively aware he would hit his target.

Briefly, he considered letting Lady Isla keep her secret. Her relationship with Grayburn was none of his affair.

But . . .

"What are ye hiding? I sense the situation with Grayburn is more fraught than ye be letting on."

"I cannot imagine what you mean, Captain."

She said the words primly, spine straight and unbending.

Tavish couldn't stem a bark of laughter.

"I'm right pleased to discover you're still a terrible liar, lass."

She glared at him then, blue eyes snapping. "A true gentleman would not press a lady thus."

"Aye, well, we both know you and yours don't consider me to be much of a gentleman, no matter my parentage nor conduct. Why are ye so *afeart* to tell your brother?"

Tavish relaxed back into the bench, stretching his long legs out and resting one heel on an obliging stone, his kilt fluttering around his thighs.

He didn't miss how her eyes swept over his person, raking his body from ear lobes to ankles.

Tavish braced his hands behind his head, ensuring she could look her fill. However, one glance at his smiling face, and she turned away again, lips pressed tight.

"*Och*, I ken ye might not be keen to share a confidence with myself," he coaxed, "but I need to know what has occurred. Knowledge is our best defense at this point."

Her shoulders slumped. The tiniest capitulation.

"As I'm sure you recall, Gray was incensed when he found out about—" She motioned at the space between them. "You and I scarcely spoke after that."

No, they hadn't. Just once. A spectacularly incendiary conversation that shattered everything between them.

Her fingers twisted in the ribbon ties of her reticule.

"What happened?"

Lady Isla paused for a moment and then shook her head.

"The precise particulars scarcely matter now." Though she might have meant the words to be sharp, they emerged soft-edged and forlorn. "Needless to say, Gray was incensed over our attachment and abused me abominably. He claimed he would rather I had died than taken up with a Balfour."

Tavish made a noise of disgust.

Damn Grayburn to hell.

"Most significantly . . ." She took in a slow breath. "Gray threatened to cast me out of the family."

"Pardon?" Tavish reared back. "He truly said that?"

"Yes. I believe his precise words were, 'Let this be one thing in your teetering life that you do not doubt, Isla. Should you so much as nod at a gentleman without my approval, I will see you cast from this family.'"

"I'm not sure Grayburn can do that."

Isla laughed, a bitter crack of sound. "I assure you, he most certainly can. Dukes can do anything they wish."

"Aye, but the scandal of such an action . . . Grayburn would wish to avoid it."

"Perhaps, but you forget that my brother detests scandal and Balfours in equal measure. I cannot say which side his hatred would favor. Given Gray's wrath over the mere thought of us courting, I cannot fathom his rage once he discovers we are married. I do not think the threat of scandal will stay his hand."

"Why didn't you tell me this? Ye were my—" Tavish cut off the rest— *Ye were my wife.*

Wife. Past tense.

"When?!" The word burst from her. "When was I to have told you? When you betrayed my trust? When you refused to listen, took your commission, and left me so very alone?"

The whip of her hurt cracked across Tavish's skin.

"I tried to tell you, *Captain.*" She leaned into the honorific. "I begged you to take me away with you. To not leave me to Gray's cruel mercy."

A terrible sort of clanging started in Tavish's ears. He *should* have listened. He *should* have known there was more to her furious pleading that day.

But . . . they had both been so young. So inexperienced with love and relationships and the harsh realities of life outside their own wee sphere.

"Ye should have written me," he bit out. "I begged ye to write me. I would have found a way to send for ye."

How, he could scarcely say. But Tavish knew his younger self and the wild pattering of his love for Isla. He would have done anything to have her with him.

"Write you? By what means? Assuming I could send a letter without Gray's knowledge, I didn't know where to direct your post," she huffed, eyes glittering. "It's not as if you wrote me or sent any word to help ease the path."

"Ye made me swear not to write ye. I honored that vow." *Even though it nearly killed me*, he didn't add.

Pain rose in Tavish's chest—old and well-worn. It had taken years for the agony of her loss to fade. Endless nights spent staring at the ceiling or tent canvas or the sky full of stars, wondering if she had ever wavered in her disavowal of him. If she would ever forgive him for his actions or repent of her own.

She clearly hadn't.

He had mourned her loss and was now ready to move on to a new life—one no longer haunted by her shadow.

"Enough." She scoffed, retrieving a handkerchief from her reticule. "I refuse to wallow in our shared past, Captain. We were both young and foolish and, therefore, behaved foolishly." She swiped at her eyes. "It scarcely matters now."

Tavish unclenched his jaw. He was rather sure it still mattered greatly, but he hadn't the privilege of knowing her inner thoughts anymore.

He took a slow breath.

"So . . . Grayburn?" He returned them to their original topic.

"I am sure you understand why telling him has been risky. If I am cast out, I have no recourse and nowhere to go. Until this week, you were a continent away and completely unreachable. Your family certainly wouldn't have taken me in—your father hates Gray just as much as Gray detests your father. I did not wish to find myself tossed into the street without funds or friends."

"Surely Grayburn is not so heartless at that?"

"I haven't dared to find out." She gave a mirthless laugh. "All that to say, I must find the right moment to tell him. Wisdom is paramount in this instance."

Tavish nodded. "I agree."

She sat up straighter and her expression closed, shuttering all her fierceness as if it had never existed. As if she had met a quota for emotion for the day and refused to shed another tear.

When next she spoke, her voice was level. All business.

"This brings us back to my question: What is your plan at present, Captain?"

"I have been corresponding with a solicitor in Aberdeen. Thankfully, Scotland is much more forgiving on the topic of divorce than England. All it requires is a judge's decision." Tavish resisted the urge to stare at her profile, to catalog every wee difference from her younger self and store it for later examination. "My solicitor feels that a divorce on the basis of my desertion should not be difficult to obtain. We have never lived under the same roof, and I have never contributed to your upkeep. We will need to file the case and then endure the procurator fiscal asking difficult questions of us both. But I believe if we present the enmity between our families and my—" He paused, taking in a deep breath before saying what needed to be said. "—my inability to provide financially for yourself, it should all come right."

"Yes. I seem to remember that being your primary concern. You married me and then realized you hadn't the wherewithal to keep me."

"My circumstances, unfortunately, have not materially improved since then."

"Perhaps you should opportune Gray to pay you off again." She lifted her chin. "It worked so well last time, after all."

So cutting, those words. So unlike the lass he had loved. It took all of Tavish's strength not to wince.

"Isla—"

"Forgive me. That was rude." She held out a gloved palm on a sigh. "Our past is behind us now. As you say, it should be a thing of naught to dissolve our union. It is not as if it were a true marriage in any sense of the word."

Tavish swallowed.

He had scarcely kissed her after their vows, much less indulged in the more pleasant activities between husband and wife. Had Tavish known then, he might have insisted upon consummation. But no, they had both assumed there would be an entire lifetime for such things.

More the fool him.

In hindsight, though difficult, their immediate parting had been a blessing. Tavish assumed Isla was still a maid. That fact would temper Gray's fury when the time came, as well as assuage any qualms a future husband may have.

"Once we have a meeting date set with the procurator fiscal, that would be the logical point to disclose our marriage to Grayburn," Tavish said. "I am happy to be present when you tell him."

Isla loosed a sharp huff. "I cannot imagine the conversation will go better for your presence. Quite the opposite, in fact."

"Well . . . know that I am willing."

"When do you think we will hear from the procurator fiscal?"

"I cannot say, as we have yet to file our case. I will be leaving tomorrow for a week or two, but I will call upon my solicitor to formulate a plan of action and ascertain the timing of dissolving . . ." He waved a hand between them.

"Oh. Leaving so soon?"

Tavish bristled at the scorn in her tone. *How like you*, it said. *Barely arrived and already abandoning me.*

This Lady Isla, angry and cutting, was new to him.

Well . . . perhaps not entirely new. He had seen this caustic side of her on that night seven years ago when they came apart.

"I apologize, my lady, if that upsets yourself—"

"Nothing you could do now would overset me, Captain."

She stared straight ahead, jaw clenched, refusing to acknowledge the irony in her words.

"I have much to settle before quitting Scotland. I don't wish to leave anything undone."

"Quitting Scotland?" She turned to him.

"Aye. I'm shipping off to America."

"Oh."

Tavish could see it in her eyes, the vague snap of interest, the wondering as to what he would do there.

He paused, curious if she would inquire.

She did not.

"Very well. I shall wait to hear from you, then." Lady Isla stood, their interview at an end. "Good day, Captain." She bobbed a curtsy, sparing him nary a glance as she pivoted and walked away.

Tavish watched her go—the sway of her hips, the upright lift of her head. He looked away before the flame he had long carried for her ignited in his chest.

Hopefully, a week spent with Ross and Fletch—hunting and discussing the details of their proposed venture in Pennsylvania—would see his head straight.

So when next Tavish saw Lady Isla, he would have forgotten all the reasons why he had loved her in the first place.

SEVEN YEARS EARLIER

Tavish paced in the wee clearing, anxious for Isla to arrive.

Instead of climbing the slope of Cairnfell, today he was meeting her at its base on the north side. Here, the River Northcairn swung inward in a slow loop, creating a hollow around a quiet pool of water against a granite cliff. Secluded and remote, it was difficult to find unless one knew the way through the dense underbrush.

He tilted his head upward, his skin eager for the sunshine after months of drab skies.

Each year, April would steal a day or two from July, warm lazy afternoons that brimmed with light. Today was precisely such a day. Hot enough that Tavish couldn't help a longing glance at the dark pool of water. A swim would be just the thing to chase away the lingering remnants of winter.

A twig snapped. He whirled around just as Isla emerged from the surrounding forest, the broad smile on her face somehow brighter than the sun overhead. She dropped a basket covered with a muslin cloth on a nearby rock before racing to him.

"Tavish!" She breathed his name on a happy sigh, throwing herself into his arms.

He wrapped his hands around her waist and pulled her into his chest, breathing in the heady scent of her lavender soap and clean skin. Her head tucked neatly into the side of his neck, slotting into his body like the final piece of a puzzle.

"I missed you," she whispered into his throat, lips grazing his skin and igniting a wee fire there.

But then, all of him felt afire near Isla.

What had begun as a meeting between friends had evolved over the past months . . . moving into something deeper and more profound.

At times, Tavish marveled at the depth of his affection for this lass. He was merely seventeen years of age; Isla, only sixteen. Surely, neither of them was old enough to form a true lasting connection. The sort of love that a life could be built on.

And yet . . .

It thrummed within him. A bone-deep assurance that had been steadily growing over the past weeks and months.

He loved her.

Not as a boy loved a friend or as some calf-love flutter of infatuation. No.

Tavish loved Isla as a man loves a woman.

He adored the way her laugh shook her shoulders. How her eyes never failed to track a bluejay or robin in flight. How she became agitated and loud over any slight toward a friend, himself included.

How their thoughts and dreams felt like two halves of a whole, and when they conversed, it seemed as if they were the only two people to see reality through the same eyes. They were strange creatures, he and Isla.

He knew she felt like an outsider in her family—the only girl, the one her brothers usually ignored, just as her father had before them.

Tavish was lost in a different way within his own family. There simply wasn't enough money or love to go around. The demands of his other siblings had always been louder than his own, and so Tavish faded into the background—the afterthought. The son no one ever asked after or fretted over.

Having a person of his own was a profound gift. Someone he could confide in, who trusted him with her own confidences. Their snatched bits of time were never enough. The longer this secretive relationship went on, the more unbearable it became.

He wanted to spend every hour of every day with her.

They hadn't kissed. Not yet. Their minds were so attuned that Tavish already understood her thoughts.

Until he and Isla kissed, they could pretend that this wasn't happening. That they weren't scions of the Montagues and Capulets, falling in love. Everyone knew Romeo and Juliet ended in disaster.

But did Tavish and Isla have to endure the same fate?

Today, Isla pulled back first from their embrace, a grin on her lips. "I have come prepared!"

Bouncing on tiptoe beside the pool, she turned back to her abandoned basket. Instead of the scones or cheese he had supposed, she removed the top to reveal a towel. She unfurled it proudly.

It took Tavish a moment to understand.

He laughed. "Today is the day, lass?"

She nodded, eyes lit with excitement. "Today, Tavish Balfour, I will learn to swim."

"Huzzah!"

Tavish had been trying for weeks to coax her into learning to swim. It was a lifesaving skill and one that most gentlewomen never learned, for obvious reasons. Unless a lady had a brother or father or husband who wished her to learn—or she was scandalously daring, as Tavish's Isla—a lady would never be so unclothed in company.

Isla clasped her hands. "I can scarcely believe I am going to undertake this. You have described the basics, but as you've said, I need practical experience. I am determined! So turn around, if you please, while I disrobe to my shift."

He jolted at her words.

Och, he spent far too much time trying *not* to imagine Isla in her shift. What had he gotten himself into?

On a steadying breath, Tavish did as he was bid, turning around and shucking his own jacket, waistcoat, neckcloth, socks, and shoes. After a moment's consideration, he pulled his shirt over his head, too, leaving him in only his breeks. The sun felt heavenly on his bare chest.

Behind him, he could hear Isla moving . . . the rustle of her clothing, the shuffling of her feet. It was almost unbearably intimate. A preview of his yearned-for future.

Tavish was unsure if swimming together was the most brilliant idea he had ever had. Or, categorically, the worst.

The urge to turn around, to swing her into his arms, was almost overwhelming.

Instead, he took three steps to the water's edge and dove in. The icy water swallowed him whole, jolting his system and instantly cooling his ardor. He and Callum had spent many an afternoon swimming here over the years. Tavish doubted there was an inch of the swimming hole he hadn't memorized. He stroked across the pool to where the water met the cliff face. A wee ledge rested there, the perfect height for sitting. He slid onto it, water lapping at his breastbone.

Finally, he dared a glance toward Isla.

She stood at the edge of the pool where it sloped up a grassy bank, the white of her shift a stark contrast against the dark cliffs and trees. Sunlight rimmed her from behind, catching the indistinct outline of her narrow waist and the length of her legs.

He forgot to breathe.

Some faint voice in his brain suggested closing his eyes, but he could no more look away than Aladdin beholding his Cave of Wonders.

She dipped a tentative toe in the water and shuddered before shooting him an accusing look.

"You didn't mention the water would be baltic."

"I did. Ye simply chose not to believe me."

She dipped a toe again and hopped backward, shaking her head.

"Ye can't ease into the cold, lass. Ye have to jump in, all or nothing." He pushed off the ledge, swimming across to the bank where she stood. "Once you're in the water, it's not half bad. As I've said, it's the first minute that is the worst."

Standing half out of the water, he extended a hand.

Isla's eyes flew wide, her gaze instantly engrossed with cataloging every feature of his bare chest.

Gooseflesh flared across his skin.

"Isla?"

Her gaze jerked upward to meet his eyes, a rosy blush on her cheeks. She looked so young in that moment. Her hair straight and uncurled around her face, the smattering of freckles stark on her cheekbones.

A girl hovering on the edge of womanhood.

At times, Tavish swore he could hear in her words the woman she would become. She would be speaking—about the plight of women in the local poorhouse, about the flawed logic of the minister's sermon, about her dreams for a house of her own to run and manage—and he would see an older version of her laid over top the current. As if he could envision the woman she would be five, ten, or even thirty years from now.

He longed to know every iteration of her in every period of her life.

"Come, lass." He waved a hand. "I ken my body is bonnie enough to be a distraction, but ye must resist temptation and forge onward."

She rolled her eyes, but her blush deepened regardless. A large breath swelled her chest. Biting her lower lip, she reached for his hand, stepping fully into the water with a gasp. The grassy bank quickly turned to moss in the water, and Tavish well knew how slippery it could be underfoot. Though he was holding her hand fast, her left foot slid out from under her.

Shrieking, she grabbed for his arm, nearly pulling him under with the sudden collapse of her weight into his. Tavish managed to steady her, but not before they both splashed into the water, buried up to their necks. Isla's legs ended up half atop his own in the water, an arm around his neck.

She wheezed at the cold, her hand fisting into his hair. Gently, Tavish wrapped his arms around her waist, steadying her.

"I have ye, lass."

She nodded, but he could feel the cold trembling of her body.

"Let's get ye moving," he said. "The more ye work your muscles, the warmer ye will feel."

Holding her at arm's length, he walked backward into the pool. She scrambled to hold onto him.

"What did I tell ye before? When we discussed this?"

"L-let the buoyancy of the w-water hold me aloft," she chattered.

"Precisely."

Slowly, Tavish showed her how she could float on her back before moving to a basic swimming motion. Before long, Isla was treading water and doing a rudimentary sort of paddling around the pond.

She insisted on exploring the small ledge at the back of the pool, sitting as she kicked her feet, water lapping against her collarbones.

Tavish sat beside her, an arm braced behind her back.

"Thank you," she said, looking up at him. Water clung to her eyelashes. He ached to kiss them away.

"For teaching ye to swim?"

"Yes . . . and for teaching me to be brave."

"*Och*, lass, I'm not sure ye needed any lessons in that."

Isla's hand cupped his cheek, her wee fingers cold against his skin. Her blue eyes searched his.

"I'm tired of this in-between," she murmured. "The knowing of not-knowing."

Tavish smiled. How like her, those words. And how like him to immediately understand them—

I want to know what it is like to kiss you. I want to decide that we will fight to be together.

Bending down, Tavish pressed his forehead to hers. "Are ye sure, lass?"

"As sure as I've ever been of anything, Tavish Balfour."

"Here?"

"Yes."

"Now?"

She smiled, looking around them—the dark water swirling against their bodies, the black cliff at their back, the trees and grass rimming the pool, the sunlight glittering on its surface.

She turned back to him.

"Yes. Now."

Her grip tightened on his head and, stretching upward, she pressed her lips to his—soft, fleeting, tentative.

A riot erupted in Tavish's chest—the wonder of her trust warring with the urge to chase her mouth and feast.

She went to pull back, but Tavish stopped her with one hand around her waist. His hand trembled, caught between opposing desires.

Isla touched a finger to his lips. A finger that also trembled, he noticed.

"You appear so . . ." Her voice drifted off.

"Appear so . . . what?"

"Yearning," she finished.

He nearly laughed. Of course, he yearned. He ached and craved.

Capturing her fingers, he pressed a slow kiss into her palm.

Her lungs caught.

It was all the permission Tavish needed.

Shifting his hand to the back of her neck, he tilted her chin upward, his mouth unerringly bending to hers.

Her lips were chilled, soft and pliant, and he sucked her gasp into his lungs.

She was the sweetest thing he had ever tasted.

Lady Isla Kinsey wasn't the first lass he had kissed.

But by all that was holy, Tavish intended she would be the last.

Her hand in Gray's, Isla stepped from the carriage onto the gravel drive, shaking out her skirts. Taking in a lungful of Highland air, she smiled up at the elegant facade of Kingswell House.

At last, they had arrived.

Hope felt buoyant in her chest.

Yes, a week-long house party with Colonel Archer and his parents was precisely the reprieve that Isla required. A week of deepening her relationship with the colonel and coming to better know the man behind his unperturbed surface. A space to ponder her impending divorce, her long-awaited future at Malton Hill, and how best to maneuver the chess-board of her relationship with Gray through both obstacles.

Honestly, a woman's work was never done.

Though she had traveled scarcely fifty miles north from Pettercairn, being somewhere new—a place the ghost of Tavish Balfour did not haunt—was like waking up to sunshine after weeks of never-ending rain.

She could breathe again.

Kingswell House was just as Gray had reported—modern and imposing. No one would ever call it a hunting lodge. *Palace* was a more apt descriptor.

Built in a similar style to Dunmore, the house featured a pedimented, Palladian facade, sweeping front stairs, and symmetrical tall windows. In short, it appeared a comfortable location to spend a week when deciding whether or not to marry a gentleman.

At her side, Gray proffered his arm, a smile on his lips. Isla knew her brother felt similarly relieved to be out of the Balfours' circle.

They hadn't quite reached the stairs when the front door opened and their hosts streamed out to greet them—Lord and Lady Milmouth with Colonel Archer on their heels. A series of servants followed, intent on the trunks strapped to the gleaming ducal carriage.

"At last!" Lady Milmouth grasped Isla's hands, pressing them warmly. "We had nearly despaired of seeing you today."

The lady and her husband were cut of standard, English stock— broad cheekbones and foreheads, slightly florid cheeks, sturdy of figure.

"I apologize for our tardy arrival. The road was rather boggy outside Aberdeen." Gray shook Lord Milmouth's hand, followed by Colonel Archer.

The colonel wasted no time in bowing low over Isla's knuckles.

"Lady Isla," he murmured, his eyes glowing with warmth.

He was a younger version of his parents—brown hair, blue eyes, and a chin that would soften rapidly with age. His even features and expressive face lent him a boyish handsomeness. There was a sort of trusting goodness about Colonel Edward Archer. He was a gentleman who smiled with ease and always saw the best in people and situations.

A man Isla would be content to call her husband.

More to the point, she doubted Colonel Archer would ever make her cry. First, he was far too amiable and conciliatory. And second, the colonel simply didn't tug at her heart in what she now recognized as a sort of obsession.

Isla had experienced the frantic love of youth. How had Shakespeare put it? *Love is merely a madness.*

Yes, that rather summed it up. Such mawkish, immature love *was* a madness, destined for Bedlam.

Better a truer affection built on respect and sensible feeling, on constancy and a calm steadiness.

In short, the emotions she felt for Colonel Archer.

Isla smiled at the man in question and murmured greetings to his parents.

"We are so glad you have arrived!" Lady Milmouth pressed her palms together. "Please, come!" She motioned for them to follow her.

Colonel Archer offered Isla his arm. She wrapped her fingers around his elbow, appreciating the leashed strength under her fingertips.

Isla could envision their future together. She would bear his children and host dinner parties and embroider handkerchiefs in her spare time. When in London, she would attend the theater and, when in the country, walk the paths around Malton Hill.

It was the life she craved. She only needed to disentangle herself from Tavish Balfour first.

They climbed the stairs, Lady Milmouth asking questions and clucking over the trials of a carriage journey. Like her son, there was an affable generosity to her ladyship, a sense of sincerity and wide-eyed delight with the world. As if her ladyship simply couldn't fathom that terrible things might happen to those in her immediate orbit. Had Dr. Johnson included portraits to illustrate words in his dictionary, Isla supposed an etching of Lady Milmouth would appear beside the word *guileless.*

It was yet one more mark in Colonel Archer's favor—a mother that Isla would happily call her own.

They crossed into the front entry hall with its white marble floor, three symmetrically-placed pedimented doorways, and two parallel fireplaces on the left and right walls. The butler hurried forward to take Isla's pelisse and bonnet, as well as Gray's coat and top hat.

"Let me show you to your rooms," Lady Milmouth said with a motherly tilt of her head. "You must be exhausted after your long journey."

A loud burst of laughter—both feminine and masculine—carried through one of the pedimented doorways. A *crowd* of laughter, to be precise.

Isla paused, glancing at Gray. Wasn't this to be a stay with just Lord and Lady Milmouth and their second son? A week of Isla and Colonel Archer deepening their relationship, while Gray tromped through fields, shot his fill of pheasant and grouse, and solidified his political alliance with Lord Milmouth.

Gray looked to their hostess with a slight frown.

"Ah, yes, our other guests." Lady Milmouth cleared her throat.

"There are others besides ourselves?" Gray lifted his eyebrows.

It was a rather intimidating lift, as Isla well knew.

Lady Milmouth was not immune. She flushed, hands clasped at her waist.

"Yes." She gave a fluttery laugh. "You see, my sister, Lady Forsyth and her husband, Sir John Forsyth—of the Southampton Forsyths, not the Suffolk—were longing for a stay in the country, and I simply couldn't bear to disappoint them. They have come with their two daughters and have brought the daughter of another dear friend."

"Emmeline loves nothing more than to have a house full of people," Lord Milmouth said on a fond laugh. "Why return to London when we can ask half of London to join us here?"

"It is true. I do adore hosting a merry house party," Lady Milmouth sighed, flitting a tentative glance at Gray.

"Emmeline assures me that the other guests shan't get in the way of our discussions, Grayburn," Lord Milmouth added.

"Not too much, at least. But I know that single gentlemen always appreciate the company of well-bred young ladies." Lady Milmouth smiled brightly at Gray.

A bit too brightly, per Isla's intuition.

Ah.

Of course.

What self-respecting matron could permit a handsome bachelor duke to idle away his days without attempting some match-making?

Enter three eligible young women—all with close ties to Lady Milmouth—who would now spend the week vying for Gray's attention.

After all, what mamma did not wish her daughter to marry the Duke of Grayburn?

The tight clench of Gray's jaw indicated that he saw through the ploy.

Isla had to pinch her lips together to prevent a smile escaping.

Hah! She rather liked the idea of watching Gray squirm for a week.

Laughter sounded again from the next-door room.

"And the gentlemen?" Gray ground out.

"Oh, yes!" Lady Milmouth beamed. "Of course, I couldn't leave our numbers unsettled. Edward was kind enough to invite a pair of fellow officers from his time in the army—his closest friends, actually—to ensure that each lady has a gentlemanly arm to escort her into dinner and such."

Colonel Archer grinned at his mother. "We shall make a jovial bunch this week, I dare—"

A whoop sounded from the drawing room—male voices rising in unison. A rush of footsteps quickly followed.

Two gentlemen burst into the entrance hall, one after the other.

The man in front had an affable grin on his face.

The gentleman on his heels, however.

Gray hissed in a breath.

Isla nearly gasped.

"Ho, Fletch!" the first man called, seizing Colonel Archer's shoulder in a strong grip. "Remember that night in Porto when we were deep in our cups over . . . . *Och,* I beg your pardon."

The gentleman paused, noting the new arrivals.

"The last of our guests has arrived," Colonel Archer said.

Isla stared in horror as Captain Tavish Balfour halted beside the men.

Tavish.

Tavish was here.

Ehr . . . Captain Balfour. Thinking of him as *Tavish* would be ruinous.

Captain Balfour, who was a close friend—a confidante even—of Colonel Archer.

Isla could scarcely breathe through her shock.

Her separately constructed worlds—i.e., her secret marriage and her role as Lady Isla—had just collided.

Isla had never considered herself to be the swooning sort of lady.

Such missishness was for women of lesser constitution. But the room decidedly spun when she met Captain Balfour's somber gray eyes.

It was little consolation that he appeared as surprised as herself.

Lady Milmouth grinned, oblivious to the undercurrents. "Ah, there you are, gentlemen! Your Grace, Lady Isla, may I introduce Captain Ross and Captain Balfour, two officers who served with our Edward?"

Colonel Archer smiled brightly, clearly delighted for Isla to meet his friends.

The dear man. He hadn't a clue.

Isla pressed a hand to her midriff.

Gray said nothing. Isla dared a glance at him. He rather resembled a furious bull, nostrils flared beneath wide eyes.

Captain Balfour continued to gaze at her, expression impassive. He stood a hair taller than the other gentlemen. Though he wasn't dressed in the height of fashion like Colonel Archer, nor commanded the might of a wealthy dukedom like Gray, Captain Balfour was the man who drew eyes in the room. The sheer gravity of him. As if he were a mountain, unmoved and unyielding.

Silence descended.

Isla couldn't spare a syllable, her throat too dry. Gray and Captain Balfour likely felt the same. The other four people merely glanced at each other, obviously attempting to understand why the temperature in the room had abruptly chilled several degrees.

It was Lord Milmouth who finally broke the stalemate.

"Balfour?" His brow pinched, his head turning to Captain Balfour. "As in . . ."

"Aye, my lord. My father is the Earl of Northcairn. I am the second son, after my elder brother, Lord Cairnfell."

"Ah." Lord Milmouth's head went back before his gaze shifted to Gray. "I see."

Lady Milmouth glanced between the men, looking confused for a fraction of a second . . . and then realization sank in. She flushed a truly remarkable shade of scarlet.

Everyone in Polite Society knew of the enmity between Northcairn and Grayburn. But as Northcairn and his progeny rarely attended *ton* events—Gray had ensured they were hardly received anymore—their ill-fated meetings were not treacherous shoals that hostesses were called upon to navigate with any regularity.

By inviting members from two hostile families, Lady Milmouth had made a most colossal blunder.

"Oh! Oh, no!" Her ladyship fluttered a hand to her bosom. "I hadn't the slightest idea . . . Edward merely invited his friends and didn't mention their familial connections, you see . . . we rarely stand on ceremony when here at Kingswell House, so I didn't think . . . and Edward's friends had just arrived before you, so there hasn't been a moment to ascertain . . ."

Poor Colonel Archer looked back and forth between everyone, his expression confused. Isla nearly sighed. His innocent soul likely couldn't fathom the depth of hostility that existed between the Balfours and the Kinseys. Would he be similarly unruffled by her foolish marriage to one of his closest friends?

Oh, what a tangled web we weave . . .

Mr. Walter Scott had the right of things.

Isla feared she would be sick.

"Our rooms, if you please, Lady Milmouth." Gray kept his eyes trained on Captain Balfour as he spoke. A warning if Isla had ever seen one.

Her ladyship spared one more glance for Captain Balfour and then squared her shoulders.

"Of course. You must wish to rest, Your Grace. Please follow me."

Isla trailed her brother, gaze studiously avoiding Captain Balfour.

But she felt the burning press of his eyes regardless.

LADY MILMOUTH SHOWED Isla and Gray to their rooms, apologizing on a loop, hands wringing in misery, tears brightening her eyes.

"I simply didn't know. Oh dear, what a disaster! I am so desperately sorry for any distress this has caused you both. And here we were, so hopeful for a wonderful week!"

Her ladyship's anxiety matched the jittery nervousness that had taken hold of Isla's limbs.

Lord help her! What was she to do?

Perhaps Gray would insist they leave at daybreak. Or demand Captain Balfour be shown the door. Or goad Captain Balfour into a bout of fisticuffs over tea and scones and have him arrested for brawling.

Isla hardly knew which outcome she would prefer.

After changing her clothing and tidying her hair and sternly ordering her hands to *stoptremblingthisinstant!*, Isla knocked on Gray's bedchamber door.

Gray's valet answered, bowing her into the room. Like herself, her brother had already changed out of his traveling attire and was currently staring into a mirror, straightening the cuffs of a tight-fitting blue tailcoat.

Gray met her gaze in the reflection and then nodded at his valet to leave. The man closed the door quietly behind him. Gray gave his sleeves one final tug.

"We are not staying with Balfour in residence." Trust her brother to get directly to the point. "I refuse to put you in his orbit."

So.

They would be leaving.

The knot of dread beneath Isla's breastbone did not loosen at the thought as she might have supposed.

Why?

The answer arrived immediately—

Leaving solved nothing.

If she wished to continue her suit with Colonel Archer, she needed to learn to navigate his relationship with Captain Balfour. She had to face this challenge, not shrink from it.

Fortunately, Captain Balfour had said he was leaving for America. Soon, he would be an ocean away. Which meant Tavish Balfour wouldn't be a regular fixture in her life with Edward Archer, thank goodness.

But that didn't solve the problem of this week-long house party.

Isla crossed to the window.

Naturally, the Duke of Grayburn had been put in one of the finest rooms in the house—a large tester bed, a sitting area before the fire, as well as two enormous windows overlooking the Italian parterre garden and the rising mountains to the west.

Isla cleared her throat. "Lady Milmouth is excessively distressed over this *faux pas*. I would hate to ruin her house party due to our intransigence over—"

"Her ladyship should have had the intelligence to ascertain who Archer was inviting. Asking a few pertinent questions as to the origins of one's guests is the duty of any worthy hostess!" Gray snapped from behind.

"That is potentially my future mother-in-law you speak of, Gray. If you find her ladyship so lacking, shall I decline to continue my attachment to Colonel Archer? Will you toss away any hope of a political alliance with Lord Milmouth?"

Silence.

Isla stared out the window where an evening breeze shook the Scots pine. She could feel Gray seething at her back.

"I believe . . ." On a deep breath, she continued through lips gone numb. "I believe I can tolerate a week of seeing Captain Balfour here and there."

Or, more accurately, she needed to *learn* how to tolerate a week of seeing the captain here and there.

If she couldn't manage basic social interactions with Captain Balfour—if his mere presence overset her and rendered her what? maudlin? lovesick?—then it would be better to know now. Though to what end, she couldn't say.

She had no desire to return to what they had been. And she certainly wouldn't be forfeiting Malton Hill and her community there. She liked Colonel Archer. If she wanted a life with him, she needed to fight her way through this bramble.

Gray snorted. "I do not wish to witness you *tolerate* his presence, as you say. If Balfour were any sort of gentleman, he could recuse himself immediately to spare your feelings."

"My feelings are utterly indifferent, Gray."

"Are they, though?" His tone held a knowing condescension that raised the fine hairs on the back of her neck.

They never spoke of this, she and Gray. In fact, after his harsh words that night seven years ago, they hadn't spoken of Tavish Balfour until his reappearance last week.

Isla wrapped an arm around her middle. "You don't trust me."

Gray said nothing, though the weight of his anger pressed against her shoulder blades.

"You don't trust that I have changed." She whirled, meeting his hazel eyes. "You don't trust that I am sincere when I say I will not be returning to my youthful self. I was barely two weeks past my seventeenth birthday when those events occurred, Gray. I am now seven years older and no longer a child. Please give me credit for understanding my own mind."

He stared at her before turning away, pacing to the fireplace and back again, his limp making an agitated appearance.

Isla could feel it warring within him. His black hatred for all Balfours—Captain Balfour, in particular—competing with his desire for her to marry Colonel Archer and ally their family with the Earls of Milmouth.

Gray ran a finger under his neckcloth, as if fighting the urge to wrench the restricting garment off his neck.

"There are also three other young ladies currently under this roof," Isla continued.

"Pardon?" Gray paused, a frown denting his brow. "Why are they part of this equation?"

Isla nearly rolled her eyes at his cluelessness.

"You are hardly so obtuse, Gray. If you throw around the weight of your ducal authority and insist Captain Balfour depart, possibly taking Captain Ross with him—which, of course, you are within your rights to do—the ladies' undivided attention will devolve upon you and you alone."

Gray clenched his jaw and pivoted back toward the fireplace, resuming his pacing.

"Despite our feelings on the matter," Isla said, "Captain Balfour is also the son of an earl. He is not inconsequential, at least not to these ladies and their mammas."

"As if Balfour has two tuppence to rub together to support a bride," Gray snarled. "Can you even imagine him marrying?"

Unfortunately, Isla could. She *had*. Something hot and tasting of ash settled on her tongue at the vision of Captain Balfour taking another bride.

This would not do. She would not feel jealous over Captain Balfour's future—and surely past—paramours.

The longer she spoke with Gray, the more Isla was convinced this week would be a blessing. She would see Captain Balfour every day and be able to compare him to Colonel Archer. To understand, quite clearly, why she had disavowed Tavish Balfour in the first place.

This was her chance to confront and finally bury any lingering tendresse for *that man* before he disappeared into the wilds of America forever.

Isla folded her arms. "You are angry because you know I am right."

Gray didn't deny it. He merely continued his pacing.

"I want to know Colonel Archer better. You want to court Lord Milmouth as an ally. Both of those objectives become more difficult if Captain Balfour leaves. We can be civil for a week, Gray."

"But can he?"

"Of course, he can. He is just as changed as I am. Neither of us will return to what we once were."

But just saying the words caused that pang again. That fathomless old grief that rippled below her surface.

"And what *were* you, precisely, to one another, Isla?" Gray paused, a hand braced on the mantelpiece.

The question caused Isla to take a step back.

Everything.

The answer surged forward with no effort.

We were everything. An entire universe unto ourselves.

Gray might have uncovered the fact of her relationship with Tavish, but he had never known the profound depth of it.

"What does it matter?" she whispered through a throat gone dry. "It has been dead and buried for seven long years."

Her brother lifted an eyebrow, pinning her in place with his hazel eyes.

Silence stretched, pulling taut.

Finally, Gray spoke. "For your sake, as well as his, I hope you are correct."

10

Tavish descended the stairs for dinner, his mood as sour as the wine Ross had once made out of grapes from an abandoned vineyard outside Cadiz.

Fletch had been there, too, come to think of it.

Damn and blast.

Seeing Isla standing in the entrance hall, Gray thunderous at her side . . .

The saber that flayed his upper cheek had been somehow less jarring.

But, as of yet, Lord and Lady Milmouth had not asked Tavish to leave, though his effects had been discreetly relocated to another bedroom two floors up from where he had been. The footman who saw to the move flushed when Tavish asked him why.

"I b-believe her ladyship wished for more s-space between yourself and His Grace," the man had stammered.

Of course. Tavish could hardly fault Lady Milmouth for moving him as far as possible from Grayburn. Heaven forbid the duke encounter Tavish at random. His Grace's tranquility was not to be disturbed.

Regardless, Tavish dressed for dinner and left his room, muscles tense, waiting for the guillotine blade to fall. He was halfway down the second flight of stairs when Ross hailed him from behind.

"Ho there, Balfour!"

Tavish paused, waiting for his friend to join him. Like himself, Captain George Ross was the son of a Scottish gentleman. Unlike Tavish, Ross's father owned the lucrative Bracklamore whisky distillery, and Ross himself had a pretty property in Moray with tenants and a thousand acres of decent farmland.

Tavish and Ross had served side-by-side from the first day Tavish arrived in the 95th Rifles. The 95th was different from other rank-and-file regiments. They were the crack elite troops charged with slipping ahead of advancing forces and removing enemy officers before they took the battlefield. To aid in this, Rifles worked in pairs—one shooting his Baker rifle while his partner reloaded.

Until the point of their rank advancement, Ross had been Tavish's partner. To say that Tavish had no better friend would be a gross understatement. He would trust Ross with his life and had on more occasions than he could count.

"Ye looked about ready to cast up your accounts seeing Grayburn and his sister here." Ross said the words easily, but Tavish registered the concern in his friend's eyes. "Is all well?"

"As well as could be, I ken." Tavish shrugged.

"I cannot believe that Fletch forgot about your family rivalry with the Dukes of Grayburn."

Rivalry? Tavish would have gone with *vitriolic hatred* himself.

"We both know Fletch has no head for these sorts of things," Tavish said. "Though Lady Milmouth should have been more aware of who she was inviting."

Ross twisted his mouth and glanced about the stairwell, checking no one else was near.

"This is the same duke who instigated the ruination of your sister, correct?" he murmured.

"Aye. The very same."

"Bloody hell. Will ye stay the week then?"

Och, that was the question, was it not? Haring off felt too much like ceding the field to enemy forces, something Tavish had never done with ease.

But staying and having to make polite with Grayburn, all while pretending Isla was a stranger to him . . .

"It would be a shame if ye left," Ross continued. "We've much to discuss with Fletch."

"Agreed."

That was also the truth. Fletch was the third partner in their whisky endeavor. He brought needed capital while Ross contributed knowledge, and Tavish brute labor, some capital, and an intense desire to succeed. This was to have been their week to hammer out the fine details of their plan. Grayburn and Isla would be a hindrance to that.

"I am sure Grayburn will avoid us as surely as we avoid him," Tavish said.

"Aye. If nothing else, the young ladies will have him dancing a merry jig."

"True. The ladies did seem decidedly eager for His Grace's arrival." The thought cheered Tavish immensely.

He rather liked the picture of His Lofty Dukeship dodging impertinent questions and incessant flirtation. From what Tavish had already deduced from the Misses Forsyth and Miss Crowley, they would no doubt pester Grayburn nigh to death. Prudence and restraint were two characteristics he had yet to see the young women embody.

As Tavish and Ross crossed the landing toward the final run of stairs, Fletch came striding from the family wing, a hand lifted in greeting.

Tavish couldn't recall when Colonel Edward Archer had become *Fletch*. It was some sliding progression from *Archer* to *Arrow* to *Fletcher* to *Fletch* in the eccentric way that nicknames developed. The moniker had stuck for years now.

As usual, his friend sported a wide grin. The sort Tavish couldn't help but mirror.

"Gentlemen." Fletch stopped before Tavish and Ross. "I see you have yourselves sorted." He nodded toward their evening attire.

Tavish had long resisted dipping into the nest egg of funds he had from the sale of his commission, but he had realized that a few elegant pieces of clothing would be a necessity for civilian life. His dark green superfine coat, striped waistcoat, and tight-cut breeches spoke to that this evening. After all, a gentleman did not continue in regimentals after selling out of the military.

"Is all well?" Fletch continued, meeting Tavish's gaze.

Tavish understood his friend's unspoken question—are you content to spend a week under the same roof as the Duke of Grayburn?

"Of course," Tavish lied smoothly. "As long as other guests are comfortable with my presence."

It was the correct answer, as Fletch's shoulders relaxed and his smile broadened. "Yes. The other guests are content."

Tavish *highly* doubted that.

"I am glad." Fletch clasped Tavish's shoulder. "The week would be dreary without you, my friend."

Ross lifted a skeptical eyebrow. "Even with so many comely ladies present?"

Fletch snorted. "Two of those ladies are my cousins, I will have you know."

"People marry their cousins all the time," Ross countered.

"Hah! Caroline and Anne are more like sisters than cousins. The thought of marrying either—" Fletch shuddered. "But they are fine girls, of course. The finest! Either of you should be so lucky. And Miss Crowley is charming."

"Indeed," Ross chuckled. "Why do I feel like ye have no interest there either?"

Fletch laughed and promptly changed the subject. "And you, Balfour? Have you come up with a plan to resolve . . . matters?"

It was an oblique reference to Tavish's marriage. Aside from those who were present at said wedding, Ross and Fletch were the only two other people who knew of its existence, though even they did not know the identity of the lady.

Tavish hadn't meant to tell anyone, but Fletch and Ross had caught him deep in his cups after the Battle of Tarbes. Though their own casualties had been relatively light, the slaughter had been great among the French. The loss of life had weighed on Tavish's soul, for not the first nor the last time.

Usually, Ross and Fletch would leave to find solace elsewhere—Ross in the arms of whatever woman he could find; Fletch with his Spanish paramour.

But that night, his friends had remained at Tavish's side. Together, they had drunk enough French wine to float a small boat, becoming more loose-lipped with each glass.

"Why don't you ever touch a woman?" Fletch had asked.

"Aye! I have long held that question." Ross saluted with his cup.

"Not once have I caught you kissing a lady-bird or even gazing at a comely bosom." Fletch.

"Do ye not like the lasses, Balfour?" Ross.

The question caught Tavish off guard. Of course, he liked the lasses and had a more than healthy appreciation of a fine bosom.

However, he had made sacred vows to one particular lass, and regardless of her feelings on the matter, he intended to honor their marriage.

Ross and Fletch teased Tavish for nearly thirty minutes before he admitted the whole to them.

"I am married." He stared into the ruby depths of his glass, as if it could conjure some clarity alongside the headache he would have come morning.

"Married?!" Ross slapped the table. "And we are only now hearing of this?!"

"It's complicated." Tavish pinched the bridge of his nose.

"Complicated . . . how?" Fletch asked.

"Our marriage was a handfasting, and her family is unaware of our attachment. We didn't part on the best of terms."

"But . . . you are her husband." Fletch frowned. "She is bound to you."

"Aye, but she is not pleased with that fact. My death would surely be a relief."

"Oof! That's a fine pickle then." Fletch belched. "So who is this lucky woman?"

"I shan't be disclosing that information. She is a lady, and I will not harm her good name by uttering it."

A long silence ensued.

Ross finally roused himself, swirling his wine in his cup. "Ye do realize that divorce is possible in Scotland."

"Aye."

"And adultery is generally considered the surest way to go about it."

"Aye."

"And still . . ." Ross raised an eyebrow at him. An unspoken question. A wondering.

Tavish drained the rest of his cup. "I don't have it in me to dishonor my marriage vows and betray my wife. We will simply have to find another way of dissolving our union, she and I."

"So you won't—" Fletch made a vaguely rude gesture. "—until you have dissolved your marriage?"

"That's about the right of it."

And that had been that.

Both Fletch and Ross knew that Tavish intended to dissolve his marriage before embarking for America.

Folding his arms, Tavish looked at his friends hovering a few steps above him.

"Aye," he said. "I spoke with a solicitor in Aberdeen about a possible divorce. As I have never contributed to the lady's upkeep, the matter should be fairly straightforward on the basis of desertion. And the lady herself is in agreement."

"Ye saw her?" Ross leaned forward.

"Aye." *And I will see her again in mere seconds,* he declined to add.

"How did that go?" Fletch asked.

"About as one would expect. Plenty of tense silences and a host of words left unsaid."

"Do ye ken she still loves your sorry carcass?" Ross asked.

Tavish recalled Isla's icy gaze, her clipped words.

"Not a chance in hell. And I will thank both of ye for guarding this secret with your lives. As usual, I plead with you on your honor not to mention it to anyone, for the lady's sake." The last thing Tavish needed was one of his friends mentioning his marriage this week.

Fletch motioned for them to continue down the stairs.

"So why no interest in Miss Crowley, Fletch?" Tavish changed the subject.

"My sights are set on a different lady."

"Are they now?" Ross matched their friend's smile.

They reached the bottom of the stairs, a murmur of voices humming from the drawing room across the way.

Fletch paused and turned around to face Tavish and Ross. "There is no harm in telling you both, as it will become plain soon enough. I have recently requested and have been granted permission to court—" Fletch paused, a sort of happy wonder taking over his features. He took a step back, peering into the drawing room. "Ah, you can see her perfectly from here."

He motioned for his friends to come closer. Tavish did so, looking in the same direction as Fletch.

There, perched on a settee and rimmed in fading sunlight, sat Lady Isla speaking with Lady Milmouth.

A terrible ringing commenced in Tavish's ears.

"Truly?!" Ross's eyebrows rose, as if impressed. "Grayburn gave ye permission to court his sister?"

"Yes," Fletch said, that same wonder in his voice. "It scarcely seems real." He clapped a hand to Tavish's shoulder. "I know that you don't approve of Grayburn as a rule, but even you must own that his sister is as lovely and refined a lady as has ever lived."

"Aye," Tavish managed over a throat gone sandpaper dry.

"I shall count on you both to assist me," Fletch continued. "Keep the other ladies diverted, so I can spend more time with Lady Isla. I hope to settle our betrothal soon, possibly even by the end of this week."

Only later, as he lay staring at the canopy above his bed, did Tavish realize *that* had been the point—the precise juncture in time where he should have confessed that Isla was the lady he had married.

However, in the moment standing with Fletch and Ross, Tavish was too stunned to utter another syllable. The word *betrothal* rolled around his brain like a billiard ball, knocking all other thoughts aside.

And in that wake, two facts blinded him to any other reality.

One, Isla had known when they spoke atop Cairnfell. She knew she was being courted by another gentleman with the intent of marriage.

And two, she hadn't said a damn word of it to Tavish. Regardless of what had happened and would happen between them, pursuing a second marriage *before* securing a divorce definitely resided in the column entitled *Details I Must Tell Tavish.*

He wanted to rage. To scramble up the sides of Cairnfell and bellow his fury.

Instead, he shuttered his expression and grimly followed Fletch and Ross into the drawing room.

11

SEVEN YEARS EARLIER

JUNE 30, 1810
PETTERCAIRN, SCOTLAND

Isla buried her face in Tavish's chest, hands clasped around his waist. She adored the perfect way her frame nestled into his, as if his body had been made for the simple purpose of supporting hers.

"I never get to hold ye long enough." His chin rested on the top of her head. "I want ye with me every minute of the day, not these wee stolen hours."

Haar had settled over the landscape—great sheets of fog rolling in off the North Sea and blanketing the coast in an ethereal mist.

Today, Isla and Tavish were standing in a copse of dense brush halfway up Cairnfell. It was discreet and difficult to find unless you knew where to look, particularly in the *haar*. No one should discover them here.

And yet, Isla worried.

She worried that Gray would learn of these meetings and would send her away. Or that Lord Northcairn would uncover them and forbid Tavish from seeing her. Or that a comet would fall from the sky in a great pillar of fire and obliterate them all.

Her worries were not precisely bound by logic.

"I miss you, too." Lifting to tiptoe, Isla pressed a kiss to the underside of his jaw. "The worst is watching you walk away, not knowing if or when I'll be in your arms again."

Tavish tightened said arms. "I always fear each time will be our last together."

Isla pulled back, looking up into his beloved face. The warmth in his gray eyes, the tumble of his red hair across his forehead. She pressed a finger to his impossibly full lips, marveling at their give. He kissed her fingertip.

Would it ever grow old, she wondered? Touching him like this? Tavish touching her in return?

She rather thought it wouldn't.

"I love you," she whispered.

He kissed her forehead. "And I love ye, lass."

He had said the words to her for the first time three weeks past, and she had immediately echoed them.

Now, it had nearly become a benediction.

I miss you, and I love you.

Until we meet again, and I love you.

As if the words simply could not be repeated enough.

She saw him, and it was akin to coming alive, like the Tuscan sun-flowers Miss Farnsworth had once described. *Girasole*, they were called in Italian, which translated as *turns-toward-the-sun*. Or *sun-turners*.

Isla felt like that. Tavish was her sun, and whenever he appeared, her entire soul rotated in his direction, helplessly drawn to his brilliant light.

Finally, she understood the profundity of every poet who had scribbled lines about love. What had Shakespeare said?

Love alters not with his brief hours and weeks,
But bears it out even to the edge of doom.

Yes! That was the precise sentiment. Isla would cast herself to the very edge of doom—beyond, even!—before she would cease loving Tavish Balfour.

"What are we to do, Tavish?" she whispered.

Their situation felt untenable—a band stretched too taut that could snap at the slightest disturbance.

They never spoke of the future. But the deeper she fell in love, the less Isla could envision a life without Tavish.

He stroked her cheek with his thumb. "Ye do know that in Scotland, we don't need permission to marry."

"Yes. It's why the English fly north to Gretna Green to tie the knot."

"Aye. Anyone can marry here, even at our ages. It only requires two witnesses."

"Is that all?"

Isla hadn't thought . . .

Or, rather, she *had* thought. About *it*. Marriage and all its attendant activities . . . at great length and in shocking detail. She had even gone so far as to bribe one of the housemaids to tell her precisely what occurred in the marriage bed between a man and a woman.

She supposed most gently-born ladies would swoon over what the maid had described. Isla, however, had hung on every word. And then, to imagine engaging in that activity with Tavish. *Her* Tavish.

The thought left her flushed and warm with a terrible, empty yearning deep in her belly.

"I have given it some thought. How we could go about a marriage . . ." Tavish began. "Or, rather, that is . . . if ye should like . . ." A ruddy flush crawled up his neck.

"Are you . . ." Isla stepped out of his arms. "Are you asking me to marry you, Tavish Balfour?"

He tugged on his neckcloth. "And if I am?"

Euphoria. That was the only word Isla could summon to describe the emotion that battered her breastbone.

Married.

To Tavish.

YES!

"Well," she said, breathless. "If you ask me to marry you, I expect you to do it proper-like."

"Proper-like?"

She pointed at the ground. "On your knees, of course. And including many flowery things about my person and your adoration of my virtues."

He grinned.

But he did not kneel. Instead, he grasped her hands loosely in his.

"I can't offer ye much, Isla Kinsey."

"Are you proposing?"

"Am I on my knees?"

"No."

"Precisely. I am merely discussing. Exploring possibilities. We both know, if we were to marry, it would be against our families' wishes. My father will refuse to harbor us."

"Yes, and Gray will not release my dowry to you."

"I don't want your dowry."

"You should." She smiled. "I understand it's thirty thousand pounds plus a pretty estate in Gloucestershire called Malton Hill. I've never seen the house, but I'm told it's a lovely old Tudor building."

His eyebrows lifted. "I would hate for ye to lose it."

She placed a hand to his cheek. "But I would be gaining you."

He kissed her lips. "All is not lost. I have a bit of money set by. My own inheritance from my mother. It's not something that my father can deny me. It won't be much to begin our life together, but I am hale and hearty and determined to succeed. I shall explore options and ensure there is a future for us."

"Yes! I will be at your side, cheering you on with every step."

Tavish bent down and kissed her lips again. "Someday, our families will see the error of their ways and reconcile."

"We merely need to set the example."

"Aye."

He kissed her longer, lips clinging. Isla stepped into his body, eager to deepen their embrace.

Instead, he held her away from him.

Isla cocked her head in confusion.

And then clapped her hands over her mouth as Tavish dropped to his knees.

12

Isla cut her beef into precise squares, the murmur of voices washing over her from every corner of the dining room table.

If this had been a normal sort of house party, she would have found the food and company delightful.

The situation of the dining room at Kingswell House was everything a hostess desired—a long, elegant table set with fine Sèvres china and polished silver cutlery, blush ranunculus and white roses spilling from vases, a gentle fire flickering in the hearth.

The food was excellent—tender beef in a well-set aspic atop flaky puff pastry—courtesy of Lady Milmouth's skilled French cook.

The company laughed and talked at ease, particularly Colonel Archer at Isla's elbow. Even Gray, seated to the right of Lord Milmouth at the head of the table, had managed to relax into a semblance of his London self. Her brother charmed Lady Forsyth at his elbow and laughed at a quip Lord Milmouth offered.

All in all, it should have been an enchanting evening.

But the weight of Captain Balfour's presence pressed down on every lighter emotion Isla might feel.

He sat down the table from Isla. Miss Lydia Crowley, a pretty young lady with sparkling dark eyes and a far-too-generous bosom, sat to his right and repeatedly drew him into conversation.

Isla wanted nothing more than to ignore the captain completely. But the man himself made that task difficult.

First was the matter of his clothing. Not once had she seen Tavish Balfour in evening attire. Most certainly not kitted out like a Corinthian of the first stare as he was this evening. The fact that Captain Balfour wore his well-tailored coat with the practiced ease of a high-born gentleman overset her thinking.

Obviously, he *was* a high-born gentleman. But Isla had never specifically envisioned him at a *ton* event. She had never considered how he would draw the eye. How he would stand out as a particularly spectacular example of aristocratic breeding.

Clearly, she lacked imagination.

Had she no prior knowledge of him before this evening, Isla would have found herself drawn in. She would currently be stealing furtive glances of his handsome profile. Perhaps even admiring how the crisp brightness of his neckcloth and the high collar of his coat accentuated the deep dent in his chin and the fullness of his pillow lips.

She once had tried to determine how many features of his face could hold a pencil without assistance. The perfect dent in his chin? Yes. The deep shadow under his bottom lip? Absolutely, yes.

Truly, his lips were nearly obscene. Far too full for a man. How was a woman to think of anything other than how those lips would feel atop her own? Or remember, once she had kissed them, that they felt like silk-covered goose down . . . which truthfully was a hundred times worse. Had the man no mercy?

Isla tried to concentrate on Colonel Archer's voice in her ear. To make banal replies to his questions. Yes, the weather had been lovely of late. Yes, her bedchamber was to her liking.

But Miss Crowley's tinkling laughter and murmured questions constantly intruded, particularly when Captain Balfour, those damnable pillow lips pursed into a smile, leaned his head down to better hear the lady.

Abruptly, Isla remembered being sixteen years old and giggling with Tavish as they attempted to best each other at draughts. Her mind had raced for words, anything to fuel the rumble of his laughter. Surely, her expression then had mimicked Miss Crowley's now, flushing and gazing up at Captain Balfour with awestruck delight.

Isla feared she had lost that open-hearted girl somewhere along the way.

Granted, Captain Balfour didn't smile the same now either, Isla noted. Not his true smile. The one that had once caused her pulse to skip with gladness. The smile that mirrored his heart in his eyes.

But what did Isla know? Perhaps Captain Balfour didn't smile like that anymore.

He is a stranger, she reminded herself. *He is not the boy you knew. Your Tavish died long ago.*

If only the present weren't so determined to resurrect the past. To force Isla to ponder the boy he had been and the man he had become. To confront and understand the changes in her own self.

But . . . this was what she had wanted. Why she had encouraged Gray to remain at Kingswell House. A week of penance to purge any lingering sentiment for Tavish Balfour.

Surely navigating the treacherous shoals of her memories would become easier as the days passed.

Unfortunately, relinquishing the men to their port and withdrawing with the ladies did not grant Isla the expected reprieve.

Lady Milmouth instantly cozied up with Lady Forsyth before the fire, leaving Isla alone with Miss Forsyth, Miss Anne Forsyth, and Miss Crowley. As young unmarried ladies were wont to do, their conversation rapidly turned to the unattached gentlemen.

"Do you not find Captain Balfour excessively handsome?" Miss Crowley asked. "I think he is the most well-favored gentleman here."

"You are only saying that because he complimented your gown, Lydia." Miss Anne Forsyth nodded to the pink silk of Miss Crowley's evening dress.

Miss Crowley flushed. "Yes, but he complimented it so prettily."

Miss Forsyth fixed her younger sister with a *look*. "I know you find Captain Balfour to your liking, too, Anne. You are just sore that he didn't compliment your gown, as well."

Miss Anne Forsyth glared. Isla had the distinct sense that, were they not in company, Miss Anne might have stuck out her tongue at her sister.

"I agree with Lydia," Miss Forsyth continued. "There is simply something arresting about Captain Balfour. As if the entire world could fracture to pieces, and he would simply set about tidying up. I cannot imagine anything would overset him."

"I agree. Such self-possession would be an excellent quality in a husband," Miss Crowley added with another blush.

Oh, gracious.

It was all Isla could do not to press a hand to her stomach.

This was *her* husband the young ladies discussed.

"What do you think, Lady Isla?" Miss Forsyth asked.

"Of . . . Captain Balfour?" Isla managed to croak.

"Yes." Miss Crowley leaned forward. "I know your family is not friendly with the Balfours, but surely there is no harm in appreciating the fine figure of an attractive man?"

Isla opened her mouth, but struggled to form words. What was she to say?

Why, yes, I do find the captain decidedly alluring. His kisses rather melt one's knees.

Or, perhaps . . .

I am not sure he would make the best of husbands, to be truthful. It's been over seven years since our own wedding, and in that time, I don't think we've spent above an hour in one another's company.

But even as the thoughts tumbled through, she recalled Tavish on their wedding day. How they had stood before a retired doctor and his wife in Stonehaven and pledged their vows.

It always astonished Isla how easily she could recall that moment. The wide wonder in Tavish's gray eyes. As if he could scarcely believe that this moment had finally—*finally!*—arrived. That they would be bound as one, never to be parted.

His hand had trembled in hers. Her tears had wet the tartan ribbon of their handfasting. He had kissed her afterward, a tender touching of lips. A promise of a world to come.

She still kept that strip of tartan, along with the written witness of their marriage vows, tucked in a box slid to the back of a drawer.

Perhaps, she would burn that ribbon . . . maybe on the day their divorce became final.

The silence stretched too long.

Miss Anne Forsyth pursed her lips at Miss Crowley. "You place Lady Isla in a most indelicate situation, Lydia. She cannot say anything lavish about Captain Balfour without betraying her family. Besides, we know Lady Isla's interests lie elsewhere." She aimed a pointed look at Lady Milmouth, implying Isla's connection with Colonel Archer.

Isla willed herself not to blush.

Miss Crowley at least had the decency to appear abashed. "My apologies, Lady Isla."

"There is no need for an apology."

Silence descended.

"Lady Isla, may we ask you a question?" Miss Forsyth motioned to her sister and friend.

"Of course."

"Do you consider it likely that your brother will speak a full sentence to any of us this week?"

Oh.

The abrupt change in topic had Isla sitting upright in her seat.

"Gray?"

All three young ladies nodded.

Miss Crowley tittered. "Your brother is so handsome and noble, Lady Isla, one scarcely notices his faint limp."

Right.

The fact of Gray's uneven legs was rather common knowledge. No one ever spoke of it directly, of course, but Isla overheard whispered conversations about both her brothers. People always voiced the same question: What dreadful sin had the previous Duke of Grayburn committed to so kindle the wrath of God? After all, two sons with a similar deformity must be a sign of divine displeasure.

Such whispers were one of the many reasons why Matt never ventured into company.

"But will His Grace speak with any of us?" Miss Forsyth pressed.

"Gray is rather . . ." How to finish that sentence? Circumspect? Uninterested in marriage at the moment?

In short, Isla could scarcely imagine her brother looking at any woman in fondness or—*shudder*—love. Gray kept a healthy distance between himself and tenderness.

She assumed that eventually, when he decided to take a bride, he would meticulously survey the field, make a list, and conduct interviews before choosing the most eligible young woman to marry. No love or passion involved.

Fortunately, the gentlemen chose that moment to enter from the dining room.

Unfortunately, Isla met Captain Balfour's gaze as he stepped into the drawing room.

They both looked away almost instantly, but the intensity of his gray eyes burned in her mind's eye.

He wanted to speak with her. Alone. Isla was sure of it.

The fact discomfited her. She didn't wish to be so attuned to his thoughts. To know with just the briefest of glances what he was thinking.

She didn't dare look in his direction again, but it didn't stop her from watching him in reflection—the mirror over the fireplace, the gleam of a silver vase, the panes of the large windows overlooking the back garden.

The week promised to be a long one.

AS ISLA INTUITED, she found a folded bit of foolscap slipped under her bedchamber door when she retired for the night. It gleamed a stark-white on the edge of the Aubusson carpet.

She snatched it up with trembling fingers.

Foolish man.

Captain Balfour would get them both in trouble.

Thankfully, he had the wisdom to write his message in their cipher. At least if the paper were discovered, Isla could plead ignorance.

Still.

NQ EOCV CKQYT . . .

Unlike his last message, this one encompassed several lines of text and took a minute to decode.

We must speak. There is an empty bedchamber directly above your own. Meet me there at one a.m. Be discreet.

Isla blew out an exasperated breath.

Be discreet?!

Not meeting at all would be discreet! A clandestine assignation was the very definition of *in*discreet.

She did not enjoy being treated like one of his soldiers—a green recruit who would jump to obey his commands.

Perhaps, she would write her own message in reply.

FJ!

He would understand the word *No!* well enough.

Instead, she tucked the message into her traveling desk and brooded, staring into the fire until her lady's maid arrived to help Isla undress and prepare for bed.

She shouldn't meet with him. It only encouraged his domineering behavior.

She *wouldn't* meet with him.

No, she would not. Let *him* stew, for once.

She tucked into bed with that very intention. But questions tossed and turned in her brain, making sleep elusive.

What *did* Captain Balfour have to say to her? He was to have met with a solicitor in Aberdeen already. Perhaps there was news to report?

How did he know that the bedchamber above hers was empty? Had he bribed a pretty housemaid?

Isla glared at her bed canopy in frustration.

Regrettably, curiosity got the better of her.

When the mantel clock struck one, Isla was already out of bed, pulling on her dressing gown, wrapping a dark shawl around her shoulders, and shuffling in stockinged feet to her bedroom door.

The hallway outside her door loomed in shadows. Nothing stirred.

On soundless steps, Isla moved down the hall to the staircase.

She wanted to be indignant and furious. Summon all the righteous anger she would need to fend off the confusion Captain Balfour inspired.

Instead, her heart beat swiftly, and the tiniest thrill chased her spine.

Was she . . . ?

Was she *excited*, dash it all?

She could feel it rising inside her . . . an enlivening of sorts. Or, perhaps, a lost fragment of self.

It wasn't a swell or a torrent. More like a gentle trickle of anticipation. A faint echo of the sensation she had felt when racing up the path to Cairnfell. That eager chasing of something forbidden.

Perhaps those years ago, she had merely been swept up in the exhilaration of an illicit connection—notes written in secret code, hidden messages, a handsome boy who filled her ears with honeyed words and the intoxicating rumble of his laughter.

And if Tavish had been Colonel Archer or Captain Ross or some other gentleman, would she have felt the same excitement?

Isla truthfully couldn't say.

The knowledge was a rather appalling insight into her character. Her future needed to be based on something other than reckless thrills and a desire for entertainment.

Her association with Tavish Balfour couldn't end soon enough.

She found the empty bedroom easily. It was the only one with the door slightly ajar.

Isla pushed it open.

A bed sat to the left. A fireplace to the right.

But straight ahead . . .

He rested on the sill of the single window, the shutters opened to let in moonlight. The dim glow streamed around his broad shoulders and painted him in hulking shadows. Only the quicksilver of his eyes glittered, mirroring the starlight at his back.

He felt . . . elemental. Solid. If her Tavish had been laughter and sunrise, Captain Balfour was steel and midnight.

It should have terrified her. Or, at the very least, been cause for a modicum of trepidation.

But that disturbing solitary thread of thrill remained.

Isla closed the door and leaned back into it. Her hands remained behind her, clasping the door handle. As if it could spare her the force of him. Or steady her in the onslaught of memory. Or, at the very least, provide a quick escape.

"Why am I here?" she whispered. "I assume you spoke with your solicitor and set things in motion with the procurator fiscal, as you said you would. Has anything changed from our last conversation?"

He shook his head, a single stroke to the left.

She gripped the door handle tighter.

Pushing off the windowsill, he crossed to her. Isla drew herself up, standing as tall as possible. He still loomed. Not threatening, per se. Just . . . large.

"Then why summon me here?" Isla continued, tongue darting out to lick her lips. "We risk much if we are caught."

That seemed to amuse him. His lip pillows quirked upward in the low light.

"The horror," he deadpanned. "What would follow should we be found together, yourself and I? A duel for your honor? Demands that we marry?"

Darkly ironic, those words.

"A marriage that might stick this time, you mean? I don't think you want that outcome any more than I do."

"So I've heard."

"Pardon?"

"I count Edward Archer among my closest friends. He has saved my life—and I his—more times than I can quickly count. I would die for that man." A pause. "I did not, however, expect to hand him my *wife*."

TAVISH WATCHED HIS words land, emotions fluttering across Isla's face.

Surprise and resolve.

That was how Tavish would label the flare of her eyes and slight lift of her jaw.

Aye, the light was dim, but she faced the window, capturing what there was of the waxing moon.

"And what of it?" Her chin edged higher. "Your esteem of Colonel Archer only does him credit and proves my good sense. I anticipate that you and I will both remarry eventually. Colonel Archer is an excellent choice. I should think you happy to see me well-married and content."

Tavish ground his teeth, as he could scarcely disagree. Fletch was the best of men.

"You seemed to find Miss Crowley's ample bosom alluring this evening," Isla continued. "I am sure it will be no hardship to unearth a lady to console you in the wake of my loss."

As you have no doubt done in the past, her tone added.

Her words slashed outward. Tavish felt their bite, the cut unexpected and stinging.

Was this the woman she had always been fated to become? This withdrawn and caustic creature?

Fletch thought of her as everything elegant and refined—more complimentary words than *cool* or *unfeeling*—but Tavish had once known the wild color within her. He had reveled in it.

What happened to that girl? Or had she never really existed? Tavish would not be the first man to see only what he wished in a woman.

He didn't disabuse her notion that he might have sought solace elsewhere. She clearly had not been loyal to him or their marital vows—in thought, certainly, if not in some small deed.

A man did have his pride, after all.

"You have no right to this fit of jealousy," she finished.

"Jealousy? This has naught to do with jealousy, lass, and everything to do with communication."

At least, that was the reason he told himself.

"Communication?" she scoffed.

"Aye! Like it or not, your actions still affect myself. If ye go dragging another innocent gentleman—"

"Another?!"

"—into this quagmire, it may prove a fly in the ointment."

Her eyes narrowed at him.

"Our current course for divorce depends upon us both presenting unimpeachable reasons for wanting to secure said divorce," he continued. "If ye are betrothed to another, it undermines everything."

"How? Because this still sounds like you're simply jealous."

"How?! *Och*, ye go from a wife deserted by her husband to a scheming shrew intent on more money than I can provide. And given that both Fletch and I are the second sons of an earl, our case would prove easy to—"

"Fletch?"

"Archer," Tavish amended. "His nickname is Fletch."

"I see. And what is yours?"

"My what?"

"Your nickname?"

"Not *bastard*, as I'm sure you're thinking."

"Truly? But it is so fitting."

Tavish couldn't stop a startled laugh.

"Hush! Someone will hear." She glanced toward the door at her back.

"Unlikely. I'm the only guest on this floor, as it was determined that the stench of my presence was too close to your august elder brother. The other bedchambers are empty. And your room is the one below this one."

"How do you know?"

He tapped his nose. "Reconnaissance." He took a step toward her. "Fletch being in the middle of this complicates everything. Have ye told him you're married?"

She shook her head just once—*No.*

Dread sank through Tavish's bones.

"Lass, I *cannot* keep this secret from Fletch. He is one of my closest frie—"

"You must. Our marriage isn't your secret alone to disclose. I do not wish to tell Colonel Archer about it until he and I have decided we suit. Until then, the point is moot."

"Fletch will view it as the most craven betrayal on my part when he finds out. More importantly, I don't ken he will react favorably to ye keeping the fact of your marriage from him. He will justly view your actions as duplicitous."

"Perhaps, but I am the one who will have to deal with the aftermath of Colonel Archer's reaction." She tapped her chest. "And I would like to tell him in my own way and my own time. You owe me that, at least."

The dread tightened around Tavish's ribcage.

He refused to relinquish his friendship with Fletch. But would Tavish ever be able to stand in the same room as Fletch and his new bride without longing to punch something?

Tavish wasn't sure.

Bloody hell, but this was a *fankle*, a knot of Gordian proportions. Suddenly, he was infinitely grateful there would soon be a vast ocean between himself and Lady Isla.

She stared at him, eyes snapping. The faint moonlight caressed her skin, turning it into the finest alabaster.

He hated that Fletch probably already knew what her skin felt like under his lips—silk and heat and rose petals.

Dammit.

Tavish probably *was* jealous.

"Promise me, Captain Balfour," she whispered.

Not Tavish.

Certainly not *darling* or *love*.

Captain Balfour.

Why did the reality of moving from sweethearts to strangers have to be lined with spikes that abraded the wound of her loss?

But in this, he decided to acquiesce. Isla was Tavish's wife currently; therefore, his loyalty should be to her first. And as Fletch's potential future wife, Isla deserved to control how and when he learned of her prior marriage.

"Very well," he nodded. "But be careful, lass. Try not to toy with Fletch this week. Maybe wait until after the house party to deepen your connection."

Anything to prevent Tavish from having to watch Fletch openly court her.

"You would like that, wouldn't you?"

"Pardon?"

"A reason to force me to remain true to you. To avoid other gentlemen."

"Enough!" He leaned down. "Your comment earlier about Miss Crowley's—how did ye phrase it?—*ample bosom*? Was that not jealousy, too? I'm not the only one struggling with this change in our circumstances."

"Hah!" She pointed a finger at his face. "So you admit you *are* jealous!"

Whip quick, Tavish wrapped his palm around her raised wrist—the reflex as habitual as lifting a rifle to his shoulder. A ghost of the boy he had been, endlessly reaching for her, snatching any excuse to feel her body against his.

The shocking warmth of her skin singed his nerves and raised gooseflesh along his arm.

She gasped.

Their hands remained frozen, locked in the air between them.

I can't believe you dared to touch me! her rapid breaths said.

I can scarcely believe it either, his own breathing replied.

But if this were to be the last time he would touch his wife, Tavish refused to relinquish her. Not until she tugged on her wrist or demanded her freedom.

She did no such thing.

He could feel the bird-flutter of her heartbeat under his fingertips.

With infinite care, he lifted her arm and pressed a kiss to the sensitive hollow on the inside of her wrist. A brush of his lips to the pulse that trembled there.

He had thought to tease her, to show her that she, too, still felt the tug of their connection.

Oh, but the jest was on him.

Her skin smelled like lavender in August. Once, he and his men had stumbled upon a lavender field in bloom outside Guadalajara. Purple-blue flowers stretched across a low valley, perfuming the air. It had been a feast for the senses—the buzz of lazy bees, the sun-drenched smell. They had discovered a beehive and gorged themselves on day-old bread slathered with lavender honey. It had felt like venturing into the Elysian Fields themselves.

Touching Isla's skin after a drought of seven years evoked that afternoon—a surge of longing and hunger and wild yearning. An ache to recapture a fleeting instant of luminous contentment.

Helpless, he kissed her wrist again, lingering this time.

Her breathing caught, a wee catch in the back of her throat. That unguarded sound, coupled with the frantic tattoo of her heartbeat, sent triumph flaring through his veins.

"Ye are not unmoved either, lass. The thump of your pulse betrays ye." He nuzzled her palm before pressing a kiss there. "Admit it."

His words broke the spell.

Her fingers curled inward, and she pulled on her wrist, demanding to be set free.

He released her instantly.

They stared at one another, a scant foot of space between them. Their harsh breaths filled the air.

How easy it would be to cross those final few inches and let his mouth find hers. To rediscover if her kisses still ignited flames in his chest.

He remained rooted in place.

"I am sorry that Colonel Archer—Fletch—is your close friend. But that means you know, as well as I, what a good man he is. I don't . . ." She drifted off.

"Ye don't what, lass?"

"I don't want you." She said the words slowly, as if pulled from deep within. "I don't want the life you could offer me. Not anymore."

The truths punched through the hazy lust of his thinking.

I don't want you.

Reality washed over him, as brisk as a *dooking* in the North Sea in January.

I don't want you.

Tavish took a step back, nodding.

Of course.

Eejit.

Why would she want him when someone like Fletch was an option? And she wasn't wrong. Fletch *was* a good man.

"Aye." He cleared his throat. "Aye. Of course. I agree. Ye deserve better than I can offer ye."

"Captain, I—"

He stopped her with a slice of his hand. "There is nothing more to say between ourselves. Ye have the right of it. I will rely on yourself to tell Fletch about our marriage when the moment is right. Just . . . delay the betrothal until after I meet with the procurator fiscal."

She met his gaze and nodded once before leaving as quietly as she had come.

But not before Tavish noticed her hand, the one he had kissed, clenched tight into a fist.

13

SEVEN YEARS EARLIER

AUGUST 25, 1810
PETTERCAIRN, SCOTLAND

Arranging all the pieces for a secret marriage was a Herculean task. It had taken Tavish nearly two months.

Isla could only disappear for a few hours at a time without raising alarm, so they had only a small window in which to enact their plans.

The legal requirements for handfasting in Scotland were straightforward—a couple needed only to declare their vows before two witnesses. In practice, however, it was best to ensure that the chosen witnesses were well-known members of a town. This explained why the local blacksmith often performed handfastings in Gretna Green. When he signed his name to a document, everyone knew his identity.

Tavish had chosen a doctor in Stonehaven—a pillar of the community—to witness their handfasting. A man far enough away from Pettercairn that he had no ties to either the Dukes of Grayburn or the Earls of Northcairn. In fact, the good doctor had likely not even known their identities. But in exchange for a few coins, he had tied the ribbon of handfasting around their clasped hands.

The moment had been . . .

How could Tavish think to describe it?

The fluttering weight of Isla's slight hand in his. The love and adoration in her eyes as they spoke their vows. The warble in his voice as he slid the slim band of gold onto her finger. The surety in his veins that this—this!—was the best decision he would ever make.

It scarcely mattered what the future held for him. With Isla at his side, they could conquer anything.

They bid the doctor and his wife goodbye, the man promising to deliver a copy of their wedding lines to the local sheriff for recording.

The most difficult hurdle had been accomplished. They were married, and there was ought either of their families could do about that. Tavish had his small inheritance. It wasn't much, but it would be enough provided they lived frugally.

Now, they rode for home astride Callum's hunter, Goliath. Tavish had borrowed the horse without mentioning his plans. Isla's arms wrapped around his waist from behind, her face pressed into the space between his shoulder blades. Despite the discomfort, traveling via horseback had been a wise decision, enabling them to quickly exit the road whenever necessary. They couldn't risk being seen by someone who would recognize them. Not until they were ready to tell their families.

"Almost there," Tavish murmured, nudging Goliath over the last bridge before Cairnfell.

They had been gone longer than he had hoped. The roads had been busy today, and he and Isla had tucked into the trees every half mile or so to permit a farmer or carriage to roll past.

Tavish urged Goliath forward, turning the last bend before the narrow track split. The right fork continued past Cairnfell and onto Balfour land. The left fork crossed the River Southcairn and carried on into Grayburn's estate.

This was it. The place where they would separate.

Tavish had wanted desperately to find a way for them to manage a few hours alone after their marriage. A wee space for them to talk and laugh and, he fervently prayed, consummate their union.

But he had to abandon the dream once he realized how far afield they needed to travel in order to declare their vows. Covering twelve miles in each direction in under four hours—a handfasting occurring in the middle—had been grueling. He could feel Isla's weariness seeping into his back. Unfortunately, she still had a mile to walk before reaching home. With any luck, she would only receive a scolding for her tardiness.

Pulling Goliath to a halt, Tavish stopped before the crossroads.

Wind rustled the trees that lined the narrow road and tugged at the ends of his great coat. A lone hawk called overhead. Somewhere in the distance, sheep lowed.

Thankfully, this was not a well-traveled road. More of a rural trackway than a thoroughfare.

Curling his left leg over the pommel, Tavish dismounted, reaching for Isla. She slid off Goliath and into his arms with a soft moan of relief. He pulled her tight against him.

His wife!

The words reverberated in his mind, echoing like bells on Christmas morning and every whit as joyful.

How he adored her. The feel of her body melting into his. The sink of her chest as she exhaled in contentment. The way her hands slipped under his great coat and jacket to fist the fabric of his waistcoat, as if she intended to hold him forever.

She had slipped his wedding ring off her finger, threading it through the ribbon of their handfasting and stowing it in her pocket alongside their marriage lines for safety.

Soon, they would never again have to hide their love.

"Two days," he whispered in her ear.

"Two days," she returned.

That was when they would leave in truth. The escape had been planned in detail.

They would each leave letters for their families, outlining what they had done. Then, they would abscond. Marrying beforehand had been a calculated decision. If they eloped, it gave Grayburn reason to chase them and potentially stop their nuptials. But if they were already married, there would be nothing he could do.

"I don't want to leave you," Isla sighed into his neckcloth. "I want us to be together every hour of the day. No more caution or secrecy. Just you and I, hand-in-hand, running into the sunshine of our future."

Tavish basked in the happiness of that image for one deep breath.

He needed to let her go. She must hurry home.

And yet, he struggled to release her. It felt akin to dragging his own heart from his chest.

Instead, he bent his head and kissed her.

He intended it to be a quick kiss of parting. A promise of things to come. But one kiss became two . . . and then became twenty.

Bloody hell, how he loved this lass. How blessed to have found her. To know that she would be the companion of his soul from now until his dying breath.

One of her hands threaded into his hair, pulling his head more firmly against her own. Tavish lost himself in the delicious joy of kissing his wife.

"Ye need to go, lass," he murmured against her mouth. "They might come looking for ye."

"I don't want to leave."

"Isla—"

His clever wife inhaled his words, nibbling them from his lips.

Tavish had just dipped his head to feast on the sensitive place below her right ear, the spot that always made her moan, when Isla let out a horrified scream.

He lurched upright as she shoved him away.

"You damn, miscreant curr!" a stern English voice snarled. "I will kill you for this!"

Tavish whirled to see the Duke of Grayburn descending on him from up the road, face a glowing coal of rage, walking stick swinging like a cricket bat, his limp pronounced.

"Go!" Isla pushed Tavish's shoulder.

"Isla—"

"Go! He won't hurt me. GO!" She shoved him toward Goliath.

"Isla!"

"Gray *will* harm you! Don't be a stubborn idiot. Go!"

Though it went against everything Tavish thought himself to be, he swung onto Goliath's back and whirled away, kicking the horse into a gallop.

Away from Grayburn.

Away from Isla.

Once Tavish gained the bend, he slowed, pausing to look back.

If Grayburn so much as laid a hand on her—

The duke faced Isla down, yelling and flushed. But his arms remained at his side, one hand clenched around his walking stick. He did not appear to be physically threatening her.

Grayburn whipped his head upright, his gaze finding Tavish. If the man had a gun, Tavish would already be dead.

He wheeled Goliath for home, a knot of dread twisting in his gut.

Damnation.

How, after all his precautions and detailed scenarios, had he not anticipated the worst?

14

Touching Lady Isla had been a colossal mistake.

A tactical error that Tavish, as a longtime soldier, should have known to avoid.

Seven years.

Seven years without so much as laying a bare fingertip to a woman's skin.

And now this . . .

Even hours on, staring at his ceiling in the light of dawn, he recalled the satiny give of her wrist and replayed the wee carnal snatch in her breathing. Evidence that she hadn't been unaffected. That his touch still meant something to her.

If he thought about it too long, Tavish felt concussed—his head woozy and senses spinning.

And he had definitely thought about it overlong.

I don't want you.

Och, the other bit from last night that wouldn't leave him be.

Sitting up, he kicked his legs out of bed and slumped forward, his head between his hands.

Of course, he knew in his rational mind that Isla didn't want him. What sensible lady *would* want the poverty and struggle of a life spent with him?

And even if he had funds and a secure future, who was to say Isla wanted the man he had become? Seven years of war had changed him, just as the passage of years had given Isla ample time to regret her youthful indiscretions.

However, knowing a fact and truly accepting it were two rather disparate things.

Tavish knew she didn't want him. But hearing the words low and harsh from her lips had rattled something inside. Some dormant yearning he had assumed long dead.

She didn't want him. But he feared a neglected wee corner of his heart still wanted her.

Lifting his head, Tavish stared at the rain lashing the window panes. The maids had been in earlier to open the shutters, light the fire, and leave a pitcher of warm water. A cup of hot chocolate and plate of fresh scones rested on the bedside table.

Small luxuries, but ones Tavish had rarely experienced since . . . well, since Mariah's ruination, at the very least. Luxuries that Isla surely took for granted and ones Tavish would likely never be able to provide.

Such logic did nothing to soothe his longing for the lass he had left. His wife. The woman he had loved and now understood he would likely love until the day he died. A girl who perhaps had only existed in his adolescent perception and memory.

The Isla of the present didn't want the man he had become.

He needed to respect her wishes and let her go.

RAIN KEPT THE guests indoors.

After breakfast, the ladies retreated with Lady Milmouth and Lady Forsyth to do . . . whatever ladies do. Something about ribbons or embroidery. Tavish was unclear on the particulars.

Grayburn disappeared with Lord Milmouth and Sir John Forsyth.

Tavish played billiards with Ross and Fletch, the three of them talking of everything and nothing. The guilt of Tavish's secret marriage weighed heavily—smarting with each clack of the billiard balls—yet there was nothing to do but bite his tongue and carry on.

After Fletch won twice, they retired to the warm fire in the library, meticulously discussing their plans for Pennsylvania. Tavish and Ross intended to relocate to the United States and begin work there, keeping Fletch up-to-date with frequent letters.

As usual, Fletch became animated as they spoke, hands gesturing and words spilling easily. He was the most gregarious of their wee group, enthusiastic and excitable. A puppy of a person, Ross often described him.

Ross, by contrast, was quick with a dry remark or teasing quip. More of a cat than a puppy, he would say.

Tavish knew himself to be the cool-headed one. The soldier who, the more intense the fighting, the more calm and clear his thinking. Quiet and observing but swift to act when circumstances required it.

"Ye be a bird of prey, Balfour," Ross had once said. "Silently circling, cataloging every detail before diving into action, like a raptor falling from the sky to snatch up a mouse."

A far cry from the often brash boy Tavish had been. Years of war and battle had a way of refining a man to steel.

As ever, talking with his friends felt like slipping into a comfortable boot. How many fires had they shared? Divvied up rations, passed around a bottle, discussed their hopes and dreams?

After lunch, the young ladies joined the gentlemen in the library. Thankfully, Grayburn remained absent.

"You gentlemen were quite the topic of conversation earlier," Miss Forsyth announced.

"Oh, yes!" Miss Crowley clasped her hands before her bosom. "We should dearly love to hear of your time with the Rifles."

She glanced at Tavish with what could only be described as avid interest. He made a note to do nothing to raise the girl's expectations. She was lovely, but not for him.

Fletch laughed that easy laugh of his. "I cannot imagine even a fraction of what occurred would be appropriate for a lady's ears."

"Surely there is something you can tell us?" Miss Anne Forsyth said.

Lady Isla stood to one side, hands folded at her waist. Nothing indicated she would be adding her voice to the ladies' enthusiasm, though curiosity danced in her gaze.

Compared to the others, she appeared mature and poised and, to be blunt, expensive. The lace trimming of her rose muslin gown must have cost a small fortune.

As a lad, church had been the only place Tavish witnessed Isla in company. Then, she had always been in motion, expression animated and smile at the ready. Before this house party, he would have supposed her to be unchanged—the vibrant center of any gathering, a bright light drawing all to her flame.

However, like himself, she had become quieter over the years, more observant. Only her hair remained the same—already slipping from its curl, strands dangling straight beside her face.

But there was still an arresting quality to her. A sense of mystery in her composure. A spark in her eyes that promised a quick wit and unusual depth of thought, if only a gentleman could break through the shell of her exterior.

I don't want you.

Tavish glanced away before anyone realized he had been staring overlong.

"Do ye have maps, Fletch?" Ross asked. "We could show the ladies our movements and describe the sights we saw in Spain and Portugal."

"Brilliant!" Fletch grinned.

Fletch took charge. He sent a footman to collect tin soldiers from the nursery and flipped through his father's collection of rolled maps. A few minutes later, they had a map of the Iberian Peninsula spread out on the table in the middle of the library, tin soldiers sitting in a basket.

"Ross and I were stationed in the Peninsula in 1808, almost from the beginning of Wellington's action there." Fletch lifted two soldiers from the basket and placed them atop the town of Óbidos on the Portuguese coast north of Lisbon.

Fletch moved the toy soldiers through the various battles he and Ross had seen. Ross added wry commentary along the way.

"Ah, yes, Corunna, where my first pair of boots disintegrated to dust."

"It was about then that I decided I didn't mind the taste of weevil. A bit like mustard."

"I'm fairly certain we counted the leaves on trees to entertain ourselves over those weeks."

They spoke of the reputation of the Rifles, the deadly accuracy of their aim over great distances. How the *Crapaud*—the French soldiers (said with a hint of contempt)—would scatter when they learned that the Rifles would join the attack.

All the while, rain pattered against the windows, and a fire popped in the hearth, attempting to bat away the chill.

"It wasn't until after Bussaco in the autumn of 1810 that Balfour joined us." Fletch added a third soldier to their ranks, grinning at Tavish.

"Lieutenant James Westover made captain and transferred to another company." Tavish folded his arms across his chest. "I took his place."

"Ah, Westover! I miss him." Fletch gave a fond smile. "Capital fellow."

"Crack shot, as well," Ross added.

From there, the ladies asked enthusiastic questions, which Fletch and Ross readily answered. If anyone noticed that Tavish and Lady Isla remained generally silent, they didn't remark on it.

For his part, Tavish ruthlessly avoided even looking at her. But he felt her in the room. A weight on his spirit. Or perhaps just a rising bit of self-consciousness.

The whole affair was rather bizarre, he decided. A clash of two worlds that he had always viewed as utterly separate: his relationship with Lady Isla Kinsey and his time serving as a soldier. It felt odd that Fletch and Ross should know her—not as his wife, but as the beautiful, wealthy lady that Fletch would likely marry.

Did she feel anything as his friends spoke? Did she wonder about all that was not said? The hunger and deprivation they suffered during the retreat to Ciudad Rodrigo, waiting for supplies to arrive. An event Fletch summed up as being "a bit unpleasant." The terror of the Battle of Vitoria where their own dead had carpeted the battlefield. Horrifying bloodshed Ross described as "rather disheartening."

If Isla saw between the lines to what was not said, she didn't show it. Her expression remained polite, but Tavish thought he saw something occasionally flicker. A slight wince over their privations, perhaps. A faint lift of an eyebrow at Miss Crowley's incessant questions.

The topic of the war with Napoleon continued through dinner.

However, when the gentlemen joined the ladies in the drawing room, Lady Milmouth declared the women would provide musical entertainment instead of dunning the gentlemen for more war stories.

Grayburn, of course, nodded his approval. As usual, His Grace was dressed as if he were spending an evening with the Prince Regent at Carlton House instead of with friends in the Scottish Highlands. The duke's initial anger toward Tavish's presence had been replaced with a determined indifference to simply pretend that he didn't exist.

And so the company sat as Miss Forsyth played a pretty Bach minuet and then sang a pair of Italian arias with her sister to polite applause. Miss Crowley demurred to perform, insisting she was out of practice.

"Lady Isla, you must grace us next," Fletch encouraged.

"Please." Grayburn motioned toward the piano with a languid hand. "Your playing is always welcome."

Tavish resisted a frown. He hadn't known Isla played. If she had mentioned it, he couldn't recall. But, naturally, the daughter of the Duke of Grayburn would have been tutored in music. Such things were expected of young ladies.

"Hear, hear, Lady Isla. Your abilities at the keyboard must be celebrated," Fletch said before turning to Tavish and Ross. "Her ladyship is a fair angel when she plays. Her melodies transport me to heaven."

Something ugly twisted in Tavish's gut. Fletch knew this part of her. He had heard her play before—and more than once, by the sound of it.

While Tavish . . . hadn't even known.

Isla blushed. "You give me too much credit, Colonel Archer."

"Play for us, Lady Isla, and let the company judge for themselves."

With some reluctance, Isla sat at the pianoforte, sorting through music before settling on a concerto by Herr Beethoven.

What followed was fifteen minutes of astonishing musical virtuosity. Her fingers flew across the keyboard with ease, notes ringing soft and then loud, dynamics coaxing emotion from the instrument.

Tavish was, indeed, transported to heaven.

It was the oddest feeling—a deep sense of admiration and astonishment at her skill and mastery. But even more acute, a pang of loss. That this brilliant talent had been there all along—Isla had to have begun learning at a young age—and Tavish simply . . . hadn't known.

But . . . why would he? Isla had probably practiced every day right after being drilled on French verbs and before *plein aire* drawing lessons. The study as natural a part of her life as eating and sleeping. It likely hadn't occurred to her to mention it to a husband who had never seen her in that sphere. They had only ever met alone, isolated from the world and society.

How many other things had he not known about her?

Isla finished to enthusiastic applause, her smile radiant. The same smile he once assumed she bestowed on him alone.

Even in that he had been mistaken.

She did not look his way as she returned to her seat. Not even a flicker of a glance.

I don't want you, she had said.

And as Tavish excused himself for bed, he understood—perhaps better than he ever—precisely why. Because, despite being her husband, he wasn't sure he knew her in any real way.

THE NEXT MORNING dawned bright and cheery as if the elements wished to apologize for the dreary weather of the day before.

The morning post arrived, and Isla spent an hour propped against her headboard, reviewing the letters that had arrived from Malton Hill—one each from Mrs. Sumsion and Mrs. White, as well as a long missive from Mr. Cranston, Isla's steward.

Her heart sank as she read his words about one of her tenant farmers:

> *Mr. Tippets passed away unexpectedly on Friday last. It is a dreadful business, as you can well imagine. Poor Mrs. Tippets is beside herself with grief and worry. She knows she cannot pay their rent nor work the farmland alone, not with four small children underfoot. I cannot bear to evict them, knowing they will end up in the poor house or worse. I am sure you feel the same. What course of action would you like to take?*

Isla let the letter flutter to the counterpane.

Mr. Cranston asked an excellent question—what *did* she wish to do in this instance?

Situations like this were what made being mistress of Malton Hill so challenging, and yet, rewarding. Here, her actions dramatically affected people's lives.

In this instance, of course, Isla wouldn't cast Mrs. Tippets and her children out on their ears. But neither could she let them live rent-free on her property indefinitely. What would be an equitable yet compassionate solution?

Isla spent far too long pondering options, reaching no conclusions, before dressing for the day.

Consequently, she was the last to arrive in the breakfast room, the rest of the party already dining on toast soldiers and coddled eggs.

The gentlemen lurched to their feet with murmured greetings. Colonel Archer even took a half step toward her, as if he would see to her care, but Gray hastened to pull out a chair with a solemn, "Good morning, sister," before turning to prepare her a plate from the sideboard.

It was her brother's typical behavior toward her—polite and solicitous, particularly in company. Think what you would about Gray—and Isla had certainly thought plenty over the years—his manners were always impeccable. Only a Balfour sent him lashing out in fury.

Speaking of which . . .

Captain Balfour sat directly across from her. He appeared just as intimidating and stoic today, his coat brushed with military precision. Sunlight tangled in the strands of gold in his auburn hair, setting them to shimmer.

Their eyes briefly met before Isla looked away. But not before she saw the vexation there.

Captain Balfour was in a sour mood.

She disliked that his moods were still known to her. He had been discomfited yesterday as the ladies asked questions about the soldiers' experiences. Something about the set of his shoulders let her know that Captain Ross and Colonel Archer had omitted important details. Probably *all* the important details. Did she even wish to understand the horrors Captain Balfour had suffered over the years?

Of course, this morning, the ladies immediately returned to the topic of war.

"You cannot imagine, Colonel Archer, the tremblings we ladies experienced yesterday as you described the role of the Rifles in Wellington's army." Miss Crowley clasped her hands under her chin.

"Yes," Miss Anne Forsyth added, looking at her cousin. "I cannot fathom how your aim with the rifle can be so true, Edward. It boggles the mind, the distances you spoke of and the Rifles' accuracy across them. How is such a thing even possible?"

Gracious. The ladies should endeavor to be more circumspect in their ogling. Isla barely stopped an eye roll as she pushed her own eggs around her plate. Given her letter this morning, she felt the differences between herself and the other young ladies keenly. Miss Forsyth had clearly never debated the fate of a kindly widow and four fatherless children.

"You must have more faith in me, Anne. In all of us." Colonel Archer waved a hand to indicate his fellow officers. "It was a bit of a lark at times to see who could shoot the farthest with the greatest accuracy."

Isla frowned. "But surely war is not such a game, sir. You practiced accuracy in order to—" She halted. "Or, rather, I cannot imagine . . ."

She trailed off, unable to complete either thought in company. Helplessly, her gaze tangled with that of Captain Balfour across the table. She read the truth there, turbulent and churning.

Yes, the men had certainly seen horrors, just as Isla witnessed hardship and suffering at Malton Hill. Such was the nature of life.

The room fell into silence. Gray shifted at Isla's side, but said nothing.

Colonel Archer, amiable as ever, stepped into the conversational void.

"Sometimes, a bit of sport was just the thing we soldiers needed," he said before turning to Captain Ross. "Do you remember the time Balfour shot a playing card out of Lieutenant Wilson's hand at two hundred paces? It was the most incredible—"

Gray snorted.

It was a decidedly indelicate noise.

Every head swung his way.

"Two hundred paces? As in, two hundred yards?" Gray fixed Captain Balfour with a contemptuous lift of one eyebrow. "Impossible. A man can scarcely see that far, much less make an accurate shot."

Colonel Archer sat back in his seat, lips pressed together in amusement. The gentleman was almost ridiculously affable, Isla decided. What would it take to spark the smallest flash of irritation?

Though she had to admit she shared her brother's skepticism. She doubted her Tavish had rarely fired a rifle before enlisting, much less been a crack shot. It beggared belief that he could have developed such a true aim so quickly.

"I assure you I do not exaggerate, Your Grace," Colonel Archer said. "I saw the whole with my own eyes. It was an astonishing feat of marksmanship."

"Aye," Captain Ross chimed in, "and made all the more remarkable because Lieutenant Wilson *knew* that Captain Balfour wouldn't strike his hand."

Captain Balfour, notably, said nothing in his own defense. Merely spooned jam onto a roll and took a bite, as casual as you please.

Gray watched him chew, though when next the duke spoke, it was to Colonel Archer.

"I do not doubt what you *thought* you saw, Archer. Only Balfour's abilities." Gray's tone implied that perhaps some trickery had been afoot. That Captain Balfour's impressive display had been duplicitous.

If Gray thought to dampen Colonel Archer's enthusiasm, he was greatly mistaken. "Hah! Your Grace, with all due respect, you didn't serve and fight alongside Captain Balfour for nearly seven years like Ross and I. I've seen Balfour make a shot like that more times than I can count. He could have taken the shot at three hundred paces and still hit his mark."

"Aye," Captain Ross agreed. "Balfour is ridiculously modest, but he was generally considered one of the best shots in the Rifles."

"And that," Colonel Archer added, "is tantamount to saying he is one of the best shots in the whole of the British Empire."

Gray merely lifted his eyebrows.

Captain Balfour continued to eat his roll, as if the conversation were of no consequence.

Silence descended once more.

Isla reached for her tea, her throat suddenly gone dry. She still struggled to imagine her Tavish as a crack shot. Though, she thought wryly, his long-ago aim at her heart had been true.

Captain Balfour's gaze flicked to hers. It was the tiniest movement, but Isla saw the dark amusement there. He found Gray's protests entertaining. Which meant that his friends' words were true.

The reaction was also a smidgen of her Tavish. Though she had never seen him around others, she supposed he would be like this. Content to permit friends to talk up his strengths before proving them correct in some way. A jest of sorts.

Isla disliked seeing her Tavish in Captain Balfour. It abraded the scab atop the wound of his loss.

He is a stranger to you, she reminded herself. Just listening to him and his fellow officers talk about fighting in Spain and Portugal yesterday . . . the camaraderie of their relationship, the way they would complete one another's sentences, the shared jokes and knowing looks.

Captain Balfour had lived a lifetime of experiences without her.

It was the indomitable Miss Crowley who broke the quiet. "'Tis a pity you gentlemen do not have your rifles here, so we could put the claim to the test."

The beatific smile that lit Colonel Archer's face probably caused lilies to bloom somewhere in the Amazon.

"My dear Miss Crowley, my mother requested we bring our regimentals. Therefore, I am more than pleased to inform you that we former officers do, indeed, have rifles and uniforms in our possession. Do we not, gentlemen?" He looked to his friends.

Captain Balfour and Captain Ross both nodded.

Colonel Archer stood, giving Gray a brief bow. "Your Grace, may I formally invite you to test your shooting skills against those of His Majesty's Rifles. Perhaps that will help you understand why the Rifles were one of the most respected and feared regiments in Wellington's army."

Isla was watching Captain Balfour as Colonel Archer spoke. The wicked delight in his eyes said it all.

If Isla's suspicions were proven correct, Gray was about to be thoroughly schooled.

SEVEN YEARS EARLIER

AUGUST 25, 1810
PETTERCAIRN, SCOTLAND

Isla had never suspected that her eldest brother harbored such rage. It glowed, incandescent, from the red tips of his ears to the furious growl of his voice.

After discovering her with Tavish, Gray marched her across the fields, through the front door of Dunmore, and into his private study.

He motioned for Isla to sit in a chair beside the fire before kicking the door shut behind him with a crash that caused her to jump.

She had meant what she told Tavish. Gray would not physically harm her. Even now, he hadn't laid a finger on her.

But . . . she had never met this Gray. This towering thundercloud of wrath that set her limbs to shaking.

He stared down at her, chest heaving, nostrils flaring.

"You are just like her," he spat. "Her face. Her voice. Her eyes."

"Her?" Isla whispered.

"Yes, *her*! Our whore of a mother!"

Isla recoiled. Whatever she had expected him to say, it wasn't that.

"P-pardon?"

"Our mother. A whore." He enunciated each syllable with brutal precision. "And you, her bastard get."

The disgusted curl of his lip said it all.

Isla simply stared at him, unable to comprehend the horror of his words.

Whore? Bastard?

Surely, he didn't mean . . .

"G-Gray—" Isla hiccupped.

"Silence!" He swiped an arm through the air.

On a grunt, he clawed at his neckcloth, tearing it from his neck and tossing it atop the mess of papers and books on his desk. His coat and waistcoat soon followed.

He stood over her in shirtsleeves, chest heaving.

"Father told me much on his deathbed. Before then, I merely thought our mother a bit of a flibbertigibbet. A flighty woman who shirked her duties as wife and mother. However, the truth is much darker. Our mother was disgusted by my birth and the deformity of my foot that soon became apparent." Gray paced before his desk, limping badly. "Then, Matthias was born. Mother—No! I refuse to even refer to her as my mother!—*that woman* refused my father his matrimonial due entirely. 'Never again will I come to your bed,' she told him. 'I have borne you two sons with deformities of limb. I refuse to bear a third.' My father was devastated, as he had thought their marriage to be a love match. The more fool him."

Isla panted in terror, palms pressed to the arms of her chair. Every word out of Gray's mouth altered a piece of her childhood and her place within their family.

"Eventually, *that woman* sought the comfort of other men, reveling in the arms of anyone but those of her rightful husband. *You*—" Gray lifted a scathing hand in her direction. "—are the unwanted result."

Unwanted.

Bastard.

Tears blurred the room.

Isla's understanding of her existence shifted, coming into sharp focus as if through a spyglass. Each harsh epithet her father—not her father!—uttered. Each well of silence. Each vicious scolding and act of petty tyranny.

How the old duke must have detested her and the betrayal she represented.

"At the time of your birth, our mother begged my father to have mercy on you. To not cast you off to an indifferent fate. Because you were female and could never inherit, Father, in the benevolence of his heart, agreed. He hid the scandal of your illegitimacy as our mother wished.

"But unbeknownst to you, your entire life has been hanging by a thread. At any time, Father was prepared to denounce you as his child and cast you off. All he needed was a reason. You do not know the *half* of what he endured for you—everything that occurred with our mother—and out of compassion, he stayed his hand."

Isla struggled to breathe.

She felt as if some giant had scooped up all the facts of her life—mother, father, brother, her sense of belonging—tossed the lot into an enormous jute bag, and then dashed it upon a cliff face. Every last element—each last shred of self—shattering upon impact.

And still, Gray was not done. "Knowing what he had suffered, my father bestowed on me the same power to denounce you. He left a declaration in my keeping—written in his own hand and witnessed by his solicitor—that you are not his daughter. A way for me to divest myself of any obligation toward you, should the task of keeping you prove too high. Little do you know the humiliations I have already suffered for your sake."

"W-what humiliations?" Isla managed to hiccup. Their mother was dead. What did Gray refer to? What explanation could make sense of this?

He laughed, a single bark of sound. "Hah! As if I would disclose such secrets to you. You, who are no better than the circumstances of your birth, indulging in the lusts of your body with a *Balfour*, no less. I would rather you had died than take up with the likes of them. Do you not feel a speck of loyalty to our family?"

Isla's stomach clenched, and she staggered to the piss pot in the corner, heaving into it.

Gray's manner toward her had cooled over the past two years; now she knew why.

"You should be casting up your accounts," Gray raged behind her. "No Balfour would ever love you. They are duplicitous to the core, the lot of them! That boy is using you as a weapon to cut at the heart of Kinsey blood. Little does he know you haven't a drop of it flowing in your veins. Maybe I should denounce you and wash my hands of this business. Let Balfour have you."

Hands shaking, Isla pulled a handkerchief from her pocket, wiping her mouth.

She dared a glance at Gray then.

His anger . . . Isla was prepared for.

But his revulsion . . . this loathing. As if she were of no more significance than a pair of wet, reeking socks he couldn't thrust far or fast enough from his person.

She had no defense.

In every scenario she had imagined, Gray still loved her. Yes, he might have become more aloof in recent years, but Isla assumed he hadn't altered so fundamentally as to become a different person. He was the brother who dried her tears. The one she had pledged to love and support, and he in return. Never once had she considered that her loving brother might be gone forever.

But this . . .

This man was the Duke of Grayburn, furious and embittered. Resentful of all she represented—their mother's adultery and the old duke's cuckolding. And now her own betrayal with a Balfour.

The trembling started with her fingers before quickly spreading up her arms to her torso, until all of her was wracked by the same horror-stricken emotion.

"Fortunately for you, I am the same forbearing man my father was. I will grant you a reprieve this time, but you will never speak with Balfour again," Gray said, his voice terrifyingly quiet. "Let this be one thing in your teetering life that you do not doubt, Isla. Should you so much as nod at a gentleman without my approval, I will see you cast from this family. You will associate with whom I tell you to associate. You will marry whom I tell you to marry. Am I clear?"

Isla simply stared at him, too shocked to speak.

"AM I CLEAR?!" he roared.

She nodded, tears dripping down her neck.

"Get out." He jerked his chin toward the door.

Isla raced to her bedchamber, the crackle of Gray's temper nipping at her heels.

Her life had just been shredded to tatters.

But one powerful truth still remained—

Tavish and I are married, and there is nothing Gray can do about it.

Hallelujah.

Isla grasped onto that thought with both hands, holding it as the lifeline it was.

She didn't have to stay here and endure the edge of Gray's bitterness. His vitriol for their mother's heartless betrayal of the old duke. The humiliations that Isla's very existence caused.

Tavish would save her. He would enfold her in his arms and promise all would be well, vowing she never had to see Gray again. Together, they would steal away, leaving her brother and all his terrible words far behind.

Isla merely had to reach her husband.

16

Two hours later, the guests convened on a long stretch of grass behind the house.

Isla found herself walking beside the other young ladies, all of whom bounced with excitement over the impending shooting competition.

Miss Crowley was in particular alt. "Look! My hands tremble from exhilaration, and the gentlemen have yet to begin."

Isla stood to one side as the former soldiers sat on stools, assessing and preparing their weapons and shot. In addition to the three officers, both Gray and Lord Milmouth intended to try their hands at shooting targets. Sir John Forsyth had begged off participating, claiming a dodgy shoulder, but still appeared eager to watch the contest.

Lord Milmouth was directing servants to set up the shooting range.

Gray watched everything with equanimity, hands clasped behind his back as he spoke with Sir John. A footman stood behind the gentlemen, a rifle for the duke leaning against his shoulder. Heaven forfend that Isla's brother dirty his person with the mechanics of preparing a weapon. That was a job for servants.

She longed to roll her eyes.

The three officers had changed into their uniforms. Isla had never seen the uniform of the 95th Rifles. She was unsure what she had expected, but the somber green of their attire was not it. The entire uniform was green—from trousers to coat to trim to the top of their tall, conical hats.

Didn't British soldiers typically wear red-and-white uniforms? They were called "redcoats" for a reason, after all.

Miss Forsyth had the same question, which Captain Ross happily answered.

"Aye, ye do have the right of it, Miss Forsyth. Generally, army soldiers do wear red." He sighted down his rifle. "But we Rifles creep in advance of the main body of troops and disable enemy officers before engaging in the field. The green of our uniforms helps us blend into the forest and shrubs, aiding our stealth."

Oh.

That sounded . . .

Isla swallowed.

Disable? Surely, he meant *eliminate.* And *aiding our stealth* seemed a more pleasant way of saying, *ensuring we were difficult to see and kill.*

Her eyes strayed to Captain Balfour. The uniform was close-cut, accentuating the ridiculous breadth of his shoulders and the strength of his arms. He lifted his rifle to his eye, sighting down the barrel with practiced ease. As if he had done so a thousand times or more. Which . . . he probably had.

She hated this—witnessing the actions that had changed her Tavish into Captain Balfour. She hated knowing the suffering and terror and slaughter—the repetitive actions, again and again—that formed him into this aloof, stern soldier.

Most importantly, she hated that he had *chosen* this. He chose to leave her and enlist in the army. He chose to join the Rifles. He chose to become this . . . this calculating warrior.

Isla looked away to the surrounding trees before Gray caught her staring.

Like its grand counterparts south of the border, the landscape of Kingswell House was an elegant combination of natural beauty and deliberately curated wilderness. The lawn stretched into the distance, a long rectangular strip. To the left, a row of pine trees rimmed the grass. To the right, the lawn ran into a lake of deliberate design. The water's even bank and charming center island—complete with a miniature gothic-arched folly—proclaimed the whole to be man-made. The architect, likely some protégé of Inigo Jones, had even constructed a lovely wooden bridge to connect the bank with the island. The bridge arched high over the water, its picturesque wooden railing covered in clinging moss.

But despite borrowing elements from estates farther south, no one would mistake this for English scenery. The mountains quickly rose to the west, looming over the small glen. Instead of oaks or beech, Scots pines with prickly needles and wide-spreading branches towered overhead. If England's hills and valleys murmured a polite "How do you do?", Scotland's glens and granite cliffs brandished a dirk and barked, "*Och*, what ye be doin' on ma land?!"

The countryside here would never be a genteel, well-mannered thing.

The officers stood up, rifles in hand, their preparations complete. Lord Milmouth finished directing a pair of grooms to set up a wooden target a good one hundred and fifty yards down the lawn. A square piece of paper with an inked circle drawn in the middle fluttered on the target. Nearby, spare sheets of foolscap rested on a small table, a rock on top to prevent them from blowing away.

Miss Crowley and Miss Anne Forsyth clapped in eagerness.

"I am utterly breathless with anticipation," Miss Crowley said, hands clasped to her ample bosom. Isla was beginning to think the motion deliberate. What better way to direct a gentleman's attention to said bosom?

Captain Balfour sent the girl a fleeting smile that set her to blushing. Isla gritted her teeth.

Ridiculous.

Lord Milmouth waved from down the field that all was ready and began walking toward them, feet striding wide as he paced the lawn. He stopped before reaching the gentlemen.

"Fifty paces," his lordship called and directed a groom to place a marker.

His lordship repeated the process, coming closer to them. "One hundred paces."

A groom placed a marker.

Lord Milmouth paced out three more markers—one hundred and fifty, two hundred, and two hundred and fifty paces.

"Do we need more than this?" his lordship asked as he rejoined their group.

Colonel Archer shrugged. "Let us see how we get on. I know Balfour is frighteningly accurate, even at three hundred paces."

Three hundred yards? Isla thought. Though she didn't wish to doubt Captain Balfour's abilities, most of her sided with Gray. How was such a feat even possible?

"Grayburn." Colonel Archer nodded to Isla's brother. "We shall give you the first go."

"Thank you." For his part, Gray shrugged out of his greatcoat and tight-fitting tailcoat, handing them to the waiting footman who, in turn, then handed him the prepared rifle.

"Ladies, you would be advised to back up and give the gentlemen space. We should hate for any accidents to occur. The bridge shall give you a decent vantage point and is about halfway along our shooting gallery." Lord Milmouth pointed to the arched bridge over the lake and the steps leading to it. "Also, I brought this to assist you in verifying our aim." He handed a spyglass to Isla. The metal barrel felt cold in her hand.

With gasps of excitement, Miss Crowley and Miss Anne Forsyth all but ran to the bridge. Isla and Miss Forsyth followed in a more decorous fashion.

By the time Isla gained the bridge, the men had walked up to the closest mark—fifty paces. Squinting, Isla noted that the sheet of paper tacked to the target had the number fifty written across the top in black letters.

Ah.

So they were to use a different target sheet for each range, likely comparing the accuracy between distances.

Gray lifted the gun to his shoulder and took time to line up the shot before pressing the trigger. The gun bucked in his hands, a sharp *crack* ringing out.

Isla lifted the spyglass to her eye, bringing the target into close focus. A hole punctured the foolscap just outside the black center. A groom darted forward and wrote on the target with a pencil—a letter G, it appeared—indicating where Gray's shot had landed.

Isla handed the spyglass to Miss Forsyth, indicating the ladies should cycle through turns just as the gentlemen did.

Lord Milmouth was next. His shot landed on the edge of the black circle.

Captain Ross shot, his bullet piercing the target dead center.

Everyone clapped, and even Gray lifted an impressed eyebrow.

The grooms marked the location and then placed a tuft of cotton in the hole, stopping it up.

"Oh! The cotton will show the men if the next shooter hits the center, as well," Miss Anne Forsyth said.

As if hearing her words as a challenge, Colonel Archer took aim and fired. His shot knocked the cotton plug out of the hole, enlarging it and shaking the foolscap. Once again, grooms marked the shooter and stuffed the center of the target with another bit of cotton.

Then Captain Balfour stepped up.

"Do you think he truly is as excellent a shot as Colonel Archer supposes?" Miss Crowley asked, leaning forward, gaze expectant and eager. She handed the spyglass back to Isla.

"We shall see," Miss Forsyth said.

Unlike the other gentlemen who had taken several seconds to line up and calculate their shots, Captain Balfour lifted the rifle to his shoulder, sighted, and fired in one fluid motion, as if the rifle were nothing more than an extension of his arm.

Crack!

It seemed impossible that such insouciance could result in accuracy, and yet . . .

The bit of cotton covering the hole in the center of the target evaporated, the paper not so much as fluttering.

"Oh, gracious!" Miss Crowley exclaimed.

Isla peered through the spyglass. Captain Balfour's bullet had indeed only struck the cotton plug, passing cleanly through the hole left by his comrades' bullets.

Such precision was . . . impressive.

Isla lowered the spyglass, passing it to the other ladies. Her heart hammered like thundering hooves in her chest while her mind scrambled to reconcile the boy she had loved with this . . . this . . . competent, focused soldier.

The men reloaded and backed up to the marker for one hundred paces.

The scene repeated itself. Gray's shot went a little wider, as did Lord Milmouth's. The three officers shot dead center again.

At one hundred and fifty yards, the differences between the military officers and the others became more pronounced. Gray's shot barely hit the target and pasted a scowl on his face. Lord Milmouth missed altogether.

Captain Ross and Colonel Archer landed shots within the blackened-out center of the foolscap.

Captain Balfour was the only one to hit the target dead center. Again.

The men walked toward the two-hundred-yard marker, passing the bridge where the ladies stood.

Predictably, Miss Crowley raced down the stairs to speak with them. Isla and the others followed at a more sedate pace.

As they approached, the gentlemen were ribbing Captain Balfour good-naturedly over his bad manners in always besting them.

Gray stomped alongside them, forehead frowning. Isla found the irritation of his pricked ducal pride rather comical. Her brother was so used to being the lord of anything and everything he touched. To be bested so thoroughly by someone else—a Balfour, no less! the horror!—must be trying his patience.

Isla suppressed a smile.

"Give someone else a chance for once, Balfour!" Captain Ross was saying.

"I can't help it if your shots are inconsistent, Ross," Captain Balfour retorted. "Perhaps ye should practice more and laze about less."

He glanced to the side as Isla approached.

"Your shooting has been remarkable," Miss Crowley gushed.

"Why, thank you." Colonel Archer gave a theatrical bow, setting everyone to laughing. His head lifted, and he fixed Isla with a warm smile. "What think you, Lady Isla? Have we wooed you with our shooting prowess?"

He was openly flirting with her, but then, his romantic intentions were hardly a secret. However, it would have been easier to bear without the hot press of Captain Balfour's gaze.

"Indeed, you have." Isla blushed, ordering her eyes not to flicker in Captain Balfour's direction. "To be honest, Colonel, I was unaware my own brother was such an excellent shot. Grayburn has been hiding his talents."

Isla wasn't sure if she said the words as a compliment or to further needle her brother. Regardless, Gray gave her a ducal nod of thanks.

"Yes, I wager it is the purview of brothers to learn skills without their sisters' knowledge." Colonel Archer grasped Lord Milmouth's shoulder. "My father taught me to shoot well away from our womanfolk's hearing."

"Aye," Captain Ross added. "'Tis how Balfour and I learned to shoot, too."

"Truly?" Miss Crowley turned to Captain Balfour, her expression eager.

Honestly.

Isla barely suppressed a sigh.

Captain Balfour nodded. "My elder brother, Lord Cairnfell, is a wee bit of a crack shot himself. He and I would attempt to outshoot one another as lads. It's why I was asked to join the 95th regiment so quickly. I already had years of experience shooting at targets."

The sparse flash of information landed with a whip-like *thwack* across Isla's psyche.

Callum? Her Tavish had learned to shoot because of Callum? And more to the point, Tavish had been a crack shot back then . . . even as she married him. Why hadn't he ever mentioned it?

It seemed like a fairly critical bit of information for a wife to know about her own husband. Not something she learned seven years on: *Oh, by the way, darling, I am actually one of the most celebrated sharpshooters in*

His Majesty's army. My marksmanship is talked about in hushed tones and circulated through admirers as if I am a demigod.

A terrible sort of tremor swept through her.

Here she was, upset that her Tavish had died in every real sense; but instead, she was quickly realizing that she had perhaps never known him. That even the boy she had loved had been a figment of her imagination. Or, at the very least, an incomplete picture.

The longer she was here—observing him around people and friends, in settings they had never experienced together—the more she realized how narrow her vision of him had been. How much of himself he had kept from her.

Was he thinking the same—that he had only known the smallest part of her?

Of a surety, her years at Malton Hill had changed her, just as the military had changed Captain Balfour. They had both lived nearly a full tenth of a lifetime without the other.

No wonder he felt like a stranger.

"Come along then." Colonel Archer rallied the gentlemen. "Let us bring this to a close and permit Balfour to impress us all."

Captain Balfour chuckled and walked on.

Gray scowled.

Colonel Archer noticed.

"Cheer up, Grayburn." He clapped Gray on the back as they strolled up the field, words carrying back to Isla. "You are not the first man to assume Balfour's self-deprecating manner means he doesn't know his way around a rifle. Your families may not be particularly friendly, but even you must admit Balfour is a damn fine shot."

Isla couldn't hear her brother's reply, but she supposed it was some variation of the clichéd, "Over my dead body."

The ladies turned back to the bridge, hurrying up the stairs.

Shooting from the two-hundred-yard point went as Colonel Archer predicted.

Both Gray and Lord Milmouth missed the target entirely.

Colonel Archer landed his bullet inside the black, to much jubilation from the ladies.

Captain Ross hit the edge of the black.

Captain Balfour did his signature lift-aim-fire and . . .

. . . hit the target dead center.

They moved to the final marker, two hundred and fifty yards.

The last scenario played out similarly—Gray and Lord Milmouth missed the target. Colonel Archer and Captain Ross both landed shots outside the black circle.

Only Captain Balfour remained steady. Lift, aim, fire—and a hole bloomed dead center.

Both Colonel Archer and Captain Ross whooped with joy.

Even the younger ladies bounced and cheered as the wooden bridge trembled.

The men walked back toward the targets, Gray limping slightly—the only sign of his feelings over being summarily beaten by a Balfour.

Unsurprisingly, the younger ladies swarmed after the gentlemen. The grooms rushed forward with the shot paper targets, and the gentlemen and ladies gathered round to examine them.

Isla followed more slowly, trying to gather her feelings into some coherent whole. On the one hand, admiration and astonishment stuffed her thoughts to stupefaction. On the other hand, she felt vastly . . . betrayed. Or was it lost? Because even seven years ago, she hadn't known the full breadth of Tavish Balfour.

It didn't help that she could hear Miss Crowley mooning over Captain Balfour's shots even from a distance. They could probably hear her in the next county.

"I'm telling you, it is not a fluke," Colonel Archer was saying as Isla stopped behind the group. "Balfour always shoots like this. Years! I have endured years of being bested in this manner. An honest gentleman knows when to raise the white flag of surrender and simply admit his admiration."

Gray folded his arms, lips pressed tightly. He was trying to remain aloof and unaffected—a good sport and all that. But the clench of his fist betrayed him.

For his part, Captain Balfour pointedly ignored Gray. Too pointedly.

Colonel Archer, bless his pure soul, did not catch on to the undercurrents.

"Balfour, are you up for one more challenge?" he asked.

"Of course." Captain Balfour rested the barrel of his rifle on his shoulder.

With a wink for the ladies, Colonel Archer pulled a playing card from his jacket pocket.

Miss Crowley gasped. "You're not going to hold it as a target, are you, Colonel?"

"Nae," Captain Balfour spoke up. "He won't."

"I won't?" Colonel Archer lifted an eyebrow.

"Nae. If I must shoot playing cards, place them on the posts." He waved to the targets. "No need to tempt Fate today."

"Afraid you'll miss, Balfour? Harm your friend?" Gray said, his tone biting.

Captain Balfour shrugged. "Not particularly. But given the distance I intend to shoot from, the slightest change in the wind could mean the difference between life and death." He leveled a cool gaze on Gray. "And a competent soldier doesn't permit ego to obscure the value of another soul. Accidents happen. And I don't want one of my good friends to be the victim."

Silence for a moment.

"Well spoken, Balfour," Lord Milmouth said. "I know your cool thinking saved Edward's life many times over. You will forever have our admiration and thanks."

Captain Balfour tilted his head toward his lordship before looking at Colonel Archer.

"Place three cards on the post at random and stand back from the target." Captain Balfour's eyes flicked to Isla before sliding to the rest of the women. "You ladies should likely go resume your perch. No accidents, remember?"

And with that, he turned his back and began walking toward the shooting lines. Miss Crowley shivered and then skipped several steps to catch up with him, walking at his side, chattering loudly.

Isla followed the rest of the ladies down the lawn and up the steps of the bridge, Miss Crowley reluctantly leaving Captain Balfour's side.

Isla turned to watch Captain Balfour continue walking away from the target. He paused at the two hundred and fifty marker, assessed the wind with a finger in the air, and then continued to walk away from the target with deliberate steps.

Even standing on tiptoe, Isla struggled to see him. She walked backward up the steep bridge, trying to keep Captain Balfour in view. The ladies followed her. The sloping arch of the bridge, along with the accumulation of moss, made the wood planks somewhat slippery. But a firm hand on the railing grounded Isla.

Captain Balfour paced another fifty yards.

Isla knew because she counted them.

Three hundred yards from the target.

Isla was a little more than half that distance, and the three playing cards tacked to the target's surface appeared as small white dots. How could Captain Balfour even *see* the playing cards from three hundred yards, much less hit one of them?

The men stood back from the target, but still close enough to have a clear view of where the bullets might land.

Unlike with his previous shots, Captain Balfour took a moment to center himself. He looked to the targets, lifted his rifle, and fired.

He was so far distant that Isla saw the bright yellow flash of the bullet exiting the rifle before the *crack* of the retort reached her ears.

The card to the left exploded.

Isla had scarcely drawn a breath. She whirled back to Captain Balfour to find him reloading his rifle with shocking speed.

The ladies erupted into euphoric applause, clapping and voices carrying.

Captain Balfour knelt, one knee in the grass.

Lift. Aim. Fire.

The playing card to the right disintegrated.

Miss Crowley squealed in delight, jumping up and down, grabbing Isla's elbow from behind. Isla tightened her grip on the handrail.

The level of Captain Balfour's skill simply boggled her mind.

Not a fluke.

Not an instance of luck.

No. Tavish Balfour displayed an almost mythical ability.

Why had he never told her?!

Methodically, Captain Balfour reloaded.

He moved from kneeling to sitting on the ground, propping the barrel of the rifle on his toes with the butt of the rifle against his shoulder.

He aimed.

Crack!

The third card disappeared.

Colonel Archer whooped, tossing his hat in the air. The three other ladies cheered, raising their arms and calling their zeal.

Captain Balfour leapt to standing, waved to them, and began walking back toward the targets. The gentlemen were gathered together, bending to pick pieces of the playing cards out of the grass.

"He is truly the most remarkable—" Miss Crowley pushed past Isla in a rush to greet Captain Balfour.

But in the girl's haste, her feet slipped on the mossy planks, pitching her sideways. Her shoulder caught Isla in the chest.

Isla stumbled back, careening into the wooden railing with force.

The handrail pressed against the small of her back for the space of a heartbeat.

Then, with a loud snap, the wood gave way.

Isla teetered on the edge for one terrified second, arms wind-milling, frantic for purchase.

But then gravity asserted itself, pulling her down to the water below.

Isla barely managed to scream before splashing into the cold depths of the lake.

17

Tavish was sprinting toward the lake before Isla hit the water.

He had watched the whole happen with nauseating horror. Miss Crowley blundering into Isla. Isla staggering backward into the railing that, with a sickening crack, gave way.

The white flutter of Isla falling would likely haunt his nightmares— her arms reaching skyward, the muslin of her dress rippling in the air.

No!

That had been his only thought.

No!

His rifle had landed somewhere on the lawn, tossed aside in his desperation to reach her, hat ripping from his head with the force of his strides.

The moment felt like being in the midst of a battle. When time slowed and his senses became heightened and he could see with acute clarity how he needed to act and behave.

Someone was screaming. Perhaps several someones. Shapes flickered in his periphery.

Nothing else mattered beyond saving Isla.

His wife.

His love.

Reaching the lake's edge, he plunged through the surface in a shallow dive, the frigid water washing over him. He scarcely noticed it. Arms stroking, he powered across the lake toward the bridge, desperate to reach her.

Thank God Isla had surfaced. She gasped for breath, neck arched upward and face barely exposed, arms moving as she tried to tread water.

And then he was there, grabbing onto her elbow, pulling her into him.

"I have ye," he panted. "Isla, ye be safe."

She clawed onto his arm, blue eyes flaring wide.

"Stuck," she wheezed, head threatening to sink beneath the water once more. "My skirts . . . caught . . ."

He didn't wait for her to finish. Filling his lungs, he sank below the surface, eyes open and searching for the problem.

The cotton muslin of her gown fanned out in the murky water, making it difficult to immediately discern the problem.

He caught a blurred glimpse of her white legs moving in efficient circles to keep her head afloat. Dimly, his brain noted that she was treading water proficiently, particularly given her tangled state . . . and with more skill than he remembered her possessing.

She was stuck. How? And where?

He scanned, looking for the snag.

There!

A section of her skirts was tangled in the branches of a fallen log. Diving down, dodging her legs, he grabbed a handful of the fabric and pulled.

Once. Twice.

His lungs screamed for air by the time he ripped the muslin free.

He kicked upward, surfacing with a great gasp.

And then she was there, arms extending, cold fingers grasping his neck and shoulders.

"Tavish." The intimate whimper of her voice enveloping him.

Isla's voice. That of the girl he loved.

"I have ye, lass," he panted, a hand wrapping around her waist. "Ye be safe with me."

Her eyes met his, open and tender. A window to the soft heart of her.

The years melted away, vanishing like hoarfrost in the warmth of summer sun.

They were just Isla and Tavish. Best friends, reaching for one another as they always had. The press of her hands—one clinging to his shoulder, the other on his chest—and the soft give of her body under his palms.

A second passed.

Maybe two.

The briefest flash of fantasy where the past seven years had never happened. A wee liminal space where they still loved each other. Where their hearts still beat in harmony, and she still wanted a life with him.

And then reality came crashing back down.

The Isla before him was not the lass he had known—her body more rounded, her cheekbones and jaw more refined.

Her gaze shuttered, and she pushed away, treading water. "I can swim without assistance, Captain."

Shouting intruded from overhead.

Tavish glanced up to see Miss Forsyth and Miss Crowley sobbing on the bridge, staring down in horror.

Och.

He was an acquaintance effecting a rescue, not a husband desperate to save his wife.

"Let's get ye to shore," he said, breathing hard.

Isla nodded.

Tavish turned, giving her his back. "If ye wish, ye can hold my shoulders, and I'll tow ye to the bank."

The firm weight of her hand grasped the side of his neck.

Slowly, Tavish kicked for the shoreline.

"Ye be a better swimmer than I recall," he couldn't help but say.

She said nothing for a long moment.

And then, "The swimming hole is precisely where you left it. I might have practiced over the years."

He barely stopped a grin.

That's my lass, was his first thought. Chased quickly by a second—*She is not for yourself.*

A glance at the edge of the lake confirmed this.

The other gentlemen were just now arriving, calling and reaching for Isla. Grayburn shook out his greatcoat.

Tavish's feet brushed against the silty bottom of the lake. Pushing upright, he dragged Isla forward.

Suddenly, Grayburn was in front of them, wrapping Isla in his great-coat to preserve her modesty and lifting her out of the water. But not before Tavish got a glimpse of her lush body from behind, the dripping muslin of her gown quite translucent.

Oof.

Yet one more thing to haunt his dreams.

"Thank you, Balfour," Fletch said, as Tavish stood in the water to his waist, catching his breath. "Your bravery and abilities know no bounds."

Grayburn, predictably, snorted as he set his sister on her feet on the grass.

Fletch frowned. "Come now, Grayburn. Even you must admit that we just witnessed a tremendous act of heroism. How many times must we tell you: Balfour is *always* like this. The finest shot. The first into the breach of danger. The clearest head amid a crisis."

"'Twas miraculous to witness," Lord Milmouth added. "Such quick thinking. You saved the lady's life, Captain Balfour."

"Indeed, you did." Fletch turned to Tavish. "Lady Isla appeared stuck, and you freed her. Thank goodness her ladyship knows how to swim." He shot Grayburn a bright smile. Because who else would have taught the lady to swim?

And still, Grayburn said nothing. Though he did give Tavish a look of such bitter vitriol, it could strip paint. The duke ushered Isla away from the bank, limping as he walked away.

Frown deepening, Fletch turned to follow them, asking after Lady Isla.

It was left to Ross to extend a hand and pull Tavish from the lake.

"Like Fletch said, always the hero," his friend said with a wry smile.

Tavish stepped onto the grassy bank. Water sluiced off his body, weighing down the wool of his regimentals and squishing between his toes in his boots.

The panic of the moment over, he started to shiver.

Damnation.

Ross grabbed his shoulder. "Are ye well?"

Tavish nodded, bending and bracing his hands on his knees to stem the trembling. Combat had always been like this—a few minutes of tense, calculated action followed by a shaking nervous attack once the danger had passed.

Taking a few more deep breaths, Tavish managed to stand upright.

"It still catches me off-guard, even after all this time," Ross continued.

"Pardon?"

"Your ability to react instantly to a crisis. It's almost preternatural. Ye were nearly in the lake by the time the rest of us gentlemen even realized something was amiss. Nothing escapes ye."

Not where my wife is concerned, at least, Tavish thought, the words sour.

He glanced to where Isla stood, shivering in Grayburn's coat.

Ross followed his looking. "Lady Isla appears to be in decent spirits. Wet and cold, but no harm done."

Tavish grunted.

He took a few steps, grimacing as the water squelched in his boots.

Blast.

It was going to take some work to save his footwear. Fortunately, they were sturdy leather. Only an idiot wore boots that couldn't get wet, given the Scottish weather. But this was a bit extreme.

Granted, focusing on his boots was merely a distraction from everything else. The terror that Isla had been hurt. The sense of their years apart slipping away. The press of her body against his once more.

His hands thrummed with the lingering feel of her. The soft give of her skin, the generous curve of her waist. That was new. The Isla of his memories had been slight, more girl than woman.

But this Isla . . .

Tavish closed his eyes, bracing his hands on his knees once more.

Yearning swelled his chest like a sponge soaking up rainwater until it was nigh to bursting.

Dammit all to hell.

He loved her.

He still loved her.

Of all the moments to experience an earth-shattering truth . . . with Grayburn not even ten paces away and Fletch clucking like a mother hen over Isla.

Tavish feared he was going to be sick.

Bloody hell.

He had likely never stopped loving her.

He might have buried the emotion deep within, but she had always held the key to unlock him.

Tavish had loved the girl Isla had been. The wild unconventionality of her. The fierceness with which she met challenges.

Aye, she was no longer that girl.

But now, Tavish was rapidly coming to adore the strong, resilient woman she had become. The sort of woman to stare down the barrel of a rifle and keep her chin high. This new version of Isla might be a stranger in many ways, but Tavish already knew the heart of her. That had never and would never change.

How he loved her!

It was a part of his essence, of the very fragments that made him.

Tavish existed. Therefore, he loved Isla Kinsey.

A truth as sure as any philosopher's aphorism.

Years. He had spent years slogging through the mud of Portugal and shedding blood in Spain. And he realized now that he had done it all in some small measure to protect her. That as long as he fought and rallied his men and became the deadliest of soldiers, she would be safe at home in Dunmore.

He had lived his life knowing that she existed. That elsewhere on this planet, she breathed and laughed and loved in some joy-filled heaven.

And that had been enough to soothe the beast of his regret.

Until now.

Ross placed a hand on his back.

"Are ye well, Balfour?" he asked, voice low.

Tavish wanted to say *nae.*

He managed a nod instead.

I don't want you.

The echo of her words reverberated through him.

Aye, he might yet be sick.

He *had* to let her go.

"Ho, Balfour!" Fletch called.

Tavish sucked in a stuttering breath and lifted his head as his friend approached.

"Are you unwell?" Fletch looked him over. It was the practiced eye of a commanding officer searching a soldier for a battle wound.

It hurt to meet his friend's concerned gaze. To know the pain that he would cause this good man. How terrible to lose Isla and Fletch in one awful stroke of Fate. At least they would have one another.

The thought wasn't as comforting as Tavish wished.

"I'm . . ." *Lovesick? Unnerved? Fair out of my mind with regret?* Tavish went with, ". . . well."

Fletch's gaze turned skeptical.

"Truly, I am," Tavish continued.

"Ye look like hell," Ross said.

"Go to the devil," Tavish shot back, but his heart wasn't in it.

"That's a bit better." Ross looked at Fletch. "But it lacks his usual bite."

"Mmm." Fletch stared at him.

Damn these two and their perceptive eyes. They would ferret out this secret.

"How is the lady?" Tavish asked.

"About as well as you," Fletch said. "Cold and wet but glad to be alive."

Tavish nodded.

"Grayburn behaved abominably." Fletch glanced back at the duke. "Not even a word of kindness for your actions. Your families are not friendly, and still you ran to save the lady. That alone should be acknowledged."

And what was Tavish to say to that? "Any of ye would have done the same. I just happened to be the first to notice the lady fall."

"For the love—" Fletch bit off his words. "Just once, I would like to see you claim something for yourself, Balfour. A mere smile of glory or a smug expression of ego. Something."

Tavish managed a sharp laugh.

"I think he's gone a wee bitty *fou*. Addled in the head." Ross slapped his back. "How much pond water did ye drink?"

Tavish shoved him off.

"Well, you may not accept it," Fletch said, "but I cannot express the depth of my gratitude, Balfour. You saved my lady and—"

Tavish cut him off with a slice of the hand. "No thanks are necessary, Fletch."

His friend merely stared, expression bewildered. "Someday, I will find a way to repay the debts between us."

"Fletch, someday I am sure to do something that will have me groveling for your forgiveness. When that happens, I thank ye for remembering this moment."

"As you say." Fletch rolled his eyes, assuming Tavish was in jest. "Come on, then. Let's get you dry before pneumonia sets in."

18

SEVEN YEARS EARLIER

AUGUST 26, 1810
PETTERCAIRN, SCOTLAND

Tavish waited until after dinner to corner Lord Northcairn in his study.

Tavish's pulse had been drumming at the base of his tongue for hours. He prayed Isla was safe, that Gray had raged but not harmed her.

After much thought, Tavish realized that their plan remained the same—secure the funds of his inheritance and rescue Isla.

It was merely a wee bit more complicated now.

But once he had Isla free, they could decide together where to go. Only then would Tavish tell his father about their marriage. At the moment, he needed his father's unwitting support. Forgiveness would be easier to receive than permission.

An affectionate man, Lord Northcairn doted on his children and usually excused their foibles. For example, Callum had a knack for trouble—namely gambling, ladies of ill repute, and acts of daring-do—and Da' had regularly brushed off his exploits.

So Tavish assumed that his father would eventually come around to the idea of a Kinsey as a daughter-in-law. But he wanted to ease into telling him.

"Ah, Tavish." His father beamed, waving him into his study. The fire in the hearth cast shadows along the wooden paneling on the walls and decorative plaster overhead. "Come to join me for a spot of whisky, lad?"

"O' course."

Alcohol would only help this discussion.

They sat before the fire, sipping at their tumblers, speaking of inanities—the chance of some fishing later on in the week, Mr. McKay's prized hound who had just whelped a litter of auspicious puppies.

Finally, Tavish found his opening.

"So, Da', I turned eighteen this month, and thoughts of my future have been circling in my head. I know that Mamma left me a wee inheritance. I have begun thinking of how I can best use those monies for my . . ."

Tavish trailed off. The longer he spoke of his inheritance, the darker his father's expression became until it resembled a funerary shroud.

"Da'? What is it?"

Lord Northcairn sat forward, skin suddenly haggard and gray.

"I . . ." He swallowed, as if some ghastly truth were stuck in his craw. "I am so sorry, son. There is no inheritance."

"Pardon?"

His father ran a shaking hand over his face. "Just that. The money is gone."

"How?! It was set aside for me. Legally, it is mine." Tavish could hear the panic in his voice.

"Aye. And ye can take me to court and demand I pay it, but I'm telling ye lad, there is no money to be had."

"But . . . ye be an earl? Our lands and tenants bring in regular revenue."

"Aye, but that merely supports us day-to-day at present. There be no excess."

Tavish lurched to his feet, desperate to move, hopeful that simply shifting positions in the room might afford a solution. "But what about Mariah's situation? She won a large settlement for breach of promise from Lord Stafford at the last Court of Sessions."

"Gone."

Tavish stared down at his father, noting the hunch in the man's shoulders, the bleak anger in his gaze.

"How? How can all that money be gone?"

Lord Northcairn sighed. "That bastard Grayburn."

"Grayburn?"

"Aye. When Mariah was in London last year, unbeknownst to any of us, Grayburn lured Callum into the depths of some of the worst gaming hells in London. Your brother racked up significant debts that had to be settled."

A terrible ringing started in Tavish's ears. A numbness spread to his limbs and whispered of catastrophe.

"Every last cent I could muster went to settle Callum's markers. Your inheritance. Your sisters' dowries. The monies from Mariah's settlement. We were hardly flush with cash before this, but now, we are paupered."

His father shrugged his shoulders. As if the complete disintegration of their finances and the future of all his children were a cloak, easily shaken off and discarded.

I have a wife to support! Tavish nearly yelled. *Why did you save Callum from the consequences of his piss-poor decisions and leave the rest of us to suffer for it?*

Damn his brother and his poor judgment. And damn Grayburn for being the devil who birthed it all. One more woe to lay at Grayburn's feet.

Tavish remained silent. Devastation and Panic were fighting cockerels in his chest, each warring for dominance. Callum would probably wager on their fight and lose.

So bitter those thoughts.

Tavish breathed through the cacophony of anger. Would plowing a fist into Callum's face, the crack of bone on bone, be as satisfying as he currently imagined? He rather thought it would.

"What am I to do then?" Tavish met his father's gaze, his fury barely in check. "Ye will cast me off into the world without a farthing? Without a thought for my future?!"

Lord Northcairn looked away to the fire. "I cannot say. Like most other gentlemen, ye will have to plot your own course."

In other words, *I protected the honor of my heir, and the rest of ye can sort yourselves.*

The horror of Tavish's situation sank deeper.

What was he to do?

He had a *wife*. A girl whom he loved more than life, more than breath, and who now relied on him to keep her housed and clothed and . . . happy.

Tavish knew it would be wiser to stay. To talk with his father. To explore, perhaps, other avenues and ideas for a profession.

Instead, he stood and walked out. Across the great hall, down the main staircase, and through the front door. He left the walls of his ancestors, hiking across their land. Climbing until he summited the slipping shale of the cairn of Cairnfell itself.

Head back, he roared his fury. His despair. His helplessness.

The north wind roared back. Merciless. Scouring the tears from his cheeks and offering no help beyond a pounding headache and a hoarse voice.

THE NEXT DAY, a letter arrived for Tavish. Unfranked and sealed with unstamped red wax, he already knew its sender before he unfolded the foolscap.

He withdrew to his bedchamber to read its contents.

Balfour,

I will be brief.

You will never speak with my sister again. I do not know what your intention has been with this scheme. Perhaps you think to ruin Lady Isla and harm our family for the slights you assume you have been dealt. I do not care. Your association with her ends this moment.

Tavish paused, absorbing the words.

Grayburn didn't know about their marriage. Isla hadn't told him.

Tavish was unsure if he felt relieved or frustrated. If the duke knew of their marriage, then Tavish would have a legal claim on Isla, one that superseded her brother's. His Grace would have to let them be together.

But as it was . . .

The letter continued:

I know your family is paupered. Your brother's indiscretions are numerous and well-known. You have no prospects beyond the dubious legacy of your father's title and your family name, tarnished as it is by your older siblings' behavior.

Tavish clenched his jaw. The dishonor that had fallen upon Mariah had its origins with Grayburn. And if his father was to be believed, Grayburn had deliberately led Callum down the primrose path to destruction. Yes, both his siblings had made mistakes, but the root of those mistakes lay at Grayburn's feet.

Therefore, I offer you a reprieve. I am prepared to purchase you a commission in the 92nd Regiment. It is far better than you deserve, but I cannot have you here, sniffing around my sister. Take my offer. Leave and never return.

But know this: If I ever see you again—if you so much as breathe the same air Lady Isla breathes—I will put a bullet through your heart, damn the consequences.

Grayburn

That was it.

Tavish's legs gave way, and he slumped to his knees on the floor. A supplicant, pleading for some glimmer of hope.

What am I to do?

The question spun in his mind, a child's top whirring, granting him no surcease.

Whichever way he examined the situation, there was no solution. No route for him to provide for Isla without pursuing a career. The military was the best—and, possibly, his only—solution.

But . . . it would mean a separation from Isla for a time. Until he could get his feet under him and come for her. Despite Grayburn's demands, Tavish would not agree to never return. He would forswear himself in that oath. Promising to never see Isla would be akin to pledging to hold one's breath indefinitely—an impossible task.

No.

Grayburn could threaten all he wished, but unlike the devastation the duke had wreaked on the Balfour family, His Grace would never come between Tavish and the woman he loved.

19

August 5, 1817
Kingswell House
Aberdeenshire, Scotland

Isla stared into the fire, desperate to reorder her thoughts after her impromptu swim in the lake.

She snuggled into the warmth of a blanket around her shoulders and sipped a cup of tea. Her wet hair spilled loose, cascading down the back of her armchair and slowly drying. The housekeeper and a maid had left Isla to rest.

"Recover your strength, ye poor lamb," the housekeeper had said.

A hot bath and a change of clothing had done wonders to restore Isla physically.

Emotionally, however . . .

She didn't think a nap was going to cure what ailed her.

It didn't help matters that Miss Crowley had talked for nine minutes without taking a breath—Isla had timed the girl—about Captain Balfour's heroism.

"Oh, Lady Isla, you should have seen it," she had rhapsodized, eyes glowing with hearts as Isla stood dripping in the entry hall, Lady Milmouth and the housekeeper fussing to fetch towels and arrange a bath. "The way Captain Balfour reacted when you went under. He was like an arrow flying to the mark, tossing his rifle, his hat tearing from his head. Like . . . like a hero of legend, bolting into the breach to rescue a fellow soldier from enemy fire. But instead, he raced to save the sister of his sworn enemy. 'Tis a nobleness of spirit my poor heart can scarcely fathom. Look—" She extended a shaking hand. "I tremble still. How shall I ever sleep?"

Isla wasn't sure whether to laugh or cry.

But then, she could hardly fault Miss Crowley for her enthusiasm. Regardless of the boy Tavish had been or the imposing Captain Balfour he was now, the man commanded attention.

His display *had* been astonishing. And Isla knew him well enough to understand that if Miss Crowley had been the one to tumble into the lake, Tavish would have acted just as quickly.

I have ye, lass. Ye be safe with me.

Just remembering his rumbled words sent gooseflesh pebbling Isla's upper arms.

For the smallest fraction of a second, when he had tugged her skirts free and surfaced to ensure she was well, he had felt like *her* Tavish. Wry and gentle. Open and concerned. As if the past seven years had never happened.

It had been terrifyingly disorienting. The sense of something long dormant shaking awake.

But then she had touched him, and the aura disintegrated. This Tavish was too big, too strong. The hard planes of his chest under her palm had been . . . astonishing.

And now, hours on, Isla felt . . .

Oh, what did she feel?

Confused, certainly. Overwhelmed. Unsure.

The longer she was in his company, the harder it became to separate the Tavish of then from the Tavish of now.

On a sigh, she shifted in her chair, setting down her teacup and tucking her feet underneath her.

Her logical brain knew that a life with Tavish wasn't what she wanted. She had a crystal-clear vision for her future—Malton Hill with tenants' needs to address and the resilient woman she was there. A future that didn't involve living in poverty with a Scot, no matter how physically alluring, compelling, or skilled with a rifle.

But her heart . . .

Her heart was a shambles. The girl she had been longed for him still, for the joy and happiness they had once shared. She probably always would.

And yet, Isla recognized that even her remembered joy and happiness were likely a counterfeit. A replacement for the love lost with her mother's death. A heady combination of tasting a forbidden fruit and rebelling against Gray's abrupt cooling in demeanor.

A knock sounded on her bedchamber door.

"Come," she called.

Her brother stepped into the room, shutting the door firmly behind him.

Thinking of Gray . . .

"Are you recovered?" he asked without preamble.

As usual, he was dressed to perfection, not a hair out of place. She had soaked through his greatcoat when he lifted her from the lake, dampening his jacket. Surely, he had cursed her name for spotting his attire.

"Yes. I am quite well, simply tired and chilled," she returned.

He nodded, gaze assessing, his hazel eyes turbulent. His father's hazel eyes. A color so very different from Isla's own blue or the green of their mother. A forever reminder that Isla was not a Kinsey in truth.

Gray crossed to the window, limping slightly. The sight did not portend a calm conversation about her health.

Her brother surveyed the late afternoon light, but his hands twitched, tugging ends of his coat sleeves, as if desperate to cast them from his body.

Once, Isla would have fretted over the volatility of his moods. Now, she simply wished to no longer be subjected to them.

Silence stretched.

Gray had come for a purpose. He would get to the point.

"You will do me the courtesy of stating how you learned to swim," he said at last.

Ah.

So that was his concern.

Not a question or a request, of course. A demand.

"What does it matter how I learned, Gray? The skill saved my life. Every lady should know how to swim."

Gray whirled on her, fire igniting in his gaze. The setting sun poured through the window beside him, burnishing his hair and turning it into a lion's mane.

"Be that as it may, Isla, a lady only learns to swim"—he ticked off his fingers—"if her father, a brother, or her husband teach her. Learning any other way is reprehensible. Our father certainly didn't teach you. Neither did Matthias nor I. You have no husband. So again, I ask, who taught you how to swim? Was it *that man?*"

You have no husband.

Hah!

"Captain Balfour? He has a name, Gray." Isla looked away to the fire. "I refuse to speak with you when you are seething over the Balfours. No good will come of it."

Silence.

Isla so rarely disobeyed him—fear made her tread carefully around Gray's temper—that her recalcitrance stunned her brother into silence.

Lifting her chin, she looked at him. Really looked at him. The scowling brows under his lion-mane hair. The stern slash of his mouth.

The horror of his temper the evening he had found her with Tavish would never abate. The aftermath of that fury had been horrific. What lay in store for her now?

Words crowded Isla's throat—quarreling, fractious things she could scarcely contain.

Will you toss me out for insubordination, Gray? What will you do once you learn I am married to that man?

Why do you hold the circumstances of my birth like a knife to my throat?

Tavish had rattled something loose within her. A need, perhaps, to shrug off the last vestiges of the compliant, passive self she had so loathed as a young woman.

Or maybe her courage had a simpler origin: Tavish had returned, and Isla finally felt like someone would stand beside her in a crisis. A person who would reach out a hand and say, "Grab hold. I have ye," just as Tavish had earlier.

And how tragic that Isla didn't believe her brother would help her but intrinsically trusted her soon-to-be former husband.

Rather telling, that.

"Isla," Gray finally said on a deep breath. "Please answer me."

"So what if Captain Balfour was the one to teach me, Gray?" Isla threw up her hands. "He is my past. And the past will occasionally intrude on the present, particularly when the knowledge I learned *then* might save my life *now*. Also, may I remind you, Captain Balfour is the gentleman who jumped into the lake to save me. Not you. Not Colonel Archer. Captain Balfour was my savior. And he was the only gentleman present who *knew* I could swim."

"Do not attempt to turn this argument back on me."

"I'm merely stating facts."

"When and how did he teach you, Isla?"

"Enough. I'm not speaking with you like this." Isla pushed to standing.

Gray tracked her movements. "You will do me the courtesy of answering my questions, Isla."

"Why, Gray? Are you going to summon a doctor next? Demand proof I am still a virgin?"

"If I must." He looked away, muttering something that sounded like *damnable Balfours*. "At the very least, I wish to know if I need to bloody that man for his impertinence toward you."

You can try.

Fortunately, Isla stopped that sentence in time.

"Enough! I never engaged in such intimate activities with *that man*, as you call him." Not for lack of wanting to engage in intimate activities, she declined to add. And not for lack of planning to engage in them. "When will you stop punishing me for a brief lapse in judgment seven years ago?"

Gray pivoted, head shaking. "The more I learn of your dalliance with Balfour, the less 'brief' I think it was. How deep was your involvement there?"

"I've already said all I intend to say, Gray. I am yet a maid. You needn't worry that you are selling damaged goods to Colonel Archer." Gray at least had the decency to wince at her choice of words. "I have no intention of revisiting the mistakes of my youth. My goals and dreams for the future are focused on Malton Hill, as well you know. Can you please do me the honor of believing me?"

Her brother stared at her, plumbing her gaze as if he would ferret out all her secrets.

"I have spoken with both Colonel Archer and Lord Milmouth about a marriage contract." Gray changed the topic.

"Oh. Have you?" Isla hated the faint tremor in her voice.

Botheration. With Tavish consuming her thoughts, Isla had rather lost the plot on her week here.

"Yes," Gray said. "Nothing official, naturally. Nothing binding. But all is in readiness."

"I see."

You said you would wait for my consent before acting, she wanted to add. Events were moving faster than she had considered.

"Are you going to tell Colonel Archer about your involvement with Balfour?" Gray turned for the door.

"Of course. He deserves to know. But as it is my secret to tell, I thank you for letting me be the one to tell it."

Gray nodded. Just once. "See that you do. As you said, Malton Hill is your goal. Only my approval will see the estate safely into your hands. I am trusting you to act properly, Isla. Do not disappoint me."

And then he was gone.

HOURS LATER, ISLA sat reading before the fire—hair dry now and tied into a thick braid, heart quiet after an evening spent free of her brother and the other house guests.

The hallway floorboards creaked outside her bedroom, and a note appeared under the door.

Isla stared at the folded foolscap, white and damning against the wood.

No need to wonder who it was from. Only one person in this house would be slipping her a note.

She contemplated not reading it. Just tossing it onto the fire and pretending she had never received it. After all, no good would come of deepening her relationship with Tavish at this point.

She had her sights set on Malton Hill and her life there—the laughter of Mrs. White over dinner, the comfort of Dr. Sumsion's sermons and Mrs. Sumsion's wry commentary afterward. Isla's community and the place where her decisions made an impact.

After some pondering, she had decided on a course of action for the now-widowed Mrs. Tippets and her children. The local seamstress, Mrs. Bolton, was in need of a new assistant, and Isla knew Mrs. Tippets to be skilled with a needle. Surely with the right encouragement, Mrs. Boulton would hire her. Moreover, Mrs. Bolton had a wee apartment above her shop where Mrs. Tippets could live and work. Isla would write Mr. Cranston in the morning and propose the solution.

Any interaction with Tavish Balfour threatened to upend the very real good Isla did at Malton Hill.

But the bit of foolscap, stark against the dark floor, caused her heart to pang. Its presence indicated concern and, perhaps, tenderness.

Soft footsteps sounded overhead.

Capitulating, Isla picked up the paper.

YSQ DJO NQWW? VYK . . .

She translated:

> *Are you well? Tap the ceiling with a poker once if yes. Twice if you require rescuing. Three times, and I shall bring the cavalry.*

Isla didn't wish to smile. She didn't wish to be charmed.

And yet . . .

Here, again, were shades of her Tavish. Just as in the lake earlier, the moment felt disorienting. A ghost of the past transposed over the present, rendering her light-headed.

The Isla of seven years ago would have tapped three times, daring him to act outrageously.

Now . . .

She picked up the fire poker and, standing on a chair, tapped the ceiling with the handle. Just once.

She imagined him in that room overhead, crouched down and listening attentively. How had he hoped she would react?

Swallowing, Isla returned the poker to its stand.

After a few minutes, the footsteps retreated, and another door closed with a faint *snick*—Tavish retreating to his own bedchamber.

Emotion gathered in her throat, as unwelcome as it was unexpected. That same well-worn grief, a king tide rushing into her chest and threatening to spill over its banks.

With a stern shake of her head, Isla banished it.

Malton Hill and her people there.

That was her goal.

She merely needed to keep her eyes on the prize.

20

SEVEN YEARS EARLIER

AUGUST 31, 1810
PETTERCAIRN, SCOTLAND

Days.

It had been days since Isla's wedding and not a word from Tavish.

Granted, Gray had confined Isla to her bedchamber. A footman tracked her every movement the one hour a day she was permitted to stroll in the garden.

But still . . .

Tavish was resourceful, and Gray's servants bribeable.

Why hadn't he contacted her? What had Gray done?

Fear for Tavish kept Isla up most nights. Sleep, when it did come, was fitful. She would race through dark woods, screaming for Tavish but never finding him, before awaking with a lurch, heart thudding and throat dry.

Gray refused to speak with her.

In retaliation, on day three, Isla stopped eating.

Tray after tray was sent down to the kitchen, strawberry tarts and roasted pigeon untouched. Isla controlled so little in her world. But her meals she could rule with an iron fist.

Cast me out, her actions screamed. *I dare you.*

Tavish wouldn't care if she were illegitimate. If Gray renounced her, then she could join her husband. They could run away and start their life together.

On the sixth day, Gray stormed into her room, a footman at his heels carrying a tray laden with Isla's favorite foods.

"You will eat," he demanded. "I grow tired of this childish display of temper."

Isla merely stared at him—light-headed with hunger, limbs weary—hoping her gaze appeared as dead as she felt.

"I will eat when I am no longer a prisoner. Until then, you can watch me starve and know that your uncaring hand has caused it." She turned to look out the window.

Gray had ranted for another five minutes. Isla ignored him.

Her stomach knotted in pain, but she scarcely noticed. Her heart felt fractured and shattered in ways she hadn't known hearts could break.

Set me free, she silently pleaded. *Let me find solace with the one person who loves me.*

The next day, a doctor arrived. He listened to her pulse and bled her a little.

"We must balance the melancholic spirit," he said to Gray, as a footman carried the bloody bowl away. "She merely needs rest and food. That will see her right as rain."

Gray had nodded, but his hazel eyes remained turbulent and watchful.

Isla met his gaze boldly over the doctor's shoulder.

I dare you, she said with her expression. *Cast me out, Gray.*

Her brother looked away first, a frown between his brows, arms folded across his chest.

He didn't cast her out.

Isla wasn't sure if she should be encouraged that he still retained enough human decency to care about her welfare, or furious that he preferred control over all else.

On day eight, her fifth day of not eating, the gnawing hunger penetrated the fog of her grief. Her body demanded to live. Isla ate a small bite of a scone and then crumbled the rest so Gray wouldn't know.

She did the same on the ninth and tenth days.

On the eleventh day, she discovered a note under a plate of shortbread.

ISLA FOUND TAVISH waiting at the old bridge—the one that crossed over the River Southcairn and led to Cairnfell—just as his note had said he would.

Night had fallen hours ago, but Isla would know the cant of her beloved's head anywhere.

Just that single glimpse—

How she had missed him! Her husband! Her love!

Isla raced down the path, the tears on her cheeks from both happiness and relief. The handle of her valise sat heavy in her fist, biting into the wedding ring on her finger.

His note had been terse and simple, written in their cipher:

Meet me at the old bridge on Wednesday at midnight.

Isla hadn't known, at first, how she would accomplish the deed.

But just the day before, Gray had called off the footman guarding her door. And in a show of obedience, Isla began eating again yesterday and today.

Thankfully, the lack of a guard meant she could slip out of the house to meet Tavish. To run away with him.

She hadn't felt an ounce of guilt as she packed her bag with all the items she could manage. Her possessions were meager, but fribbles like pretty frocks and bonnet ribbons mattered little when the entirety of her future trembled in the balance.

Tavish stood tall beside Goliath, caped greatcoat falling to his ankles, saddle bags bulging.

Somehow, though it had not even been two weeks, he looked older. His demeanor more upright and rigid. His eyes more seeing.

What had happened? What terror had Gray enacted?

"Tavish!" she whispered on a hoarse voice, dropping her bag and sprinting to him.

He lifted her into his arms, spinning around. She grabbed his head and kissed him, tasting her tears on his lips.

At last!

He had found a way!

They were free!

She would climb onto Goliath, and they would ride off to a new life together—just the two of them. No more need to conceal their love. No more Gray and his cruel truths and hateful words.

Jubilation made her giddy. She covered his face in kisses, her lips desperate to touch every inch of his skin—the crease of his closed eyelids, the smooth patch beside his earlobe.

"You're here," she breathed. "I love you. I missed you. Hallelujah, you're here!"

It was a miracle she had survived so many days without him. She couldn't hold or caress him sufficiently. Finally, after one last deep kiss, he pulled her hands from his body.

Of course. They needed to be on their way.

She looked up into his shadowed face.

"I'm ready to go with you. You didn't say, but I brought my valise." She gestured to where she had dropped it on the path. "Let me grab it."

She pivoted, but he stayed her with a gentle hand at her elbow.

That was her first clue that anything was amiss.

"Isla . . ." he began, a catch in his voice.

A chill dropped down her spine. She turned back to him.

Something was wrong.

"What happened?" She clutched his fingers in hers. "What did Gray do?"

Tavish . . . crumpled. There was no other way to describe it. His shoulders pitched inward, and he shook loose her hand, his arms dangling useless by his side. The shadowy features of his face puckered.

In the dim moonlight, the glitter of his eyes found hers.

"I'm leaving, Isla." He said the words quietly, but they still struck Isla with a bracing *thwack*.

I am leaving. No *we*.

She refused to accept what he might be saying.

"I know, love. That's why I'm here. I'm leaving with you."

Silence.

And then—

"Isla . . . I can't . . ." A breath. "I can't take ye. Not yet."

"What do you mean, Tavish? Of course, you can take me. You have your inheritance. You would buy a commission, you said, with a little set by for us."

He winced. "There is no money, Isla. Callum spent my inheritance. He lost it. Gambling."

"Pardon? How is that even possible?"

Tavish laughed, a terrible, caustic sound that resembled Gray too much for her liking.

Isla flinched.

"I don't ken how it's possible, but Callum managed it." Tone so bitter. "I'm paupered, Isla. I haven't two sous to rub together, much less funds to support a wife."

Isla blinked up at him, unable to truly fathom what he was saying.

"But you're leaving." She pointed to the saddle bags thrown over Goliath's rump.

He nodded.

Isla took a step backward. "I don't . . . I don't understand."

"Isla . . . I am enlisting."

"Without a commission?"

"Nae. With a commission."

"But . . . but you just said there is no money for that."

He sighed, as if defeat sat heavy on his shoulders. "Isla . . ."

It hit her with blinding clarity. "Gray. Gray is forcing you away."

He nodded again. A sharp up-down movement.

"He offered to buy me a commission provided I leave and never return. Immediately."

The betrayal took a long moment to land.

It started as a buzzing in her head that quickly migrated to a strange panicked quaking of her limbs.

"I'm taking Callum's horse," he continued on a sharp laugh. "I didn't ask him if I could. It's the least my dear brother can do to repay me for his selfishness."

This bitter Tavish was new to her. A man whose words emerged as barbed spikes.

"But . . . but what about me? I'm your wife." She hated that her own voice sounded small and shaking.

"Ye will be safer if ye remain here."

"Safe? How will I be safe?!"

"Has Gray harmed ye? Ye said he wouldn't."

The image of Gray rose—looming over her in his study, his words battering like a fist. *Our mother. A whore. And you, her bastard get.*

"He has broken my heart, Tavish! Matters are not—"

"But has he hurt ye?"

"No. Not physically, but—"

"Then ye will be safe here."

"I don't feel safe!"

"But ye will be."

No!

Tavish wasn't listening. He didn't know that she was illegitimate. That Gray despised her for it. Before this moment, Isla had thought Tavish wouldn't care about her parentage. But now . . . when he appeared so ready to turn his back on her *before* even knowing that critical bit of information . . .

"We're married, Tavish!" She lifted her left hand, pointing to his wedding ring gleaming there. "You can't leave me! Again, I'm your *wife*! You have an obligation to me."

"I ken that, Isla. And I want us to be together, but I require an income before we can set up a household together. That's why I'm taking this commission."

The panic spread to Isla's heart. She feared the organ would punch through her chest and collapse to the ground at her feet, her lifeblood pouring loose.

"And giving me up?! Permitting Gray to buy you off?"

"No!" He ran an agitated hand through his hair. "That's not what I'm saying. I will find a way to return for ye, Isla. I'm not planning on holding to my word with Grayburn."

"I cannot stay here. Gray is . . . or rather, Gray told me . . ." The confession of her illegitimacy froze on her tongue. She couldn't risk Tavish turning away from her, too. "I cannot bear it!"

"Isla, I can't take ye with me at the moment. I am to report to Shorncliffe in Kent for training with the 92nd Highlanders. There isn't a place—"

"Officers take their wives on campaign."

"Aye, they do, but I know nothing of the mechanics of it. Ye will simply have to wait until I can save the necessary funds and find a way to send for ye."

"Save funds?! What if you cannot save sufficient?" The nervous energy thudding her heart blackened her thoughts. Rationality fled.

All Isla could see was the desolation of Tavish's betrayal.

He had promised they would be together. She had married him based on that promise.

Instead, he had allied himself with Gray.

And now . . .

Now, he was leaving. Perhaps never to return.

"I don't know!" The sentence burst from him on a frustrated rush. "I don't know, Isla. Our plans unraveled and now every obstacle feels insurmountable and . . . and . . . I don't know what to do. We're both so young and inexperienced and . . ." He drifted off on a huff.

Regret.

That was what Isla heard in the breaths between his words. Regret that he had married her. Regret that she now hung like a millstone about his neck.

Just as Gray regretted the burden of her life.

The cuckoo in the nest. Unwanted. A noxious millstone to bear.

Isla took a step back from Tavish. Then two.

"Isla." He reached for her.

But she was already shaking her head, tucking her hands to her chest and wrenching his wedding ring from her finger.

"You are trying to twist the reasons for your actions, Tavish, but they all reach the same conclusion—you are letting Gray buy you off. You decided to take his money and run. You can take this, too!"

She hurled the ring at his chest. It bounced off, clinking to the path at their feet.

Tavish scarcely glanced at it.

"Love, that isn't at all what I'm saying, and ye ken it."

"I'm not your love!" she hissed. "If you l-loved me, you would take m-me with you."

"Isla." He reached for her then, trying to pull her into his chest. "I'm promising to return for you. Ye be twisting *my* words, too."

"No!" She wrenched free, dancing back.

"Ye must look at this logically, Isla. As an adult with a mature perspective. I ken that ye be not even a month seventeen, but we must—"

"So I'm a child now, too?!"

"Please, lass. Don't do this. I want ye as my wife."

She heard the pleading in his voice, but something had fractured within her. Some deep mooring that Gray's cruelty had loosened. And now with the harsh battering of Tavish's plans, her ties to rationality snapped entirely.

"Go then! Go and never come back!"

"Isla—"

"You cannot call me a child, and yet consider me a wife in the same sentence. You cannot tell me to behave like an adult, and yet dismiss my reasons as immature. I might be a *child*—" She leaned on the word with acidic scorn. "—but even I know that this isn't what a marriage should be."

"We're both new to this, lass, but that—"

"No! We stand together. We go together. That's the only marriage I want!"

"Isla. Please stop."

"Don't bother sending for me. I won't come! Don't write me, as I surely will not write you!"

She hated that her self-pitying demands sounded like those of a child. Angry and taunting.

"Ye will change your mind, Isla. Ye must!"

"I won't!"

"I'll write ye as soon as I can. I'll arrange some way for ye to receive—"

"No! Do not write me! I don't want to hear from you. I shan't read anything you send. I'll burn it unopened!"

The following silence rang with the echo of her fury.

She could hear the harsh exhale of his breaths. As if, like her, he was seconds from screaming his rage.

Finally, Tavish shifted on his feet, lungs settling, gaze shuttering. His actions declared that, unlike her weak, juvenile self, he was capable of controlling his emotions.

"Very well, Isla. I won't write ye. I will wait for you to write me." So measured and precise those words, maturely shifting the decision back into her hands. "Ye can send me letters through Mariah. She doesn't know about us. No one does. But I know she will help, if ye explain—"

"Go to the devil, Tavish Balfour."

Spinning on her heel, Isla picked up her abandoned valise and walked home.

ISLA RETURNED TO Dunmore as if in a fog.

She unpacked her bag, crawled into bed, and didn't stir.

Once again, food was sent back down to the kitchen, uneaten. Not born of stubbornness but of a deep melancholy of spirits.

Tavish refused to listen to her. To understand why she couldn't bear remaining under Gray's merciless thumb.

Instead, when faced with the loss of his inheritance, Tavish had accepted Gray's offer and left for a separate life—one that wouldn't contain her.

What did Tavish think she would do without him? What future did he envision for her? What waiting? His plan sounded like more hope than any logical reasoning. At best, it was a thin excuse to abandon her, as if she were a burden he regretted taking on.

Tavish was gone and would likely be killed.

She would never see him again.

What was the point of life?

Her thoughts probably were childish. Petulant, even. But her heart simply overflowed with too much *feeling*, and Isla didn't know how to channel it.

The doctor came and went, Gray on his heels. Gray even went so far as to place a warm hand on her forehead, his own brow furrowed.

She didn't care.

Let him watch me die, she thought. *Let him see what he has wrought.*

The housekeeper asked her questions that she didn't hear.

It was Matt—dear, kind Matt—in the end, who reached a hand into the darkness and tugged her toward the barest hint of light.

Sitting beside her bed, he laid his single palm on hers.

"Come, Isla," he said. "I cannot bear another moment of this. Neither can Gray. He has said we can away, just you and I. Somewhere free of memories. A new place. One ready to nurture our happiness."

The next day, a footman lifted Isla into a carriage heading south to Malton Hill.

21

August 6, 1817
Kingswell House
Aberdeenshire, Scotland

Tavish stared out the library window of Kingswell House, trying to recall another time in his life when he had felt so lost, so helpless.

After his mother's death, perhaps. Definitely that first year in the Rifles following his break with Isla.

Regardless, for a man who had spent the past seven years avoiding death through a combination of quick thinking and decisive action, such bafflement was unwelcome.

The cause of his dazed state currently sat on the back terrace, her head bent over a book, oblivious to Tavish watching her through the window.

After an afternoon and evening spent in her room, Isla had reemerged this morning for breakfast, fresh-faced and no worse for wear after her unexpected *dooking* in the lake.

She had smiled warmly at Fletch, answered the flurry of questions from the Misses Forsyth, and aside from thanking him once more for helping her from the lake, had all but ignored Tavish.

It was as things must be. He knew this.

Fletch offered Isla a life that Tavish could not . . . and that was before factoring in her substantial dowry. Fletch was the man she wanted, not Tavish.

But as he stood at the library window, staring as she turned a page, he could scarcely suppress his longing.

Aye, she had been lovely as a lass.

But now . . .

The gentle arch of her spine reminded him of tulips bending on a May breeze. Her lips moved, mouthing soundless words that might as well have been an incantation. He certainly felt ensorcelled as his gaze traced the smooth column of her throat and that one recalcitrant tendril of hair beside her chin, slipping defiantly from its curl.

But it was more than her physical beauty that arrested him. Tavish knew her soul, the tumble and turn of her mind. Every last atom of her blazing with fire and life and—

"I would recommend not letting Grayburn or Fletch see you staring at Lady Isla like that."

The sudden voice at Tavish's elbow caused him to start.

"Damnation, Ross!" Tavish placed a hand over his pounding heart.

Ross laughed. "I'm in earnest. Ye know better than to even glance Lady Isla's way after Grayburn's reaction yesterday, much less stare as if she hangs the sun and moon. Ye might have saved her life—and both of us know that can forge a powerful bond—but you will be horsewhipped or challenged to a duel if ye don't beat a hasty retreat."

"Aye." Tavish swallowed around the boulder lodged in his chest—the one with the words *I don't want you* chiseled upon it.

A dent appeared between Ross's brows. "Why so glum?"

Tavish tried to smile, to summon a quip that would assure Ross of Tavish's indifference toward Isla.

Instead, he grimaced and looked away before Ross could see the misery etched into his face. His friend knew him well enough to logic his way to the truth.

And even then, Tavish couldn't stop his gaze from drifting back to Isla once more.

In his periphery, Ross's eyes widened to the size of saucers.

"No." His friend's chin went up.

Tavish said nothing.

"No, no, no." Ross shook his head before glancing to Isla and then back to Tavish. "Surely, what I'm thinking cannot be true."

Tavish managed a deep breath, but no more. He feared he couldn't speak without the yearning in his chest erupting outward.

And maybe, just maybe, he was tired of no one else knowing the reality of his pain.

Ross grabbed his arm, forcibly turning him away from the window and Isla, brow furrowed as he dragged Tavish back into the gloom of the library.

"Ye forget how well I know ye. I can tell when you be keeping a secret, ye bawbag," Ross hissed. "Ye must tell me I'm wrong. Because my brain has drawn a straight line between several facts. One, ye grew up on lands adjacent to Grayburn's. Two, ye seem to be a wee bit preoccupied with Lady Isla. Three, ye be secretly married. And four, ye don't want anyone to know of your secret marriage to protect your lady wife. Tell me, Tavish Balfour, that there are no links between these four things. I need to be assured that the mind-numbing revelation I am experiencing is ludicrous."

Unable to summon words, Tavish merely looked at his friend, letting all the misery of his soul flood his face.

Ross staggered back a step, jaw flapping open for a solid six seconds. Again, his eyes darted from Tavish to Isla and then back to Tavish.

"Ye bloody *eejit*!" Ross hissed. "Do ye want to die?!"

Tavish sighed and crossed back to the window. Ross followed.

Isla had loosened her bonnet ribbons to reveal a wee strip of skin between the bottom of the bonnet and the collar of her dress—a delectable two inches of her nape that Tavish longed to kiss.

"Grayburn is going to kill ye," Ross said.

"He will try."

"Ye still love her."

"Aye." Tavish lifted a helpless hand in her direction, as if to say, *How could any man resist* that?

"Why aren't ye fighting to preserve your marriage?"

"And how would I do that, Ross? Spirit her away to live in a cabin in rural Pennsylvania? I don't have the means to support a highborn lady. Besides, she doesn't want me."

"How do you know that?"

Tavish gave Ross a *look*. "Because she said, and I quote, 'I don't want you.'"

Ross winced. "*Och*, but you love her."

"Aye. More than life. But when ye truly love someone, ye want their happiness. And if that happiness doesn't involve yourself, then ye give them the happiness they do want. I love Isla enough to grant her freedom. I want her to find the sort of love I feel for her."

Ross snorted, scrubbing a hand over his face. "And just when we all thought ye couldn't possibly be any more bloody noble. Fletch is . . . *Och*, bollocking hell! Fletch!"

"Aye. Fletch." Tavish shot Ross a side-eye. "Isla made me promise not to tell him. She wishes to control when and how he learns of this."

Silence for a long beat.

They both watched Isla turn another page in her book, her elegant gloved fingers tracing the lines.

"No wonder ye've never touched a woman in all the years I've known ye. I wouldn't either, had I such a bonnie lass waiting for me at home."

"Ross." A warning. "She was never waiting. Our marriage was over as soon as it began. I'm the *eejit* still holding a candle, unwilling to blow out the flame of my love."

More silence.

Isla turned another page.

"I'm not sure Fletch will forgive ye. For not telling him, that is."

"Aye." Tavish pinched the bridge of his nose. "I don't know what to do. I can't . . . I can't manage this. What I feel and—"

"Balfour! Ross!" Fletch's voice boomed outside the library door.

Ross gave Tavish a look of sympathy. Fletch bounded into the room—smiling, happy, and oblivious. The sight cut Tavish like a dagger.

"There you two are!" Fletch said on a laugh. "The ladies are asking for you. Or rather, the ladies were hoping Ross here would assist them with untangling some knitting wool in the morning room." His gaze turned to Tavish. "And Balfour, can I persuade you to assist me with an important matter?"

GRAVEL CRUNCHED UNDER Tavish's boots as he walked the path that snaked through the trees and around the lake.

Ahead of him, Isla strolled arm-in-arm with Fletch, her ear lifted to hear whatever tender endearments he had to whisper.

Tavish looked away before he caved to the temptation to pound his fist into one of the surrounding trees.

A chaperone.

Fletch had requested Tavish act as a *chaperone* for his "courting campaign"—Fletch's words—of Lady Isla.

The pity in Ross's eyes would have been comical had the situation not been so tragic—Tavish chaperoning his *wife* as another man wooed her.

He challenged Shakespeare himself to concoct a situation more absurd.

In truth, Fletch didn't need a chaperone to take a stroll with Lady Isla. As long as a couple remained in easily visible locales—like the gravel paths surrounding Kingswell—there was little concern for a lady's reputation.

No, Fletch wanted a friend along for plausible deniability. With a trusted third person present, Fletch could steal a kiss or two from his lady love without placing her upstanding character in danger.

For Tavish, the thought of having to turn his back while Isla kissed another man was almost unbearable. It was one thing to know a gentleman courted Isla. But another thing entirely to have to witness it. To assist and encourage it.

For her part, Isla appeared oblivious to the men's machinations.

She walked with ease, head canted toward Fletch. However, she did occasionally glance back at Tavish, as if ascertaining his distance or unable to shake the weight of his presence.

Maybe Tavish *should* leave Kingswell. Grayburn clearly wished him to. At breakfast, the duke had met Tavish's gaze over the rim of his teacup, eyes flaring with a dark warning. His Grace had ridden off with Lord Milmouth shortly after. To what end, Tavish hadn't a clue. Something pompous and lordly, no doubt. The two gentlemen were endlessly discussing political matters, likely shoring up their soon-to-be familial alliance.

As for Tavish . . . leaving Kingswell felt a wee bit like ceding the battlefield, and the soldier in him simply couldn't do that. And there were still matters to be discussed with Fletch and Ross about Pennsylvania.

At least, those were the excuses Tavish told himself. But he was honest enough to recognize the deeper reason: As much as it battered his heart, he simply couldn't tear himself from Isla until circumstances forced their separation. These would likely be the last few days he would ever spend in her company, and even though situations like playing chaperone pierced him to his core, the thought of not experiencing them hurt more.

Isla had always been a woman who sparkled like snow on a sunny day, blinding him to responsibility and wisdom. He had never had any sense of self-preservation when it came to her.

Ahead, Isla laughed at something Fletch said, and Fletch looked at her with adoration.

Tavish watched in misery.

He couldn't blame Fletch.

Isla was irresistible—a butterfly's wing, entrancing and urging a hunter in pursuit. The iridescent flash of her wit. The flutter of her laugh. The clever dance of her mind.

Letting out a slow breath, Tavish pretended to study the forest—a mix of poplar and larch trees with more exotic rhododendron bushes sprawling underneath. The lake glimmered through the branches, and the occasional break in the foliage offered stunning views of the surrounding mountains covered in purple heather in bloom.

Isla and Fletch continued their engrossing conversation.

She asked questions. He answered.

He pointed at something across the lake. She paused and stretched on tiptoe to see it.

She shook her head at something he said. Fletch laughed.

It was . . .

Tavish forced himself to breathe slowly—in and out, concentrating on the air moving through his lungs, the sound of his pulse in his ear. A technique he used right before a battle to settle his nerves.

It only marginally helped now.

The trio had just crossed a wee wooden bridge when a voice hailed them from the path ahead. A gamekeeper came into view, hurrying toward Fletch. Holding up a hand for Isla to stay, Fletch stepped off the path to confer with the man privately.

Tavish stopped beside Isla. She spared him a glance but said nothing.

They both watched Fletch and the man converse. The man spoke urgently, arms gesturing. Fletch put his hands on his hips, head bowed.

"Did . . . did that man just say something about poaching?" Isla murmured.

Tavish glanced around the forest. "It wouldn't surprise me. These estates cover vast tracts of land. It would be difficult to keep poachers out."

Fletch clasped the man's shoulder before walking back to Tavish and Isla, a frown denting his brow.

"I fear, my lady, that Mr. McCoy requires my assistance with an urgent matter. My father is away with Grayburn, so this small crisis falls to me."

"I hope all is well," Tavish said.

"Nothing I won't be able to sort, I am sure." He darted a look at Isla, indicating that he didn't wish to speak of it in front of a lady. "But I apologize that I must leave you both. Captain Balfour will see you back to the house, my lady."

"Oh!" Isla looked at Tavish with apprehension.

Fletch, naturally, misread her concern. "You will be safe in his hands, Lady Isla. Captain Balfour is the most honorable man I have ever known.

Upon my life." He pressed his hand to his chest, which Tavish thought was doing it a bit brown.

"I-I am sure." A blush flooded her cheeks.

"Thank you, Balfour." Fletch clasped Tavish's hand before striding off with the gamekeeper toward the house.

Isla and Tavish watched both men disappear around a bend. Birds chirped overhead, and wind rustled the trees. A lazy bee bobbed through.

"Well," Tavish said into the silence. "That did not turn out as I expected."

"What *did* you expect?"

He shrugged, shoving his hands into the pockets of his greatcoat before he did something stupid, like offer her his arm.

"The way ye two were cozying into one another, I figured I was going to have to pretend to examine a bush while ye indulged in a kiss or two."

If he thought Isla had been blushing before, it was nothing compared to the red that now scorched her face.

"Tavish!" she hissed.

He chuckled. "Am I Tavish now?"

She merely glared at him. "I am hardly so wanton as to kiss another man in front of my husband, no matter how estranged. I could feel your gaze drilling my shoulder blades. Please assume I have a modicum of sense and propriety."

"Oh?" Tavish tried to keep his voice light despite the jealousy gathering beneath his ribs. "So ye would wait until I absented myself? Or ye have yet to kiss another man besides me?"

Her eyes narrowed. "Such cruel words are unbecoming of you, Tavish Balfour. I will not remain here and be slandered thus. Good day."

With a toss of her head, Isla stomped down the path, away from him.

Shame washed Tavish from head to toe.

He hurried after her.

"Isla, please stop."

She took one more step. Then two, before whirling to face him, arms crossed over her chest.

"I'm sorry," Tavish said. "I didn't . . ." *Deep breath.* "Ye be right. That was cruel and unbecoming of me. This situation is . . . difficult. And seeing ye, it . . . it has stirred up the sediment of everything . . ."

She looked at him for a long moment before jerking her gaze to the landscape—the trees rustling and the clouds scudding overhead, growing thicker at the horizon.

Finally, she spoke. "Thank you for apologizing."

"It's the least a gentleman can do—acknowledge his mistakes and take ownership of them."

She continued to study the sky . . . then swallowed. "You wouldn't have been so quick to apologize. *Then* . . . I mean."

Her words caught him off guard.

"I was a bit arse-headed . . . *then*." He smiled, a faint thing. "That is the problem with youth—ye don't think through the consequences of actions as carefully as ye should."

She snorted. "That shall be the title of the memoir we eventually pen—*On Things Unpondered and Misunderstood*. I will begin with chapter one—'A Calamitous Marriage.'"

Tavish winced, letting out a harsh breath.

"Sorry. That was uncalled for, too." She waved a hand. "I was just as rash and impulsive as yourself. *Then*."

"And here I assumed it was my charming manner and handsome face that made ye throw caution to the wind and marry me."

She shook her head, a grin now teasing her own lips. "Pigheadedness and a desire for adventure, I should think."

But not love.

She didn't add that, but Tavish sensed the words anyway.

He mimed a dagger to his heart.

They stared at each other until he sensed that something had eased within her. Or perhaps within himself.

He gave an exaggerated survey of the path. "Well, ye now have another rash decision before ye, my lady. Would ye like to return to the house the way we came, which will see ye arrived shortly? Or . . ." Here, he lifted an eyebrow. A wee challenge. ". . . would ye like to continue your stroll around the lake with those menacing clouds lurking on the horizon there and my dubious person for company? I do come highly recommended, as Fletch stated. The most honorable of men."

He laced that last with a bit of irony, as they both knew there was nothing honorable in their current deception.

Isla followed his gaze, searching up and then down the path. As ever, Tavish could practically see the gears whirring in her brain, weighing the curiosity of speaking with him against her dread of Grayburn discovering her with a Balfour.

Past Tavish would have added something more. A "go on" or "trust me." Pushing her to be more unconventional, less fearful.

But the Tavish of now knew better.

This needed to be her decision alone.

Finally, she nodded and met his eyes with a faint smile.

With a toss of her chin, she pivoted and began walking down the path that led away from the house, the cant of her head indicating he should follow.

Back turned to him, Isla didn't see his wide grin or the happy lift in his chest.

Tavish rushed after her.

I sla's pace didn't falter as Tavish fell into step beside her.

But then, she mused, he had never been one to deliberate. Quick to action. That was Tavish Balfour.

She had decided to prolong their walk for one simple reason:

Isla wanted to know *this* man—the person her erstwhile husband had become. Perhaps the man he had always been, and she had simply been too young, too inexperienced, too . . . *something* to see it.

After studying him over the past several days—listening to his friends speak of him, watching him interact with others, and the ready admiration he inspired—a dreadful curiosity had lodged in her soul.

Yes, they were both still intent on divorce. But that didn't mean Isla couldn't learn more about the experiences that had formed his character these past seven years. If nothing else, she and he had once been friends. And she wanted to know more about her friend before he disappeared forever into the wilds of America.

They walked in silence for a few minutes. Like herself, Isla could practically feel Tavish churning with questions he evidently refused to ask.

"We were speaking of you," she said into the quiet.

"Pardon?"

"I suspect you wish to know what Colonel Archer and I were discussing. The answer, it turns out, is you."

"Ye were discussing me? Why?"

Isla spared him an amused glance. "Our Colonel Archer is quite sure you hang the moon. He admires you greatly."

She didn't miss Tavish's wince.

For her part, Isla couldn't help but compare the two men.

Yes, they were both handsome in their way. Colonel Archer with his ready smiles and kind eyes that glinted with good humor. Tavish with his rugged jaw and quiet, looming presence.

But in other ways, the difference was stark.

Colonel Archer was careful in his pursuit of her—flirtatious but cautious. He treated her like a prized orchid, something with a fussy temperament that had to be kept in a well-regulated glasshouse. A delicate creature.

Tavish, however . . .

In many ways, being around Tavish was like stepping into a forgotten room in her soul—a place of sunshine and security she had once reveled in dwelling. There, Isla was accepted precisely as she was, and perhaps more importantly, as she wished to be.

But outside that room, he felt like a stranger.

The paradox of him overwhelmed her. Known, yet unknown.

That terrible grief bucked again—sorrow and betrayal she thought long dead and buried alongside the girl she had been. Emotions she had supposed her time at Malton Hill had healed.

"What did Fletch have to say about me?" Tavish asked. "He exaggerates, I assure ye."

Isla shook her head. "You do realize that comments like that only confirm his high opinion, not lessen it?"

"Fletch has the incredible gift of seeing the best in people. He inspires fierce loyalty. It's what made him such a tremendous commanding officer in the army, and why he counts so many of us as his closest friends."

"Well, he spoke at length about your bravery."

"Ah."

"He told me . . . he told me of your heroism in *killing*—" She choked on the word. On the imagined scene of Tavish being tasked with taking others' lives, war or no. "—killing a French general. He described how you took the shot—half lying down as you did for that final shot yesterday. Well over three hundred yards distant with a stiff breeze blowing. An impossible shot, Colonel Archer declared. And yet, you downed the general with ease. And then reloaded, aimed, and fired again, killing the officer who ran to assist his fallen leader."

The most astonishing thing I've ever seen, Colonel Archer had said. *It's been four years, and it's still talked about in hushed reverence.*

Little did Colonel Archer understand how Isla would react to his storytelling. The horror of it. Of imagining *her* Tavish bearing the physical and moral responsibility of that act. The boy she knew would have grieved over taking another's life.

Tavish said nothing.

"You don't speak because I assume that scene still haunts you," she continued. "That, yes, you did what you must that day—and the thousand days before and after it—knowing that your actions saved more lives than the ones you took. But it didn't leave you unmarked."

They walked in silence, listening to the rustle of wind through the leaves and the call of starlings quarreling in the trees. The clouds continued to darken overhead. It would likely rain before luncheon.

Finally, Tavish cleared his throat. "Ye be correct, of course. Our actions as Rifles saved more lives than the ones we ended. But that doesn't mean the lives we took had no value. That French general had a wife and three daughters waiting for him at home. Four women who surely suffered greatly because of the general's loss. I learned of this later from a prisoner of war we took. There are no winners in war. Only horror and heartbreak."

Isla had to take several steadying breaths. Anything to tamp down the knot of *painangergrief* that filled her throat.

"I know they all see you as a hero. And they should. You are! But . . ."

He clasped his hands behind his back. "But?"

"I hate it," she whispered. "I hate that you had to become exception-ally good at killing others in order to survive."

Isla paused and looked up at him. Really looked.

His gray eyes held storms, thundering clouds and tumultuous winds. Pain and loss and the moments in between when he had to pretend the pain and loss had never happened. Had he relegated her and their rela-tionship to that same in-between place?

"I hate . . . I hate that it feels like I never knew you." Her hand closed into a fist, as if she could contain the sting of that truth. "I just knew some version of you. But not all of you. I didn't know that you could shoot a gun, much less that you were a crack shot. I didn't know you were quiet in company but always observant of others. I didn't *know*." Her voice broke. "And now I wonder how much else I didn't know. How deluded I was. How naive."

His hand lifted, as if he would cup her cheek or pull her against his chest. Because, as she knew, it wasn't in his nature to see her suffering and not offer comfort.

His hand hung there between them for a moment before dropping. As if he recalled just in time that offering her comfort was not something he was permitted to do anymore.

And that terrible grief swelled under her breastbone. How much lon-ger would she be able to keep it at bay? To see him and not . . . remember all that had been lost?

"Ye knew me, Isla. Ye knew me as no one else has, before or since. Ye may not have known the outward bits of me. Shooting a rifle, my abil-ities there, that is merely one of a thousand things that I *do*. But those skills are not who I *am*. They are not the heart of me—the soul ye knew and loved."

It hurt to look at him. To see her Tavish peeking out from his gaze. It surged upward—the disorienting feeling she had experienced in the lake just yesterday. Somehow, she inhabited two places at once—the devastat-ed girl who had lost her lover and all hope in one awful stroke, and the resilient, thriving woman who had risen from the ashes of that girl.

Without meaning to, her eyes dropped to his mouth, to those pillow lips that still surfaced in her dreams. Her pulse thumped when she dared to recall how they had felt pressed to her wrist. The soft give of them, followed by the gentle rasp of his night whiskers against her skin.

Just the memory caused a disturbing weakness in her knees.

Attraction hummed between them like a living thing. Like a band strung too taut, just waiting for that final bit of pressure to snap.

She lingered too long, staring, lost in memory.

Who knew what might have happened had Mother Nature not intervened.

A large wet raindrop splashed onto her nose.

Isla startled and looked to the heavens, only to receive three additional raindrops to the face for her trouble.

"Blast!" Tavish nodded to the lake, where a wall of rain rushed across the water toward them.

Whirling, Isla scanned the landscape for some sort of shelter.

"There!" She pointed toward an outcropping up the path, rocks overhanging a small hollow. Without thinking, she grabbed his hand and began running.

They reached the hollow just as the worst of the rain hit.

Dashing inside, they stood shoulder to shoulder, watching the rain cascade in sheets, dimpling the lake and shaking the leaves.

"Quick thinking. Spotting this." Tavish squeezed her hand in approbation.

At which point, Isla realized she was still holding it.

His hand, that was.

She dropped her grip as if scorched.

Out of the corner of her eye, she caught Tavish's grin. The wretch likely understood her every action.

The thought made her frown. And maybe huff a sigh.

"Am I so transparent to you?"

He laughed then. "Nae, lass. Not always."

She huffed again.

"Though I will admit," he continued, "sometimes reading ye feels as easy as a book."

Hearing him echo her own thoughts . . . a shiver traveled her spine.

She nudged him with her shoulder. It was meant to be a display of annoyance, but as he didn't move an inch, it only reinforced the hard solidity of his body.

He said nothing for a long while, both of them staring out from their small grotto as rain hammered the landscape.

"I feel it, too." His words so quiet, she almost didn't hear them. "The sense that there are wee bits of ye I never learned. Or perhaps never clearly saw. For example, I didn't know ye play the piano with such skill. I sat in awe listening to ye the other night."

Isla flushed at the compliment. "Yes. Pianos were rather in short supply atop Cairnfell, so I was never able to give you a proper demonstration."

"I imagine ye have other talents I have yet to see."

"We were so young. Am I so changed then?"

"No more than myself. But I remember that wild lass, standing atop the cairn, screaming her rage into the wind. The lass who bravely took my hand and stepped into the swimming hole that day. And I wonder . . . what happened to that lass? Or was I merely seeing what I wished?"

"Gray happened," Isla whispered around the sudden ache in her throat. "That's what befell that lass."

"He hurt ye?"

"Not physically. Never that. Just . . . my mind. My soul. He was angry and cutting. My life always balanced on a knife's edge." One of a thousand reasons why Isla had found such joy at Malton Hill. It was the one place Gray never intruded.

"A knife's edge," Tavish repeated slowly. "Ye mentioned his threats to cast ye out. Is that what ye refer to?"

Isla swallowed, refusing to let tears fall. She had already shed a lifetime of them over her parents' betrayals, over Gray and his changeable nature.

Rain continued to patter down, the world a soft hush. The heat from Tavish's large body saturated her left side. The scent of damp wool and his cologne—bergamot and sandalwood and an exotic spice she couldn't quite pin down—engulfed her senses. She was torn between gulping it in or breathing through her mouth to avoid it entirely.

But then that rather summed up how she felt about Tavish as a whole—did she want to run far and fast from him? Or grab hold of those broad shoulders and lose herself in his kiss?

Standing beside him now felt like times past. When he would take her hand and they would talk and everything else would simply . . . melt away.

How she had missed this. The ability to speak without worrying about what the other person might think or say.

"There is more . . ." she began.

Out of the corner of her eye, she watched Tavish lift an eyebrow. "More? To the situation with Gray?"

Isla nodded. "Given everything . . . and what is yet to come with our divorce . . . you should know all."

"All?"

She didn't speak for a moment, rallying her courage.

"Remember how Gray withdrew from me after my father died? Began treating me like my father had?"

"Aye. Ye were right upset. The pressing duties of the dukedom made him distant, ye thought."

"The dukedom had nothing to do with it, unfortunately." She swallowed before continuing, "On his deathbed, my father informed Gray that I was not his daughter."

Tavish hissed in a breath. "Pardon?!"

"Just that. My mother had refused to share my father's bed after Matthias's birth. She had borne him two sons, she said, both with deformities of the limbs. She refused to birth another. Eventually, she sought physical comfort elsewhere."

"With whom?"

"I don't know who my natural father might be. Gray may know, but he has never said. Obviously, he found the truth about our mother difficult to bear. I think he views her infidelity as the most craven betrayal, both of her marital vows and the dukedom. The horror that she would so cavalierly heap scandal on our heads. Gray's reasons scarcely matter, I suppose. The moment he learned the truth of our mother and my birth, I became an unwelcome millstone around his neck. A physical manifestation of scandal and betrayal. That night, when Gray found you and me together . . . he marched me home and, with cutting words, informed me of my illegitimate status."

Tavish's chin lifted on a sharp jerk.

"You thought you were marrying a duke's daughter, but in fact, you tied yourself to a cuckoo in the nest," she continued, unable to stem her bitterness.

"Ye ken well that your parentage, noble or otherwise, was never of concern to me."

She rallied, flattening her palms against her skirts. "Perhaps not. But *I* care. My father didn't denounce me as illegitimate at birth, mostly to protect the family reputation, Gray said. But—" Here, she paused, shoring up her defenses. "—but my father *did* leave a letter in Gray's keeping. A declaration in his own hand that I am not his daughter. He gave it to Gray in case my brother ever wished to divest himself of any obligation toward me."

"Oh, Isla," Tavish breathed. "Gray told ye that he would publish the letter unless you gave me up?"

"Yes."

"How could ye not have told me this?"

"I tried, Tavish! During that last conversation, but . . ." She fluttered a hand.

"I was too stubborn to listen."

Isla nodded, blinking rapidly.

"I'm so sorry, Isla. I should have realized. I should have—"

"Enough. We could both drown in the regret of our decisions then. But, in hindsight, we both know our marriage was a catastrophic mistake."

He let out a gust of air. His shoulder brushed against hers and unleashed a small riot in her midsection.

She shouldn't be standing beside him in this narrow space.

"Are you truly going to marry Fletch?"

Right.

There was that, too.

"Of course. If he'll have me. He will make a good husband." The words came out almost as a reflex.

She had scarcely given Colonel Archer a second thought since leaving his side.

Rather telling, that.

But what else could she do? She wanted to remain Lady Isla Kinsey, the legal daughter of the Duke of Grayburn. She wanted Malton Hill.

She loved the woman she became there—her confidence and sense of purpose, the people like Mrs. Tippets who relied upon her. She would not abandon them to an uncertain fate under Gray's indifferent care.

Tavish doesn't know about Malton Hill, Isla thought. *He doesn't know the person I became. The rebirth I experienced. He doesn't understand why I wish to marry someone—anyone, really—like Colonel Archer. Why retaining my dowry is so important.*

She liked Colonel Archer. More importantly, *Gray* liked Colonel Archer.

Ergo . . . she would marry him.

"But ye don't love him," Tavish grunted.

A statement. Not a question.

"How do you know that?" She pivoted to face him in the small hollow.

The rain had morphed from a raging tempest to a more docile drizzle. They would likely be on their way back to the house soon.

Tavish made no move to leave their secluded grotto. Instead, he mirrored her actions, turning toward her.

She had to look up and up to meet his gaze.

Gracious, but he was close. So close, the scant six inches of space between them arced with electricity.

"How do you know I don't love Colonel Archer?" she repeated.

"Because I know what ye look like when you're in love, lass. And this—" He waved a hand to indicate her entire person. "—this isn't it. Ye've decided ye want the life Fletch offers—a comfortable house, a fine carriage, expensive gowns, and servants to wait on ye—but the man himself is fairly irrelevant."

As ever, she found his rapier-sharp dissection of her thoughts unnerving.

"It is not wrong to shun a life of poverty."

"A life of poverty with myself, ye mean?"

"I didn't say that."

"What about love?"

"I cannot say what true love is. Not anymore. I thought I was in love once, but perhaps what you saw was more a form of obsession and mania than true love—emotions that end in pain rather than fulfillment. Perhaps the respect and quiet admiration I feel for Colonel Archer is more the genuine definition of enduring love."

"Is that what ye tell yourself?"

"Yes."

Deliberately . . . as if it were a test of some sort . . . he closed that remaining half-foot between them, bringing his chest flush with hers.

Isla's heart lurched to a gallop.

She could step back. The grotto was small, but not so confining that she couldn't move away from him.

She *should* step back.

It was only . . .

Her head tilted back of its own accord, taking in the new difference between them in height. Perhaps Tavish had always been this tall. Perhaps it was her own memories that had diminished him. Somehow, she had needed to shrink how much he had meant to her in order to accommodate his loss.

But now, he filled her vision. Literally larger than her dreams had ever painted him.

His hand found hers again, prying it from her side and gently lacing their fingers together.

It was a dare, she realized. Again, he was challenging her. Offering her choices. A different way of seeing and being.

Are ye sure it's Fletch ye want, lass? the press of his hand in hers said.

Slowly, so slowly, his head bent down. He hovered just above her mouth, the warmth of his breath skimming her skin . . . giving her all the time in the world to change her mind, to step back or tug her hand away. Anything, really, to interrupt the downward slide of gravity drawing his lips to hers.

Isla didn't so much as twitch.

She gasped when his mouth touched hers. The barest of brushes. A feather press of soft lips. Fleeting and gone too soon.

He lifted his head just enough to peer at her.

Tavish's eyes. Open and honest and desperately hungry. Wild eyes. A reflection of the terrified pounding of her heart.

"Isla . . ." he exhaled, those same eyes dropping again to her mouth. As if she undid him. As if within the two wee syllables of her name, he could find salvation.

His head bent again, and she raised to tiptoe. Eager. No . . . *desperate*. She had to know if reality matched her memories. If his kisses still burned like lava in her blood.

Their lips touched, faint as an owl's wing in moonlight—

Voices intruded.

Loud voices.

Male voices, calling and coming closer.

Isla and Tavish lurched apart as if jolted by lightning, shifting as far from one another as possible in the small space.

"Gray," Isla choked, recognizing the timbre of her brother's deep bass.

"Of all the bloody luck." Tavish met her gaze, and she watched him retreat—yearning icing over as sure as a pond in January.

Turning away, he walked into the rain.

TAVISH STEPPED FROM the hollow, his senses reeling from the feel of Isla pressed against him, his lips still tingling from the shadowed caress of hers.

She insisted she didn't want him. Not in any permanent sense.

But by all that was holy, he wanted her. Not just the physical charms of her person—though he decidedly wanted those, too—but the clever snap of her wit, the fierce tenacity of her mind.

He wanted the girl she had been and the woman she had become. He wanted a lifetime exploring every iteration of the person she would grow to be.

The longing felt too vast to accommodate. Like trying to wrap his arms around the sun and hold it tight. Surely, he would be scorched to dust.

Thankfully, the cool drizzle of rain cooled his ardor.

Tavish looked up the path, gravel glistening.

"Here they are, Grayburn." Fletch came into view, the duke on his heels.

Both men were soaked from the rain, caped greatcoats drenched and the brims of their top hats dripping.

Fletch waved, a broad smile on his face. Were he a puppy in truth, his tail would be wagging.

Grayburn scowled, limp pronounced, his brow as dark and ominous as the clouds overhead—more or less His Grace's permanent expression with any situation that involved a Balfour.

Tavish lifted a hand in greeting.

"Really, Grayburn," Fletch continued as they drew near. "How many times must I tell you? Despite the differences between your families, you can depend upon Balfour's honor as a gentleman."

The duke's glower turned thunderous. Tavish could practically see the man biting back a ranting tirade—enumerating Tavish's base behavior towards Isla in the past, His Grace's surety of a repetition of said behavior, and how he would enact retribution. However, propriety stilled Grayburn's tongue. His Grace couldn't disclose Tavish's past behavior without implicating his sister and damaging her reputation.

And so he clenched his jaw and seethed in silence.

Tavish was petty enough to revel in Grayburn's discomfort, particularly after Isla's revelations just minutes ago.

Fletch stopped in front of Tavish, peering around his shoulder to Isla still standing out of the rain. Grayburn walked past the two of them to his sister.

"Grayburn was convinced you were ravishing Lady Isla in the woods." Fletch gave an abbreviated eye roll, as if the very notion were absurd in the extreme.

Guilt wrapped around Tavish's ribcage and squeezed. Had the gentlemen taken another five minutes to arrive, he very well may have been ravishing Isla in the woods.

Bloody hell.

This was a debacle.

"I have assured His Grace in no uncertain terms that you are not that sort of gentleman." Fletch looked to where Grayburn was speaking quietly to Isla. "But he simply refuses to believe me."

Tavish experienced a surge of affection. Isla deserved a husband like Fletch—loyal and good. He would worship her until the day he died.

So would Tavish, for that matter, but probably with less reverence and more passion.

"The history between our families is deeply unpleasant, as well ye know," Tavish said. "I do not fault Grayburn for his concerns."

"Yet another reason why we all admire you so, Balfour. You spare kind words for your enemies. You always have."

Grayburn and Isla approached them, her hand threaded through her brother's elbow.

"The rain has cleared. Archer, would you be so kind as to accompany Lady Isla back to the house?" Grayburn extended Isla's hand toward Fletch. "I shall join you both momentarily. I merely wish a brief word with Captain Balfour."

The murderous look Grayburn gave Tavish didn't instill confidence that the brief word would be a pleasant one.

Fletch glanced at Tavish in concern, silently asking if he needed assistance. Tavish gave a faint shake of his head. Grayburn would bluster, but if it came to fisticuffs, Tavish knew he could hold his own.

Fletch and Isla had scarcely gone thirty feet before Grayburn whirled on Tavish.

"I don't know what game you are playing at here, Balfour, but you will not win."

Tavish couldn't stop a snort. "No game, Grayburn."

"Spare me your prevarication. Why else were you out in this forest alone with Lady Isla?"

"*Och*, I could scarcely leave your sister unaccompanied in the woods. As Fletch said, I am an honorable man, despite your lowering opinion."

"We both know that to be a lie. Your past actions have been anything but honorable in regards to my sister."

"Hah! Like your actions toward my own sister and brother?"

Grayburn reared back. "As I suspected, you are panting after Isla in some unwarranted bid for revenge. There isn't a thimbleful of honor between all you Balfours. Lady Isla is not for the likes of you. Do not think for one minute that you can sniff around her skirts, reclaim her affections, and receive one farthing of her dowry. I will see her cast out of our family first."

Deep, long-buried rage swelled Tavish's chest.

"Unlike yourself, Grayburn, I don't ruin gently-bred ladies for sport."

The duke went icily still. "What, precisely, are you accusing me of, Balfour? I have never—and would never—ruin a *lady*."

The implication being that Mariah was no lady.

Tavish pinched his lips to stem a tirade of anger.

When he trusted himself to speak, he returned to the topic at hand. "I have no designs upon Lady Isla's dowry or her familial connections, Grayburn. Upon my honor as a gentleman."

Upon her person, however . . . Tavish most definitely had aspirations there. *That* he would not deny. He wouldn't act upon those designs, but he held them.

Fortunately, Grayburn didn't notice the omission.

"A gentleman," the duke sneered. "What use is your word?"

Tavish gritted his teeth. "My honor is as valuable as your own, all things considered."

"You *dare* to besmirch my hon—"

"Enough, Grayburn." Tavish held up a palm. "Ye dislike me. Ye consider me a fortune-hunter and rakehell or worse. Ye wish me dead. But none of those opinions change the fundamental nature of who I am—"

"A libertine like your brother? Or a light-skirt like your sister?"

It was an unforgivable insult.

Anger charred Tavish's veins.

This bastard had ensured Mariah's disgrace and dragged Callum to his doom.

But the soldier in Tavish saw the tactic for what it was—Grayburn was baiting him. Challenging him to lash out. To strike. And then what? The duke would accuse Tavish of assault? Have him arrested?

Powerful men had certainly reacted more brutally with less justification.

Tavish wasn't a boy, quick to temper and imprudence. One didn't survive seven years of constant war without learning to keep a level head when provoked.

"Careful, Grayburn." Tavish leaned forward. "We both know the true reason ye say such things about Lady Mariah. Ye be jealous that it wasn't yourself to whom she offered her virtue."

It was a low strike, but given how Grayburn hissed and stepped back, Tavish knew his bullet had struck true. He had long suspected that Grayburn harbored a tendre for Mariah—the man expended far too much effort in church attempting *not* to look at her—and here was proof.

"No true gentleman would speak so crudely of a lady," Tavish continued, "and Lady Mariah *is* a lady, no matter your insinuation, to say nothing of your ruinous behavior toward her."

"Pardon?!" The duke's eyes flared in surprise. "Again, what are you accusing me of here, Balfour? You think *I* somehow orchestrated your sister's ruination?"

"Orchestrated? Encouraged? The end result was the same. Spare me your protestations of innocence, Grayburn. We both know that ye have treated my own sister with much greater disrespect than I have ever displayed toward your own. At least my past intentions toward your sister were always honorable."

"How dare you! I shall ensure that—"

"I've said my piece, Grayburn. Your threats are hollow. Fortunately, I do not require your approbation in order to live my life. Good day."

With that, Tavish pivoted and walked off toward the woods, away from Grayburn and Isla and Fletch.

Anything, really, to prevent himself from plowing his fist into the duke's smug face.

It took ten minutes of brisk walking to regain his temper.

Tavish needed to keep his distance from Lady Isla for the remainder of the house party. No good would come of them rekindling their physical attraction to one another, even if the phantom brush of her lips burned in his memory.

Aye, he loved her, but she had made her future goals clear. If he cared for her at all, he would respect her intentions and help her achieve them.

From now on, all he could be was a distant friend.

23

The kiss had been a mistake.

Isla knew it the moment she heard Gray's aristocratic voice coming up the path.

The following hours only proved her right.

She endured Gray's lecture on the evils of being caught alone with Tavish. Never mind that had she been snugged with Colonel Archer in a grotto in the woods, Gray wouldn't have said a word.

She wrote to Mr. Cranston and outlined her plan for assisting Mrs. Tippets and her children.

Over dinner, Isla smiled at Colonel Archer and talked with Lady Milmouth and watched Miss Crowley flirt relentlessly with Tavish.

All the while, reliving that life-ruining kiss.

It had been a horrific mistake, Isla decided, but not for the obvious logical reasons.

Because, in hindsight . . . it had scarcely even *been* a kiss. The faintest touch of lips. So light and quick, it was over before she had properly registered its occurrence. An indistinct caress, as hazy and vague as shadows drifting through mist.

In summation—the most dissatisfying kiss in the history of womankind.

It hadn't been enough of a kiss for objective comparison to Tavish's past kisses. It certainly hadn't been enough to resurrect his ghost, much less banish it forever. It most definitely hadn't quenched her curiosity or desire.

Quite the opposite, in fact.

Their brief kiss felt akin to the lingering coals of a fire. Just enough heat to set a fuse to smoking, but hardly sufficient to ignite a blaze.

And now that fuse of desire smoldered. It smoked and glowed and craved the final hot spark needed to burst into flame.

Isla knew she should smother that flicker of desire. Shut the metaphorical chimney flue and suffocate it entirely. No good would come of fanning the spark into a conflagration.

Worse, she kept replaying Tavish's tortured whisper of her name—

"Isla . . ."

In her mind, ellipses trailed off the end leading . . . where? What words had he intended to say at the end of those dots?

Maddening.

And even more maddening, she would likely never know.

Their week at Kingswell House ended in just three days. Tavish would continue his preparations for America and whatever he intended to do there. She would return to Dunmore with Gray and envision a life as Mrs. Archer of Malton Hill.

She would, perhaps, see Tavish once he had a hearing with the procurator fiscal, at which time she would tell Gray about her marriage. Isla and Tavish would likely have to appear before a judge . . .

. . . and that would be that.

Her marriage would dissolve, and Tavish would leave, never to cross her path again.

And that felt . . .

It felt . . .

The only word she could summon was *unbearable.*

Unendurable.

It would not do.

Isla struggled to swallow the thousand unanswered questions hovering on her tongue.

What were Tavish's plans in America? How, precisely, had he ended up in the 95th Rifles? What series of events had led to the scar on his cheek? Had he ever, as he charged into rifle fire or reloaded behind a barricade, thought of her and wished desperately for one more hour in her arms?

Had this past week—the weight of their glances, the brush of their hands, the barest press of their lips in the grotto—unmoored him as thoroughly as it had her?

Yet, despite these questions, she spoke not a word to him.

Malton Hill. That is your goal, she reminded herself. *Stay in Gray's good graces, retain your dowry and the lady you have fought to become.*

For his part, Tavish mirrored her actions. He didn't speak to her directly and rarely even looked her way. Heaven knew what Gray had threatened.

But Tavish was clearly just as aware of her as Isla was of him.

The morning after their kiss-that-was-scarcely-a-kiss, the company congregated in the breakfast room. Gray had yet to make an appearance, thank goodness, improving Isla's mood. Miss Crowley insisted Tavish sit between her and Isla, placing Tavish on Isla's left side.

Across the table, Miss Forsyth kept up a steady barrage of impertinent questions regarding Gray.

"Do you think he intends to marry soon?"

"I cannot say." Isla stirred her tea.

"Have you noticed him favoring a specific young lady?"

"My brother is the soul of discretion, Miss Forsyth. He would never raise expectations."

The girl was relentless. The longer her interrogation went on, the more frustration built in Isla's chest. She didn't want to discuss her brother, but neither did she wish to give Miss Forsyth a stern set-down. Such was not Isla's way.

"But if His Grace *were* to show partiality toward a young lady, what would he do or say?" Miss Forsyth asked.

Before Isla could respond, she felt a warm weight pressing into her thigh under the table—Tavish's leg resting against her own, steady and supporting.

I'm here, it said. *I see ye.*

It was a shocking breach of etiquette but one unseen underneath the tablecloth.

Isla sipped her tea, steadying her breathing and willing her blush away. She dared a peek at Tavish from beneath her lashes.

His lips were slightly pinched, as if suppressing a grin. As if he found this situation rather absurd.

Abruptly, she found herself fighting a smile of her own. Miss Forsyth's increasingly brazen questions about Gray *were* ridiculous, now that Isla considered them in that light.

"A gentleman will always keep his feelings close, Miss Forsyth," Tavish said, drawing the girl's attention. "It is to Lady Isla's credit that she does not break her brother's confidence. Miss Crowley has suggested boating on the lake today. What say ye?"

The conversation shifted after that, but Tavish kept his leg pressed to hers. Isla was sure he meant it as a silent bolstering, but the touch abraded her already frayed nerves.

The next day, Isla lost one of her gloves while on a walk. It was a favorite glove, and she and the ladies spent the better part of an hour retracing their steps in search of it, but to no avail. They told their woes to the gentlemen over lunch, who made suitable noises of sympathy. Tavish didn't say a word.

But lo, when Isla went to retire that night, there was her glove—muddy and a bit worse for wear—waiting on her dressing table.

She found a note inside, written in their code.

Because I ken how much ye detest cold hands.

The dear man.

How was she to manage the pang beneath her breastbone? With each kindness, each act of caring, a bit more of her succumbed to him. She may not know the man Tavish had become, but the soul of him, as he said, was the same.

But how she longed to know the man, too. To relearn the crags and valleys of his heart. To bask in the warmth of his deep baritone and simply listen. She would see him smiling with Miss Crowley or offering to assist Lady Milmouth or sharing a memory with Captain Ross . . . and that pang would intensify. A craving to claim Tavish as her own once more.

It was the purest madness.

On the final day of the house party, Isla could scarcely think.

She felt as if she walked the cliff's edge of Cairnfell itself. A thin line where one wrong step could send her tumbling into catastrophe.

She and Tavish had leapt from that cliff's edge once and had both paid a heavy price.

Remember Malton Hill became her almost hourly chant.

It was the only thing that saved her sanity—pondering her community and work there. The one that marriage to Colonel Archer could give her.

The colonel had hinted on two separate occasions that he wished to speak with her. Alone.

Isla had pretended to misunderstand his meaning both times.

If he proposed, and if Isla said yes, Lady Milmouth would insist upon an impromptu celebration. Isla couldn't bear forcing her current husband to celebrate her impending nuptials to another man.

The final evening drew to a close, and they all said brief goodbyes in the drawing room, promising to see one another in the morning before departure.

Tavish had slipped from the room unnoticed an hour before.

There would be no goodbye between them.

A dreadful weight lodged in Isla's stomach as she made her way upstairs.

Gray rapped on her chamber door just before she climbed into bed.

"Archer has requested a private audience with you before we depart tomorrow," her brother said without preamble.

Though entirely expected, the announcement landed with the clang of a prison door.

Isla could scarcely say why.

Colonel Archer represented the future she wanted—Malton Hill and her stewardship of its lands and people. She had known this was coming. And the timing was excellent, as she sensed Tavish would be gone before sunrise.

Gone.

Just conjuring the word caused her grief to ripple.

"Of course," she said through lips gone numb.

She would have to tell the colonel of her marriage before accepting him. Honor demanded no less. The hour of reckoning bore down on her like a runaway carriage.

"Excellent. I will inform Archer that he may have an audience after breakfast. I had planned to leave before luncheon, but perhaps we should consider extending our stay for a day or two. Permit you and Archer to celebrate and plan your life together."

"Of course," she repeated on a nod.

"Good night, Sister. Sleep well."

Gray closed the door behind him. The warning in his tone hung in the air. *Sleep soundly and stay put* was his unspoken demand.

Isla crawled into bed and snuffed her candle. The bed canopy loomed overhead.

She thought of Malton Hill and the woman she was there—strong, independent, flourishing. She could easily imagine her steward, Mr. Cranston, pushing his spectacles up his nose as they discussed wool yields and plans for refurbishing tenant cottages along the river. Or hear the rattle of her châtelaine as she counted silver with the housekeeper and went over the household accounts.

How she wanted that life!

Seven years ago, Tavish had nothing to recommend him. That hadn't changed. He was still penniless without any clear prospects. A future with him remained shrouded in want and uncertainty. Assuming Tavish even wished for a life with her, of course.

And yet . . . the thought of leaving him without even saying a proper goodbye, without a private discussion that offered her a modicum of closure . . .

No note magically appeared under her door.

She did not pen one of her own.

Nothing occurred to spur her to action.

But that bit of fuse continued to smolder. To crave and yearn.

She tossed and turned. Events of the past week played over and over in her mind.

The flash of Tavish's rifle.

Gone.

The clutch of his palm at her waist in the water.

"*Isla . . .*"

The faint, feather-touch of his lips.

She wanted to wrench open the shutters, toss up the sash, and scream into the summer night.

Argh!

She drummed her feet against the mattress, instead.

This simply wouldn't do.

With an exasperated huff, she tossed off the counterpane and drew on her dressing gown. Slipping out her door, she glided on bare feet down the hall and up the stairs.

The vacant bedroom beside Tavish's was just as quiet as it had been the first night of the house party.

This was as near to him as she dared come. To sit in the room beside his—a wall firmly between them—and whisper her goodbyes.

It would have to be enough.

She closed the door behind her with a soft *snick*.

Directly opposite the door, the window stood with shutters open, light from the full moon flooding the room.

A four-poster bed rested to the left, curtains tied back and counterpane neatly pressed. It was a sizable piece of furniture—thick, rectangular bedposts supporting a heavy wooden canopy. The sort of furniture at home during the reign of the Stewarts.

To the right sat a marble fireplace with a clock ticking the hour on the mantelpiece. A painting hung on the wall above—the wall that separated Tavish's bedroom from this one.

Was he lying in bed there, thinking of her? Wishing for a few last words, but unwilling to risk it?

As she stepped farther into the room, the ghostly shadow of her reflection flickered in a mirror to the right of the window. Her eyes appeared huge, wide and apprehensive. A glance out the window revealed the kitchen garden and the lake in the distance, bathed in moonlight.

She felt him even before he turned the door handle.

Staring into the mirror, she watched Tavish close the door and lean against it. An echo of her position that first night of the house party, when his note had summoned her here.

Ah.

So he had been lying awake, too.

Slowly, she turned around.

The sight of him clubbed her senses.

Tall and broad, of course. That same cleft in his chin. The same pillow lips. The same eyes gleaming in the low light.

But tonight, his auburn hair was tousled, as if he had been tugging at it. His clothing was in a similar state of disarray. He wore only breeches, braces loose and dangling to his knees, and a shirt—tucked but unbuttoned and sagging open to mid-chest. Like herself, he was barefoot. Even in the low light, she could see the column of his throat and the line where his neckcloth always sat, separating the tan of his neck from the lighter skin below.

That bit of bare chest rendered her light-headed. As did the shadowy muscles moving underneath when he took three steps forward, halving the space between them.

She had seen his bare chest before. Of course, she had. When they swam in the eddying pool or lounged about on the grassy bank, drying afterward. But that had been the chest of a boy. This . . .

Her eyes drank him in. How had she thought herself prepared to face him? The whole week had been a slow seduction. Not on his part, but her own.

She had seduced herself.

And now, her only thought was for that too-faint kiss. The smoldering fuse yearning for the tiniest spark to erupt into flames.

Isla took two steps toward him before stopping herself.

The sound of her own breaths echoed in the room—too fast, too urgent.

"Isla."

She closed her eyes at the sound of her name. Gravelly and winded.

As if he, too, were seconds away from coming undone.

"Ye shouldn't be here, lass. Nothing good will come of this. This is our goodbye."

"I know."

"Fletch intends to propose to ye tomorrow. Ye should go back to bed."

"I know."

And yet, her feet remained rooted in place.

"We won't see each other again." She could hear the pleading in her voice. "Not alone. Not like this."

"Nae. We both ken it ends here. It ends now."

She nodded.

"Ye don't want me, ye said," he continued. "Not me nor the life I offer."

Malton Hill rose in her mind, mist lifting over the fields into the gold of sunrise, sheep lowing in the distance. The scritch of her quill as she met with tenants to collect rents and discuss their concerns. Mrs. Tippets with her arms around her fatherless children, eyes brimming with thanks.

"I don't." The words sounded like heartbreak to her ears.

"Well." He looked away from her. "There ye are, then."

She stared at his profile, willing him to close the distance between them. To do something to ease the weight of their memories, their longing, the pang that—

"Goodbye, Isla. I wish ye every happiness."

He spared her one final glance before dipping his head and turning for the door.

"Tavish . . ." She gasped his name, just as he had hers in the grotto.

He pivoted back to her.

Suddenly, she knew what came after those ellipses.

Tavish . . . I can't seem to stop wanting you.

Tavish . . . what are we to do?

He stood so very still, as if her thoughts diffused through the room, and he strained to hear them.

Isla would have thought him unmoved except for the flexing of his right hand, as if he fought the urge to reach for her.

And yet, he did nothing.

Merely waited.

Isla willed him to act. Any movement that would justify a response from her.

He lifted an eyebrow.

Do ye want something? that eyebrow said. *If so, ye will need to claim it yourself.*

A challenge.

Of course.

"Damn you," she hissed.

It marked the first time in her life she had uttered such words aloud.

His lips twitched at her cursing.

There's my lass, his gaze said. *The woman who exists for me alone. The one who would say, "to hell with heaven and earth," just to have me.*

She would never curse in front of Colonel Archer. Only Tavish saw this uncensored side of her.

And he knew it.

His eyes glittered, sparking in the dim light—the final burst of heat needed for combustion.

Two steps and Isla was flush against that potent chest.

Her fingers threaded into the thatch of his hair, mercilessly pulling his head down to hers.

The touch of his mouth landed like a torch to dry heather.

Flames engulfed them both.

Isla moaned.

His large hands whipped around her waist, pulling her hard against him, a groan rumbling his chest.

Isla whimpered in return.

This was no tentative brush of a kiss.

No. It was a branding. A claiming.

Once, at Malton Hill, Isla and Matthias had witnessed engineers blasting through a hill to create an offshoot of the Kennet and Avon Canal. Though they were nearly a quarter-mile distant, the ensuing roar of sound had vibrated her breastbone and shuddered the earth.

Isla felt like that detonation of gunpowder—her balance jolted and smoke billowing from her skin to touch the sky. The explosion obliterated every thought but Tavish and the delirious pleasure of threading her fingers into his hair.

Angling his head between her palms, she feasted on his lips—sucking first the top, then the bottom into her mouth—teeth clicking in eagerness.

He growled his approval.

An arm braced under her buttocks, he lifted her backward not once breaking their kiss. Her spine encountered the bedpost, her feet barely touching the ground.

Bent over her, he devoured.

Like she was bread after weeks—no, years!—of hunger.

Like she was salvation and damnation all in one.

His lips moved from her mouth to her throat, then lowered to graze her collarbones before returning to her mouth and starting anew.

His hands were everywhere, slipping inside her dressing gown to clutch fistfuls of her chemise.

She felt fevered. Frenzied, even.

Seven years!

Seven long years she had hungered and yearned for this passion. This claiming.

This inferno of desire she had only ever felt with him.

TAVISH WAS A man possessed.

He had intended to leave, to walk away before either of them did something regrettable. Kissing Isla that day on the path, no matter how brief, had been a colossal mistake.

Because it had taken up residence in his brain, that fleeting taste of her.

He felt akin to a former drunkard receiving a thimble of gin. Just enough to inflame the craving for another swallow but not nearly enough to quench it. And now, Tavish had dunked his head in the stuff, and he couldn't drink fast enough.

But like a drunkard with gin, he feared no amount of Isla would satisfy him. He would need a lifetime, a hundred lifetimes, of just this—of touching, of tasting, of devouring her.

The sound of her choking gasp when his tongue found that sensitive spot where her neck met her shoulder.

The curving arch of her spine that pushed her soft bosom to his chest.

The taste of her mouth, the honey and peppermint of her tooth powder.

Slow down. Ye need to slow down.

He knew this. He did.

If they continued, they would end up naked on the bed at her back.

He tried to hold onto the thread of that logic, willing it to douse the wildfire consuming them both.

But all his brain could summon was the devotion in her eyes as she gazed at him over the ribbon of their handfasting. And the seven years of lonely nights and aching want for his wife between that moment and this.

Her lips on his skin had never felt more vital.

That she matched him—kiss for kiss, touch for touch—only fanned the flames.

She *did* want him, no matter what she said.

Her teeth nipped his throat, drawing a deep hum of approval from his lungs.

She skimmed her hand inside the open collar of his shirt, laving a kiss to his sternum, before tugging at the cotton fabric, wanting it free. He helped her, pulling his shirttails from his breeches. And then her palms were underneath, skimming across his bare skin, moving from his spine to his stomach and back again.

It was . . .

Words failed.

Her body felt pliant as putty and just as yielding. He couldn't pull her close enough, couldn't kiss enough of her.

He was crazed, dizzy on need and want and the love pounding in his veins.

Later, he couldn't say what broke through the lust-filled haze of his thoughts.

Some deeply ingrained instinct that had seen him survive the horrors of war, year after year. The same instinct that told him when and how to direct a bullet to his chosen target.

An infinitesimal sound. A shift in the air. Something.

A silent warning shouted at Tavish to duck.

Just as the Duke of Grayburn's fist sailed through the space that his head had occupied.

24

Tavish staggered sideways, whirling to a crouch. Every sense alert, cataloging the danger.

His heart was a kettle drum against his ribs.

Grayburn filled his vision—a silk banyan thrown over shirtsleeves and trousers—mouth twisted in rage.

"Damned mongrel curr!" the duke snarled, lunging for Tavish. The abrupt motion sent both the man's mule slippers flying, pitching Grayburn forward.

Isla screamed.

Tavish dodged again, pivoting as Grayburn stumbled and fought to regain his balance, roaring obscenities.

"Gray! Stop!" Isla sobbed, drawing her own dressing gown around her body.

Tavish darted to place himself between his wife and her brother. As ever, instinctively protecting her.

Grayburn bellowed, taking three uneven steps before having his elbows seized by Ross and Fletch, who Tavish finally noticed were in the room as well.

"You miserable. Scheming! BASTARD!" Grayburn raged, pulling against the hands that held him. "I will see you hanged for this! I will destroy you! How DARE YOU TOUCH HER!"

Isla was weeping at Tavish's back, deep hiccupping sobs.

Chest heaving, Tavish's military training snicked into place. He assessed the room with clinical precision.

Someone had placed a large candelabra on a chest beside the open door.

Grayburn continued to pull against the other men's hold, the maroon of his banyan matching the red of his face. He was barefoot, his slippers discarded. Tonight marked the only time Tavish had ever seen the duke without shoes, making the lacking two-inches of his right leg glaringly apparent in the slope of his shoulders.

Holding Grayburn's right arm, Ross looked at Tavish with understanding and pity.

But it was Fletch, grasping Grayburn's left arm, who held Tavish's attention.

His friend appeared shattered—the very image of heartbreak. Good, kind Fletch who had saved Tavish from enemy fire at the Battle of Badajoz. The man who had rallied Tavish's spirits and championed him at every step and never once wavered in his loyalty.

Grayburn shrugged free, straightening his banyan with brisk movements, his face shuttering in the candlelight. The duke's icy facade had been restored. Limping, he rammed his feet back into his slippers, the thick sole of the right mule instantly correcting his gait.

He turned back to Tavish with a sneer. "I would challenge you to a duel, Balfour, but your carcass isn't worthy of the honor of me filling it with lead."

Tavish only half-heard Grayburn's threats. The man's rancor was an ancient thing, well-worn and expected.

But Fletch's devastation . . . his look of bewilderment and confusion. Like the entire world had turned upside down, and he couldn't make sense of reality.

"I don't understand." Fletch shook his head. "Ross and I caught Grayburn coming out of Lady Isla's room. She had vanished, and His Grace was convinced that she was with you, Balfour. Which . . . I assumed to be laughable. Ross and I followed His Grace to your room, certain we would find you there, fast asleep. Because . . . I know you. You would never—"

"He's a dishonorable bastard, Archer," Grayburn spat. "I've been telling you this in no uncertain terms all week. This isn't the first time Balfour has been sniffing about my sister."

"No . . . b-but . . . I don't . . ." Fletch stared at Tavish. "I don't understand, Balfour. In all the years I've known you, I've never seen you *touch* a woman. You've never even looked longingly at a lady, no matter how comely. You are as celibate as a monk!" His voice picked up steam. "You told Ross and me that you were married! Married! That you would honor your vows to your wife! And now you do this?!" He pointed toward Isla. "Seduce the woman you know I am courting? Have you gone mad?!"

Tavish was watching Grayburn as Fletch spoke. The word *married* struck the duke as true as an enemy barrage. His Grace took a staggering step backward, his wide and horrified gaze dropping to his sister.

It was easily the most raw emotion Tavish had ever seen the man display.

I suppose he is human after all, some part of Tavish mused.

"*Isla!*" Her name emerged from Grayburn's lips as half curse, half horror.

Fletch looked to Grayburn and then back to Tavish, his expression confused . . . before the truth dawned. His jaw went slack.

"Ye are correct, Fletch. I will *always* honor my marriage vows. That has not changed." Tavish took in a slow breath, his head helplessly tilting to Isla hiding behind him. "However, there is no dishonor in a man kissing his wife."

Grayburn continued to stand frighteningly still. As if he had just been dealt a mortal wound and, though his intellect knew himself done for, his body had yet to crumple. His gaze darted from Isla to Tavish and then back again.

Fletch shook his head, equally as stunned. "You're married . . . to Lady Isla?"

Tavish nodded.

"How long?" Fletch asked.

"Seven years."

Grayburn's nostrils flared.

Fletch winced. "I kissed her." He pointed to Isla. "She let me kiss her, even knowing that she was . . ."

He trailed off.

Tavish briefly closed his eyes, the sting of Fletch's words biting deep. Isla sobbed anew.

"At least you were more loyal to her than she was to you," Fletch continued, voice hurt and baffled.

Grayburn had gone from red-faced to white-lipped.

Isla touched Tavish's sleeve, her chest hiccupping.

"*G-Gray?*" she gasped around his arm.

Tavish hated the pleading in her tone. The fear and worry.

Without a word, Grayburn pivoted and left the room, the silk of his banyan flaring behind him.

"Gray! No! Wait!" Isla called, dashing after him.

"Isla!" Tavish reached for her.

Why? He didn't know. Only that Grayburn was in a towering fury and would not be kind to her gentle heart. And Tavish, more than anything, wanted to spare her more pain.

She pushed out of his grip and raced after her brother.

Tavish took one step to follow, only to be stopped by Fletch's fist punching with brutal force. Pain exploded in Tavish's cheek. He staggered sideways from the blow and looked back at his friend.

Fletch stood shaking out his hand.

"That was for not telling me!" he raged. "I deserved to know! You owed me that much, Balfour!"

"I should have told ye," Tavish nodded, wiping away blood from his nose. "Not that it's an excuse, but Isla begged me not to. She wanted to control how and when ye learned. I think she intended to tell ye this morning, when ye proposed."

"Your wife, you mean?! When I proposed marriage to your *wife*!" Fletch was pacing now.

"Aye. My wife."

A flurry of footsteps sounded in the hallway. Lord Milmouth appeared in a nightshirt and cap, a banyan loosely drawn around his shoulders and a candle held aloft. The ladies crowded behind him, standing on tiptoe, eyes wide.

His lordship's gaze flicked between his son still shaking his hand and Tavish dripping blood.

"I say," his lordship rumbled, "what the blazes is going on? Lady Isla in hysterics and Grayburn in a thunderous fury? And now this?"

Tavish looked at his two friends. Somehow, despite everything, they still understood each other. Fletch jerked his chin toward the door, turning to stare out the window.

"Later, my lord." Ross politely, but firmly, shut the door in their faces.

"But what happened?!" Tavish heard Miss Crowley say, a bit too loudly. "Why is Captain Balfour bleeding?"

Ross handed Tavish a handkerchief, which he took with murmured thanks. His eye would be properly black and blue by tomorrow. He could already feel it pulsing.

"You knew!" Fletch pointed an accusing finger at Ross.

Ross held up his hands, palms out. "I put the clues together a few days ago, Fletch. I haven't known long. Balfour requested that Lady Isla be the one to tell ye. I wasn't going to betray the lady like that."

Fletch growled and returned to his pacing.

"I've hurt my hand," he muttered, flexing his fingers. "Damn you and your hard head, Balfour. You won't even permit a fellow the pleasure of punching you properly."

Tavish watched Fletch as he crossed from the fireplace to the window and back again.

"I still intend to divorce her, Fletch."

"After that panting display?!"

"She doesn't want me."

Fletch laughed. A caustic burst of sound. "If that kiss wasn't the very definition of wanting, then I haven't the foggiest notion of what the hell wanting is! She certainly didn't kiss me like that."

Tavish flinched, but soldiered on. "I have nothing to offer her, Fletch, as well ye know. I'm no better than a pauper. That hasn't changed."

Fletch continued in his pacing.

"Well, at least I know now you're human," his friend muttered. "I had wondered at times."

Tavish dabbed at his nose. "Far too human."

Human enough to feel the reverberating cracks of the evening's events.

He was well and truly wrecked . . . in every sense of the word.

Finally, Fletch stopped and faced him. The man's expression hardened, moving from that of a friend to the fierce colonel the French army had feared.

"I think you and Ross should leave at first light." Fletch crossed to the door. "After the events of tonight . . . I need some space to ponder my next steps and whether my future will include either of you at all."

He exited with a loud *clack*.

ISLA POUNDED ON Gray's bedroom door.

"Gray! Speak with me!"

She had flown down the hallway after her brother, nearly colliding with Lord Milmouth and the rest of the guests coming upstairs. Apologizing, she had pushed past them, trying to catch Gray. He was limping badly, a sure sign of his wrath.

He had slammed into his room and locked the door before she could reach him.

"Gray!" she called.

She needed to speak with him. To explain what had happened before he made a rash decision.

Of all the ways for him to learn of her marriage . . .

Lungs hiccupping, she leaned her forehead against the cold wood. The tears continued to fall.

What was she to do? She refused to abandon Malton Hill and her community.

How could she have behaved so stupidly? Clearly, seven years of regret had taught her nothing. The first chance she got, she had thrown herself into Tavish Balfour's arms, greedily feasting on his kisses.

That deep grief welled upward at the mere thought of Tavish and everything they had once been. Everything she had lost and forgotten.

As a girl, she remembered hearing of a ghastly flood that had destroyed a Swiss village. Part of the mountain above the town collapsed into a nearby lake, sending a towering wall of water crashing into the village and burying it under hundreds of feet of debris.

If loosed, she feared her grief would swallow her in a similar fashion, burying her so deep, she would be lost forever.

Her chest spasmed, breath coming in stuttering gasps.

No!

Through sheer willpower, she pushed the tide of emotion back down.

She would think about Tavish later . . . about those few transcendent minutes in his arms and the implication of Colonel Archer's words to him—*I've never seen you touch a woman . . . celibate as a monk! . . . she let me kiss her, even knowing . . .*

A trembling, anxious energy seized her limbs, crushing her ribcage and shaking her shoulders. Her breathing stuttered, and the world went dark at the edges.

Pressing a hand to Gray's door, Isla forced air in and out of her lungs, anything to stem the attack of panicking terror.

A few minutes later, she heard the other guests retreating downstairs.

She couldn't endure Miss Crowley's questions or Lord Milmouth's reproachful face.

Swiping at her tears, she silently willed Gray to open his door one last time before retreating to her own bedchamber.

FIVE HOURS LATER, as the first light of dawn washed the sky, Isla waited downstairs in the entrance hall, her trunk packed.

She knew her brother.

He would depart at first light with minimal leave-taking. Anything to avoid witnessing the stench of her scandal being paraded before others.

And, for once, she was unsure if Gray would permit her to accompany him.

Slowly, the sun crested the horizon, washing the world in golden sunlight. Her eyes were scratchy and surely red-rimmed but dry. Unlike the last time her world crumbled, she would not tumble into melancholy and listlessness.

No. This time, she had Malton Hill and a reason to fight.

She had to try to make things right with Gray, to at least attempt a reconciliation. Anything, really, to convince him of the necessity of his help in ending her marriage.

As she expected, the ducal carriage rolled around from the stables and stopped before the front stairs.

There was no sign of Gray, but Isla brooked no chances. She ordered her trunk strapped to the back of the carriage and then accepted the hand of a footman who assisted her inside.

Her behavior was a blatant challenge, and well she knew it. But as Gray hadn't ordered the servants to refuse her . . .

If Gray intended to cast her out, he would have to do it publicly in front of Lord and Lady Milmouth. And Isla was betting her brother was too scandal-averse to make such a scene.

As a peace offering, she sat with her back to the horses. Typically, a gentleman would take the rear-facing seat, ceding the preferred forward-facing side of a conveyance to a lady. But Gray suffered from nausea after traveling too long, particularly when sitting against the flow of motion.

A typical carriage ride would end with Gray slowly turning an alarming shade of green until Isla forced him to sit beside her.

Today, she surrendered her seat in a show of humility.

Gray arrived a short while later, walking stick in hand and gait still uneven . . . which did not bode well for their conversation.

He scarcely glanced at her as he took his seat and rapped the ceiling, indicating the coachman should spring the horses.

Carriage in motion, Gray stared out the window, one hand resting atop his walking stick, his gloved fingers opening and closing around its brass top. With an irritated toss of his head, he tugged off his top hat, setting it on the seat beside him. A few minutes later, his gloves followed, landing inside his hat. He ran a hand through his hair, standing the tawny strands on end before turning back to the window.

Yes. Gray was incandescent with rage.

Usually, he could resist his fidgeting and loathing of confining clothing.

Not today, however.

Isla said nothing until they crossed the gate marking the entrance to Kingswell House.

"Captain Balfour and I intend to divorce." Isla kept her tone even and factual. "He has already made inquiries into the matter."

Gray flexed his fingers, jaw tensing. The only indication he had heard her.

"I still intend to marry a gentleman who meets with your approval," she continued. "Perhaps . . . perhaps even Colonel Archer, if he will still have me."

That got her brother's attention.

Ever so slowly, his head rotated toward her, the gold flecks in his hazel eyes flashing fire.

"Before last night, I had considered you to be a lady of some sense, Isla Kinsey. But now?" He laughed, an acidic sound.

Isla recoiled as if scalded.

Gray leaned forward. "What gentleman of reputation, pray tell, would marry a divorced, scandalous woman?" A slice of his head. "None. Not. One. You are naive in the extreme if you think Milmouth or Archer will even associate with you after this, much less consider allying themselves with your reputation."

"Perhaps, but—"

"But NOTHING!" Gray roared.

Isla recoiled. This was the Gray of that dreadful night long ago, the last time he caught her kissing Tavish Balfour. The Gray she hadn't seen since, but lived in fear of. The one who looked like her brother, but was anything but brotherly.

"You idiotic, stupid slattern of a woman! You will drag us all into your disgrace!" he continued, eyes blazing. "And I had thought our light-skirt of a mother to be beyond the pale! At least Father managed to keep that quiet."

A terrible trembling started in Isla's legs.

"Once word of this gets out, not one gentleman will have you, Isla. Not. One! You are as good as dead to Polite Society!"

Isla's natural instinct was to retreat, to cower before Gray's fury.

But she was no longer that terrified girl.

The woman she had become at Malton Hill reared up within her. The one who had stood up to angry tenants thinking they could run roughshod over their young landlord. The one who had argued for better work conditions for the poor house and a school for the village children. The woman who, just this week, had hatched a plan to save a young widow and her children from penury.

"I'm married, Gray! To the son of an Earl of the Realm. You may hate Lord Northcairn and his children, but that doesn't diminish the fact that they are members of the Peerage. It's not as if Tavish and I have carried on in sin! There has been no sinning at all!"

"That kiss was the very *definition* of sin!" Gray let out a shout of laughter. "It appeared akin to how a sailor falls upon a harlot after too long at sea. The sort of kiss a man bestows right before he tups a woman senseless against an alleyway wall. Or a bedpost, in your case."

A dreadful blush scorched Isla's cheeks, her ears burning from his crude language. Frustration and anger and helplessness mounted in her chest, that trembling spreading from her legs to her abdomen to her hands.

Tears clogged her throat. Why, why, WHY as a woman must emotion coalesce in tears? Why couldn't she scream her rage and pound her fists in fury like a man?!

Instead, she bit the inside of her lower lip, willing back the sting in her eyes. Anything to stop the rising flood. Were it to overtake her, she wasn't sure she would survive.

She stared at her brother, praying, hoping she could unearth some vestige of the kind heart she knew he had once possessed.

"Piers," she said, his given name emerging on a tremor.

The name she hadn't used since he assumed the dukedom.

The name he wore when last he loved her.

He recoiled. Not much, but enough for Isla to see his Christian name had landed with a *thwack*.

"Please. You once loved me. You once cared about me and about my happiness—" Her voice cracked. A single tear broke loose, splashing on her cheek. "I need your help, Piers. I made a terrible mistake, one I have regretted for years. Please."

Gray made a dismissive noise, giving her his profile. "Marry in haste, repent at leisure . . . isn't that how the saying goes?"

Another tear fell.

"Piers, I know that my reputation is potentially damaged. Long ago, you, Matt, and I promised to be one another's support. To never turn our backs on one another. I have tried to be that for you. I have been your hostess during the Season and tended your household. But now, I need your help in return. If anyone could find a way out of this debacle without the news of my divorce landing in the gossip rags—without it becoming public knowledge—it would be you. Please."

She wasn't above begging for her future. For the woman she wished to be.

"That kiss was not one of regret, Isla." Gray still didn't look at her. "That kiss was a homecoming, not a departure."

"And what if it was?!" She threw up her hands, crying in earnest now. "It doesn't matter. I want Malton Hill and her people. I don't want a future with Tavish Balfour!"

"Poverty, you mean. You don't want a future of *poverty*. The man, however . . . I think you would happily take him if you could have your dowry, too . . . which will never happen as long as my heart continues to beat."

Isla struggled to draw air. The trembling had reached her chin, causing her words to warble.

"H-he is essentially a s-stranger, Piers."

"And how well did you know him before you married? His prospects haven't changed, Isla! He might be an earl's son, but that is all he has to recommend himself."

"Please, Piers. If you can find even a single thread of love for me—"

"Bah!" He looked out the window once more, giving her his shoulder and dismissing the rest of the conversation.

Isla wept . . . silent, fat drops of despair.

That frightening tremor of panic and anxiety rose again, banding her lungs and making it difficult to draw air.

She fought to tamp it down, to avoid sinking into the morass of sorrow and pain and fear she could sense rolling toward her. That immense wall of water and churning debris that would see her subsumed into grief.

Pressing a hand to her stomach, she fought to breathe.

The carriage rolled on, tackle clanking.

Gray's hand flexed atop his walking stick—once, twice—the inset ruby of his ducal signet ring flashing. A small but potent symbol of his complete power over her.

Finally, he looked back to her, his gaze moving dispassionately over her face. Utterly unmoved by her distress.

"You plead for my love and forbearance, Isla." His tone was as chilly as his expression. "But I am not the one who has been inconstant here. I have long considered your future and your happiness. You have always had my support, more than you can comprehend. Despite your bastard status, I have safeguarded your dowry and ensured you are luxuriously clothed and housed and given every opportunity afforded a lady of your station. I have run off fortune hunters—Tavish Balfour being merely the first of a long string of them, I assure you—and made contacts with every eligible gentleman in the *ton*. I have ignored the lowly stench of your birth and refused to publish my father's letter. Instead, I have labored for years to ensure *your* happiness and well-being!"

"I am th-thankful for—"

"No! You are most certainly *not* thankful! You are a wailing child, upset that you have been caught. You dislike having to face the consequences of your poor choices."

The grief rose. The wall of emotion rushed toward her with terrifying speed, white caps frothing and churning.

"Gray! Piers, please, if you would just—"

"Isla, you have recklessly put your *own* sensibilities and desires before your duty and responsibility to our family name. You have taken the Kinsey name—the one my father and I have so generously allowed you to keep—and slathered it in the foul stench of scandal, proving once and for all that you are no better than your illegitimate birth. And now, like my father before me, I am forced to shelter and care for a duplicitous woman. It is not to be borne!"

Gray shook his head now, teeth grinding in anger.

"No," he muttered, almost to himself. "I will not bear it."

He fixed her with a long, weighty stare. All the fine hairs on Isla's arms flared to attention.

Her chest heaved, the raging tempest towering overhead.

"I think, dear sister . . . it is time you understood the consequences of the choice you have made."

The merciless timbre of his voice cut deep.

Isla tried to speak, to plead her case.

But the monster of her grief crashed, burying her under its weight.

Isla crumpled to the carriage floor, tears drenching her skirts.

25

"Well, I must say that visit could have gone a wee bit better," Ross sighed, clucking his horse. "I'm not sure Fletch is going to forgive ye."

Tavish nudged Goliath forward, resisting the urge to answer with a grunt. His left cheek throbbed, and his eye was half-swollen shut. For once, his exterior appearance matched the wretchedness of his internal one.

However, given that Ross was still at Tavish's side, the man deserved better than a guttural reply.

"Perhaps not," Tavish said. "All I can do is hope for a mending of our friendship given time."

To his dying day, Tavish would regret how Fletch had uncovered the fact of his and Isla's marriage. It had been as cowardly and selfish an act as Tavish had ever committed.

Fletch was more than justified in his anger.

Tavish had awakened to find a note pushed under his bedroom door. At first, his foolish heart had assumed it was from Isla. That she wished to speak with him, or reconcile, or throw herself upon his chest and profess her love.

More the *eejit*, him.

Instead, he had found Fletch's black scrawl. A wounded diatribe against Tavish and his betrayal of their friendship. The letter ended with a bleak parting shot:

> Given the breach of trust between us, I think it best to sever both our financial ties and those bands that once bound us tight as brothers.

Flowery but to the point—*we are no longer friends, and I will not be going into business with ye.*

As if Tavish's spirits could sink any lower.

Isla had departed at dawn with Grayburn.

She had fallen upon Tavish like his lips held the meaning of life. Like she were famished and his body the only sustenance that would satisfy.

And then she had left without a word.

Tavish struggled to feel anger over her actions. Instead, he harbored a bone-deep sadness. He had always known this was how things would end with them. She had made her intentions clear from the beginning—*I don't want you. I don't want the life of poverty and hardship you offer.*

As for Fletch . . .

"He struggles to hold a grudge, Fletch does," Tavish said.

"Aye. But perhaps he hasn't been sufficiently motivated in the past. Time will tell, I ken." Ross shrugged. "In the meantime, I'm unsure what you and I are to do. Fletch was to provide a substantial amount of our needed capital. We cannot move forward with our plans in Pennsylvania without an investor."

Tavish nodded. He was twice an *eejit* for not foreseeing this outcome with Fletch.

"Do ye have anyone in mind?" Tavish asked. "Would your father be interested?"

"Nae. If anything, my father would be happy to see the whole plan scuppered. He wants me home, managing my wee estate, and contemplating marriage."

They rode in silence for a long moment.

"Would it . . ." Ross began. "Would it be so terrible if we backed out of our plans?"

Aye! Tavish wanted to snap. Some days, the only thing keeping him upright was the thought of the green hills of Pennsylvania and his fields of rye growing there. A tangible something that prevented his future from feeling so very bleak.

Ross took his silence as encouragement.

"Once ye be free of Lady Isla, ye could marry anew. A lass whose family supports your suit and provides ye with a dowry. Combined with your funds from the sale of your commission . . ." He drifted off.

Och, Tavish didn't want a different wife. He liked the one he already had, thank ye very much. But as she currently had no interest in remaining married to him . . .

"A new lady's dowry would have to be truly spectacular to support us in any meaningful way."

"Aye, but if it included property. An estate, even . . . ye could have ongoing income."

Tavish looked out over the countryside—the hills covered in purple heather, smoke rising from the occasional stone farmhouse—wondering if there would ever come a time when his life felt settled. Anytime Tavish wanted something—his inheritance, the woman he loved—it was stripped from him.

"Have ye considered politics?" Ross asked, seemingly from nowhere.

"Pardon?" Tavish turned to stare at his friend, the motion causing his eye to pulse in pain.

"Merely that ye have presence. Your father is an earl with a position in Lords. Ye could put for a seat in Commons. Between that and the right wife, ye could live quite comfortably."

"Do I look like a politician type?"

"Nae. But I think that would be part of the appeal. Ye are a bit of a war hero. Ye could do some shooting exhibitions and use the momentum to boost your abilities to take on Westminster."

"Have ye gone *doolally*? Perhaps Fletch knocked your head last night, too, because ye be speaking utter nonsense."

Ross merely shrugged again.

They rode in silence for a few more minutes.

"Why all this talk of new wives, estates, and politics? It appears to me ye want to back out of our endeavor," Tavish said. "Ye ken I won't hold ye to any part of it."

"I admit that I see the wisdom in my father's advice. And now that our funding has disappeared . . ." Ross drifted off. "However, I won't leave yourself unsettled."

"I'm not yours to tend to, Ross."

"Aye, but I value ye as a friend and, as such, your happiness matters."

"Well, I'd rather . . ."

Whatever Tavish intended to say died on his lips.

They had just rounded a corner and there, in the distance, a woman sat on a log beside the road. Dressed in a light blue pelisse and a straw bonnet, she was bent in half, palms covering her face, shoulders shaking with sobs.

He recognized her instantly.

"That bloody bastard!" Tavish hissed, kicking Goliath into a gallop to reach her.

He threw himself from the saddle before the enormous hunter had fully stopped.

Damn Grayburn and his cold, black heart.

"Isla." He crouched in front of her, pulling her hands from her face. "Love. Darling. What's happened?"

She lifted her head, tears clinging to her lashes, strands of blonde hair hanging limply beside her jaw. She had never looked more miserable or more heartbreakingly beautiful.

"Isla," he whispered again, a hand raising to thumb away her tears. Anything to offer her comfort.

However, she didn't lean into his palm or sigh with relief to see him.

Instead, her lovely face contorted in rage.

She placed both palms on his chest and shoved. Hard.

Tavish toppled backward, landing on his bottom in the dirt with an *oof*.

Isla stood and stomped down the road, away from him.

Ross swung from his saddle beside Tavish, taking Goliath's reins in his hand.

Tavish rolled to his feet, brushing off his buckskins as Isla strode away. She made it about twenty feet before stopping in the middle of the road, her bonneted head turned away, her hands balled into fists. She stood there for several seconds before tipping her head back . . .

. . . and letting loose a heart-rending scream.

The sound came from deep within her chest—harsh, desperate, and so anguished. To Tavish's ears, it was the sound of every lady abandoned by a lover. Every mother who learned of her son's death on a battlefield. Every woman who suffered the impotence and rage of what it so often meant to be female.

Tavish closed the distance between them, stopping at her side.

She glanced at him, silently daring him to curb her actions.

As if he would ever clip her wings.

She screamed again. That gut-wrenching noise he had once taught her.

And Tavish . . . did nothing. He stood and let her unleash pain.

Isla roared several times, her bonnet slipping from her head and hanging down her back, before turning toward him. Tavish reached for her, but again, she rejected his help.

Instead, with a sob, she beat her fists against his ribs. He tightened his muscles and let her vent her rage.

Because *she* knew: Unlike every other man in her life, Tavish would bear her fury. He would let her expend it on his body and would hold her in the aftermath.

Because *he* knew that her anger was actually grief and pain in disguise.

Because their minds, as ever, were uncannily attuned.

The anger in her fists decreased with each strike, until slowly, she crumpled—slumping into him, her hands balled against his chest. She *greited*, forehead pressed to his collarbones.

"He c-cast m-me out, Tavish," she hiccupped. "He s-said he was d-done. That y-you were c-coming behind us, and I w-was yours to d-deal with now."

Tavish pulled her against him, pressing a kiss to her forehead. "He's an arse-headed blackguard, Isla, and I should have plowed my fist into his face last night."

If Tavish thought his words would help, he was mistaken. She collapsed into dreadful wracking sobs that sounded as if her very being were coming undone.

Perhaps it was.

I don't want you.

And yet, Gray had forced her to be with Tavish anyway.

Gently, Tavish lifted her into his arms, cradling her close as he walked back to Ross and Goliath. His friend's gaze held only empathy and understanding. Setting Isla in front of his saddle, Tavish swung up behind her and gathered her to his chest. She melted into him—one hand clutching his lapel, the other snaking inside his coat and around his waist to grip a fistful of his waistcoat, her face pressed to his shirt.

He nudged Goliath to walk on, letting the sounds of her heartbroken sobs drift along the road behind them.

TAVISH, ISLA, AND Ross arrived late at an inn on the southwest outskirts of Aberdeen, the distance between Kingswell and Castle Balfour being too great to travel in one day. They would spend the night here and then go their separate ways come morning—Ross to his family north, and Tavish to his in the south.

While Ross saw to the horses, Tavish stepped into the entryway and requested two rooms—one for Captain Ross, the other for Captain Balfour and Mrs. Balfour.

The innkeep frowned at Tavish's black eye, but only asked if they had a preference for a room to the back or front of the building.

Tavish kept a tight arm around Isla's waist as he spoke with the man. Her *greiting* had been replaced by a chilling silence. A sort of lethargic melancholy that worried Tavish far more than her weeping ever would.

Isla didn't so much as twitch when the innkeep asked, "Would Mrs. Balfour like a bath to be drawn?"

Tavish nodded for her and then followed a maid to their bedchamber. He studiously did *not* look at the single bed to the left of the door.

Why torment himself? Isla would never be joining him there. Not now. Not ever.

He waited until the maids had finished pouring hot water into a hip bath before turning for the door.

"I will sort this out, Isla, and convince Grayburn to see reason. Don't despair. Not yet."

"Thank you," she whispered, gaze dead and unseeing. "Thank you for . . . for all of this." She gestured at the room.

Silence descended.

Tavish didn't know how to reply. *My pleasure* certainly felt out of place.

He went with, "I'll be in the bedchamber through the wall there with Ross, if ye have need of me."

She didn't reply, merely nodded, her face splotchy and eyes bloodshot.

Ross raised an eyebrow when Tavish knocked on his door.

"I don't wish to discuss it," Tavish said, entering the room.

To Ross's credit, he spent the rest of the evening acting as if Tavish didn't have a wife sleeping on the opposite side of the hearth.

And just as he had many times in the past, Tavish blew out the lamp and lay down to sleep beside Ross. Brothers in arms and all that. At least they were on a mattress this time and not wrapped in their greatcoats on the hard earth.

Neither of them spoke. They merely listened to the creak of floorboards and the scuttle of some rodent in the attic overhead.

Finally, Ross sighed. "The problem, Balfour, is that ye don't want a different wife, do ye?"

"Nae."

"Ye want to find a way to keep the one ye have."

"Aye."

If Tavish could establish an income, he might be able to provide for Isla—a way for them to move forward together. Or, if she refused him entirely, it would distract him from the pain of losing her yet again.

He felt more than saw Ross nod. "I'll ask around for another investor."

The olive branch . . . the kindness of it . . .

A rush of emotion surged in Tavish's chest. "Thank ye, Ross."

Ross didn't reply directly, just turned to his side, away from Tavish.

"Don't even think of giving me a wee cuddle," he said over his shoulder. "Save it for that bonnie wife of yours."

Tavish chuckled. "Goodnight, Ross."

CASTLE BALFOUR GLOWED in the fading sunlight.

Tavish was unsure if he was happy to be home or dreading the coming confrontation.

Would his family be any more welcoming of the belated news of his nuptials than Gray had been?

Truthfully, events could go either way.

Isla rode behind him, her hands clasped around his waist, her head drooping in weariness between his shoulder blades. In some ways, their travel south had been a depressing repeat of their journey after tying the knot of their handfasting. The same road. The same horse, even. But this time, instead of the intoxicating hope of their longed-for future together, Tavish shouldered the leaden weight of Isla's despair.

Tavish pulled Goliath to a stop before the castle's front doors, dismounting and turning to help Isla down. She slid off the horse with a soft groan, her feet wobbling as they hit the gravel. His poor lass was unaccustomed to riding for such long periods. Tavish clutched her to him for a brief moment, ignoring the enormous eyes of the groom who had come to take Goliath away and likely recognized Lady Isla in the process. Every servant in a twenty-mile radius would have a report of this within days. Who knew what the local gossip mill would make of it.

It remained to be seen if Tavish and Isla could keep the truth of their marriage and eventual divorce hidden. Though without Grayburn's ducal assistance, news of their divorce would land in the scandal sheets almost immediately.

More to the point, without Grayburn's support, what would become of Isla? Tavish would never force her to remain in their marriage, but neither would he cast her out into the world.

Bloody hell, but this was a mess.

"Come," Tavish wrapped an arm around her, turning for the stairs to the front door.

It opened with a *clack*.

"Tavish!" called Elsie.

"Finally!" yelled Edmund.

The twins raced down the stairs, only to come to a stumbling halt once they realized Tavish had his arm around a lady.

For her part, Isla pushed away from him, a hand tentatively going to her crumpled bonnet before attempting to smooth her pelisse, the fine garment heavily wrinkled from their journey.

Tavish took her hand and wrapped it through his elbow.

"Who's this?" Edmund frowned, looking at Isla.

Elsie elbowed him. Hard.

"Ow! What's that for?" he scowled at his twin.

Elsie rolled her eyes. "Lady Isla," she curtsied, pretty as a picture.

Bless Mariah. She had obviously been instilling manners in one of the twins.

"Lady who?" Edmund said, far too loudly.

Elsie leaned into her twin's ear to whisper. Tavish heard *Grayburn* and *sister* and *recognize her from church services*. To his credit, Edmund's eyes widened as she spoke, his gaze darting between Tavish and Isla before landing on the place where Isla clutched Tavish's elbow.

"Why does Tavish have a black eye?" Edmund asked.

Elsie shrugged.

"Oh, gracious! There ye two wee hellions be," Mariah said, coming to the door. "Why are ye yapping at Tavish—"

Mariah broke off with a start as her gaze landed on Isla and then fluttered up to Tavish's swollen eye.

The butler, Jameson, finally appeared, his gray hair fluttering in his haste to reach the door.

"So sorry, Lady Mariah." The man panted. "I was polishing silver in the kitchen and didn't hear the bell . . ." He, too, trailed off.

Tavish smiled, though he was rather sure it came off as more of a grimace. He hazarded a glance at Isla. She was staring past Mariah's shoulder, her gaze unfocused, face sagging in exhaustion.

Mariah—good, gentle Mariah—walked down the steps and took Isla's hand. "Welcome to our home, Lady Isla. I think . . ." She cleared her throat. "A servant from Dunmore delivered a trunk here a few hours ago without saying a word. I'm rapidly gathering the trunk is yours."

"Oh," Isla said, the merest puff of sound.

Her eyes filled with tears. Tavish had never been a violent man, but witnessing Isla's misery yet again . . .

More than once over the past two days, he had imagined lying in wait for Grayburn and burying a bullet in his thick skull. Anything to enact retribution for Isla's pain.

"Thank ye, Mariah," Tavish murmured.

His sister nodded, glancing once more at his black-and-blue face. "Come. Let us get ye settled with a wee bit of dinner in your bellies. Afterward, I'm sure Da' will have questions."

"YE'VE GONE AND married who?!" Lord Northcairn sat forward in his leather armchair, his face turning a deep shade of red. "Surely, I didn't hear ye right just now, Tavish. Because no son of mine would act with such incredible stupidity."

Tavish barely avoided rolling his eyes at the irony in their father's accusation.

In the chair opposite their father, Callum set his tumbler of whisky down on a side table with a clatter.

For her part, Mariah stared into the fire, her feet tucked against the stool where she sat.

Only Tavish was standing, a glass of much-needed whisky in his hand.

Candles cast long shadows on the walls. Two floors above them, Isla slept in a guest bedroom. The house had been in such an uproar after Tavish's arrival, it had taken some settling before he had a chance to face his father with the news.

"Seven years ago, I married Lady Isla Balfour," Tavish repeated. "A handfasting. Outside Stonehaven."

Callum pinched the bridge of his nose.

Mariah closed her eyes, as if in pain.

Their father, however, lurched to his feet, his expression a thundercloud. "Married? Ye married a spawn of that . . . that . . ." He glanced at Mariah, censoring what would likely have been a spectacularly profane epithet. "After everything that Grayburn has done to this family. His cruelty to Mariah and dishonor toward your brother. Ye would betray us all by allying yourself with . . . with . . . them?!"

"Allying myself?!" Tavish snapped, the strain of the past week catching up to him. "I assure ye, Grayburn is no happier about this than yourselves!"

He resisted mentioning that Isla wasn't actually a Kinsey, in the end. So technically, Tavish hadn't allied himself with *them*. He doubted that wee detail would matter to his father. Or if it did, Lord Northcairn would crow the fact of old Grayburn's cuckolding from the rooftops, ensuring everyone knew of Isla's illegitimacy.

"*Och*, that's a fine lie to tell yourself, lad!"

"Is that what happened to your eye?" Callum asked. "Grayburn's displeasure?"

"Nae, this is courtesy of my friend who was courting Lady Isla."

Mariah made a helpless noise of distress.

"Lady Isla and I intend to divorce on the basis of desertion," Tavish continued.

"Divorce?!" Lord Northcairn turned a rather alarming shade of puce. "Divorce?! Ye would add scandal to betrayal, after everything we have already endured? Have ye no sense of your duty to this family at all?!"

"Da'," Callum said, reproof in his tone.

Tavish clenched his jaw, tossing back the last of his whisky. Bitter words stacked on his tongue, angry accusations about his own inheritance and Callum's ruinous behavior and their father's utter disregard for Tavish's future.

Tavish swallowed the vitriol down. He wanted his father's cooperation, not a fight.

"My goal is to keep the fact of my marriage and divorce quiet."

"Out of the newspapers, you mean," Mariah added.

"Precisely. If all is done with discretion, then there will be no scandal, particularly if I had some assistance with the matter." Tavish glanced meaningfully at their father.

Lord Northcairn made a sound of disgust. "I'll have none of this." He drew his hand in a sharp line. "The fact that ye married a Kinsey at all is beyond the pale. Ye can both rot in your disgrace! Ye and your *wife* will be out of my house and my sight by morning!"

He stomped from the room, shutting the door with a *boom* that rattled the window panes.

Silence echoed in the aftermath.

Crossing to a sideboard, Tavish poured himself another finger of whisky. He could feel his siblings staring at his back.

"Da' will come around eventually," Callum said. "Give him a few months to grow accustomed to this news."

Tavish gritted his teeth. He didn't have a few months. There were problems to solve now.

"So it was Grayburn who purchased your commission." Mariah said the words as a fact, not a question. "Not a distant, generous uncle."

Tavish nodded. A single slice of his head.

"Grayburn knew? About your marriage?" she asked.

"Nae. He merely knew there was a connection between Isla and myself. He learned of our marriage three days ago and cast Isla out."

"What will ye do?" Callum asked.

"Divorce her, if Grayburn will agree to take her back under his wing. It's what Isla wishes." Tavish turned back to his siblings. "I have little beyond the funds from my commission to offer her. It's not enough to support a lady. Not at the moment."

Callum winced. "Ye ken I will be eternally sorry about your inheritance, Tavish. Someday, somehow, I will find a way to make it up to ye."

Tavish clenched his jaw at the apology offered far too late. "I'm sorry, too."

"Ye don't want to divorce her," Mariah intuited.

Tavish laughed. "It doesn't matter what I want, Mariah. Isla doesn't want me. It will take some weeks, perhaps even months, to sort out, particularly with Grayburn being recalcitrant and Da' refusing to help. I had hoped that we might stay here in the interim, but . . ." He sent a telling look at the door their father had just slammed.

Tavish drained his tumbler in one long gulp. Perhaps if he got drunk enough, he could forget his difficulties for a few hours. Though he doubted there was enough whisky in all of Scotland to make him forget the bleak despair in Isla's eyes at the thought of being well and truly stuck with him for a husband.

"Ye have nowhere to go," Mariah said. Again, not a question.

"Nae."

His sister rose to her feet, hands smoothing her gown. "I believe I have an idea. A wee way that Callum and I can help."

26

"Here we are," Lady Mariah said, leading the way up the ancient spiral staircase of Cairnfell Castle.

Isla followed, the heat of Tavish's large body at her back.

After crying for the better part of two days, a melancholic numbness had set in, as if the tidal wave of her grief had annihilated every other emotion with its weight.

Her inner landscape resembled the aftermath of a flood—mud and tree limbs pushed against rocks, houses knocked from their foundations. Labels fluttered from each destroyed thing: Love, Belonging, Family, Hope.

And yet . . . Tavish remained—stalwart and true.

That realization seemed momentous, but the feeling struggled to reach her.

The stairs opened up to the great hall of the old castle. Isla stepped into the room, Tavish at her side.

Neither of them said a word to one another. In fact, they had exchanged only a handful of perfunctory sentences since their incendiary kiss rather literally burned both their lives to ash.

Isla's nerves still felt raw and scorched.

Surely, they were both remembering their previous encounters at Cairnfell Castle.

But what had once been a damp, chilly room cluttered with sparse bits of furniture had now been refurbished into a more habitable space.

Lady Mariah noticed their surprise. "I have been slowly bringing the old castle back to life when I can find the time and spare a shilling or two."

"Ye've done wonders here, Mariah," Tavish said, voice sincere.

Isla agreed. Gone were the rickety table and mismatched wooden chairs. The sooty fireplace and cold flagstones underfoot.

The walls had been plastered a gleaming white and hung with faded tapestries, while a rug had been laid on the floor. The furniture was still mismatched, but now a worn velvet sofa and a pair of stuffed armchairs sat before the hearth. A sturdy table surrounded by four chairs and a sideboard with dishes and crockery took up the other half of the space.

"I'm glad ye like the changes. I couldn't bear to watch this place crumble to ruin if I could help it." Lady Mariah managed a wan smile.

Even in a simple day gown and apron, she looked astonishingly beautiful—dark hair pulled back with loose curls framing her face, her striking blue eyes always flashing with humor or exasperation or some other emotion.

That same sadness weighed on Isla. In another lifetime, she and Lady Mariah would likely have been fast friends. One more thing lost.

"I've been raiding the attics at Castle Balfour for discarded furniture and linens. The tapestries were a particularly nice discovery. A bit worse for wear, but still serviceable and warm." Lady Mariah beckoned. "Come see. I've refitted the bedchamber, as well."

She led them through the door to the left of the fireplace where a decrepit bed pallet and moldering mattress had once resided.

Like the great hall, this room, too, had been plastered and a carpet laid. A fireplace stood just to the right inside the door, the opposite side of the enormous fireplace in the great hall, both sharing the same solitary chimney.

Before the hearth, a large tester bed with a deep tick, heavy counterpane, and woolen bed curtains dominated the space.

Isla sucked in a slow breath.

Lady Mariah continued to talk, pointing out a small writing desk and washstand before retrieving a set of towels from a wardrobe.

But all Isla could do was stare at the bed. It looked decidedly . . . matrimonial.

Tavish touched her arm from behind, the slightest of brushes.

"I'll be sleeping in front of the fire in the great hall," he murmured in her ear. "Ye will have this bedchamber as your own."

Isla blinked, unsure how she felt about his words.

For one, they showed his uncanny understanding of her thoughts. The two of them were, even now, nearly an extension of one another.

Moreover, the memory of their kisses continued to thrum between them. Isla found it appalling. How, after all the damage that attraction had wreaked, could she still feel the pull of it? Would she have the presence of mind to reject him if he *did* join her in that bed?

She turned away before she could imagine the scene—his enormous chest curving around her body and pulling her to him.

Lady Mariah bustled back into the great hall.

"As we discussed, Callum and I will do our best to prevent others from learning of your presence here," she said. "Jameson and several other trusted servants have agreed to help us keep you both hidden. I have already put it about that Lady Isla left this morning to visit friends in Edinburgh. Tavish, ye are supposedly off sorting matters with Captain Ross. Lord Northcairn never comes up here—the steep incline is too much for his heart, even on a horse—so he is not a concern. The reprieve will give ye both a couple of weeks to sort yourselves out. In the meantime, I will send up meals from the kitchens as I am able."

"There is no need for that, Mariah," Tavish said. "Ye have already done much. If ye could muster some supplies, I can cook well enough for us."

Lady Mariah lifted one elegant eyebrow in question.

"Soldiers cook for themselves in the army," he explained. "I became rather handy at the basics. Just deliver some daily bread and possibly the occasional pastry or sweet." He quirked a grin.

"Ye always had a sweet tooth," Lady Mariah sighed. "Very well. That's settled then. A trusted groom will deliver your trunks this afternoon. I will send up a maid every other day or so to collect laundry and tidy up, if ye need. Until then, I'll bid ye both adieu."

Tavish motioned to his sister. "I'll see ye out."

The great hall rang with silence in the wake of their departure. Isla unpinned her bonnet and set it on the table, ignoring the tremor in her hand.

The indistinct murmur of Tavish's voice carried up the stairwell. Lady Mariah said something in response. The great door closed below, and he reappeared in the doorway.

There was a sense of waiting about him. As if he expected Isla to do or say something specific. What? She hadn't a clue.

"So . . . what are our plans?" Her voice sounded overly loud to her ears.

Crossing the room, Tavish pulled off his hat and tossed it onto the table. He had donned a kilt today in the blue-and-gold Balfour tartan, shedding the finery he had worn at Kingswell House. His coat and waistcoat were neatly pressed, but loose and well-worn.

He gave her an assessing look once again. The skin around his blackened eye was slowly fading from blue and green to a rather sickly yellow.

"At the moment, there isn't much to do besides wait. Hopefully, we will hear soon from my solicitor about proceeding with our divorce." Tavish paced the perimeter of the room, studying the tapestries. "I also assume your brother will need a week or two to cool his temper and begin to see reason."

"Tossing me from the family will have social repercussions he will wish to minimize. Gray hates scandal, as I've said."

"Precisely. I am confident Grayburn will come around to some sort of reconciliation with yourself. That reconciliation will go better if I am well on my way to being out of the picture. In short, it's all just an enormous tartan knot that we will pick, stitch by stitch, to untangle."

"And once we untangle it?"

He stopped and looked back at her. "Ye will be free."

Abruptly, the room seemed far too small to hold the enormity of their shared history. Isla felt like a thief returning to the scene of a crime.

Once, she would have loved nothing more than to marry Tavish and set up house together in this small tower. Now that she had achieved her wish, she and Tavish were scrambling to unravel it.

The irony.

"Free," she repeated.

"Aye . . . free from this," he said quietly.

She gave him a questioning glance. For once, she wasn't quite following the trail of his thoughts.

"This." He gestured to the space around them. "The humbleness of this existence. 'Tis why I left seven years ago. That lass I had wed deserved so much more than this lowly life."

He picked up a pewter plate from the sideboard. A far cry from the fine silver dishes and Sèvres china of Dunmore.

And yet . . .

"I don't think that lass would have cared," Isla said, sadness whispering between each syllable. "All she wanted was you."

AFTER MARIAH'S DEPARTURE, the hours crawled by.

Some foodstuffs and their trunks were delivered. Isla unpacked her things. When at Dunmore, her lady's maid would take care of smoothing her dresses and seeing them properly hung in a wardrobe. But at Malton Hill, Isla had typically done for herself.

She carefully hung her few gowns and underclothes on pegs in the wardrobe and placed her shoes underneath in a neat row.

But once everything was put away, there was little else to occupy the hours.

She took her book, *Waverly,* by Mr. Walter Scott into the great hall, intending to curl onto the sofa and read. But she hadn't the stomach for swashbuckling tales of doomed Jacobites—naive idealists who couldn't accept the harsh reality of their world.

It felt a bit too on the nose.

Tavish, on the other hand, scarcely stopped moving.

Once he settled his effects, Isla watched as he shed his coat, leaving him in his kilt, waistcoat, and shirtsleeves. From there, he sharpened an axe and chopped wood beside the oaken front door before carrying it upstairs, kilt swinging, to stack it neatly against the wall to the right of the fireplace.

With each movement, Isla felt she was witnessing him settle back into his Scottish skin after so many years away. A relaxing, perhaps, of the militant Captain Balfour.

He laid a fire, and once it crackled in the hearth, he pulled a stool close to the flames, toasting bread for their luncheon. A crock of *crowdie* cheese, a jar of marmalade, a loaf of bread, and a plate covered with a pretty embroidered cloth sat on a side table at his elbow.

Isla studied him from her perch on the sofa, that unfortunate pull of attraction still humming.

She noted the flex of his biceps against the thin linen of his shirtsleeves. The ease with which he balanced on the balls of his feet, calves flexing in his woolen stockings, gently coaxing the fire to life. The confident way he cut the bread into uniform slices and slipped them onto a skewer for toasting.

Colonel Archer's words to Tavish on that fateful night would not let her be—*I've never seen you touch a woman. You are as celibate as a monk!*

Was that true? Had Tavish spent the past seven years as chaste as a priest, loyal to her and their marriage vows?

The notion held a lovelorn sort of ache. As she was growing and changing at Malton Hill and planning a future without him, he had been doggedly faithful to her. Year after year, as he slogged through winter mud in Portugal and baked beneath summer sun in Spain, Isla had been there, in his thoughts and desires.

If she pondered it too long—Tavish languishing in some far-off clime, heart stalwart and true—a stone lodged in her stomach.

And then to see him now—still beside her, still loyal—his broad shoulders flexing as he lifted a slice of bread from the fire . . .

Finally, she could bear the wondering no longer.

"Is it true what Colonel Archer said?" she asked, leaning forward on the sofa.

"Pardon?"

He handed her a plate of perfectly toasted bread slathered in a thick layer of soft *crowdie* cheese, topped with a drizzle of marmalade and a sprinkle of salt. It smelled heavenly.

"Is it true that you never touched a woman in all your years in the army?" she asked.

Tavish shifted on his stool before the fire, toasting iron extended over the flames. He spared her a glance over his shoulder.

"Of course. Ye think I would betray ye like that?" His tone held a hint of incredulity.

"I wouldn't have blamed you if you had." She touched the crust of her bread on her plate.

He was silent for a moment.

"Because ye kissed Fletch?" He asked the question without inflection, not a trace of accusation.

Which somehow made it worse. Because his anger, she could counter. She could use it to stoke her own ire. But to feel his understanding and perhaps a hint of melancholy . . .

That merely added more weight to her regret.

"Yes." *Just the once*, she wanted to add. *It meant nothing.*

She didn't. Because, though it was the truth, saying the words felt too much like a child brushing off bad behavior. And at the time, the kiss hadn't meant nothing. She had hoped it would be a beginning to something. A promise of sorts.

Though now, in hindsight, she had to wonder.

Colonel Archer's kiss had been pleasant, but certainly not the all-consuming incineration she experienced with Tavish.

Which type of kiss was the result of genuine, long-lasting love? She couldn't say.

"And others?" He rotated his own toast over the flames, as if her answer mattered not at all. But the white grip of his knuckles on the skewer betrayed him. "You kissed others?"

"And others," she whispered.

He glanced at her again, as if he had heard her regret that time.

She took a bite of her toast. The contrasting warm crunch of the bread, the creamy tang of the *crowdie*, and the sweet yet bitter punch of the marmalade should have quickened her senses.

Instead, the whole stuck in her throat.

He pulled his toast off the skewer with practiced ease, setting the hot bread on a plate balanced on his thigh. Pushing aside the cloth-covered plate, he reached for the crock of *crowdie*.

She watched as he prepared his own slice as he had hers—*crowdie*, marmalade, and a pinch of salt. And then, as was his wont, he took an obscene bite.

That peek of her Tavish felt like a gleam of sun in January—the faintest echo of summer . . . of a season, now lost, when life had burst with bright happiness.

To think, she was the last woman he had touched.

Well, of course, she was. It had only been four days since they had nearly combusted in each other's arms.

But before that. From their first kiss almost eight years ago to this moment, she had been the only woman whose cheek he had caressed, the only one who had made his body crackle with heat and his chest rumble with desire.

The very idea felt almost too large to accept. To think he esteemed her to such an extent, even after all this time.

The well of her shame sank deeper.

"Don't," he said, swallowing. "There is no need to mire yourself in guilt. What's done is done."

She nodded. And then, on a deep breath, offered him an olive branch.

"I have realized this week that those other gentlemen were all weak imitations. Somehow, I had diminished . . ." She motioned to the space between them. "But now . . ."

She drifted off. Because trying to say the words aloud sent the truth of them burrowing deep.

In a very real sense, after Tavish left, she had needed to reduce what they were to each other in order to preserve her sanity. Because if what they had together had splintered so easily, what did that say about her? About him? Surely, the fault had to have been in the shallowness of their relationship in the first place.

But now . . . she didn't know.

She waited for that pang of grief to tremor as it always did when she thought of their past, of what she had lost . . . but in the present moment—sitting before him, watching him watch her—nothing came.

Perhaps these past days had scoured the pain away.

Toast in hand, Tavish unfolded his large body from the stool before the fire and, after a moment's debate over where to sit—an armchair or the sofa—he sank down beside her on the sofa. Their bodies didn't touch, but she felt the heat of him everywhere regardless.

They each took a bite of their toast, chewing slowly.

Tavish swallowed. "Ye have lived years of experiences that I cannot fathom, just as I have lived events that you cannot imagine. But as I've said, ye still know me better than anyone before or since. I consider ye the person closest to my heart. I would never—I *could* never—taint the memory of our past love—" *Deep breath.* "—by seeking comfort in another's arms. It would be akin to dining on pig slop after a rare and most elegant feast."

Isla watched as he took another bite of toast. The afternoon sun filtered through the window behind them, burnishing his auburn hair. Vividly, she remembered the silken texture of it against her palms. How, when her nails scraped his scalp, he had growled, low and deep.

He brushed a loose crumb from his lips and then set his plate aside before angling his body toward hers.

"Isla, the truth is . . ." He took in another long breath before meeting her eyes.

Her heart stuttered.

His gaze was pure Tavish. *Her* Tavish. The open, sweet boy she had known. The boy, she was rapidly realizing, who had not vanished but had simply grown into this remarkable man.

"The truth is . . . ," he swallowed, "as long as we are married . . . I would not want my first experience with . . . with intimacy to be with anyone but yourself."

It took a moment for the impact of his words to land.

First experience . . .

Did he mean . . . ?

She turned to the left.

Set her own plate down on a side table.

Stared ahead for the space of three heartbeats.

And then looked back to him.

"First experience with intimacy?" she repeated.

He nodded, an eyebrow lifting as if to say, *Yes, it is precisely as ye be thinking.*

"But . . . I had always assumed, given your father and Callum and their behavior, that you had . . . before we married, of course . . ."

A blush scalded her skin. She had never asked him. At sixteen, she had been far too shy—too *timid*, forever that word—to voice such a probing question.

Tavish shook his head. Slowly, so slowly, he reached for her hand where it lay between them on the cushion. His fingers engulfed hers, the rough calluses on his palms brushing over her skin and flaring gooseflesh up her arm.

"Sometimes—" His index finger traced a blue vein on the back of her hand. "—sometimes, seeing such lascivious behavior in a father or a brother has the opposite effect. I didn't want to behave like them— to view women as mere things to be consumed by my lust. And once you and I became friends . . . I couldn't imagine being with anyone but yourself."

He smiled at the end of that—a sad, forlorn gesture. As if to say, *more the fool me.*

"So we're both virgins?" For once, Isla chose to be direct.

He nodded.

It shouldn't have mattered. Not really. It changed nothing. And yet

. . .

Somehow, it did.

It meant that they were equals. That they had both, from the beginning, held on to the promise of one another. Even herself, try as she might to let it go.

Again, no grief thrummed at the thought. No pain at their youthful ignorance.

Instead, Isla felt . . .

She felt something akin to gladness. A sense of relief that the girl she had been wasn't simply naive and suffering from a blind devotion she had mistakenly labeled as love.

No.

Tavish Balfour had been worthy of her heart. He had been true and loyal and resolute in his devotion, then and now.

She sat with that feeling for a long moment. Remembering how thoroughly she had loved him.

Colonel Archer was correct—Tavish was the most honorable of gentlemen.

He sat back on a sigh. "It is of no import now, I ken. But I felt ye should know."

His words were casual, as if he expected they would drop the topic. As if it held no more interest for him.

But for Isla, she feared she was now blinking into the light of a new dawn.

Because if her love for him was not some tainted facsimile—if it had, indeed, been soul-deep and true—what was she to do now? How was she to weigh the very real needs and wants of her future against the power of that remembered love?

He brushed the back of her hand one last time before releasing his grip. Twisting, he lifted the cloth-covered plate off the side table, setting it on the couch between them.

Isla raised her eyebrows in question.

"I ken that in the bustle of everything, ye have forgotten."

"Forgotten?"

"Aye." He lifted the cloth off the plate, revealing a lovely iced Savoy cake, prettily decorated with sugared pansies.

"A cake?" Isla laughed.

Tavish smiled, small but tender. "Happy birthday, Isla."

Oh!

She blinked, mind rapidly counting the days.

"Is it truly the twelfth?"

"Aye."

"Why . . . I utterly forgot!" she laughed. "You procured us a cake!"

He chuckled. "Mariah helped. I merely asked."

Isla stared, emotions racing by so fast she struggled to catch hold of any one—surprise, bewilderment, gratitude.

"Also, there is this." He tugged a small velvet pouch from his pocket. "A wee gift."

Shaking her head in astonishment, Isla took the velvet bag. "When did you possibly have the time to acquire a gift?"

"I bought it for ye years ago in Portugal . . . on our first birthday apart."

"And you kept it all these years?"

"Of course, I did. I've kept everything, lass."

There was a weight behind his words that caused emotion to tighten in Isla's throat.

Fingers trembling, she tugged open the pouch and tipped its contents into her palm. A round locket of deep blue enamel tumbled out. Isla gasped, examining the lovely bit of jewelry—royal blue enamel on one side, and a golden spiked sun nestled into the center on the other.

"Because ye have always been akin to the sun to me—a cheery bit of happiness."

Isla swallowed back tears.

Pressing the small clasp, she opened the locket, finding it empty.

"I had intended to place a lock of my hair in the center, but . . ." Tavish trailed off on a shrug.

Isla turned the locket over in her hand, reveling in the solid heft of the gold, the smooth enamel cool against her skin.

"You carried it all these years?"

"Aye." He gave another soft smile. "I couldn't discard it any more than I could purge your memory. The locket is yours now."

"Thank you. I will treasure it." She gently tucked the locket back into the velvet bag, clutching the whole in her fist.

Turning, he reached for a knife to cut the cake.

"But it's your birthday, too," Isla murmured. "And I have nothing . . ."

Abruptly, it felt the cruelest thing . . . that he had remembered and wanted to ensure her birthday didn't go uncelebrated. While at the same time, neglecting his own.

It was such a . . . a *Tavish* thing to do.

"I have a pudding." He pointed a knife at the Savoy cake. "I don't need much else."

"Tavish—" she began and then broke off.

He met her gaze.

What was she to say? *I fear I might be falling in love with you again?* That wouldn't be kind.

And yet, she couldn't stop staring at him. At the wee mole near his left eyebrow that she had loved to kiss. The whorl in his wavy hair near his nape where she used to press a finger.

He met her gaze for a long moment before focusing his attention on the cake between them. "Ye can't be giving me looks like that, lass."

"Looks?"

"Aye. Your whole heart in your eyes."

She nodded, as that was an accurate description. A tear slipped out. She turned from him to brush it away.

"Ye don't want me," he continued, tossing those words back at her once more. He cut a large slice of cake, sliding it onto her plate.

"No . . . no, I misspoke that night," she whispered.

Pausing, he looked at her.

"It's not that I don't want you, Tavish." *I want you more than I can express.* "It's that I want . . . I want my home more."

"Your home?"

"Yes. Malton Hill."

27

Tavish stilled at Isla's words.

"Malton Hill?" He searched his memory, cutting himself a slice of the Savoy cake. The scent of citrus, butter, and brandy wafted upward. "The estate that is part of your dowry?"

"Yes."

He might have felt stung over her admission—that he mattered less to her than a pile of masonry and adjacent land—but something in the fervor of her tone stopped him.

She answered the question in his eyes.

"I went there after we parted, and . . ." She held her plate with her own slice of cake. "Matthias accompanied me. I was so distraught, so melancholy . . . even Gray must have been concerned, as he made the plan for us to go."

Tavish mentally winced, relaxing back into the sofa. "How selfish of me not to inquire after yourself. I grieved your loss during my first two years in the army. Perhaps even longer. I waited for a letter from ye, hoping against hope that ye would write. That we could mend what had broken between us."

It felt bleak to recall those years. The letters he would scribble to her and then toss into the fire before he was foolish enough to post them. The dangerous risks he took as a soldier simply because he didn't value his life enough to be careful.

"At times," he continued, "I think being transferred to the Rifles is the only thing that saved me. It gave me a higher purpose at a time when I needed it most. Of course, ye would have searched for a similar sense of purpose." He took a bite of cake, but it tasted more of regret than sugar and lemon.

"Yes." She nodded, eyes going bright once again, though no tears fell. "I did. Need a purpose, that is. And I found one at Malton Hill."

Tavish let out a long breath, trying to order his riotous thoughts.

First, Isla *did* want him. That knowledge felt momentous. Like he should cup her cheek and bring her in for a pulse-pounding kiss.

And second, like himself, Isla had suffered greatly in his absence. Of course, she had. But he had never imagined it as a crushing force that had caused her to reach for a new cause. One that, like the army for him, had bent and reformed her desires and priorities.

"Tell me," he urged, suddenly desperate to know, to relearn each piece of her. "Every last experience. Every reason ye love Malton Hill so much."

Because it was painfully obvious that she did.

She laughed and finally pulled a handkerchief from her pocket, dabbing her eyes. "I didn't mean to fall so thoroughly in love with the estate. But I arrived with my heart full of affection and desperate for an outlet—or perhaps it was too newly wounded and quick to empty—but . . . Oh, Tavish. Malton Hill is so beautiful! Like a jewel box nestled into the green hills outside of Tetbury—honey-colored limestone and arched Tudor windows set with thick, wavy glass. Gray calls the house an antiquated pile, and I suppose he is right, as it has acres of wood paneling and plastered ceilings that haven't been fashionable in at least two hundred years. But it is *my* antiquated pile."

It was as if she were describing a beloved child, the way her eyes softened and her voice took on an almost astonished quality. As if she could scarcely believe something so clever and wonderful existed, and that she had been the one chosen to care for it.

Oh, Isla.

She broke off a small piece of their birthday cake, chewing it slowly. "Don't mistake me. It isn't a grand estate like Dunmore with corridors of bedchambers and a room for every hour of the day. It's a modest country house, polite in its manner rather than extravagant. Big enough to be grand in its own way, but small enough to feel like home. My home."

The sort of fine house Tavish was unable to provide.

That bit went unspoken, of course.

"It sounds like a wee paradise," he said instead. "I can picture ye thriving in a place like that."

And he could.

In his mind's eye, she strolled through airy rooms, dappled with English sunshine, a beatific smile upon her lips. A man joined her there—someone with Fletch's expressive face and merry demeanor. Children spilled in, blond-haired and rosy-cheeked, speaking in elegant English tones.

A scene that would never include Tavish.

Something of his bitterness, no matter how slight, must have spilled out.

"Tavish, you mistake my meaning. The house is certainly lovely, but even if the house burned tomorrow . . . it's the people of Malton Hill who hold my heart. The previous Duke of Grayburn had neglected them. When compared to the vast holdings of the dukedom, Malton Hill is the smallest of properties. Gray hadn't had the time to assess everything yet, so he was unaware of its shambolic state."

Side by side on the sofa, both eating their birthday cake, Tavish listened as she told of arriving there, her despair and grief. And how, little by little, the house and estate awakened her. How she cast off the old steward with his slovenly ways and hired the new, bright-eyed Mr. Cranston with his modern, ingenious ideas to manage the house and farm and tenants. How she integrated with the community—dining regularly with Dr. and Mrs. Sumsion and courting a friendship with the prickly Mrs. White—until she became one of them.

The sun was dipping toward the horizon, the Savoy cake nearly gone, by the time she finished.

"I don't have much power as a woman in the larger world, but at Malton Hill, my actions make a difference. I have ensured that my tenants have sound roofs overhead and windows that don't leak. I rallied other women in the village and established a dame school for the laborers' children to learn how to read and write. I reviewed practices in the parish poor house and worked to make conditions there more humane. And in the process of doing all of that, I became someone different. A woman who knows her own mind and has the confidence to help others. Do you not see how much Malton Hill means to me?"

And he did.

Tavish could see with astonishing clarity the magnitude of her commitment to her people.

His beautiful Isla with her vast capacity for compassion would never give them up. Nor would he ever ask her to. Some things were simply more important than romantic love.

"Of course, ye would fight for those people. It's all your fierce heart knows how to do. Ye were like that as a lass, and ye remain the same today. Ye love with your whole self."

And if she heard in that an echo of her own love for him, long dead and gone, then so be it.

"I do love them. It unlocked this maternal instinct I didn't realize I possessed. A need to shelter and protect."

And here was another key to the woman she had become. A change just as profound as his own. While Tavish led and shepherded men, fighting for her safety here at home, she was doing the same work, only on the opposite end. Fighting to ensure the women and children of the men he led not only survived, but thrived—bettering their situations and learning important skills.

Yet more proof as to why he loved her so.

The sheer scope of her determination humbled him.

"I want ye to have Malton Hill, lass. I want ye to keep your people."

"It's all I dream about, to be honest. I spent two years there after you left. I would be there still, but Gray likes having me close, both to act as a hostess and to ensure I marry where he wants." So sardonic that last bit. "So we compromise. I spend half the year at Malton Hill between September and March, hiring a widow friend to act as my companion while there for propriety's sake. I then join Gray for the Season in London. Often, I can plead the month of August, too. But not this year."

"Because of Fletch?"

She nodded.

Neither of them added the other truth. Because Fletch, or any gentleman who met Grayburn's approval, would ensure Malton Hill stayed in her possession forever. Yet one more reason why she needed to be reconciled with her brother.

Tavish was certainly a glutton for punishment because one question rang in his mind.

The one most likely to pain him to hear her answer.

And yet, after a pause, he opened his mouth anyway—

"If all things were equal, if I could offer ye Malton Hill and everything else that a gentleman like Fletch could, who would ye choose?"

YOU!!

THE ANSWER shrieked in Isla's head.

As sure as breath moved in and out of her lungs, she knew the answer.

You.

I would choose you.

In a thousand lifetimes, I would choose you.

She sat impossibly still, the force of her reply stunning her senses as thoroughly as a cold plunge into the River Northcairn.

"Ye look aghast. Never mind." Tavish waved a hand. "'Twas an unfair question. Forget I asked."

Mmm.

Forgetting his question would be highly unlikely.

They moved on after that, speaking of how Tavish had met Colonel Archer and Captain Ross.

Isla listened, but her mind still reeled.

Her immediate internal reply to his question had cracked a vital part of her foundation, letting a piece of the girl she had been escape. The girl who had loved him with shattering force.

And now that force pulsed there within her breast, a vagabond reminder of her past self—of a love so deep and vast, it stretched to the horizon of her mind. And now, it hovered at the edge of her vision, eager for rebirth.

What was Isla to do?

Because this feeling meant that the innermost core of her loved Tavish yet. That, in many ways, she was still that starry-eyed girl, longing for things she had best not keep.

And, more to the point, how was she to reconcile this knowledge with her future plans? Could she return to Malton Hill, knowing that Tavish would always be the true love of her heart?

They cleaned up the dishes and tidied the room.

Isla turned for the bedchamber, but paused to watch Tavish make up his bed, concern frowning her forehead.

"Why not at least sleep on the sofa?"

With a snort, he lay on the sofa, showing her quite clearly that his tall frame could not fit.

Her frown deepened.

He grinned. "Though I find your concern touching, lass, I assure ye, I spent years sleeping on the hard ground with nothing more than my arm for a pillow. This—" He pointed to the makeshift pallet on the floor. "—is practically luxurious."

"Careful. You might be laying it on a bit thick. And saying you are accustomed to such spartan sleeping arrangements is not exactly the comfort you wish it to be."

He chuckled. "Good night, Isla."

She nodded and reluctantly retired to her bedchamber.

But hours on, sleep remained elusive.

She lay on the comfortable mattress, pillow under her cheek, his locket hanging from a chain around her neck. The enamel felt heated from her skin, as if it held the memory of their past love just as surely as every atom of her body.

Wrapping the locket in her fist, she stared at the fireplace beside the bed. It was far too easy to envision Tavish on the other side of the chimney, long body stretched before the hearth with only a blanket as a mattress.

Perhaps she should have pushed for him to join her in the bed. Not for anything else but sleep.

Yet her revelation at his question—that she would still choose him over any other gentleman—felt too raw, too jolting. And she worried that if he were in such close proximity, she might act rashly. Turn into his arms, press her body to his, and demand a repetition of their explosive kisses from earlier in the week.

Her imagination could easily supply his reaction—his warm palm on her waist, the firm press of his lips. Just the thought sent heat pulsing through her veins and pooling in her abdomen.

But she would never toy with his noble heart and raise expectations she hesitated to fulfill.

Granted, Tavish hadn't attempted a repeat of their kisses, either. But the memory of them hummed along Isla's skin whenever he was near.

She sighed and rolled onto her back, staring up at the bed's canopy, Tavish's locket still clutched in her hand.

Time.

Unlike the girl she had been, Isla knew she needed to give her realization a bit of time. A space where it could be aired in the light of day for her examination. Perhaps her jolt of remembered love for him was an aberration, a one-time occurrence that would not stand up to future scrutiny.

She still had Malton Hill foremost in her mind's eye.

Yet, speaking with Tavish about her estate . . .

His unwavering support and instant desire to assist her in achieving her goals. How like him . . . to hold her happiness above all else.

If she contemplated it too long, she felt like weeping.

Because he had always unerringly supported who *she* wanted to become—the vision she had for herself—rather than demanding she fit into the mold Polite Society required.

She prayed she could do the same for him in return.

Sleep was long in coming.

FOR ISLA, THE next few days passed in a blur of memory.

Lady Mariah sent over books from Castle Balfour's library, and Isla and Tavish exchanged favorites that they had read over the past few years.

Isla wrote letters to Mr. Cranston at Malton Hill, following up on matters with the widowed Mrs. Tippets and her children.

She and Tavish hiked the cairn and, instead of screaming in fury, they stood atop the rock and let the wind batter their clothes and tug at their hair and whip away the crack of their laughter.

But mostly, they talked, just as they had in the past . . . words and ideas, as ever, flowing easily between them.

Isla would ask a question about his time in the military, such as, "Tell me how you landed in the Rifles?"

Or, "How did you change from the Tavish I knew into Captain Balfour?"

And then Tavish would tell her of his military training—the battles fought and the friendships made.

A few hours later, he would ask something like, "What is your greatest hope for Malton Hill?" and she would describe the ongoing refurbishment of the old barns and her desire to create a successful dairy.

Back and forth, give and take.

Isla felt transported back to the girl she had been. And Tavish, with every passing hour, became more and more her Tavish.

Isla had ravaged her inner emotional landscape in venting her grief. But within the debris, new seeds had taken root. New memories of Tavish and perspectives on their love. New insights and ways of seeing him.

He hadn't changed so much as evolved. Just as she had.

And like the new seeds, her affection for him flowered and bloomed, sending out a branch here and a tendril there.

No, they were not the same people. But they still understood one another. Still saw the same beauty in the world and laughed at the same jokes. Still thought along the same paths.

They were still two halves of the same soul.

The knowledge was both euphoria and catastrophe.

What was Isla to do?

TAVISH FEARED FOR his sanity.

Each morning, Isla emerged from her bedchamber, fresh-faced and neatly dressed. And each day, the expression on her face softened a bit more—moving from impassive to warm to a happy smile upon seeing him.

And with every interaction—every look exchanged, every lively conversation—he tumbled deeper in love with her.

She was all he could see, all he could want.

If he possessed an ounce of self-preservation, he would force more distance between them.

Leaving her once had nearly ended him. But losing her again? He wasn't sure he would survive it. The first time, he had held onto hope that she would write, that there might be a reconciliation. But this time . . . with the finality of divorce and her remarriage, there would be no return.

Granted, Isla hadn't mentioned the prospect of their divorce in several days. But then, she had also never once indicated she was interested in continuing with their marriage.

Tavish could scarcely blame her.

His lacking prospects had not miraculously improved. Her understandable attachment to Malton Hill remained the same.

He knew Isla wrote letters most days to her people there. She had even described her plans to assist a widow named Mrs. Tippets in gaining employment with a local seamstress.

Isla couldn't look on suffering and not rush to help, such was the nature of her heart.

And Tavish couldn't listen to Isla's hopes and dreams without longing to help her achieve them.

Such was the nature of his heart.

And so, even though it nearly broke him, Tavish did what he could to assist her.

He wrote to Fletch, apologizing again and reiterating his support of his friend's suit for Isla's hand.

He wrote to Ross and urged his friend to stand by their business plans in Pennsylvania.

All while trying to stem his own free fall back into love with Isla.

Each day felt like running a gauntlet, dodging the punishing force of his adoration of her and praying he could make it to sunset without tripping up and doing something ruinous, like kissing her again.

The evening of their fourth day at Cairnfell, they had just finished tidying up after dinner when Isla turned to him, a hand on her hip.

"Do you dance?" she asked.

His locket rested on her chest, dangling from a gold chain and glinting in the warm light of sunset pouring through the west-facing window. She hadn't taken the locket off since he had gifted it to her. It did something to him, seeing that wee representation of his affection. Like those precious fleeting minutes so long ago when she had worn his wedding band.

"Pardon, lass?"

"Dance? You?"

"Like a Highland jig?"

She laughed. "No, like a minuet or a waltz."

Tavish stared, trying to suss out the purpose of her question. "Of course I waltz. I also carry calling cards, can recite the order of precedence from the king down to Lord Byron, and have excellent table manners. Despite my poverty and your brother's ill opinion, I am an earl's son."

"So you acquit yourself well in a ballroom?"

"I haven't received any complaints from ladies with abused toes. I believe an elderly widow once complimented my finely-turned calf."

Isla leaned down and—shamelessly, he had to add—surveyed said calves. She tapped her far-too-kissable lips as she studied them, his locket swinging with the rhythm.

"I would agree with her assessment."

Heat washed the back of Tavish's neck. He adored this bold version of Isla far too much for his sanity.

"We've never danced together, yourself and I." She lifted an eyebrow. An unmistakable challenge. Similar to the ones he remembered presenting to her.

"Nae."

"I believe a demonstration would not go amiss."

"Of my dancing ability?"

"Yes. Once the glove of challenge has been laid, a gentleman should pick it up."

A beat of silence.

"A waltz, did ye say?" he asked.

She nodded, teeth biting into her plump lower lip.

Tavish took in a slow, steadying breath. He had scarcely touched her in days, terrified that if he did, he simply wouldn't stop. And yet . . . he could deny her nothing.

Stepping in close, he snaked his right arm around her waist. A quick breath expanded her lungs. She mimicked his stance, her right palm pressing into the small of his back. Grasping her left hand in his, Tavish lifted their joined hands above their heads.

"Scandalous," Isla murmured. "You favor Mr. Wilson's waltz." She named the popular dancing master who had brought the waltz to London from Paris.

"'Tis all the rage on the Continent, lass."

The dance *was* scandalous. Their position forced them to stare into one another's eyes, bodies so close, scarcely more than two inches separated them.

Slowly, they began to turn in a slow three-four rhythm—down-up-up, down-up-up. The soft scent of lavender wafted off her skin.

She clicked her tongue. "Such shocking behavior, Captain Balfour. People will think me wanton."

Humor flashed in her tone, but he felt the tremors in her limbs as they twirled around the room in a languid circle.

That was the precise moment Tavish realized the danger of this moment. Because she filled his vision, the blaze of sunset through the window turning her skin to pearls. So close, he could count the freckles scattered across her cheekbones and feel the puff of her breath against his chin.

With each sweep of her skirts, the space between them closed—two inches became one . . . and then became no space at all. Her softness pressed against him, sending his pulse soaring.

Isla swallowed. He watched the roll of her throat with rapt fascination.

"You are indeed an excellent dancer," she whispered.

He nodded, not trusting himself to speak.

Somewhere along the way, they had stopped moving.

They stared at one another, their breaths filling the air.

Alarm bells clamored in his mind.

It would be so easy to kiss her. To release her hand, grasp her neck, and pull her mouth to his—an action he had done hundreds of times. His senses anticipated it, how her chest would rise to meet his, how she would taste.

But he knew himself. As he had intuited earlier, once he began kissing her, he wasn't sure he would ever cease. He would tumble them both onto the enormous bed in the next room.

And she *would* succumb to the wildfire of their mutual desire. He may not have much practical experience in these matters, but he could feel her yearning in the pliable sway of her body and see it in the inky black of her blown pupils.

He wouldn't permit their unruly lusts to rob her of Malton Hill and her dreams for her home. He loved her too well.

With a forced smile, he dropped his hands and stepped back with a small bow.

"Ye be an accomplished dancer yourself, lass. I imagine ye have sore feet after every ball, given the clamor of gentlemen who vie to stand up with ye."

Isla blinked, as if his words landed like a splash of cold water.

Tavish supposed he had intended them as such.

"Yes," she said, blinking again. And then, with a wee shake of her head, she turned for a seat before the fire.

Tavish told himself he was glad the spell had been broken.

For the remainder of their time here at Cairnfell, his mandate remained simple—

Do not touch Isla.

That way lay madness.

28

Isla could feel herself changing.

Day by day, she found it a bit more difficult to hold onto the dream of Malton Hill. Her happiness here with Tavish at Cairnfell rivaled the happiness she experienced at Malton Hill.

Moreover, a terrible truth had been gently taking form in her mind. She hadn't buried her love for her husband, or even abandoned it. She had simply replaced it—exchanging Tavish for Malton Hill in her affections. And now faced with them both, she could no more forgo either of them without losing a vital part of her soul.

How was that possible? And as ever, what was she to do?

On their sixth day at Cairnfell, Lady Mariah managed to slip them a lovely dinner of braised beef with roasted potatoes when she delivered the post. Though Isla appreciated Tavish's ability to create a meal with the most rudimentary ingredients, a proper dinner seated at the table was a welcome change. The weather had turned chilly with rain lashing the windows and wind guttering the fire in the hearth, making the hearty meal even more welcome.

"Any word from Captain Ross about your plans for Pennsylvania?" Isla asked, spooning potatoes onto her plate, eyes darting to the stack of letters Lady Mariah had brought. Tavish had read them, a frown between his brows.

"Nothing specific." Tavish poured himself a glass of red wine. "We're still trying to locate a third investor."

Isla knew that concerns for his future weighed heavy.

"Why did you leave the army?" she asked. "Many men make a living out of it. The wages are not so terrible, particularly for an officer such as yourself."

He took a bite of beef, chewing slowly.

Isla tried not to stare with only middling success. His eye had finally healed from Colonel Archer's battering, the skin once more smooth and golden. Sometimes, she wished she could watch Tavish for hours—tracing the lines of his body, cataloging the smooth skin at the nape of his neck or the shadowed hollow beneath his bottom lip . . . all the places she longed to press a kiss.

He was her husband. All of that lovely maleness was hers and hers alone.

For now.

The price to keep him would be immense. Perhaps higher than she wished to pay. Assuming he even wished to remain married.

It was why, when he had pulled away after their waltz last night, she hadn't protested.

"Why did I leave?" His eyes took on that haunted expression she was starting to recognize, as if he were lost in a nightmare of memory. "Because after so many years of killing and death, I think ye lose foundational parts of your soul. I could feel it happening—a sort of hardening of my humanity—and I simply couldn't bear it anymore. I never wish to become such a man."

Isla thought back to the boy he had been, standing beside Goliath on the road that night. Caving to Gray's demands. So unsure and wavering in which path to take.

And here he was now, full circle. Sure. Strong. Confident in what he wanted. The Tavish of now would always assert what was right over what was easy. He would pay the high price to remain true to his innermost self.

Yet one more reason to love him.

"But I'm sure the Rifles would take me back, if I wanted. My commanding officer was none too pleased to see me go, and unlike other regiments, the Rifles were not disbanded at the end of the war. I could re-enlist." He darted a look at her then, as if assessing her reaction.

Isla was shaking her head before he even finished his sentence. "No. Of course not."

"It would be a way to support a family," he added, voice quiet.

Ah.

They had spent days tiptoeing around the elephant of conflict in the room—the collision of their impending divorce with their renewing affection, both of which were compounded by the harsh reality of their future desires being, rather literally, a world apart.

Tavish opened the door to the discussion, but Isla wasn't sure she wanted to step through it. Because she feared heartbreak sat on the other side, and she wasn't prepared to confront it.

If only she didn't like him quite so well.

But with this . . .

"Return to the army?" She focused on cutting her beef. "I cannot imagine you risking your soul in such a fashion. You were wise to get out when you could."

He nodded, as if he had expected her answer.

"Ross suggested I go into politics." A rueful smile quirked his lips, as if to say, *Can ye believe such an absurd suggestion?*

But . . . Isla could.

Abruptly, she could see it. Tavish would be dazzling in politics. A gentleman with his native intelligence, analytical mind, and strong moral compass . . .

"I think you would be brilliant."

Now it was his turn to stare at her.

"You would," she continued. "You have a competent magnetism about you. As more than one person said during the house party at Kingswell—the world could crumble to pieces and you would simply set to, cleaning up the mess. I can think of no one who would better champion the nameless masses of this country than you."

Tavish was quiet for a long while after that, picking at his food.

"Does the idea alarm you?" she asked.

"Nae." He reached for his wine glass. "Merely trying to accommodate the concept. I've never thought of myself as the political type, either here or in America. But then, I ken that most professional interactions are political in one way or another. Heaven knows, I spent years leading men and acting as a mediator between their needs and those of my superiors."

"I'm not sure politics would be much different."

They moved on to speaking of other things, but she could see him turning over the idea of running for office. Of course, he would need a wife to assist him. A proper sort of wife. But when she envisioned him stepping into a London dining room, ready to woo patrons, the only wife she could picture on his arm was herself.

Hours later, the rain continued to drum overhead, and an unpleasant chill had settled into the room.

Isla frowned as Tavish began setting up his bed. They hadn't revisited his sleeping on the hard flagstones of the great hall, but for Isla, every night alone in her large bed became more difficult to tolerate, particularly if she thought of him suffering and cold.

A true wife would ensure his comfort.

"You needn't sleep here." She pointed to his makeshift pallet. "The bed is plenty large for us both."

He didn't even look up as she spoke. Merely continued to fluff a pillow and place it atop the stack of blankets.

"Tavish." Her hands went to her hips, as if preparing to scold him. Another wifely behavior, unfortunately.

He picked up a second pillow. "Isla, as I've said, I find it no bother to sleep here."

Oh! This stubborn man!

"It's pouring rain, and the temperature is falling. The great hall will be baltic by morning. Why are you resisting my decidedly sensible suggestion?"

Tavish dropped the pillow atop the blankets of his makeshift bed.

Raising his head, he fixed her with his gray eyes . . . and something dropped within his expression. A mask she hadn't realized he had been holding. And in its stead, she saw raw hunger—feral and barely contained.

Every last drop of moisture evaporated from her mouth.

"Isla."

He said her name like an epithet. Or was it a hosanna? She could scarcely say. He took one step toward her before stopping himself.

"Lass, if I crawl into that bed beside ye"—his voice a rasp—"I will not keep my hands to myself. Lying beside ye without touching ye would require greater strength of will than I possess. A sane man knows his limits." He scanned her stunned expression. "So I sleep here."

He pointed to the piled blankets.

Oh.

And . . . now all she could picture were the delightful ways he would not keep his hands to himself. The wanting as he pulled her against his body and bent his lips to hers. She could hardly breathe for the desire clouding her thoughts.

"Is that why you haven't kissed me? Or even attempted to kiss me?" Her questions emerged breathless. "There was a moment during our waltz when . . ."

The memory of their last kisses in that empty bedroom rose like a specter between them. The wild greed of his mouth pressing against hers. The delicious weight of his hands skimming her body.

He nudged his pallet with a foot, shoulders shrugging. "Ye haven't tried to kiss me either, lass. Why is that?"

Because I don't know, she thought.

Because if I kiss you again, I'm not sure I will ever stop, and I don't want lust to drive decisions about my future.

Something of her thoughts must have shown on her face.

"Exactly," he whispered. "Ye must understand, Isla, if we consummate our marriage, that will be it."

"Pardon?"

"If I have ye, if ye take me as your husband in truth, that will be it. I will not share that intimacy with yourself and then pass ye off to another." He paused, the next words emerging as if torn from his throat. "If ye kiss me, ye should know where it will lead—you and I spending our lives together."

His words landed with all the subtlety of a gunshot.

Isla barely stopped a wince.

"Because once we share our bodies with one another—if we make that commitment," he continued. "I will never let ye go. You will be mine, and I will be yours."

His lips formed a sad quirk—one that added, quite clearly, *and we both know ye don't want that.*

And yet, as she held his gaze, she realized he was wrong.

I want to choose you.

The same words from several nights before, only this time, present tense instead of conditional—*I want* instead of *I would.*

No more hypotheticals.

I want you. I want us.

The realization upended every aspect of her thinking, stilling her tongue and rendering her thoughts a stunned hum.

Nodding, she retreated to her own bed, but sleep was impossible.

Tavish's words and her own burgeoning emotions would not let her be.

This is why I left, he had said, indicating that she deserved more than the simplicity of life here at Cairnfell Castle.

And how had Isla responded?

I don't think that lass would have cared. All she wanted was you.

How dreadful to come full circle seven years on. Because Isla was rather certain she still felt the same.

Perhaps, in the end, love *was* a sort of madness, as Shakespeare claimed.

Not because of youth or stupidity or derangement, but because it was *love,* pure and simple—wild and blinding and all-encompassing.

She didn't care what life they led—she just wanted Tavish to remain at her side. Wherever he was, there she was happiest. The past few days had proven that.

But what about Malton Hill and her responsibilities there? How would her tenants fare without her oversight?

Yet even as she voiced the thought, her time at Malton Hill morphed in her mind's eye.

When there, Isla was her own mistress. No Gray peering over her shoulder and telling her what to do. No governess to correct her speech or pronounce judgment on her comportment.

Her determination to keep Malton Hill partially stemmed from her love of its people. But another significant part came from her longing to build something of her own. To have a sliver of the world that was hers alone to manage and oversee.

And Tavish had always allowed her that freedom. He would never clip her wings. It was one of the thousand reasons why she adored him.

She had loved the girl she was with Tavish, and she loved the woman she was at Malton Hill, because in every real way, both scenarios permitted her to be her fullest self.

And now . . .

She loved him anew. Fully. Completely. Just as she had loved him then.

Only this time, she loved the man he had become, not just the memory of a boy.

And that was most terrifying of all.

TAVISH WOKE THE next morning, his body fevered with longing.

He had reached the end of his tether. The tension between himself and Isla felt nigh to snapping.

This simply would not do.

Fortunately, the rain of the day before had melted away, leaving warm sun in its wake.

He rolled off his makeshift pallet, stretching as he wiped sleep from his eyes.

His gaze drifted to Isla's bedchamber door, shut to keep in the heat.

It had taken almost superhuman strength to refuse her offer last night. He wanted nothing more than to sleep at her side for the rest of his life.

Even now, it would be simple to turn the handle and step inside her bedchamber. Lift the coverlet and slide in beside her. He had spent the entire night imagining it. Her breathy sigh as he pulled her to his chest, pressing all her glorious curves to his body. Only in his dreams, her back arched in invitation, and he bent to kiss her mouth, and everything exploded into uncontrolled passion.

He turned away before temptation got the better of him. Instead, he pulled on a shirt and belted his kilt around his waist. Leaving a wee note for Isla so she wouldn't worry, he slipped out the door.

TAVISH DOVE INTO the River Northcairn, the frigid water sluicing over his body, cutting and sharp. He welcomed the unpleasant jolt, letting it blessedly dampen his ardor. Surfacing, he shook water out of his eyes, swimming for the opposite bank.

The cold felt heavenly against his skin. If he came down here every morning and night, shocking his system into obedience, perhaps he could survive the next few weeks.

He stroked across the pool, back and forth, lazily rotating like the otters who plied these same waterways.

A swish of sound or snap of a twig—some shift in the very air—alerted him to her presence.

Treading water out into the open, Tavish watched as Isla set down a basket on the grassy bank, white Turkish bath towels and a brush spilling out.

He stared, eyes not knowing where to land.

Her glorious hair was down, unbound and cascading around her shoulders. The golden strands shimmered in the sunlight, haloing her head.

Her clothing was in a similar state of dishabille, a dressing gown tied just under her bosom. The same dressing gown she had been wearing that last fateful night at Kingswell. The sight of it recalled the memory of her curves under his palms.

"I liked your idea, and I thought I might bathe." Isla lifted a bar of soap.

Bloody hell.

Had the woman no mercy?

"Here? Now?"

Even buried to the neck in snow, his body would still feel overheated.

She laughed. "Of course here and now. Unless the thought makes you uncomfortable?"

Uncomfortable? Absolutely. Just not for the reason she supposed.

She misread his hesitation. "You can turn around if the prospect offends your sensibilities."

"It wasn't my sensibilities I was considering. I am rather . . ." He glanced at his legs, treading water. ". . . unclothed, at the moment."

She lifted an elegant eyebrow before pointedly looking at his shirt and kilt folded beside her basket. "Yes. I noticed."

Damn.

Was he . . .

Was he blushing?!

Truly, Tavish couldn't remember the last time he had blushed.

"I do believe a state of undress is assumed when one bathes," she continued, voice wry.

"Aye."

Their gazes met and tangled.

Her eyebrow lifted higher, and her hands went to the ties of her dressing gown. Was she even wearing a chemise underneath?

Tavish turned around before finding out. Seeing her disrobe would shred what remained of his control.

Even as it was, he had to endure the rustling of her dressing gown falling to the ground. Her tentative footfalls into the shallows of the pool. Her stuttering gasp and faint splash as she plunged into the cold depths.

Torture.

Pure and simple.

Every coherent thought fled his overheated brain. All he could do was listen—the slosh as she washed, the soft humming under her breath, the cascade of water as she rinsed off soap.

Finally, she laughed.

"You seem rather distracted," she said from behind. Closer than he might have supposed.

The fact did nothing to cool the fire in his veins.

"Ye be naked and bathing only a few feet from my spine. A man would have to be dead and cold in the grave to not be preoccupied in such a moment, Wife."

She said nothing for a moment.

And then, on a whisper, "Wife." She cleared her throat. "You have never once called me *Wife*."

"*Och*, ye are."

"Indeed, I am . . . Husband."

The word landed with an almost exquisite pain.

Husband.

Tavish closed his eyes.

How he longed to be that in truth.

She splashed behind him again.

It was simply . . . too much.

He couldn't remain in this water another minute. Not with his yearning so close to the surface and so poorly contained. Calling him husband and deciding to keep him as such were two rather separate things.

"My fingers have gone rather pruny," he said. "Ye might want to turn your back as I get out."

"Concerned for my missish sense of modesty?"

More like my own sanity, he thought grimly.

"Something of the like."

He swam toward the bank, eyes focused on the grass there and nowhere else. And even so, he still caught a glimpse of her bare shoulders as her arms circled in the water.

He couldn't say if she watched him get out. Pondering it sent lightning crackling along his skin.

Snatching up one of the towels she had brought, he dragged it over his body, the soft cotton engulfing him. He dried off in quick movements before pulling on his kilt and belting it.

At first, he thought to return to Cairnfell Castle—remove himself from sure temptation, as it were—but he could scarcely leave his wife bathing in an outdoor pool where any stranger could happen upon her, no matter how unlikely.

Instead, he sat on the grass beside her discarded clothing—his back to the water—trying not to ponder the fact that only her dressing gown and a pair of shoes rested on the bank.

No chemise or any other sort of undergarment.

Hell and damnation.

He pinched the bridge of his nose.

Certainly, this was one of Dante's circles of Hell. The one where a man desired his wife but could never have her.

A few minutes later, he heard the sound of water sluicing off a body. Her body. That of his *wife*. Helplessly, he imagined her rising from the pool like the birth of Venus from sea foam.

"Could you hand me my towel and dressing gown?" she asked, far too close for his comfort.

He nodded. She had rendered him mute. Eyes shut tight, he stretched the items behind, her fingers brushing his as she took them.

His arms trembled with the force of holding himself back.

He couldn't bear this. They should return to the keep before his control splintered. He cleared his throat, intending to propose just that, when she sat down beside him.

Reflexively, he glanced at her.

She was, thankfully, dressed.

However, water droplets clung to her fair skin and his locket glinted around her neck, dangling just above the swell of her bosom.

Lord help him.

Oblivious to the crisis consuming him, Isla tipped her face toward the sun.

"Mmmm," she moaned. "The sunlight feels divine."

She had no mercy. His sweet, naive lass had no idea how torturous every sound and movement had become. How she was unraveling him bit by bit.

The rustling silk of her dressing gown, gaping open at the neck.

The lift of her chin exposing the smooth column of her throat.

The gooseflesh pebbling the skin over her collarbones.

Unaware, she tilted her head toward him and used her towel to wring more water out of her hair, causing the open collar of her dressing gown to sag, exposing a wee glimpse of her creamy bare shoulder.

Och.

He needed to leave.

Tavish lurched to his feet.

"I'll just . . ." What? Return to the castle without her?

"Leaving?" she asked.

He made the mistake of looking back at her.

She sat upon the grass in a disheveled heap, hair pulled to one side. Never had she looked more lovely.

She raised a hand, an unspoken request to help her up.

Swallowing, Tavish grasped her hand, still cold and slightly damp from the water. Her touch seared.

Something flickered in her gaze. A ripple of awareness. Of want. Her eyes dropped to his bare chest, as if unable to help herself.

And he knew.

His bonnie wife was every whit as affected and yearning as himself.

Her actions had been a provocation.

A deliberate seduction.

The knowledge landed in his brain with all the subtlety of cannon fire.

With a quick tug, he pulled her to her feet . . .

. . . and then kept right on pulling until she was flush with his chest.

Just as before, their bodies touched and everything combusted.

Her fingers dove into his hair, and his mouth found hers.

Theirs was less a kiss and more a collision of two fiery objects intent on incineration.

Tavish drew her tight against him, a groan shuddering his lungs.

He couldn't get enough of her—of her delectable mouth, of her breathy sighs.

Her wee hands left his head and were suddenly everywhere—skimming his chest, his shoulders, his spine—as if she were frantic to touch every inch of him at once.

She bit his lip and laved away the sting. Tavish nearly saw stars.

Just as before, some quiet part of him pleaded for sanity . . .

Ye need to stop. She doesn't want ye as a husband.

But she had called him *husband* not fifteen minutes past. And she had gazed at him as a wife gazed at a husband. Wanting—no, needing, demanding!—his touch.

And now, that was all he could picture.

Husband. Wife.

The two of them together.

29

I love him.
Oh, how I love him.

Those were the only words swinging round in Isla's brain, the only longing in her veins.

She hadn't intended to seduce Tavish. No. She well understood his warning from last night.

Her thought had been to join him in bathing and . . .

Bah! Why lie to herself?!

All rational thought had fled when she saw him treading water in the pool.

It had been untenable. Listening to his labored breathing as she had bathed. And then shamelessly watching him rise from the pool, water pouring off his broad shoulders and chasing his spine.

A truly refined lady would have looked away. Perhaps more of her mother remained than Isla would have liked, because she had tracked every motion of his body with ravenous greed.

It felt imperative—required, even—to show him with her body all the adoration brimming in her heart. To let her hands and lips declare the words her mouth still hesitated to utter.

And now she had that glorious maleness in her arms, the taste of him filling her senses. His skin had the give of silk-covered steel under her palms, warm and smooth and deliciously firm.

Husband.

The word hummed in the very air.

His mouth painted fire down the side of her neck. Isla clung to his shoulders, spine arching in an attempt to get closer. To somehow merge her essence into his.

He obliged, his strong arms banding her to him. She could feel the faint tremor in his muscles, as if his skeleton were wracked with small earthquakes. A battering ram crashing into the wall of their self-restraint and, quite frankly, any iota of wisdom.

His eager lips left her throat and returned to her mouth, plundering with punishing force.

Isla had just started to wonder why they were both still standing upright while a perfectly soft bed of green grass stretched out behind her . . .

. . . when Tavish abruptly dropped his hands from her body. Just as he had during their waltz.

The sudden loss caused her to sag. She braced her palms on his chest for support and peered up at him, a crease between her brows.

He regarded her with the same untamed hunger, but a hint of wariness had crept in. His lungs were a bellows, expanding and contracting.

"Tavish?" she gasped.

Gently, so gently, he pulled her palms from his chest and set them at her side.

He took a step back.

And then another.

Frowning, Isla stepped forward, only to have him stop her with a slice of his head.

"Isla." His voice dragged like chains over gravel.

She blinked up at him, at the sun haloing his head. She wrapped her arms around her waist, terrified of what he would say next.

"I can't . . ." He paused, eyes fluttering closed as if in pain. "I can't kiss ye and not . . ." Opening his eyes, he gave her a beseeching look. "As I've said before, we play with fire, lass. We both know that kisses such as these lead to more intimate activities. I won't have ye trifle with my affections. I meant my words from last night—if we share our bodies, I will never let ye go."

His spine straightened. Captain Balfour flickered into his expression, the iron control of a soldier.

He licked his lips.

"I love ye, Isla." The words were torn from him, ripped from the foundation of his being. "I loved ye as a lass. I love the woman ye have grown to be. I'm certain I will love every iteration of ye between now and the end of my days. Ye are woven into the very fabric of my soul."

Bending down, he picked up his shirt and the wet towels.

"I want nothing more than to spend the rest of my life proving how much I love ye. But . . ."

Silence.

She hated that string of words . . .

I love ye. But . . .

"But?" she whispered.

He sucked in a breath. "But the only thing worse than letting ye go, would be to tether ye to myself unwillingly. To watch the affection between us shrivel and decay. My lack of funds has not changed, and the prospects for my future are as they have always been. I cannot give ye Malton Hill. I cannot offer ye anything more substantial than my beating heart."

Isla couldn't move. She could scarcely breathe.

His words battered her senses.

Because she wanted to claim his magnificent heart as her own. But the fear of reaching for it turned her limbs numb.

"I want ye to be intentional about this decision, Isla," he continued. "Take all the time ye need—days or weeks or months. I will wait until ye know your own mind."

As ever, he was making her choose. Refusing to permit lust and animal attraction to cement their fates.

Isla was quite certain that thirty years from now, she would be able to call up this moment.

Tavish standing tall before her—chest bare, hair damp and disheveled from her fingers, sunlight skimming his face and turning his gray eyes to liquid silver. The rustle of trees and the burble of the river at her back. The lone call of a hawk soaring high overhead.

Her reply stuck in her throat. *I love you, Tavish. I do! But . . .*

. . . will it be enough?

As if hearing her unspoken thoughts, he shot her a sad smile.

"Ponder this choice carefully, my love," he said. "Ye know where to find me when ye wish to continue this conversation."

Leaning forward, he pressed one last kiss to her cheek—night whiskers brushing her skin and the smell of warm male skin engulfing her.

And then Tavish pivoted and disappeared up the path to the castle.

ISLA STARED AT the place where Tavish had vanished for far too long.

I love ye. But . . .

Those spare words could caption their entire relationship.

She felt the echo of them in her chest.

Ye are woven into the very fabric of my soul.

Isla loved him. Of that that she was certain. She ached for a consummation of that love.

Yet as he had said, love and lifelong commitment, particularly in the face of penury and poverty, were rather two different things.

I will never let ye go.

Just like last night, he said those words as a threat. A warning intended to control the blazing passion between them before it burned down her hopes for the future.

His actions underscored why she loved this man as she did. Even in the midst of untamed lust, Tavish still put her needs and wants above his own.

Isla pondered all this as she sat down on the grassy bank and brushed out her hair, letting it dry in the sun.

The enormity of the decision loomed large.

Once, she had committed herself to a life with him without carefully considering the ramifications.

This time . . . she would be intentional. Careful. Deliberate. Clearly understanding the repercussions. She would not toy with Tavish's affections, as he said.

Even if part of her screamed in frustration over this need for logic.

When her hair was no longer dripping, Isla braided it with quick motions and tied it off with a ribbon from her pocket.

She stared at the rippling water of the pool, hoping it would bring her some clarity.

None arrived.

On a sigh, she gathered her things and trudged back up to Cairnfell Castle.

Tavish was making their lunch when she entered the great hall. Back to her, he stood at the sideboard, slicing ham and cheese.

Unfortunately, he had donned a shirt and waistcoat overtop his kilt. Or was it fortunately? She could scarcely say.

The stiffening of his shoulders indicated he had heard her arrival.

He didn't turn around.

Isla said nothing, mostly because she didn't know what to say.

I love you and I want us to be together, hovered on her tongue. And though irrevocably true, she wouldn't declare such feelings until she was ready to commit to a lifetime of them.

"I'll have lunch ready shortly," he finally said.

"Thank you."

"The post arrived." He nudged a chin toward a small table inside the door. "Grayburn forwarded several letters to Castle Balfour for yourself."

"Ah. I suppose that is a good sign."

"He may thaw yet."

After so much tumult, Isla nearly laughed at the banality of their exchange.

She sifted through her letters—two from Mr. Cranston at Malton

Hill, one from Mrs. Sumsion. If Isla remained married to Tavish, would she ever see her estate again?

Tavish's own post remained on the side table, too. A couple of letters that appeared dreadfully official. One lay partially open, as if he had begun reading it and then tossed it aside.

Isla didn't mean to snoop, but the scrawling signature *Archer* caught her off guard.

Tavish was corresponding with Colonel Archer?

Unable to stop herself, she put a hand on the letter, smoothing the paper just enough to read a line or two.

> *. . . your nobility is as annoying as ever. That, even now, you would profess your love for your wife in one sentence and then propose I continue my suit in the next because, as you say, "I want her to have her heart's desire," is the very definition of madness. I shall have to ponder . . .*

"Isla?"

Tavish's voice caused her to jump.

She whirled to look at him, color climbing her cheeks.

"Enjoying Fletch's letter?" There was no anger or irritation in his tone. Only resignation. "Ye can read the whole if ye would like. I have no secrets from yourself."

"You wrote Colonel Archer?"

"Aye. Ye want Malton Hill. I'm doing what I can to help ye reach that goal. Ye said yourself that ye like Edward Archer. I know the man better than almost anyone; he would make ye a fine husband. Isn't that what ye want?"

It was.

A fine husband and Malton Hill.

It was what she wanted. *Had* wanted, rather.

But now . . .

Now, Isla knew she only wanted the fine husband she already possessed.

A man who loved her with breathtaking force. Who loved her enough to give her the future she wanted, even at the cost of his own happiness.

I will love every iteration of ye between now and the end of my days.

A man who stated his deepest desires and then left the choice to her. Emotion pricked her eyes.

"I see." She turned for the bedroom. "Thank you."

She all but ran through the door, shutting it behind her and leaning back against the wood.

A tear fell.

And then two.

It was simply . . . too much.

Too much love, too much longing and joy and *everything* to contain. But . . .

Oof!

No more *buts.*

No more prevarication and wavering.

Isla Kinsey loved Tavish Balfour. Full stop.

Just as he loved her.

They were woven into the very fabric of one another's souls.

How dare the man she loved not fight for his soul?

She wiped her eyes on the sleeve of her dressing gown and then met her gaze in the mirror of the small vanity.

Huh.

She appeared as undone as she felt—eyes wide, color high on her cheeks, lips still red and bee-stung from Tavish's kisses.

So this is what love looks like, she thought. *True love.*

Not a fanciful sort of passion or an inclination. Not a pleasant attachment formed from unity of thought and purpose. Not even the wild infatuation of a young girl lost in the heady delight of her first romance.

No.

This was an I-will-burn-for-you-until-the-day-I-die sort of devotion. A love that reshaped empires and incited wars and shattered two centuries of animosity between a pair of feuding families.

And between one breath and the next, Isla simply . . . knew.

The mere thought of living without him tasted of ash.

She could no more untangle the knot that bound her to Tavish Balfour than she could willfully stop her own beating heart.

Nothing else mattered beyond that. Any life she lived away from him would pale in comparison.

As he had said, he was hers.

And she was his.

TAVISH TRIED TO put some semblance of a lunch together.

But it was hard going.

His hand shook as he sliced the ham, leaving the cuts uneven. He didn't dare attempt the bread.

Finally, he set down the knife and braced both hands atop the sideboard, trying to wrestle his wayward emotions under control.

It was proving a nearly impossible task.

He shouldn't have given Isla an ultimatum. He shouldn't have blurted out the truth of his love for her. It was unfair and possibly manipulative.

Her white-lipped, stunned face would haunt his dreams.

Bloody *eejit.*

Nausea crawled up his throat.

Their situation had become impossible.

The bedroom door opened with a *snick.*

Clenching his hands into fists, Tavish turned to look at her.

He had supposed her to be changing into a day dress and pinning up her hair. Instead, she wore the same dressing gown, hair still hanging in a long braid over one shoulder. His locket gleamed against her skin. Her eyes were red-rimmed, and her cheeks held the remnants of tears.

Never had she appeared more beautiful.

As ever, his foolish heart panged to see her distress, particularly as his own actions were the likely culprit.

Tavish leaned back against the sideboard, gripping its wooden edge with tense fingers. Anything to prevent himself from reaching for her.

"I'm sorry if I have overset ye," he began. "That wasn't my intention."

"You have overset me." Tears glittered in her lovely blue eyes. "Therefore, I have a request."

"Anything, lass."

She darted a glance at the hearth. "I don't want you to sleep in front of the fire anymore."

His brows drew down. Of everything he thought she might say, this was not it.

"Pardon?"

She took a step toward him. Her hands fisted into her dressing gown, as if she were nervous.

"Husband, I don't want you to sleep in front of the fire any longer."

Tavish swallowed, his pulse a stampede of hooves against his ribs.

Surely, she didn't mean . . .

"If not in front of the fire, then where should I sleep . . . Wife?"

"With me."

"With yourself?"

She nodded, causing a tear to drop onto her cheek. Several more quickly followed.

Tavish struggled to breathe through the dawning reality of her words.

"Isla—" He took three steps toward her before stopping himself. "Are ye sure, lass? Because I meant what I said—I will not let ye go. I want ye to take all the time ye need to think through this decision. I want ye to have all ye wish for and—"

"Seven years ago, I only had o-one wish—to b-be with *you*!"

"Aye. I know. Me, too."

She nodded again, this time more fiercely.

"That is still my strongest wish—to be with you. You say you l-love me enough to set me free." She dashed a hand across her eyes. "But I want you to f-fight to keep me, Tavish Balfour! I want you to wage battles and vanquish enemies and destroy every last wall that will ever keep us apart. I want you to claim me as your own and never let me go!"

He managed a stuttering breath, but emotion rose so quickly, it stuffed his throat and nose until it found an outlet in his eyes. Swallowing, he pressed a hand to his face, anything to avoid collapsing to the floor and *greiting* like a babe.

He hadn't known.

He hadn't understood how much he wanted Isla and a life together. How desperately he longed for that outcome.

But feeling the joy of it now . . .

A terrible sob wracked him. And then another.

Damnation.

First blushing, and now this?

He couldn't remember the last time he had wept.

"Tavish." Her voice a whisper.

A hand tugged on his wrist, pulling his palm from his face.

And there she was.

His Isla.

Like himself, tears coated her cheeks.

"You c-can't cry," she hiccupped, "because then I'll c-cry, and I won't be able to s-say what I must."

"What must ye say, love?"

She smiled, so radiant. "I want you—I want *us*—to wake up each morning and choose each other." She pressed a palm to his cheek. "And I want us to keep choosing each other. Over the disapproval of our families and the uncertainty of our future. Today, t-tomorrow . . ."

She drifted off on a gasp of air.

Tavish's vision turned blurry once more.

"Forever?" he whispered.

"F-forever."

He cradled her beloved face in his hands. He brushed away her tears with his thumbs.

"Truly?" he whispered.

She nodded.

On a shaking breath, he kissed her. Not a kiss of wild hunger or desperation.

No.

A kiss of agonizing love. Of the hope of their promised life together. The kiss he had given her after their handfasting.

"Ye truly mean it?" He had to ask again.

"Y-yes!"

She laughed—a choking, hiccupping sound. The sound of more happiness than a heart could contain.

Tavish swept her into his arms, swinging her in a circle with a loud whoop of joy, before setting her down and dropping his lips to hers.

"Darling." *Kiss.* "Love." *Kiss.* "Wife."

His bright, clever wife met him kiss for kiss, caress for caress.

But . . .

"Malton Hill!" Tavish lifted his head, staring down at her. "Ye can't give up your home, lass!"

"Home is wherever you are, Tavish Balfour." She pressed a finger into the vertical crease in his chin. "I will mourn Malton Hill, but you asked me that first night here who I would choose? And the answer—" Her eyes went bright once more. "—the answer is you. I will always choose you."

"My love." He bent to her mouth once more.

But as much as Tavish wanted to lose himself in her, one more thing needed to be done. He gave her a final deep kiss before stepping back.

"Tavish?" she frowned.

"One moment, darling." He kissed the wee dent between her eyebrows and then crossed to his saddle bags stacked against the wall beside the sideboard.

It only took him seconds to retrieve what he sought.

"What is it?" Isla asked as he returned to her.

On a deep breath, Tavish opened his fist, revealing the shimmering gold of her wedding ring. The talisman he had carried through the years without her.

"Oh!" Isla gasped. "I thought it lost."

"Never. I will always keep it safe for ye."

His fierce wife lifted her gaze to his and then extended her left hand, palm down, fingers spread.

Swallowing back emotion once again, Tavish slid the wedding ring home onto her finger.

To see it there once more . . .

He lifted her fingers to his lips, pressing a kiss to the ring.

"I love ye, Wife."

"I love you, too, Husband. So much."

He kissed her again, unable to help himself.

One kiss became dozens became hundreds.

He whispered *I love ye* over and over into her skin—pressed into her collarbones and nuzzled beneath her ear.

"I fear the wait until sunset tonight will be agonizing," he murmured against her mouth.

She stilled and tilted her head back to look into his eyes.

"Tonight?" Leaning sideways in his arms, she made a production of scanning the room. "Is there anyone else present?"

"Nae."

"Are we expecting visitors?"

"Nae."

His clever wife arched a pretty eyebrow. "Then why, Husband, must we wait for darkness? I have been led to understand that nighttime is hardly a requirement for marital consummation."

Tavish laughed, the sound thrumming through his veins like quicksilver.

"Tavish Balfour, I have waited seven long years to be your wife in truth. I will be very put out if you make me wait another seven hours."

Isla took his hand in hers and pulled. Laughing, he permitted her to drag him into the bedroom. He kicked the door shut behind them and then, taking both her hands, stretched them wide.

He surveyed her, this beautiful, remarkable woman.

"What is it?" she smiled.

"Just trying to understand why a creature as vivid and lovely as yourself would take up with me."

"Now you are being ridiculous."

"Perhaps." He met her gaze and tugged, bringing her closer. "I love ye, Isla. I intend to love ye until I am old and gray."

His brilliant wife did not reply.

Instead, she wrapped her arms around his neck and kissed him.

TAVISH WOULD ALWAYS remember the next hours as some of the most beautiful and sacred of his life. The awe of giving himself wholly to another, and she in return.

Yes, there was passion, but also laughter and tenderness. A sense of a beginning just waiting to unfold.

They dozed in the aftermath, content to simply be in one another's arms.

Eventually, Tavish prepared their long-forgotten lunch, setting the tray on the bed. Resting back against the headboard, Isla's head on his shoulder, Tavish fed her tidbits of ham and slices of ripe pear.

"I'm sorry about Malton Hill," he said, cutting another strip off the pear and holding it to her lips. "I am sorry for ye to lose something ye love so well."

"I am, too, but . . . well, I'm not sure Malton Hill specifically is what I wanted, in the end."

Tavish listened as she told him of her revelation. That she mostly loved the person she was at Malton Hill—competent and in charge of her own destiny. That it was more about who she could become as a human being rather than the actuality of the place itself.

"It's why I love you so thoroughly," she finished. "Because when I am with you, I am in a constant state of becoming. You see me as Isla, nothing less or more, and will always encourage me to be my fullest self."

Tavish kissed her. "Ye know I will always love every version of ye."

"And I, you."

He smiled, lifting the lunch tray off the bed before pulling her back to his shoulder. "So . . . how many children are ye thinking we will have, lass?"

His clever Isla lifted her head to look at him in astonishment. "Tavish! You wish to discuss that now?"

"Of course."

"Why?"

He arched an eyebrow.

"Because I expect that we will be eagerly engaged in child-making activities for the foreseeable future, and I want to be prepared."

He pulled her against his chest, bending to kiss her mouth.

On a sigh, Isla melted into him.

And any coherent thoughts Tavish might have had vanished as sure as hoarfrost in the sun.

30

The next few days were the happiest of Isla's life.

She was well and truly Mrs. Balfour now, and she hadn't a moment's regret. Just seeing the wedding ring on her finger could set her cheeks to blushing.

Tavish . . . well . . .

He was precisely the attentive, affectionate husband her younger self had supposed he would be.

They lazed about in bed and took turns reading one another's favorite passages from books.

They revisited the swimming hole along the River Northcairn and had such an astonishing encounter there, Isla flushed scarlet at the memory.

They spoke of their future and tried to make a plan out of the uncertainty.

"Perhaps Matthias would like to be an investor in our whisky scheme?" Isla asked over breakfast.

Everything had become *our* and *we* and *us*.

"Do ye not think he will be incensed by our marriage?" Tavish took a bite of porridge.

"Unlikely. Matthias is more . . . understanding than Gray."

"Well, we will need funds, so it wouldn't hurt to—"

A knock sounded on the large wooden door below.

"Ah. That must be a groom from Castle Balfour with the morning post." Tavish threw down his napkin and disappeared down the stairs.

He reappeared a few minutes later, sorting through a stack of letters in his hand.

The bottommost letter made him frown.

"Tavish? What is it?"

"A letter to me franked by Grayburn."

Tavish opened the letter, only to have a separate note tumble out. He scanned the lines of the letter.

"Grayburn knows ye be staying here with me at Cairnfell. He has discreet sources, he says. I am to give ye this." He handed the note to her.

Isla took it with a lift of her eyebrow.

Gray's lines were brief and to the point.

> *Isla,*
>
> *I require your presence at Dunmore immediately. Tavish Balfour is not welcome.*
>
> *Gray*
>
> *P.S. You will be pleased with what I have to say.*

Tavish snorted as he read the note over her shoulder. "I do not believe for one moment that ye will be pleased with what your brother has to say."

"Yes, it is unlikely."

"This must be a trap of some sort."

"Perhaps."

Isla nibbled at her bottom lip, thoughts churning.

Tavish sat down in the chair beside her. "Ye be considering going to him."

It was a statement, not a question.

Drat this man for knowing her so well.

"I will need to return to Dunmore for a short visit at some point. I would like to pack up my effects—books and gowns and such—and retrieve the jewelry left to me by my mother. Gray will not deny me these things. Moreover, this would be an excellent chance to speak with Matthias about the prospect of investing in our plans for Pennsylvania."

"I agree with that ye need to return to Dunmore eventually, but I insist on being at your side when ye do."

"My love, we both know that your presence would only make matters worse. Gray specifically said you are not welcome. I do not want to give him an excuse to have you arrested."

"Grayburn might hurt you."

"Tavish, Gray has said the most hurtful, vile things to me over the years—he has battered my heart and soul—but never once has he laid a hand upon me physically. I do not anticipate that will change. But I would not put it past him to harm *you* should you accompany me."

"He can try."

"Tavish—"

"Grayburn will attempt to pry us apart."

"How? He cannot force us to divorce. We are married, thoroughly and utterly." Her cheeks pinked as she spoke.

Tavish watched her blush spread, a smile tugging at those pillow lips she loved so well. "Recalling our exploits in bed this morning, are ye?"

"Hush!" She pressed a cool hand to her face. "Ye needn't be so smug."

"And that's the thanks I get for my exertions? I do believe the words ye used earlier were *magnificent* and *remarkable*."

"Tavish!" Isla laughed.

He pressed a kiss to her cheek. "I detest the thought of ye enduring something unpleasant when I am not there to aid ye."

"I know. But please trust me. Gray may bluster and rage, but his words no longer have power to hurt me. In the end, he won't hold me hostage or lay a finger on me."

"I wish I could be sure." He reached for her hand, thumb pressing into the wedding band there.

"Be at ease, Husband. Gray has no say over me in any sense, legal or otherwise. However, I would like to speak with him. I still have concerns about Malton Hill and how he will see to his responsibilities there once I am gone."

"Do ye think Gray will neglect your people out of spite?"

It was a fair question.

"No. His quibble is with me, not the people of Malton Hill. His sense of honor will recognize that. My brother isn't perfect, but neither is he a monster."

Tavish snorted, clearly disagreeing with her.

"I shall leave this afternoon and send word from Dunmore," she continued. "If you don't hear from me by tomorrow morning, by all means, marshal your men and storm my family's august halls."

Tavish buried his face in her neck. "I don't like this."

"I know, my love." She pressed a kiss to the side of his head. "All will be well. You'll see."

ISLA STEPPED INTO Gray's study.

Her brother nodded in greeting, face impassive. However, the tapping of his fingers against his thigh betrayed his irritation.

Granted, Isla's behavior had been calibrated to needle him. Payback for the autocratic tone of his note to her.

Tavish had borrowed a small gig from Castle Balfour for Isla to drive herself to Dunmore. He accompanied her as far as the boundaries of Grayburn land.

"Return to me soon," he had said, kissing her soundly. "Ye joked about me storming Grayburn's palace, but I will do so without hesitation."

Upon stepping through the front door of Dunmore, Isla had immediately requested a bath be drawn. This had been followed by an extensive toilette and rather sumptuous luncheon.

Only then, with her belly full and an elegant London day dress upon her person, did she present herself to her brother.

He was not amused.

Gray stared as she closed the door to his study with a polite *snick*.

"You wished to see me, Brother?" she said by way of greeting.

He pointed at the leather armchair opposite his desk. Isla lifted an eyebrow but dutifully took her seat.

Leaning forward, he clasped his hands together atop the desk. "You appear in better spirits than last I saw you."

Isla barely stopped an eye roll. How like Gray. To toss her out on her ear, leave her sobbing and alone on a rural country road waiting for Tavish and Captain Ross to happen by, and then act as if they had merely been taking the air when next they spoke.

"Yes. I have rather sorted things."

"Things like Tavish Balfour? I understand you have been staying with him at Cairnfell Castle, though thankfully, the news of your indiscretion is still well hidden."

Isla didn't dignify his verbal poke with a reply. "What is it you wished to say to me, Gray?"

He studied her for a long moment. Isla couldn't discern what he was looking for, though his gaze did drop momentarily to the gold wedding band on her left ring finger.

As for herself, she felt different in Gray's presence. In the past, there had always been a thread of anxiety in their interactions. A gnawing worm of worry. The never-ending fear that Gray could not be trusted and might, at any moment, broadcast her illegitimacy and set her adrift in the world.

But now . . .

Tavish glowed bright in her mind. Even though he wasn't beside her, his strength and support buoyed her.

No matter what happened here with Gray, Tavish was hers.

"During our last conversation, you pleaded with me to assist you in unraveling the matter of your marriage." Her brother leaned back in his chair.

"I did, but I no longer require your help."

Gray continued to study her.

Silence.

Isla blinked first.

"Well, if that is all . . ." She pushed out of her chair, standing tall and turning for the door. "I shall pack my things, though I would like to discuss the needs of Malton Hill before I depart."

She was reaching for the doorknob when Gray spoke.

"I have assisted you, Sister." A pause. "With your marriage, that is."

Isla pivoted back to him.

She said nothing, waiting for him to get to the point.

Gray rose from his chair and crossed to the fireplace and the cheery fire burning there. From behind the mantel clock, he pulled a folded piece of foolscap. Unfolding it, he held the paper upright, showing her its contents.

She recognized the paper instantly.

A trickle of foreboding slithered down Isla's spine.

"My marriage vows." She crossed to him, reaching for the paper. "How ungentlemanly of you to rummage through my effects and pilfer them."

Gray lifted the paper high over his head.

Isla glared at him. She would not jump like an eager kitten to retrieve a favorite toy.

The paper represented the signed witness of her marriage to Tavish—one of two copies of the document. The good doctor had used the other to register their marriage with the sheriff.

"What is your point with this display, Gray?"

"Merely this."

With two quick steps, Gray tossed the marriage lines onto the fire.

"No!" Isla rushed for the paper, but Gray snagged her arm, stopping her.

The paper burned in a bright pillar of flame.

Jerking her arm out of his hold, Isla turned to him.

"Whatever are you doing?!"

"Destroying the proof of your marriage, Isla. Just as you requested."

Of all the—

"Gray, you cannot toss me out of a carriage in the middle of nowhere, abandon me to an unsure fate, and then act as if you give a fig what happens to me." She gestured toward the fire. "That isn't the only proof of our marriage! There were witnesses, not to mention—"

"The sheriff's registry, I know." He spoke so calmly, so conversationally. As if they were discussing the weather. As if he hadn't a single doubt as to the outcome of this conversation.

Isla stilled, a true stab of alarm racing across her skin. She took a step back.

"What did you do, Gray?" she whispered through lips gone numb.

"Precisely as you requested, Isla. *I made a terrible mistake*, you said. *One I have regretted for years now.*" He parroted her words in a dreadful falsetto. "You begged me to absolve your marriage in such a way that no one would ever know it had occurred. Once my temper had cooled sufficiently, I saw the wisdom in your request, much as it pained me. I cannot stomach an alliance with the Balfours, nor do I relish weathering the scandal of your divorce. So I acted on your behalf."

A ringing started in Isla's ears. "But the sheriff? The witnesses?"

"The good doctor and his wife passed away a few years ago. We were fortunate there, I must say. As for the sheriff . . . a careful review of his records will show no mention of your nuptials nor any copy of your vows. I assure you, I was very thorough."

"But—"

"But nothing. That document"—he pointed toward the fire—"was the last scrap of proof of your *terrible mistake*—again, your words—and I wanted you to see it burn with your own eyes. You are, thankfully, once more Lady Isla Kinsey, with no known connection to Tavish Balfour."

Isla gasped for air, as if winded from a blow to the stomach. And in a sense, perhaps she was.

Her marriage had . . . evaporated. Ephemeral as dandelion fluff in the wind.

She looked between the fire and Gray's smug, triumphant face.

"But . . . but what if I've changed my mind?"

"Changed your mind?"

Isla lifted her left hand to show him the gold band gleaming there.

"Yes!" She pointed to her wedding ring. "You cast me out, Gray! You left me with Tavish. And unlike you, he provided for me. He cared for me when no one else would. Why would you think you could treat me so callously, dissolve my marriage, say *nothing* to me of your plans, and then present the whole as if it's some grand thing you deserve a biscuit and a pat on the head for doing?!"

Given the way Gray's nostrils flared, Isla had the distinct sense that she had, perhaps, gone too far.

It was likely her comment about the biscuit.

"Let me be very clear, Isla," Gray began, the eerie calm of his voice a terrifying contrast with the anger blazing in his eyes. "I will not have you undo my efforts."

Isla raised her chin, but as her lips trembled with the force of her nerves, she feared she looked more foolish than brave.

"I don't wish my marriage to Tavish Balfour to be absolved."

Gray laughed, so caustic and sharp, Isla couldn't suppress a flinch.

"Is that so?" He walked toward her. "I never took you for such a simpleton. Do you truly think I will permit all this work to be for naught? You will not pollute our family's legacy with your base blood and poor decisions. I will not tolerate a Balfour as an in-law. You will marry a more suitable gentleman, one who will enhance our family reputation, not tarnish it."

"No." Isla lifted her chin. "I prefer the husband I already have."

"Have you heard nothing I just said?"

"I heard you. I simply reject your words."

"I have assisted you in what—"

"No! You do not get to ignore me and then make decisions about my life. I am not the mouse to your cat. You cannot bat me about like some toy!"

"Bah! I will not—"

"NO!"

Anger surged upward within Isla. The fury of a woman who, year after year, swallowed her emotions and desires. One who smiled and curtsied and chose *compliance* over and over. A girl who had given loyalty and, once upon a time, affection to the man before her and received none in return.

She stalked toward her brother.

"Piers George William Ashton Kinsey, I am a person of worth!" She poked a finger into his shoulder, punctuating her words. "You can rage and threaten me, but I am not beholden to you. I am my own woman in every legal sense. I love—" Her voice broke, emotion thick. "I love Tavish Balfour. He is the most honorable, loyal, kind man I have ever known! A thousand times the man you are, and I cannot wait to spend the rest of my life at his side!"

"If you remain with that man, you will never see a farthing from the dukedom. You will be dead to me!"

"I know! I know all this, Gray!" Isla waved her hands in a circle. "You already tossed me out of a carriage and left me to a life of destitution, remember? And Tavish was there to pick me up. To lift me into his arms and promise to help. Because that is what a man does when he loves someone! I would rather spend the rest of my life working beside the man I adore than trapped in a loveless gilded cage."

He folded his arms. "Isla, I—"

"Anger blights your life, Gray. Anger toward me, toward our mother, toward the Balfours. I once loved you with my whole heart. But your cruelty and harsh words trampled that affection to dust."

Gray looked away at that. A muscle ticked in his jaw.

Isla turned for the door. "I fear for you. If you cannot stem this blind hatred, it will cost you everything."

His nostrils flared, that same muscle in his jaw tensing. He still refused to look at her.

"You are hysterical," he scoffed, tugging on his cuffs.

She ignored his insult. "I will pack my things, say my goodbyes to Matthias, and be gone by morning. I anticipate that you and I will never speak again. Goodbye."

"Isla."

She paused with her hand on the doorknob and looked back at Gray. He stood rimmed in window light, half his face cast into shadow, eyes glittering gold. A towering thundercloud of a man. A tawny lion eager to pounce.

"You think to disobey me?" He walked toward her, steps slow. "But I assure you, you will not like the consequences that—"

"Go to hell, Gray."

She slammed the door behind her with a deafening crash.

31

Isla had promised Tavish that she would send word by morning.

However, he had experienced nearly a full twenty-four hours of incessant worry because his lovely wife had not, in point of fact, sent word.

Not a damn syllable.

Even one night away from Isla had proved difficult. Tavish refused to spend another.

The soldier in him clinically plotted his options.

One, he could rally Callum and a few grooms and storm the gates of Dunmore, as Isla had suggested.

Two, he could lie in wait until Grayburn left Dunmore and then harass the man by shooting objects around him until he gave up Isla's location.

Both options had merit.

Tavish was cleaning his rifle in preparation when a knock sounded.

At last! A message from Isla!

He took the stairs two at a time and wrenched open the door.

Fletch's handsome face greeted him.

Tavish froze.

Edward Archer was the last person he expected to see.

"Fletch!"

"May I come in?"

They spoke over the top of one another.

"Of course." Tavish waved Fletch inside and up the stairs.

As ever, his friend appeared a gentleman of wealth—tailored great-coat over a superfine tailcoat and gold-threaded waistcoat, buckskin breeches tucked into polished Hessians.

"I must say, I am surprised to see ye," Tavish said as they stepped into the great hall. "I wrote ye earlier this week to apprise ye of my situation with Isla but didn't expect a personal visit."

"Yes, well . . . I had stopped by Castle Balfour and was directed here."

"I see," Tavish said, when in fact, he did not *see*. "And ye took the time to stop by because . . . ?" He left the question dangling off ellipses.

Fletch walked the perimeter of the room, top hat twirling in his hands, poking his nose into every corner with typical Fletch-like enthusiasm. His gaze lingered on the rifle resting on a side table, mid-cleaning.

"Have I arrived at an inopportune moment?" Fletch lifted an eyebrow, his normally open expression guarded. "Your letters led me to believe my presence would be welcome."

"Nae. Ye ken I am right glad to see ye. I am merely puzzled, is all." *And eager to be off to collect my wife*, Tavish didn't add.

Fletch studied him before sighing. "Do you have any libations in this castle of yours?"

"Alcohol? For breakfast?"

"I have never known you to forgo a wee dram, as you describe it, regardless of the time of day."

Tavish shrugged, as if to say, *Ye have me there.* "We can drink while I finish cleaning my rifle."

He poured a finger of whisky into a pair of crockery mugs.

"So?" Tavish asked once they were seated across from one another before the fire. Lifting his rifle, he continued to scour rust spots off the barrel. He knew his friend—former friend?—hadn't come all this way as a courtesy call. "Ye seem to be less angry with myself?"

Fletch shrugged, sipping his whisky and watching Tavish's hands as he worked. "You are a difficult man to remain angry with, Balfour, and well you know it. I was on my way south to London and thought I'd stop in."

Tavish said nothing, waiting for Fletch to get to the point.

"Lady Isla is well?" Fletch asked.

Wasn't that the question of the hour? "I presume so. She is with Grayburn at present. I am preparing to go fetch her." Wrapping a bit of muslin around the tip of the rifle ramrod, Tavish began to clean the interior rifling of the barrel.

Fletch shot a pointed look at the rifle. "Were you?"

"Aye."

"And how are matters between you and the lady?" Fletch laid the question down carefully, as if it were a cocked pistol with a dodgy trigger—liable to fire at the slightest jolt.

The question caused Tavish to frown. "I wrote ye about it, as I said. Earlier this week."

"Ah. I must have left Kingswell before receiving your letter."

Then why are ye here? Tavish wondered.

"Isla and I have . . . mended fences," he said.

Fletch tilted his head. "Truly?"

"Aye." Tavish couldn't stop a love-drunk smile. "Isla is . . . remarkable. I'm humbled that she has chosen to remain my wife."

"You love her." A statement, not a question.

Tavish nodded. "More than life. And she, even more surprisingly, claims to love me in return."

"What do you plan to do?"

Tavish winced at that. "That part of the plan, we are still trying to piece together."

They spoke for a few minutes. Or rather, Fletch listened, and Tavish talked as he poured gun oil onto a clean bit of muslin and rubbed it into every metal surface of the rifle.

He recounted his relationship with Isla as a lad and his joy at their renewed devotion. He described his tentative hopes that Lord Matthias might join the venture to Pennsylvania and the thought that, one day, Tavish might pursue politics in Great Britain or maybe even Pennsylvania.

"I don't suppose it matters what I do," Tavish finished, setting down his rifle and moving to the washbasin to clean his hands. "With Isla beside me, everything feels possible."

"Congratulations. I am truly happy for you both." Fletch's cheerful blue eyes brimmed with honesty.

Tavish dried his hands on a hanging towel.

Silence for another moment.

"Ye must know, Fletch, how sorry I am that matters played out as they did. I never meant to deceive ye in such a way."

Fletch waved a magnanimous hand. "Though I have been stung by the loss of Lady Isla—she is, as you say, a remarkable lady—over the past week, I have begun to see matters more clearly. For one, I do not wish to marry a lady who still feels affection for another gentleman. Like yourself, I want to be first in my wife's heart. And second, I understand that you couldn't have behaved in any other manner. Your loyalty should remain with your wife, not myself."

Unaccountably, emotion rose in Tavish's chest. "Thank you. Though I don't deserve your forgiveness, I will grasp it with both hands. Ye will always be a brother in arms."

Crossing back to Fletch, Tavish extended his hand. His friend didn't hesitate to grab it. Tavish pulled the man to his feet, clapping him on the back.

"I must say, Balfour, this visit has been illuminating in the extreme." Fletch dropped his hand. "I didn't realize how little I know you."

"Pardon?" Tavish frowned. "Ye know me better than just about anyone."

Fletch paused, as if choosing his words carefully. "Perhaps . . . it's only that . . . I've never seen you so animated. You've spoken more over the past hour than I remember you speaking in an entire year. On the topic of Lady Isla, you wax voluble."

Heat tinged Tavish's cheeks. "Aye, well, I did say from the beginning that she is a bonnie lass."

"Yes, I'm sure that is part of it." His friend gave him an assessing look. "But I also wonder if I only ever knew a shadow of you—an echo of the real man. The heart of you, however . . . I believe you left that in Lady Isla's care."

"Possibly. Or perhaps, it's just that happiness sits well with me." Tavish turned and began collecting shot and black powder.

"Perhaps." Fletch's tone implied doubt. "Regardless, this conversation is actually not why I am here. I came to warn you."

Tavish lifted an eyebrow, one hand on a leather bag.

"Grayburn found a way to vanish your marriage."

Fletch's words spun in Tavish's mind like a whirlwind. He struggled to make sense of them.

"Pardon?"

"Just that. A few days ago, I received a letter from Grayburn, saying he had destroyed all evidence of your marriage to Lady Isla. Matters are as if the marriage never occurred. It was his understanding that your marriage had not been consummated—obviously, no longer the case—and if I wished to continue my courtship of Lady Isla, assuming she was amenable, Grayburn would support my suit. As I said, I no longer wish to court Lady Isla, but I wanted to make sure you knew what had occurred."

"That bloody bastard! So that was the purpose behind his summons."

"I presume you are referring to Grayburn?"

"Aye. Isla left yesterday afternoon. Grayburn demanded her presence, and she went willingly, thinking she would say goodbye to Lord Matthias, fetch her things, and return to me. She was supposed to send me word, but I have received nothing." Tavish waved a hand toward the bag. "Hence, my preparations. I fear Grayburn is up to no good."

Fletch's chin went up. "A soldier's instinct?"

"I can't say. When it comes to my wife, my reasoning is clouded. But something has occurred, or a message from Isla would have arrived by now."

"I think your worry is justified. I sensed something off with Grayburn's message."

Tavish's concern ratcheted higher. "I need to go."

Grabbing his rifle and leather bag, he turned for the pegs to the right of the stairs, the ones that held his greatcoat and top hat.

"Absolutely! We should be on our way!"

Tavish looked back to his friend. "Pardon?"

"I'm coming with you." Fletch tapped his hat on his head.

His friend's ready declaration of support tightened Tavish's throat.

"Are ye quite sure? I should hate for ye to make an enemy of Grayburn for my sake."

"Nonsense. Your enemy is my enemy. That is how friendship works, Balfour. Besides, you are more likely to get answers from Grayburn with me at your side. His Grace will hesitate to lash out at me, not wanting to anger my father."

"True."

"I would never let a fellow officer race into danger without guarding his back. Once a Rifle, always a Rifle. We go in pairs."

TAVISH AND FLETCH did take the precaution of stopping by Castle Balfour and telling Mariah their plans.

"Just so ye know where I have disappeared to," he said.

"That is hardly comforting." His sister kissed his cheek, nodding hello to Fletch. "I hope ye return with your lady love. Father will be away to Aberdeen next week, so the two of ye can come stay at the castle here, if ye'd like. I look forward to getting to know your Isla better."

Tavish thanked her and then rode toward Dunmore, Fletch at his side. They arrived just after luncheon.

They approached the house from Cairnfell rather than along one of the primary routes that would pass by a gatehouse with its keeper. In all truthfulness, Tavish had only seen Dunmore once or twice in his life. And that was as a lad with Callum when they would dare one another to sneak as close to the place as possible.

In the light of day, the honey stone facade shone, and the acres of glass panes gleamed. A grand palace for the daughter of a duke.

Why hadn't Isla written? Had Grayburn detained her, trying to force her into compliance? Or had he silenced her with some threat against Tavish?

Either option curdled his stomach.

Fletch and Tavish discussed whether or not to knock on the door with their rifles in hand.

"Though it goes against the grain, I suggest we begin with diplomacy," Fletch said. "Grayburn is surely the magistrate in these parts. No need to threaten the man with a firearm and give him reason to charge us with a crime before we have completed our reconnaissance."

Though Fletch made excellent sense, for once, Tavish deplored his friend's level head. He wanted to storm through the front door, gun cocked and ready to fire.

But Fletch won in this.

Dismounting, Tavish and Fletch handed their horses' reins to a waiting groom. The boy's eyes took in Fletch's expensive clothing—everything about the man proclaimed him an aristocrat—before widening in recognition when they touched on Tavish. Thankfully, the boy said nothing.

So far, so good.

Tavish rang the front bell.

A stuffy butler answered the door.

The man gave Tavish a thorough up and down before his eyes flickered to Fletch.

"Captain Tavish Balfour to see my wife." Tavish put the steely command of an army officer into his voice. The tone he used with underlings when he wished them to cower in fear.

Grayburn's butler was made of stern stuff because the man didn't so much as twitch. "I do not think your wife to be on these premises, Mr. Balfour. I bid you good da—"

The butler broke off as Tavish pushed his way into the house.

It appeared diplomacy was at an end.

"Sirrah!" the man gasped in outrage.

"Isla!" Tavish called.

The butler tried to grab his sleeve.

On a growl, Fletch pulled the man loose and placed himself between the butler and Tavish.

"Isla, love, where are ye?!" Tavish yelled up the stairs.

He scarcely noticed the gilt mirrors and elegant busts and acres of marble on display. In his periphery, Fletch grappled with the butler.

All Tavish's attention was on locating his wife.

A strong hand seized his arm. With automatic movements—a quick jerk of his arm and a twist of his upper body—Tavish tossed off the footman who had grabbed him. Blood pumped in his veins, his every sense alert as if this were a battlefield.

"Isla!" he shouted again, starting up the stairs.

Two more footmen raced into the entryway. Fletch had subdued the butler and pivoted to face the footmen, fists raised.

"I say!" a decidedly aristocratic voice called behind Tavish. "What is this tumult?"

Tavish pivoted on the stairs.

A gentleman stood just inside the doorway of what appeared to be a drawing room.

Lord Matthias Kinsey.

He stood tall—the sleeve of his right arm pinned up at the elbow, a book in his solitary hand.

With a stern shake of his head, Lord Matthias waved off the footmen and butler. "I have this in hand, McPherson. As you were."

"But, my lord—" the butler began.

Lord Matthias gave another severe shake of his head. "Enough." But Tavish noted how the book in his hand trembled.

Tavish walked down the staircase, Fletch joining him.

Tavish had rarely seen Lord Matthias, even as a boy. A few years older than Tavish, the gentleman had the look of Isla in the shape of his face and the watchfulness of his gaze.

"Balfour." Lord Mathias nodded.

"Lord Matthias." Tavish gave an abbreviated bow, lungs a bellows. "I am in search of my wife."

"I see." Gesturing again with the book in his hand, Lord Matthias indicated that Tavish and Fletch should step into the drawing room.

"Thank ye." Tavish righted his coat, adjusting his collar. He had not expected to find an ally in this place.

The drawing room was everything Tavish would expect of Grayburn's position and wealth. An enormous gilt mirror hovered over an equally impressive marble fireplace. Paintings by Caravaggio and Gainsborough graced the walls, and a lush Aubusson carpet rested underfoot.

Lord Matthias looked at Fletch. "And your companion?"

So polite, that sentence. As if they had merely come calling for tea.

Tavish made quick introductions, breathing heavily. He was primed for a fight, and though he had partially gotten one, Lord Matthias's gentlemanly demeanor was jarring.

"What the devil!" Grayburn's loud voice sounded in the entrance hall. "Where is that scoundrel? Someone fetch me a whip to drive him from my home!"

Excellent. Here came the fight Tavish craved.

Lord Matthias half rolled his eyes. "Gray is mostly bark, though under a bit of strain at the moment. Stand your ground, Balfour." He took a large step back, retreating to the wall just as Grayburn barreled into the room.

"You blackguard!" Grayburn speared Tavish with a dark look. "I will see criminal charges brought for this, pushing your way into my home and assaulting my staff."

The duke came up short when he noticed Fletch, arms crossed, standing at Tavish's side.

"Archer and I have come to fetch my wife, Grayburn," Tavish said. "Even you cannot hold your sister against the will of her husband."

"What wife?" the duke asked with silky ease, his glee barely masked. "You don't have a wife, Balfour."

Anger flared through Tavish's veins. Fletch had been right.

"I did as of yesterday."

"Well . . . facts change." Grayburn shrugged. "A marriage doesn't exist without evidence and witnesses, and I assure you there are neither where my sister is concerned. You are nothing to her. Now, again, you will leave before I have you arrested."

"I will see my wife—"

"Archer." Grayburn turned to Fletch, dismissing Tavish entirely. "I must admit I am somewhat disappointed to see you in Balfour's company."

Fletch didn't so much as flinch. "As I've said from the beginning, Grayburn, Balfour is the most honorable gentleman I know. That fact remains true."

Grayburn snorted. "Surely, you have better sense—"

"My wife, Duke!" Tavish snapped. "I would see Isla and—"

"That is *Lady* Isla to the likes of you."

"As *Lady* Isla might be currently carrying my bairn . . ." Tavish paused to let that tidbit of information land, "I would like to speak with her."

Grayburn's expression blanched before the red of rage reappeared.

"If you so much as touched her—"

"I'm her bloody husband, Grayburn. Of course, I touched her! I intend to touch her again!"

Grayburn took two steps toward Tavish.

"Tavish?" Isla's bright voice sounded from the entry hall.

Relief washed over Tavish, as miraculous as rain on dry soil.

"Isla! Love!" he called.

Isla walked through the doorway, a cheery smile upon her lips. Tavish's chest swelled at the sight.

As ever, she appeared as dazzling as a summer afternoon. The setting of Dunmore suited her, he noted. The elegance of the drawing room accentuated the expensive cut of her sprigged muslin dress and the intricate braiding of her coiffure.

How had it been scarcely a day since he had seen her? He took two steps forward, eager to swing her into his arms, only to be stopped by Grayburn's warning hand.

"Tavish?" Her gaze darted between Tavish and Fletch, questioning. "Colonel Archer?" She curtsied in greeting.

She did not appear to be in any distress.

Nor did she push past her brother's warning hand and cross to Tavish.

His heart trembled in his chest. What had occurred? What had Grayburn done?

"Did you not get my message, Tavish?" she asked.

"Message?" was all he could push past lips gone numb.

"Yes. The one I promised to send. I sent two, actually."

"Two?"

"Yes. One last night and then another this morning."

"I received nothing."

She frowned. "I sent them. I gave them to McPherson . . ." Her smile melted away.

Isla pivoted to Grayburn.

For his part, the duke stared over her shoulder, not meeting her gaze.

"Gray." Isla's mouth drew into a thin line.

Tavish knew that tone. It was the one that presaged a thorough tongue-lashing.

The duke's left eye twitched. "Isla."

"What happened to my letters?"

"I certainly do not know—"

"You ordered McPherson to intercept my messages to Tavish." Not a question.

"I refuse to dignify that accusation with a re—"

"How idiotic could you be?!" Isla threw up her hands. "Did you think you could just not deliver my letters to my *husband*—and he *is* my husband, no matter your meddling in our marriage—in an attempt to drive a wedge between Tavish and myself?"

"Isla, again, you are becoming hysterical—"

"I am not the delusional one here, Gray! After everything I said to you last night, you truly thought Tavish and I would abandon our love over a misunderstanding?" Isla rolled her eyes. "Honestly, Gray. Your hatred blinds you to reality."

Tavish's heart soared at his bonnie wife's spirited defense of their love.

Grayburn, however, appeared a thundercloud, dark and ominous and ready to burst.

32

Isla glared at her brother.

Gray glared right back. "You will rue the day you allied yourself with a Balfour. And when you come crawling back, begging once again for my help, you will find a deaf ear."

"Piers, we are at an end, you and I. I would have loved you to my grave, Brother. I would have been the most doting of sisters. But *you* are the one who has chosen hatred over love." She hurled her words at him. "Love cannot thrive without nourishment, and I'm tired of starving. Instead, I choose to give my love to those who will treasure it. So yes, I will happily spend my life at Tavish Balfour's side."

Isla shook her head at Gray before crossing to Tavish.

Just the sight of her husband . . .

She skipped the last few steps, throwing herself in his arms. He gathered her close, strong hands banding around her chest.

"Are ye well, love?" he whispered against her hair. "I've been half out of my mind with worry."

"I am well, darling." She cupped his beloved face. "I finished packing my things this morning. I am ready to leave. That was the gist of my lost letters. Just that I needed to say my goodbyes and secure my personal effects. Oh, and I love you."

"I love you, too."

She pressed a soft kiss to his lips. The affection flaring in his eyes said he wanted more than a mere kiss, but he was trying to behave himself.

How she loved this man.

Matthias cleared his throat.

Gray growled.

Right.

Her brothers and Colonel Archer were in the room.

She turned to face them, keeping one arm around Tavish's waist.

Colonel Archer seemed resigned, his face more serious than usual. But his quiet support of Tavish said volumes about the man's character.

Matthias appeared . . . bemused, she supposed. Isla had stayed up late with him, talking of everything and nothing. He was supportive of her marriage, even if he thought her rash to be tying herself to a man of little means.

"If your penury becomes too dire, please write," he had said.

Isla had hinted at Matthias becoming an investor in Tavish's whisky venture, and her brother hadn't rejected the idea outright. Though he did have questions and preferred to speak with Tavish directly about the proposed venture.

Gray, however . . .

Her ducal brother glowered, his gaze dropping to where Tavish held her snug to his side. It hurt that, even now, Gray was more focused on his petty need for vengeance against the Balfours than caring about her wishes as a human being.

"I suggest you remove your things from my property immediately, Isla," Gray said. "As long as you are allied with that man, you are not welcome here. Your dowry and Malton Hill are now forfeit."

Once, such words from her brother would have shattered Isla. But now? Now, she had a heart full of love and hope for a life full of affection and joy.

"I would not expect otherwise, Gray." She shifted to holding Tavish's hand, intent on the door and collecting her things. "We shall be leaving."

She had taken only one step when Colonel Archer spoke up.

"A moment, if you all please." A frown creased his forehead. "I do have one question."

Isla paused. Tavish squeezed her hand.

"What is it, Fletch?" Tavish asked.

Colonel Archer looked at Gray. "Malton Hill is forfeit?"

Gray's brow darkened.

"Why do you ask, Colonel?" Isla asked. "Gray controls my dowry."

"Yes, he does. But Grayburn spoke with me regarding all that when we were discussing a possible marriage cont—"

"I strongly suggest you remain silent, Archer." Gray clenched his jaw, his gaze drilling into Colonel Archer as if attempting to will him into silence.

Colonel Archer paused.

Matt finally stirred from his position against the wall, stepping forward. "Please go on, Colonel Archer. I am interested in hearing what you have to say."

"Matthias!" Gray shot their brother a warning look. "It is of no import."

Matt returned with a raised eyebrow. "Why silence the man then?" He motioned for Colonel Archer to continue.

Swallowing, Colonel Archer shifted on his feet. "I cannot say I know much, Lord Matthias. As I said, His Grace and I were in preliminary discussions of marriage contracts regarding Lady Isla's dowry." He gave Isla an apologetic smile. "Based on what Grayburn disclosed, I was given to understand—"

Gray made an outraged noise. "Archer, anything I disclosed was in confidence and should be—"

"What did you learn, Colonel?" Isla asked, her heart pummeling her ribcage.

Colonel Archer smiled down at her. A beatific smile.

"Malton Hill is not, in fact, tied to your dowry, Lady Isla. Yes, Grayburn controls whether or not your dowry goes with you into marriage, but he cannot control Malton Hill."

"What do you mean?" A quiver had started in her knees.

"The estate was bequeathed to you as part of your mother's will and devolved to your ownership when you came of age on your twenty-first birthday. Malton Hill has always been yours, Lady Isla, regardless of who you marry."

The knowledge took several seconds to sink in.

Isla merely stared up at Colonel Archer, her jaw sagging open.

And then a torrent of emotion rushed in—relief, surprise, blinding happiness—turning the world blurry.

"It's mine?" she whispered. "Malton Hill is truly mine?"

"As far as I understand matters, yes." Colonel Archer shrugged.

She turned to Tavish, a tear tumbling down her cheek. "Malton Hill might be mine, Tavish!"

"'Twould appear so, lass." He pressed a tender kiss to her forehead.

"Do you suppose?"

"*Och*, aye! Look at Grayburn there."

Isla wiped her tears from her eyes and turned to her brother. His red-faced fury was all the confirmation she needed.

"Gray, you cannot appropriate a property that legally is mine!" Isla shook her head.

"Agreed." Matt turned to Gray. "Not only does it go against our mother's wishes, but it is, in a word, illegal. Even for a duke."

The silence in the wake of Matt's words was damning.

Gray said nothing.

Instead, he shot them all a look of pure vitriol, turned, and walked out of the room.

Isla stared at the space he had just occupied.

Her gaze drifted back to Matt. A dent had appeared on his brow, and the book in his hand trembled.

However, he met her eyes with a quiet sort of resolution.

"I'll speak with Gray and likely involve my solicitor," Matt said. "Thank you, Colonel Archer, for bringing this to our attention. Who knows what else Gray has hidden from us in our parents' wills? It will be good to have it all out in the open." He walked toward the door.

Love for her brother swelled Isla's chest. "Thank you, Matt."

"Aye, thank ye," Tavish added.

"Think nothing of it." He paused, studying them both. "I assume you plan to remarry?"

Isla laughed, looking up at Tavish. He grinned down at her.

"I fear your sister has experienced a rather abrupt change of fortune," Tavish began.

"And we haven't had a chance to discuss it," Isla added.

"But . . ." Tavish's smile grew.

"I see." Matt swallowed, his shoulders straightening. "Isla, as Gray has bowed out, I should very much like to defend your marital interests. I insist upon a marriage contract being drawn up." He laid the words down like a gauntlet, as if he expected Tavish to object. This new assertive version of Matt caught Isla by surprise.

"Of course." Tavish's head snapped upright.

Isla held up a hand. "Matt, there is no need for—"

"Nae, he has the right of things, love. Ye are a woman of property, and your interests should be protected." Tavish kissed her forehead before glancing up at Matt. "I appreciate ye seeing to your sister's legal rights, my lord."

Matt inclined his head. "Just Matthias will do. We are to be brothers, it seems. I'll have my solicitor contact you, Balfour, regarding Malton Hill and the contracts."

"I look forward to it."

Matt smiled at Isla, love in his warm brown eyes. "I am glad to see you happy, Isla. You deserve every joy. Let me know when the marriage will occur. I should like to attend."

Isla rushed forward and wrapped her brother in a hug, pressing a kiss to his cheek. "Thank you, Matt."

He gathered her close with his arm. "My pleasure."

Isla pulled back with a smile.

"You are a good sort, Lord Matthias." Colonel Archer crossed to the door. "I will see myself out."

Matt nodded and followed. But he paused in the doorway, glancing into the entry hall. "I'm going to close this door and give you a few minutes of privacy before Gray boots you both out. I'll ensure your trunks are sent over to Castle Balfour, Isla."

He left . . . closing the door behind him.

Not one to waste time, Isla raced back to Tavish and pulled him in for a hungry kiss.

"I missed ye, lass," he murmured against her lips.

"I missed you, too."

Happiness ballooned under Isla's breastbone, stretching outward and swelling her heart nigh to bursting.

"I can't believe Malton Hill might be mine. It's almost too much joy to accept."

"Personally, I believe Grayburn's hostile reaction is all the proof ye need, my love. Were Fletch's tale not true, your brother would have simply denied it. And I have a feeling Matthias will ferret out all of Grayburn's secrets regarding your parents' wills and what ye are owed."

Isla couldn't stop the tears then.

"I get to keep you and Malton Hill . . . the first and second dearest desires of my heart."

She kissed him again, slow and lingering.

"There is the wee matter of our marriage," he whispered against her lips.

"Gray did burn our marriage lines."

"Pity that. I very much liked those marriage lines."

"Me, too."

"What say ye, my love? Shall we do this again?"

Isla smiled through her tears. "If you're asking me to marry you once more, I insist you do it proper-like, Tavish Balfour. No shirking, no matter how many times we must perform this play."

Grinning, Tavish dropped to a knee, her hands tucked into his. He gazed up at her, adoration glowing in his gray eyes.

"Lady Isla Kinsey—formerly Mrs. Isla Balfour—I have loved your beautiful self for nigh upon a decade. I delighted in calling ye my wife for seven of those years, and I should love nothing more than to call ye my wife between now and the end of time. I love ye and would be deeply honored if ye would agree to marry me once—"

Someone pounded on the drawing room door.

Isla and Tavish exchanged a wry look.

"Blast!" He stood up and pressed a quick kiss to her mouth. "I suppose I shall simply have to show you the depth of my affection later."

"I look forward to it."

Two footmen barreled into the room, followed by Gray.

"I do believe it is time for Mr. Balfour to leave these premises." Gray's voice crackled with authority.

"Never fear, we are leaving."

Tavish took a step toward the door, but Isla grabbed his arm, staying him. "One moment."

He turned back to her.

Isla looked into his adoring eyes and smiled.

And then, in front of her disapproving brother and a host of family servants, she kissed Tavish Balfour.

Openly. Thoroughly. Scandalously.

Pulling back, she took in his bemused expression.

"Yes," she breathed. "Yes, I will marry you."

It took Tavish a second, and then the most glorious smile spread across his face. He offered Isla his arm, which she happily took.

And with barely a nod at Gray, Isla grinned as Tavish led her out the front door of Dunmore and into the bright sunshine of their future.

EPILOGUE

TWO YEARS LATER

September 14, 1819
Malton Hill, Gloucestershire
England

"Baa! Baa!"

Tavish grinned as his son waved a chubby fist at the sheep grazing in the field. The sheep paid him no mind, content to munch on the green grass.

"That's right," Tavish said. "A sheep says *baa*."

Wee Fletch was just past his first birthday and could say a few words, but wasn't quite walking yet.

The toddler looked up at his father, a frown marring his face. Blue-eyed and blonde, the lad was the image of his mother. They had named him Fletcher Balfour in honor of the man who had, unwittingly, brought Isla and Tavish back together. Fletch had even stood as the lad's godfather.

"Moo?" Wee Fletch asked, his lips pursing into a perfect O with the sound. He pointed in the direction of the dairy barn.

"I'm sorry, my boy. We have to wait until Mamma is done with Mr. Cranston. Then we can go see the coos."

Wee Fletch sent a longing look toward the barn.

As today was Monday, Isla remained closeted with her steward, reviewing accounts and discussing tenant issues. Isla enjoyed running her estate, and Tavish adamantly supported her endeavors, despite the occasional busybody who voiced an opinion about Lady Isla Balfour's indecorous ways. Tavish stared down any detractors.

Just over two years ago, Tavish and Isla had wed in the parish kirk in Pettercairn. A proper marriage this time around, calling the banns for three weeks beforehand.

The first week of the banns, Dr. Sumsion had mounted the pulpit and intoned, "I publish the banns of marriage between Lady Isla Kinsey of Dunmore and Mr. Tavish Balfour of Castle Balfour . . ." The entire congregation had gasped, loudly, before dissolving into hissed talking. Dr. Sumsion had needed to pound the pulpit to regain everyone's attention.

For the next two weeks, Tavish and Isla's looming wedding had been a delicious topic of conversation, much to the delight of the nosy *nebbies* of the county. A Balfour and a Kinsey uniting in marriage. The astonishment! The scandal!

Neither the Duke of Grayburn nor Lord Northcairn attended the actual wedding, marking the first and last time His Grace and his lordship agreed upon anything.

The only crack in Grayburn's indifference came the day before Isla's wedding. A footman from Dunmore had appeared on the doorstep of Castle Balfour, a box in his hand. Tavish had watched as Isla opened it with trembling fingers. Inside, she found a stunning sapphire-and-gold parure—necklace, ear bobs, and a hair comb.

Isla had lifted Grayburn's short note, shaking her head.

> *I can no longer stomach the sight of these—a gift from my father to your mother—and so I pass them to you. May your marriage be more fortuitous than that of my parents.*
>
> *— G*

Tavish had lifted an eyebrow at Grayburn's snippy tone.

Isla had beamed with tears in her eyes.

"I don't care why he sent me this," she said to Tavish. "I love that I have something more of my mother to pass to our children. Our own history to write."

The morning of their wedding dawned clear and bright.

Every able-bodied person within a ten-mile radius packed the kirk to witness the miraculous marriage. Tavish's brothers and sisters had been particularly enthusiastic, much to Lord Northcairn's disgust.

Lord Matthias escorted his sister down the aisle to a waiting Tavish—Ross and Fletch at his side as best men.

Isla had never looked more lovely, Tavish thought. Her wedding gown—cream satin with an overlay of gold-shot netting—draped her elegant figure, and the white lilies of her bouquet perfumed the church. But it was the profound love in her blue gaze that had Tavish choking back tears. They both openly wept as they recited their vows. There wasn't a dry eye in the congregation.

Stepping from the church in a shower of rice, they had raced to the waiting carriage. Tavish would forever remember gathering his wife close and kissing her to cheers and the peals of church bells.

Tavish and Isla had immediately set out for Malton Hill. Matthias had made good on his promise to secure Isla's inheritance. Per their mother's will, Grayburn had ceded Malton Hill as well as a tidy sum left to Isla. Tavish had happily signed their marriage contracts, guaranteeing the property for Isla's own use.

As the son of an earl, Tavish knew the basics of land management and could have stepped into the role of lord of the manor, but he wanted Isla to have the primary governance of her people.

As ever, he wished his wife to have the life she chose for herself.

A grunt sounded from behind. Wee Fletch twisted in Tavish's arms, looking over his shoulder.

Turning around, they both watched as Matthias finished loading a Baker rifle, carefully pouring priming powder into the touch hole. It was tricky going with just one functional arm, but Matthias was determined to master the task.

Though quiet and retiring, Matthias had a will of steel, Tavish had come to realize. The man refused to let his disability dissuade him from his goals—in this instance, learning how to load and fire a rifle.

"Good work!" Tavish called, shifting Wee Fletch in his arms.

Three weeks past, Matthias had arrived for a lengthy visit. Isla had been ecstatic to see him, flying into her brother's embrace.

Matthias had proved a dear friend to both of them. He visited regularly and doted on Wee Fletch. Just last night, Matthias had spent over an hour attempting to teach Wee Fletch to say *Uncle Matt* with some success.

Today, however, Tavish was continuing to teach Matthias how to aim and shoot a rifle. He could have left Wee Fletch in the care of his nanny in the nursery, but Tavish adored watching his son explore the world.

"Dat?" Wee Fletch pointed toward Matthias.

"Yes, that's your Uncle Matt. Watch. He's going to fire the rifle."

"Boom!" The toddler's eyes went wide.

"Yes, boom." Tavish looked to Matthias. "Ready?"

Matthias nodded, looking down the field toward the paper target attached to a board. "I'm going to perfect my form."

"Ye absolutely will. Practice does make perfect when it comes to target shooting."

Matthias sat on the ground, adopting the supine firing position the Rifles used—back reclined, rifle butt against his shoulder, and the barrel propped on one foot. The pose enabled him to steady the gun without having to use two hands.

"Remember," Tavish encouraged. "Breathe in to focus and steady your aim, breathe out to fire."

In some ways, it astounded Tavish that Matthias was three years his senior. The man had spent so much of his life cloistered away that he had rarely participated in common activities that most men enjoyed. Watching him step into the world felt momentous.

"Hands up, lad." Tavish grinned at Wee Fletch. "Uncle Matt is going to make a boom."

Eyes still wide, the toddler instantly placed both his palms over his ears. It was patently adorable. Tavish took several steps back, moving Wee Fletch well away from any danger.

Matthias lined up the shot, took aim, and fired.

Crack!

A hole appeared inside the black circle at the center of the target.

Tavish and Wee Fletch whooped with joy.

Matthias jumped to his feet, a grin on his face. His dark hair tumbled across his forehead, his brown eyes sparking with delight.

"Matt!"

The men turned at the sound of Isla's voice.

Tavish's bonnie wife waved a hand as she crossed the lawn to them.

"What a shot!" She rushed to give her brother a hug, his larger frame dwarfing hers.

"Thank you." Matthias blushed and bent to reload the rifle.

"And how are my boys?" Isla asked, turning to Tavish and Wee Fletch.

Predictably, Fletch leaned forward, arms outstretched. "Mamma!"

Isla gathered him close, peppering his face with kisses.

Tavish lifted an eyebrow.

Isla didn't mistake his expression.

"And, of course, a kiss for you, too," she said on a laugh, reaching up a hand and pulling Tavish's mouth down to hers.

Wee Fletch pushed a palm against Tavish's cheek.

"Moo?!" he asked, waving his fist toward the barns.

"You want to see the cows, darling?" Isla asked.

"Moo!" Wee Fletch pointed again.

"Coos are of importance today." Tavish wrapped an arm around his bonnie wife, kissing her temple.

He loved nothing more than holding his two precious people in his arms.

"Well," Isla raised her eyes to his, "I suppose we should go seek them out. If I haven't told you yet today, Tavish Balfour, I love you." She darted a glance back at Matthias, still loading the rifle. "Thank you for not only taking care of me, but also the people I love."

"I love ye, too, lass."

"Remind me to show how much I love you later."

"Indeed?" Tavish laughed. "I look forward to a demonstration."

He bent down, kissing her more deeply until, once again, Wee Fletch interrupted them with a palm pushing on Tavish's cheek.

"Papa! Moo!" he said in his sternest voice, pointing emphatically toward the barns with an expression that brooked no argument.

HOURS LATER, ISLA cuddled against Tavish in their marital bed, her head resting on his shoulder.

Wee Fletch was ensconced with his nanny in the nursery, and Matt had retired an hour ago.

Tavish pulled her closer, pressing a kiss to her forehead.

This was the time of day that Isla loved most—the hours alone with Tavish when they spoke of everything and nothing.

"How fares the regiment?" she asked.

"*Och*, the same as usual. Old Colonel Patterson still prefers the sound of his own voice to any other, but John Burgess hit the target this week, so I consider that progress."

"You will make soldiers out of them yet."

Isla didn't think she would ever tire of watching Tavish integrate with life at Malton Hill. He had fallen into the community as if he had always belonged. He commanded and trained the local militia. Which meant that Isla regularly admired the masculine cut of his body in regimentals and heard the sharp bark of his voice calling drills.

It was enough to turn a lady's knees to jelly.

Most significantly, Tavish had taken to listening to local constituents at the Hare and Fox in town. He was plotting strategy in order to run for a seat in Parliament next year.

Isla could think of no one better to help govern the country.

"How are matters with Mr. Cranston?" Tavish asked, referring to her meeting earlier.

"Excellent. The harvest looks to be robust this year, though there are some concerns about the south field."

They spoke about wheat yields, the growth of the dairy farm, and their hopes for the lambing season come spring.

"And the festival?" he asked.

Isla sighed. "The Autumn Festival Committee is finalizing plans, despite Mrs. Sumsion and Mrs. White's disagreements concerning the bazaar."

"Ah."

Isla nudged him with her elbow. "I might need you to ply the ladies with your charms. See if you can't bring them around to a compromise."

"My charms?"

Isla lifted her head and grinned at him. "You know you can be devilishly charming when you wish, Tavish Balfour."

"Is that so?" He kissed her. "I feel like ye should be enumerating these charms for me."

"What if I give you a gift instead?" She placed his palm to her stomach, pressing it there.

He stilled, his gaze going wide. Sitting upright, he stared at her and then looked down to where his hand rested. Up and down.

"Are ye sure, lass?"

Isla nodded, tears pricking her eyes. "I believe so. Another babe come early summer."

"So soon?"

She gave a watery laugh. "All things considered, it's a miracle it took this long."

"*Och*, my love!" He kissed her, slow and deep, before pressing his forehead to hers. "Are ye happy then?"

"Tavish Balfour, I will always be ecstatic to welcome your child. I have hopes that this one will have your red hair and pillow lips." She kissed said lips to prove her point. "Are you happy?"

"Isla, love, I thank God every day that I get to spend my life at your side. So aside from a wee bit of terror as for your own health and safety, I am happy. Now about those charms of mine." He kissed away her tears. "Allow me to give ye a demonstration."

Isla laughed in earnest, turning her face to his and silently echoing his sentiments—

After so much heartache, she gave thanks every day for the gift of Tavish Balfour in her arms.

TAVISH AND ISLA'S CIPHER

A → Y	N → F
B → B	O → J
C → G	P → K
D → M	Q → U
E → Q	R → S
F → X	S → C
G → Z	T → V
H → P	U → O
I → L	V → H
J → R	W → N
K → T	X → A
L → W	Y → D
M → E	Z → I

AUTHOR'S NOTE

If you've made it to this page, thank you so much for reading. As usual, I can't leave a book without offering some commentary on the history of various plot points.

Cairnfell is, of course, fictional. I imagine it as a volcanic mount, similar to the ones that Edinburgh Castle and Stirling Castle are built upon.

However, the history of brothers being raised to earldoms named after rivers *does* have its basis in reality. In the early 1600s, David and John Carnegie were named the Earl of Southesk and the Earl of Northesk, respectively, after nearby rivers of the same name. Fun fact, the current Earl of Northesk is a very distant relative of the main line, descended down through a younger son of the second earl. The main line of heirs tragically went extinct in the early 2000s, so they had to go hunting back through the generations to find the next in line. We're talking four hundred years and nine generations back and then forward again to find a male heir. Can you even imagine that phone call? It would be like inheriting something that belonged to Pilgrims on the Mayflower.

Handfasting is an ancient practice, likely Celtic pagan in origin. In England, handfasting historically referred to a period of engagement before the actual church ceremony. In Scotland, however, handfasting when properly witnessed was viewed as a legal marriage (recognized civilly, though not religiously). This was why so many English flew north to be married/handfasted in Gretna Green. Handfasting was a prevalent form of marriage in the Highlands and Western Isles for hundreds (if not thousands) of years. The ceremony was simple. The couple would plight their troth and a witness would tie their hands together with a knot (hence *handfasting*), symbolizing the couple's commitment to bind their lives together. From there, a signed statement of the couple's vows were then submitted to the sheriff (not *sheriff* in the American, law-enforcement sense of the word, but more like a governor of an area, like the Sheriff of Nottingham in *Robin Hood*) and the marriage was recorded as legally occurring.

As a sidenote, in all my research I couldn't find any legal example of the other supposedly Celtic concept of handfasting—that of a trial marriage for a year and a day, at which point, the couple would decide whether or not they wish to stay married. There are definitely tales of such a thing occurring, but I couldn't find any legal basis for dissolving a handfasting after a year. In short, nothing was ever codified into law and recognized by the government. Once a couple declared their handfasting, it was for life unless they petitioned for divorce under a few allowed circumstances—adultery and abandonment being the most common.

On that note, I did a significant amount of research into divorce law in Scotland during the time period. The book *Alienated Affections: The Scottish Experience of Divorce and Separation, 1684-1830* by Leah Leneman was particularly helpful, detailing actual court cases and situations. English law was tremendously strict on the subject. Any true divorce required a new act of Parliament and would only be granted for adultery. Such barriers meant divorce remained only a luxury that the most wealthy and powerful could afford/obtain. By contrast, Scottish law was much more lax. In addition to adultery, abandonment was also considered grounds for divorce and, unlike their English cousins, the Scots were more than willing to grant a deserted wife her freedom. Divorce simply required collecting evidence and then a hearing before a judge who would make a ruling. Additionally, the cost of applying for a divorce was low, making it available to anyone. Despite the relative ease of obtaining a divorce, Scottish divorce rates remained low throughout the 19th century.

The 95th Rifles were indeed as celebrated as I describe. There are several first-hand accounts written by veterans of the Napoleonic Wars that detail their exploits, the accuracy of their shooting, and the ways they fired their rifles. The heroics I ascribe to Tavish are true to history. Thomas Plunket, a rifleman with the 95th, did indeed take out a French general and aide at the distances I described. Richard Holmes definitive book, *Redcoat: The British Soldier*, is a must-read for those wanting to learn more about the British military during this period.

I know I've mentioned this before, but for those reading one of my Scottish books for the first time, allow me to also comment on the Scottish language. I've used modern spellings of Scottish pronunciations and, even then, restricted myself to a few key words to give a Scottish flavor to the text. So at times, the accent as written is not perfectly consistent; this was done to help readability.

I have created an extensive board on Pinterest with images of things I talk about in the book. So if you want a visual of anything—including riflemen uniforms and shooting positions, Isla's locket, etc.—pop over there and explore. Just search for NicholeVan.

As usual, writing a book is this bizarre mix of working long hours alone while simultaneously rallying a village to help get the novel to publication.

A HUGE thank you to all my ARC and beta-readers who read, give suggestions, and post about my books. The Bookstagram community has pulled me through many a frustrating day of writing. I feel I cannot thank reviewers enough for the time, thought, and effort they put into posting about my books. Thank you for helping to spread the word and ensuring I can continue to write, year after year.

Also, I cannot give enough thanks to my two primary editors—Erin Rodabough and Shannon Castleton—for their tireless efforts and brilliant suggestions. They always help me take what I see as a so-so manuscript and turn it into something far beyond my own meager efforts. I love that we continue on this journey together, helping one another in our writing efforts. I also have to give a special shout-out to Marisol Barrera for her last-minute eyes and suggestions.

And lastly, I lavish all my love and appreciation on my children and husband. Thank you for your endless words of encouragement, and your patience when I retreat to my "book cave" for weeks at a time. Just . . . thank you.

READING GROUP QUESTIONS

Yes, there are reading group questions for this book. They exist mostly as a ploy to encourage readers to congregate and discuss the book, preferably with lots of good chocolate and laughter.

Please note that these questions inherently contain some spoilers.

1. How do you see the title, *A Tartan Love*, playing out in the book? What is the meaning of using *tartan* as an adjective to describe *love*? And how does it relate to the characters?

2. Once, Tavish and Isla were the best of friends. But seven years after their break-up, they view each other as strangers. Did you find this to be believable? Why or why not? Have you ever experienced this, encountering an old friend after not talking to them for years? How did it feel?

3. Isla feels trapped between two possible futures—a life with Tavish or a life shepherding her people at Malton Hill. Both choices are good. Staying married to Tavish is shrouded in uncertainty and hardship, whereas Malton Hill provides her with security and community. Have you ever faced a similar difficult choice between security and uncertainty? What did you choose?

4. How did you feel about the friendship between Tavish, Ross, and Fletch? How did you feel about Fletch forgiving Tavish in the end?

5. How did you feel about the Duke of Grayburn in the story? Is he a true villain? Or more a product of his upbringing?

6. Clearly, this book contains a lot of information about Scotland and Scottish culture. Did you learn something new or unexpected? If so, what was it?

7. Consider how this book would be as a feature film. Who plays Tavish? Who plays Isla? Gray? etc. In the movie version, what aspects of the book should be thrown out, condensed, or altered?

OTHER BOOKS BY NICHOLE VAN

THE EARLS OF CAIRNFELL

A Tartan Love
A Lass Beloved (forthcoming)
A Highland Game (forthcoming)
A Laird Undone (forthcoming)

THE PENN-LEITHS OF THISTLE MUIR

Love Practically
Adjacent But Only Just
One Kiss Alone
A Heart Sufficient
A Heart Devoted

THE BROTHERHOOD OF THE BLACK TARTAN

Suffering the Scot
Romancing the Rake
Loving a Lady
Making the Marquess
Remembering Jamie

OTHER REGENCY ROMANCES

Seeing Miss Heartstone
Devotion of the Heart
Remains of Love (a novella included in *Summer in the Highlands*)

BROTHERS *MALEDETTI*

Lovers and Madmen
Gladly Beyond
Love's Shadow
Lightning Struck
A Madness Most Discreet

THE HOUSE OF OAK

Intertwine
Divine
Clandestine
Refine
Outshine

Want more historical romance from Nichole Van?
Read on for an excerpt from *Love Practically*,
book one in The Penn-Leith's of Thistle Muir series.

LOVE PRACTICALLY

It is a truth universally acknowledged that a single lady in possession of no fortune must long to marry a duke's son.

Unfortunately, Miss Leah Penn-Leith feared she had inadvertently killed one instead.

She stared down at the unmoving form of Lieutenant Lord Dennis Battleton illuminated in the firelight. He lay slumped beside her bedroom door, eyes closed, head tilted toward the left shoulder of his red regimental coat, blood trickling from his nose.

What have I done? Whathaveldone?!

Panic tasted acrid, drying her throat.

This might be her first time attending a house party, but even Leah knew an evening of whist and laughter did not typically end in homicide.

Clutching her night rail to her chest, Leah nudged Lord Dennis's Hessian boot, jiggling the tassel.

"My lord?" she whispered.

Nothing.

Snick.

The door to her bedchamber opened.

Leah stifled a startled scream and jumped back, meeting the gaze of Mr. Fox Carnegie, Lord Dennis's close friend.

Mr. Carnegie peered into the room, skimming over her surely terrified expression, before spotting Lord Dennis's supine form beside the door jamb.

"Blast," he muttered and mumbled a string of profanity that Leah supposed would make a gently-bred lady swoon.

As she was not *quite* a gently-bred lady, she withstood the swearing with equanimity.

After all, the situation quite merited it.

Mr. Carnegie stepped into her bedchamber, quietly closing the door behind himself. It was scandalous for him to be in her room, but then so was killing a duke's son, so Leah figured the horse had already bolted from the barn.

"I-I didnae mean tae hurt him," Leah stammered on a whisper, her Scottish brogue deepening in her distress. "I awoke as he was trying tae climb into my bed. I just . . . reacted." She mimed a kicking motion.

It had been a terrifying few seconds.

First, waking to feel large hands on her hips, the smell of brandy, and murmured slurred words, "I sh-shink you've been waiting for me, love."

Then, her instinctively violent reaction, balling her body and kicking the unknown man with both feet, much like a bucking horse. Her aim had been true.

The man had staggered back, his head and shoulders hitting the wall with a resounding *thud* that rattled her bedchamber door.

Leah had scrambled out of bed, finally getting a good look at her assailant, horrified to realize she had attacked a duke's son—Lord Dennis Battleton.

Now she watched as Mr. Carnegie stooped and placed an ear to Lord Dennis's chest.

"His heart is strong," he said, voice low.

Leah nearly sobbed in relief.

Mr. Carnegie pulled back one of his friend's eyelids, studying the pupils for a second, and inspected Lord Dennis's head for more injuries.

"Why is he yet unconscious?" Leah whispered.

"I fear Lord Dennis was exceptionally deep in his cups tonight." Mr. Carnegie pulled out a handkerchief and wiped the blood dripping from his friend's nose. "The bump to the head simply sent him to sleep a mite sooner than the brandy."

For his part, Mr. Carnegie did not appear inebriated, though the smell of alcohol lingered on him as well.

"I simply need to remove Dennis from your bedchamber with no one the wiser and leave you with my most abject apologies for this unwelcome intrusion." He flashed her a grim smile, the world-weary expression at odds with his youthful face. "We must ensure this mishap does not damage your reputation nor set gossiping tongues to wagg—"

A scuffle of footsteps in the hall outside had Mr. Carnegie turning his head and muttering another low oath.

Moving quickly, he straddled his friend, wrapped his arms around the man's chest, and heaved him upright. Not unlike Leah's father hefting a fat ewe for sheering.

In short, it was an impressive feat of physical strength.

Mr. Carnegie pivoted, spinning himself and Lord Dennis around, stopping just behind Leah's bedchamber door as a knock sounded.

Leah didn't know whether to be impressed by Mr. Carnegie's quick reaction or appalled at the smooth, practiced nature of it. This was clearly not the first time Mr. Carnegie had lifted the leaden weight of a drunken friend.

Mr. Carnegie jerked his head toward the door, indicating she should answer it.

Nodding, Leah snatched a shawl from the foot of her bed, wrapping it around her shoulders. She cracked open the door.

Miss Smith and Miss Wells—two fellow guests—stood in the hallway wearing elegant London wrappers, night caps, and matching expressions of faux worry.

"Are you quite all right, Miss Penn-Leith?" Miss Smith asked, her blond braid gleaming even in the dim light.

"Yes," Miss Wells added. "We heard a *terrible* thump."

The ladies peered beyond Leah's shoulders, searching the room as if they somehow knew there were two young gentlemen concealed behind Leah's bedchamber door.

"I apologize if I gave anyone a fright." Leah pulled the shawl tighter around her shoulders and mentally grasped for a plausible lie. "I was up reading late—Miss Austen's works are so captivating, ye ken—and I stumbled over my own *muckle* foot as I was getting into bed."

As a falsehood, it wasn't particularly good.

"*Muckle?*" Miss Smith wrinkled her dainty nose. "You Scots use the oddest words."

Miss Wells giggled, standing on tiptoe, unabashedly craning her neck to see more of the bedchamber.

In Leah's peripheral vision, Mr. Carnegie made a rolling motion with one hand. *Get on with it.*

"I thank ye both for your concern," Leah began closing the door, "but all is well. I shall bid ye goodnight."

The ladies murmured a reply, and Leah shut the door fully, throwing the lock.

Now what?

Turning back to Mr. Carnegie, she watched as he eased Lord Dennis back to the floor.

"Clever," he whispered, chin gesturing toward the door. "You are a quick study."

Leah blushed. The unexpected praise sent a jolt of pleasure through her still-racing heart. Until this moment, she had never considered that her good sense and quick thinking could be used to conceal an illicit assignation and attempted homicide.

She wasn't sure whether to be proud or appalled.

Oblivious to the uproar he had caused, Lord Dennis emitted a blissful, sleepy snore.

Because . . . of course, he did.

Mr. Carnegie stepped past Leah, placing an ear to her bedroom door. "They're still nattering on," he murmured. "We'll have to wait."

Miss Smith and Miss Well's breathy giggles sounded outside as if to emphasize the point.

With a sigh, Mr. Carnegie sank down beside Lord Dennis, shoulders against the wall, wrists resting on the raised knees of his white breeches. Lord Dennis—dark-haired, stubble-cheeked, flush-nosed—snored again, snuffling in his sleep.

Leah stared down at them, unsure of the social mores when entertaining two gentlemen in her bedchamber.

Two gentlemen.

In. Her. Bedchamber.

Her mind stuttered. Surely this exemplified the sort of lascivious behavior Aunt Leith had warned her abounded in London.

Leah busied herself, stirring the fire to life and lighting a lamp on the wee writing desk. She rotated the desk chair—a worn wooden Windsor—to face Mr. Carnegie and sat gingerly, pulling her shawl tight around her shoulders and tucking her toes under the hem of her night rail.

Mr. Carnegie watched her, the lamplight flickering in his pale gaze and turning his blond hair into molten gold. His eyes were intensely blue, she noted. The color of Loch Muick on a cloudless day.

Unlike Lord Dennis, Mr. Carnegie no longer wore his coat. Instead, he sat against the wall in the red waistcoat of a regimental officer, his white shirt sleeves cuffed to the elbow. Swallowing, he tugged at his dark neckcloth, loosening and mussing it. Leah tried (and failed) not to stare at the shadowy outline of lean muscle rippling under the fine linen of his shirt as he moved.

No wonder gentlemen were required to remain precisely dressed at all times. A disheveled man invited all sorts of salacious thoughts. At the moment, Leah was hard-pressed to concentrate on anything other than the marvelous flex and pull of tendons across his bare forearms.

But then, Mr. Fox Carnegie had been drawing her eyes all week.

Leah was attending the house party—hosted by an English cousin, Mrs. Gordon—as Aunt Leith's companion. It was all part of the campaign to lift Leah out of the 'unfortunate circumstances of Isobel's marriage.' That, of course, referred to Leah's deceased mother, Isobel Leith, who had married John Penn, a Scottish gentleman farmer well below her aristocratic station.

This meant that while more refined young women were stitching samplers and perfecting their posture in a side-saddle, Leah had been darning her younger brothers' socks and galloping across the Angus glens astride her favorite gelding, helping her father and his shepherds track lost sheep.

Unfortunately, sock-darning and sheep-wrangling were not activities that gentlemen appreciated in a well-bred young lady.

But that did not deter Aunt Leith. She ruthlessly polished Leah's manners, intending to find her niece a more appropriate husband than 'some half-drunk Scottish blacksmith.' Though if Aunt Leith had actually *met* the blacksmith in Fettermill with his bulky muscles and charming wink, she would not so cavalierly dismiss the idea.

Regardless, at scarcely eighteen years old herself, Leah was at a loss as to what men *did* want in a bride. Well, aside from a large dowry and, perhaps, an equally out-sized bosom—facts she had gleaned from Miss Wells and Miss Smith as they sat giggling over luncheon.

Leah possessed none of those things—a dowry, large bosoms, or a preponderance of giggles.

But this obvious lack had not stopped her from noticing Mr. Fox Carnegie.

He had arrived in a burst of ribald laughter and youthful scuffling— Lord Dennis's, not his own. Mr. Carnegie had stood behind his friend, arms folded, expression wry and watchful. There had been a quiet sense of *noticing* about him, a steadiness that had instantly drawn Leah in.

Granted, it hadn't hurt that he looked remarkably dashing in the red coat of the 64th Regiment of Foot. The crimson wool caught the auburn highlights in his blond hair and accentuated the sharp line of his jaw. Her eyes had stubbornly followed him—noting the liquid grace of his walk, the way his shoulders tilted toward a person as he listened, the kind gentleness in his tone.

Not that Mr. Carnegie had spared a glance for the awkwardly shy Scottish lass Leah knew herself to be. None of the gentlemen in attendance did.

Though . . . Mr. Carnegie appeared to be noticing her now.

In the lamplight, his gaze skimmed her, likely taking in the unadorned linen of her night rail, the homespun wool of her thick stockings, the tattered edge of her shawl. She pulled the garment closer.

Leah knew her features were a study in nondeterminate mediocrity— bland and vacillating. Her hair was not quite blond, nor brown, nor auburn, but some unflattering mix of the three. Her hazel eyes changed color with her moods—brown to green and back again. The rest of her—body, bosom, height—remained stubbornly average.

If Mr. Carnegie found her lacking, his expression didn't show it.

He cleared his throat. "You seem to have the advantage of me, Miss . . ." His voice drifted off, a ruddy flush climbing his cheeks. "I know we were likely introduced, but my memory for faces is not the best, and I fear with all that has happened, your name has plum slipped my mind."

He said the words kindly, but Leah experienced a sinking sensation nonetheless.

She was forgettable. She knew this, and yet . . .

"Miss Leah Penn-Leith, at your service, Mr. Carnegie."

He winced. "Of course, you have the manners to remember my name."

"As your Christian name is Fox, it does have a tendency tae stick."

He smiled at that, teeth flashing and sending a zing of pleasure chasing her spine. The sensation was akin to winning first place in the jam-making contest at the Fettermill Summer Fair. (Which she had done. Twice.)

More to the point, his grin rendered him boyish and young, too young to be in a soldier's uniform. Was Mr. Carnegie even older than herself?

"I must apologize for Lord Dennis." He nodded toward his friend, sleeping beside him. "I fear he mistook your room for . . . another's."

"Another lady?" The thought was rather shocking. That Lord Dennis would have entered a woman's room, crawled into bed with her, and the lady would have . . . welcomed it?

Lascivious, indeed.

"I shall say nothing more upon the matter, as it involves some delicacy, as you might imagine."

Well, Leah *hadn't* been imagining it, but now . . .

Her eyes dropped to the long fingers dangling over his knees. What if it had been Mr. Carnegie's gentle hands reaching for her? Would she have pulled away so quickly?

She looked away, a blush scalding her skin.

"Regardless," he continued quietly, thankfully oblivious to her wayward thoughts, "I noticed when we parted that Lord Dennis had gone down the wrong corridor, so I followed hi—"

Wham!

Another door banged down the hallway, causing them both to jump. Someone giggled.

Mr. Carnegie frowned and sent a speaking glance toward the door. "I fear it might be a while before we can make an escape unseen, Miss Penn-Leith." He nudged Lord Dennis's prone body with his foot.

Leah nodded.

They sat in silence for a moment. It was a companionable sort of thing, as if they were comrades in arms, waiting to complete an important tactical mission.

Having been raised by a stoically silent father, Leah understood that silence was often a conversation unto itself.

Sometimes it could be as soothing as an embrace, as understanding as a long *blether*.

Other times, silence was a noisy thing—loud and shouty and demanding attention.

Not everyone was fluent in the language of silence, but Mr. Carnegie appeared to have mastered it. Quiet felt peaceful in his presence.

Leah liked him all the more for it.

The scent of shaving soap and sandalwood drifted over her. It was a remarkably masculine smell, the sort that rendered a young woman weak-kneed and pliable, willing to make all sorts of poor decisions.

Keep your wits about ye, Leah!

"So . . ." she began, floundering for a topic, "uhmmm, *Fox* . . . that is an unusual given name."

"I suppose," he snorted. "My father was quite fond of Mr. Charles Fox's politics. I was named in his honor."

Leah was unsure how to respond. The name *Charles Fox* was vaguely familiar. Hadn't Mr. Jamieson, the town glazier, once said something rather crude about Mr. Fox when he thought no women were present?

"He was always a bit of a radical, Mr. Fox," Mr. Carnegie continued as if he, too, were eager to have a topic to discuss. "He championed revolution, hated imperialistic warmongering, and detested our current

Hanoverian kings. My father was rather passionate about Mr. Fox's pacifistic views and democratic principles."

Something caught in Leah's chest at that.

My father was. Past tense.

She understood something about a past-tense parent.

"Do ye share your father's views then?" she asked, looking pointedly at the brass buttons on his regimental waistcoat, at the monarchy and imperialism they represented.

He followed her gaze, plucking at the sturdy red wool.

"It hardly matters now, I suppose." He shrugged and looked away, the lamplight casting his profile in stark shadow upon the wall behind.

Footsteps echoed down the hallway, drifting away from her door. Lord Dennis muttered in his sleep.

"How did ye end up as a commissioned officer then, if I may ask?"

Mr. Carnegie rested his head against the wall with a soft *thump*, as if the question troubled him. "I was orphaned last autumn, but I will not reach my majority for another two years. Worse, my father lost most of his fortune due to poor speculation, leaving me with little."

Leah's heart gave another wee lurch. So he *was* young . . . only nineteen.

"My uncle became my guardian after my father's death," he continued. "Unlike my pacifistic father, my uncle believes a man must do his duty and go to war when needed. I cannot say I relish the thought, but I must provide for myself and I have no interest in the Church. Therefore, the military is the only choice left. Uncle purchased me a commission in the 64th Foot, and here I am."

Living a life I never really wanted.

He didn't say the words, but she heard them nonetheless.

Leah knew that in-between feeling. When the smooth sailing of life crashed into a hard, unforgiving calamity.

"I ken a bit about change. My mother died two years past when my youngest brother was born—" She blink, blink, blinked before swallowing back her grief. "—and my father is still heartbroken over her loss. My younger brothers are too wee tae be without a mother, so I've had tae become their mamma."

Leah let out a slow breath, thinking about Malcolm and Ethan back home at Thistle Muir. How Malcolm, barely five, had *greited* and clung to her skirts as she walked to Uncle Leith's waiting carriage. How Ethan, scarcely two, had wailed his distress, reaching for her, fighting to get out of Cousin Elspeth's arms.

It had been too much. Leah had nearly turned back and stayed.

"Get on with ye. Go tae London," Elspeth had urged, holding Ethan tighter. As a lifelong spinster, her father's cousin had spent her years being passed like a parcel between relatives. "Get yourself a husband, lass."

Leah's father had stepped forward and pressed a soft kiss to her forehead.

"Aye," he said, voice gruff and eyes suspiciously bright. "Your mother wouldnae want ye tae be here. Go have a wee adventure. And if ye come back tae us married to some braw, young gentleman, so much the better."

Well, Fox Carnegie certainly fit the definition of a 'braw, young gentleman.'

"How challenging for you, to be raising your brothers," Mr. Carnegie replied, hair glinting in the firelight. "To take on so much, so young."

"You are kind tae say so, but we do what we must."

He sighed, a weary, body-worn sound. "You speak truth."

Silence descended.

A silence of kinship this time. A sense that, despite the differences in their upbringing and experiences, she and Fox Carnegie saw the world through a similar lens.

That they were, perhaps, cut from the same cloth.

He angled his head toward the door, listening intently. "We might finally be in the clear."

"Let me check."

Leah approached the door on light feet, pressing her ear against the dark oak.

Nothing.

Cautiously, she turned the lock and peered out into the hallway.

No one.

"How does it look?" he asked, his words close to her ear.

Leah jumped slightly, looking to him. Mr. Carnegie was scarcely a foot away. So close, she could see a faint mole to the right of his nose and count his individual eyelashes. So close, she could feel the heat of his body. So close, she would only have to lift onto tiptoe to press her mouth to his.

She blinked.

What had he asked?

"Good." Was her voice breathless? She *felt* breathless. "The coast is clear."

Nodding, he stooped down and hefted Lord Dennis upright once more. His lordship's eyes fluttered open and closed. Mr. Carnegie adjusted his hold, draping Dennis's elbow over his own shoulders and wrapping another arm around the man's waist.

"Thank you again for your kind company, Miss Penn-Leith," Mr. Carnegie whispered. "We shall remove ourselves, and let you see to your slumber."

He saluted her with his free hand and then he was gone, slipping out the door with his burden as soundlessly as he had entered it.

But the *feel* of Fox Carnegie lingered. A whiff of sandalwood. A sense of adventure in the air.

Sleep was decidedly long in coming.

Visit www.NicholeVan.com to get your copy of
Love Practically today and continue the story.

ABOUT THE AUTHOR

THE SHORT VERSION:

NICHOLE VAN IS a writer, photographer, designer and generally disorganized person. Though originally from the Rocky Mountains, she has lived all over the world, including Italy and the UK. She and her family recently returned to the US after spending six years in Scotland. Nichole currently lives in the heart of the Rockies with her husband and and three children.

THE LONG OVERACHIEVER VERSION:

AN INTERNATIONAL BESTSELLING author, Nichole Van is an artist who feels life is too short to only have one obsession. In former lives, she has been a contemporary dancer, pianist, art historian, choreographer, culinary artist and English professor.

Most notably, however, Nichole is an acclaimed photographer, winning over thirty international accolades for her work, including Portrait of the Year from WPPI in 2007. (Think Oscars for wedding and portrait photographers.) Her unique photography style has been featured in many magazines, including *Rangefinder* and *Professional Photographer*.

All that said, Nichole has always been a writer at heart. With an MA in English, she taught technical writing at Brigham Young University for ten years and has written more technical manuals than she can quickly count. She decided in late 2013 to start writing fiction and has since become an Amazon #1 bestselling author. Additionally, she has won a RONE award, as well as been a Whitney Award Finalist several years running. Her late 2018 release, *Seeing Miss Heartstone*, won the Whitney Award Winner for Best Historical Romance.

In 2017, Nichole, her husband and three children moved from the Rocky Mountains in the USA to Scotland. They lived there for six years—residing on the coast of eastern Scotland in an eighteenth century country house—before returning to the USA in 2023. Nichole currently lives in the heart of the Rockies, miles up a mountain canyon.

She is known as NicholeVan all over the web: Facebook, Instagram, Pinterest, etc. Visit http://www.NicholeVan.com to sign up for her author newsletter and be notified of new book releases.

If you enjoyed this book, please leave a short review on Amazon and/or Goodreads. Wonderful reviews are the elixir of life for authors. Even better than dark chocolate.

www.ingramcontent.com/pod-product-compliance
Lightning Source LLC
Chambersburg PA
CBHW051941240626
47153CB00005B/1576